WEST BRITON STORY

Tom O'Rourke

ISBN 978-93-80905-55-6

Typeset in Dante MT Std

First published in 2014

1 3 5 7 9 8 6 4 2

British Library Cataloguing in Publication Data.
A catalogue record for this book is available from the British Library.

Publisher: Suman Chakraborty

Quintus
An Imprint of ROMAN Books
26 York Street, London W1U 6PZ, United Kingdom
Suite 49, Park Plaza, South Block, Ground Floor, 71, Park Street, Kolkata 700016, WB, India
2nd Floor, 38/3, Andul Road, Howrah 711109, WB, India
www.quintus-books.co.uk | www.quintus-books.co.in

Printed and bound in India by
Repro India Ltd

For Lesley, Thomas and Teresa

TimeLine

559 – Birth of Rhuadrac
571 – Battle of Bedcanford and loss of the Four Towns
577 – Battle of Deorham
584 – Battle of Fethan Leag
592 – Battle of Wodensberg
593 – A New Era Begins

List of Main Characters (with suggested sound in brackets)

Acha (*At-cha*) – wife of Ceawlin
Advil – brother of Gavin, father of Cormac and Rhuadrac
Aidan (*Aden*) – King of the Dal Riada, of the Irish-Scots
Aisha (*Eyesha*) – sister of Cormac and Rhuadrac
Brocmael (*Brocmile*) – British Chieftain, King of Powys
Cadolan – a spoilt monk,
Ceawlin (*Kowlin*) – King of the Gevissas
Olric – nephew to Ceawlin
Cormac – brother of Rhuadrac, champion of Farinmael's army
Crida (*Creeda*) – a young thegn of Ceawlin
Cutha (*Kootha*) – son of Ceawlin
Willem – old comrade (shoulder-man) of Ceawlin
Uthwine (*Oothvine*) – An Engle king
Ethna – wife of Advil, mother of Cormac and Rhuadrac, an Irish princess
Farinmael (*Farinmile*) – King of Corinium
Felix – A Gaul, master of the *martiobarbuli*, warrior in Rhuadrac's war-band
Fintan – a slingsman and lyre player, a freed slave, kinsman of Cormac
Gavin – brother of Advil, uncle to Cormac and Rhuadrac
Gregor – a warrior in Rhuadrac's war-band
Gwendolyne – daughter of Farinmael
Kynon (*Kyenon*) – son of Brocmael
Little Sigfeldt – warrior in Rhuadrac's war-band

Megwei (*Megway*) – a slave-girl
Oisin (*Wahsheen*) – also, the Singer-of-Songs, kinsman of Cormac and Rhuadrac
Peg – a British woman, attendant upon Ulla
Rama Bec – a Syrian warrior in Rhuadrac's war-band
Rhuadrac – narrator, brother of Cormac
Scapthar – A tavern-brothel owner in Gaul
Scipio – An African warrior in Rhuadrac's war-band
Torquato – A Roman warrior, a freebooter in Rhuadrac's war-band
Ulla *(Oola)* – daughter of Ceawlin
Veostan *(Veeohs)* – A Scandic warrior in Rhuadrac's war-band
Aircol, Muerig,
Rhin-Gir, Constantine – various Britsh kings before the Battle of Fethan Leag

List of Unusual Place Names

Calleva:	Silchester, Roman city, south-west of Reading
Cissanceaster:	Chichester
Corinium:	Cirencester
Cunetio:	old Roman fortress, near to Malborough, Wilts
Deorham:	Dyrham, village six miles north of Bath
Fethan Leag:	near the village of Stoke Lyne, near Bicester
Forest of Baer:	Forest of Bere (Hants)
Winche:	in the region of present-day Winchester
Penwyrn:	old British fortress, possibly near Baschurch, near Shrewsbury
Uriconium:	Wroxeter, Roman city, south of Shrewsbury

Note* In two places, the modern place name was used: Bath for Acqua Sulis and Gloucester for Glevum.

Contents

You rascals, you good-for-nothings, you see me only as an old man now.

It is true – no less than sixty winters have passed since my birth so, aye, I am old.

But I have not always been old. I have lived a life, a full life, and these records are prepared for you, you scoundrels, so that you might learn something of it, and in turn might tell your own sons and daughters the story of Rhuadrac, warrior-poet, son of Advil, nephew of Gavin, and brother to mighty Cormac who was the great chieftain Farinmael's champion, and I tell too of my friend, the wild Roman mercenary of the verses, Torquato; and all of it is true.

Just as I heard the mighty Gevissa scop himself declaim in Brothers' Hall just days ago:

> *'So learn from this*
> *And understand true worth. I who am telling you*
> *Have wintered into wisdom.'*

I have set down my memory of the great battles, stories that you have heard me tell many times before: Deorham, and of Ceawlin and his daughter, Ulla; Fethan Leag and of the old King Brocmael and his son, Kynon of Powys; of the great slaughter that was Wodensberg and the calamity that befell our family there.

And we should talk of battles, for how else in this life do we achieve honour and status, glory and gold, and land for our families? How else do we show respect to the memories of our forefathers who have gone on before us? Ah! Long may such tales be told.

But you know too that my warrior days are past now. Since Wodensberg it might be that I have won some small praise and respect from the people as a poet, as a singer of verses, a scop. And it seems to me that this is right and proper too. Let us talk of great friends and warriors, but there are other matters that only a man who has lived through many seasons might dare to speak, lest he be thought weak. I wish to speak of the affairs of men and women, and of wise men's thoughts.

Aye, all of this and more is set out in my records that follow.

This life moves in mysterious ways, and no-one of us can know the final picture drawn by the threads of its pattern. For, as I say to you again, it seems to me that only through our stories, only through consideration of our actions and behaviours over a lifetime in the light of the men and the women and the things that we have known, only by that means might we better come to know ourselves and the ways of this world.

Be sure of this always at least my good, proud, dear children: I wish you all love, peace and good fortune in your lives.

⋆

So now I start my story. It is the eve of Deorham. I have seen no more than eighteen or nineteen winters, and a still-foolish boy walks with his kinsmen to the scene of that terrible battle . . .

PART I

Of the Battle of Deorham and other Matters

I

The light had not yet been completely lost.

Even in this half-light we could see, around us and all throughout the opposite hillside, the flame torches of bands of warriors in groups of five or more, perhaps as many as twenty, make their way through the thickly wooded slopes. Up at the head of the valley, its campfires already flaring out through the dusk, Farinmael's camp stood proud against the skyline. It was plain to me that all of the war-bands were converging on that place.

To our left rose up the final third of the hill, and to our right, two hundred paces below us, lay the floor of the valley. Here the Boyde, gentle tributary to the mighty River Severn to the west and south, was calm, its width no more than ten paces bank to bank. The heavy rains of yesterday had given us clean fresh air for the day's march; had flushed deep-green the fields through which we strode; so too had those rains caused the soil underfoot to soften, so that a thick layer of claylike loam formed under our boots. A keen breeze blew at our backs, as if driving us on to Farinmael's camp. The flatlands of the lower Severn had given way to sloping hills, and we had left the Boyde's banks and climbed the slope, making for the high plain that dominated the head of the valley.

So now evening had begun to fall. The sun threw its fading light upon the shadowed hillside across the valley; one farm compound sent up some woodsmoke, and a curious rose-light played upon the thatched roof of the main hut. Ahead of us we could see the forest become a dark indistinct form. Countless birds clustered in formation as they flew towards the woods.

Any passing stranger would have been in no doubt – with our mail shirts hung loosely over our shoulders, most with our swords and shields held by cross-strings against our spines, the giant with the battle-axe tied across his back from shoulder to hip – these men were Britons, and they marched to a battleground.

At our head strode my older brother, the giant Cormac, Farinmael's champion, already feared by the Saxon invaders. I walked proudly beside him. At that time I had gained some repute as a warrior, won in local disputes amongst my own people, the Britons. I had not yet encountered the Saes. With us too was Oisin, also called 'Singer-of-Songs', he of the broad shoulders and fair hair. He was a man well loved by women, amongst ordinary men a big man too, but the top of his head barely came level with Cormac's shoulders. Even as we walked he hummed some quiet tune, and he grinned and winked at me now as I looked across at him.

"So, young 'un, how does it feel to be walking to a battleground, eh? Does your heart not beat faster? Can you smell the fear in your nostrils?"

I looked at him; it was true – all day the blood had sung in my veins as I strode with my kinsmen through the valleys and hills of my homeland.

"Aye, Oisin, in truth it is like nothing else I have known in my life. The air is somehow more fresh – everything seems newly made to my eyes. See now, that hawk, just there – see how it rides the wind – see how it hovers. Look now! Those eyes – it has seen its meal – a true hunter!"

We both watched as the razor beak cut through the air and burst through the body of its slow-moving prey, brute force shuddering with shock into languid wings, sending the mute form spinning, feathers flung askew. The hawk's talons immediately seized the dying bird, taking it onto a new line, a different trajectory. That dove would find no home horizon this night.

"He has it, for sure."

Oisin looked at me then.

"A falcon. That's a good sign, it augers well for the battle. Remember this day lad. The day a man walks to his first battleground does not leave him."

So saying, he smiled at me and moved on up the track, humming to himself some favourite marching tune.

Behind him came quiet Fintan, like Oisin a distant kinsman to my mother by marriage. Fintan was a slingsman. Once a slave but now a freeman, his sling held in a pouch on his right hip, a lyre tied to his back, his nimble feet danced along the clay-heavy path with ease. He nodded at me in his quiet way as he passed me on the track, his shy kind eyes quickly looking back ahead of him.

Finally came Gavin, our uncle. His bald head emphasised the thick ruts of his forehead, and contrasted sharply with the thick black hair that covered his arms and those exposed parts of his back and chest that burst out of the old green battle jerkin that he wore. What remained of his hair was cut in the Roman style, which was short. Gavin was a veteran of many battles.

Cormac now spoke out.

"So, the matter will be settled here at Deorham, then."

He spoke to nobody in particular, but to all of us. Gavin answered him:

"Aye, the reports were right. The invader is going for the biggest prize – he seeks Bath itself. May the gods give us the strength to win this battle, for if we do not, the cities of Gloucester, Corinium and Bath will be at the mercy of the Saxons, and the western marches and Gwent will be wide open – the darkness may spread all the way to the banks of the Wye."

I looked into the lively face of my uncle. I could see from the set of his features that he was deadly serious, a rare event for that man of many elaborate tales. But the wisdom of my uncle was respected by all, and I wanted to know more. I turned back and called to my brother:

"Oi, long legs! Stop a while, I want to talk to our uncle."

Cormac glanced back at me with a sharp look and smiled. I got away with many things that he would not allow from other men. Raising his voice, he called out to the rest of our small band.

"Final rest for this march, lads! We'll take one more stop before the last climb to Farinmael's camp."

We had reached a clearing in the trees on the hill path. Ahead lay another cluster of trees, and the forest deepened as the path bore downhill. In the distance we could just make out the sound of rushing water, as the river narrowed on its journey to the head of the valley.

Cormac swung the battle-axe *Gaeallon* down from his broad shoulders.

"We will need torches for the rest of the march. Fintan, boughs please, from those trees ahead."

We spread out around the clearing; I sat down near to my uncle. Just then Cadolan arrived, but kept on walking through the clearing, disdaining to look at any of us and talking to himself as he trudged past.

"Such great haste in this world. Yet I see Farinmael's camp before me, I see the night drawing in, I know that the Saxon hordes are over the hill. Why then should I rush? The camp is going nowhere. The Saxons are going nowhere. I will be at the camp tonight. I will eat roast meat. I will drink a little wine. I will sleep. Tomorrow, the battle will come and what will happen is what God decrees should happen. Why then should I rush with the youngsters? What will come, will come."

He kept walking on through the clearing, on towards the forest. We all smiled as we saw him go. Gavin watched him reach a bend in the path and lumber around the corner.

"Ah, Cadolan the stoic, the wise man! If only his brains were as big as his belly! But then, he is usually right, too."

Cadolan was a spoilt monk; a distant kinsman of ours, a second cousin of my father. He was much older than the rest of us, the tonsure on his scalp retained in the Frankish, not Briton, style, but with a spray of white hair all around it. His beard was full and grey and black, so that it made a strange contrast with his hair. He had black sandals on his feet and black cross-gaiters that stretched up from his sandals to his knees. He wore a monk's black robe, which was ancient, tied at the waist by a plaited rope, and this plaited rope would always be slipping below his massive belly, so that he was forever rearranging it. Not only his belly was massive, his head was massive, his arms were massive – Cadolan was a massive man.

He was also a learned man, and he had taught my brother and me our letters, and I could read, write and speak in the Roman language, which I found came easily to me.

As a boy I would always ask him, pointing to his hair with an affected sweet innocence:

'Is that not your saint's halo, Cadolan?'

In turn, he would give out a good-natured roar, and make as if to hit me. He weighed his words carefully, and he never said what I wanted him to say; he confounded my expectations with his every word. But beneath his habitual world-weary mannerisms there was a good man, a wise man, for his was a gentle spirit in brutal times.

I looked now at my uncle, even as Cadolan disappeared from sight, and brought him back to the matter at hand.

"So, uncle, how does the Gevissa see this battle? Why Bath, and how do you know that this is their plan?"

Gavin looked across at me. Now, on the eve of the next great battle, when the spirits of men are agitated, perhaps as he looked at me he thought once more of my father, Advil, his brother; the wide-set eyes beneath the ridged forehead, the small mouth and Roman nose set into wide cheekbones, the heavy jaw and fair hair – my mother told me always that I shared my features with my father. Both my mother and my uncle had spoken to me many times of my father, lost at the Battle of Bedcanford some seven winters previously. There, the armies of the Four Towns had been outflanked, outwitted and destroyed by the Saxon, Cuthwulf. There had been a great massacre of our people.

My uncle had told me often how he had lain alone that night after the battle, hidden beneath foliage in the forests even as Cuthwulf's cut-throats searched for him, and made a pledge to himself, that he, Gavin, right-hand man of Farinmael, the warrior-king of Corinium, would never again underestimate the strategic abilities of the barbarian, would never again be outwitted by the heathen hordes. And that is how he had earned the respect of his fellow warriors as a man of battle strategy, a man rarely outwitted.

He gestured to my brother and me.

"If you wish to know how I see the Saxon dog's thinking, come over here whilst we rest."

We both drew nearer.

Fintan had by now returned with several boughs, a couple of which he had managed to light with the flint. My uncle gestured to Fintan to bring one over to him.

By its new light I looked across into the face of my brother – the long black hair, black brows, blue eyes set into the same wide cheekbones and heavy jaw as me. The broken nose was already testament to the proof of his warrior status. I knew that it was a matter of some pride to Gavin that Cormac had been chosen as Farinmael's champion; he had never been bested in battle, and never come near to being thrown in the wrestling contests. My father would have been proud too. Yet away from the battle and trials, in those times before Deorham, Cormac was the most quiet of men, almost childlike in his manner.

My uncle held the lit bough high with his left arm, and with a stout twig held in his right began to draw a series of lines in the dust.

"Farinmael originally thought, as I did, that those barbarians Uthwine and Ceawlin were heading west to push over the Cotswolds into the upper Severn Valley. But their progress is at odds with this belief. We know the three ancient roads that cross the great western valley to the hills beyond. There is the Cunetio Road through Verlucio to Bath; there is the second road through the old Roman camp at Cunetio, now a trade-place, to join the Calleva Road to Corinium; and thirdly, there is the hill route through the Fosse that joins Bath and Corinium."

My uncle drew a triangle in the dust.

"The Saxons will never cross the wilds of the Braden forest in our lifetimes. It is too dense, too easily defended by those who know the trails. They took the Cunetio and Corinium Road, near the point where the rivers Thames and Avon almost meet."

He scratched out the dust in a wedge shape through the centre of the triangle and drew diverging lines to the south and east of the triangle.

"We know that the barbarians have been harrying the villages on both sides of the Fosse Highway for these last few days gone by, causing such massacre that it has caused us to reach out for our Severn neighbours. They, thank the gods, have answered our call. But see, if the Saxons intend to take the upper Severn, why proceed so far down the Fosse? No, it is not the upper reaches of the Severn they seek, not the Cotswolds; it is the lower Severn Valley, for they are after Bath itself."

Both Cormac and I looked steadily at our uncle. I could see how his eyes were blazing.

"We cannot lose this fight, lads. It will be the greatest victory since Mount Badon, when the great battle leader, Arthur, drove the swine from our lands for these past seventy winters or more! We will avenge the death of your father, my brother Advil."

Cormac reached out and placed his large right hand on our uncle's shoulder.

"We walk with you, uncle. We know what is at stake tomorrow."

Gavin looked at us both, and smiled grimly.

"Aye, lads, we have known that it was only a matter of time before the heathens returned here, to our own lands. Now we will find out what the fates have in store for us all."

We stood up. Fintan and Oisin took a lighted bough each, and Cormac strode on ahead of us.

As he reached the bend in the path I saw him stop suddenly. He held up his arm, then motioned to us all to press back into the side of the hill. He came back to us. "Invaders. They have Cadolan at sword-point."

Gavin looked into Cormac's face.

"How many?"

"Four by my count. We must move now. He has moments to live."

Gavin, Cormac and I went up to the bend in the path, and with care peered around the rocks that stood there.

Cadolan was on his knees, his head in the soil, his cassock pulled down roughly over his haunches, exposing his massive white back. Four men stood around him – two held lit boughs, and a third was talking in some horrible guttural language that did not sound human to my ears. This man had his foot across Cadolan's neck, and laughed as he poked his short sword gently into his back, then he began barking at Cadolan in his strange and hellish language.

Gavin turned to Cormac.

"Get Fintan. If we charge from here he will be finished before we get within five paces of him."

Cormac brought the slingsman.

"Hit the leader. No noise. Wait for us to get into position near them."

Fintan nodded, and looked about him, then crouched and picked up a sizeable chunk of flint at the foot of the rock.

I followed my uncle and brother, circling up into the rocks. The Saxon leader's voice had grown even more strident. I could hear no sound from my teacher – he lay there on his knees.

Gavin looked back to where our kinsman stood poised at the curve in the path, his sling held in his right hand. Gavin nodded curtly. Fintan swung the sling around his head once, twice; in a practised movement the stone flew from the pouch at the top of the curve of the third circle. A moment later we heard a high-pitched curse, and the Saxon leader staggered away from Cadolan's prone body.

In two more moments we were upon them.

It was quickly done. Cormac reached the Saxons first, even as they looked at their leader's fallen body; two arcs of *Gaeallon* left three of them writhing on the ground. Gavin finished off their leader quickly, not pausing in his task.

I had barely moved, such was the sudden ferocity of my kinsmen.

Now the Saxons lay still.

Cormac pulled Cadolan to his feet. Slowly our teacher rearranged his cassock, pulling the plaited belt tight under his belly. I could see that he trembled, and his face was white.

Gavin walked over to him, and placed his hand on the monk's shoulder.

"Be calm teacher. You are safe now."

He led Cadolan over to a low rock. By now Oisin and Fintan had joined us, and we could see from the lit boughs that Cadolan could not control the movement of his lips and his eyes were closed tight.

"Here, take some of this. It will revive you."

So saying, Gavin handed the monk a silver flask, screwing off the lid as he did so.

Cadolan gulped down the clear liquid, shaking his head.

Eventually he took the flask from his mouth and passed his hand slowly down his white face. There was a cut on his forehead, the only outward sign of the event that had just occurred.

"By Christ in heaven, but I thought that my time had come then."

He closed his eyes briefly, then brought up his right arm slowly.

"But I recover now. The fear passes. Give me a few moments, then we can continue."

I stood up and moved back to the path.

I was troubled by strange thoughts. The hillside to my left was now barely a vague outline, a shadow. I saw Cormac, Oisin and Fintan search the Saxon warriors. Cormac drew out some cloth from the shoulder-fur of their leader; he held it up to the light from Oisin's bough. I could see clearly a black wolf's head silhouette outlined on the yellow cloth of the pennant. Then I saw my kinsmen roll the dead bodies of the Saxons over the lip of the hill, watched as the bodies careered lifelessly down into a copse.

Ahead of me, just above the treeline of the forest, the fires of Farinmael's camp now threw a great flare against the night sky. Somewhere below me I could hear the gentle waters of the Boyde pass through the narrow deep channel of the valley head. Still the torches of war-bands could be seen threading through the wooden slopes around us.

I imagined that my father's spirit was very close. The night sky seemed to me to be strangely black, somehow full of foreboding, as if strange creatures gathered there and were pressing to be set free.

Quietly I touched the hilt of my sword, called by me *Saesbane*, or bane of the Saxons, and recently forged for me by old Dermot, master sword maker. I drew the sword, and lifted it up to my eyes. The pommel design was of the Irish pattern. Ring within ring within ring.

I was almost overcome by some strange sense of disquiet, perhaps caused by the sudden shock of the skirmish that had just unfolded. Although I had not yet taken part in a real battle, I had been in enough local skirmishes between the Britons to know that the shock of it would pass, once the battle-spirit was upon me. Then a clear thought struck me, and I knew what it was that had so disquieted me – my noble teacher, a man of great learning, had been reduced to an incoherent fool in mere moments by the Saxon brutality. It was this new knowledge that now assailed my senses. His learning was of no value to him here; it was powerless in the face of such brutality.

I felt as if some malevolent spirit was loose in the world and that neither I, nor Cormac, nor Gavin, nor Farinmael himself had control over this spirit. It would take us where it would and only the gods themselves knew how the battle tomorrow might unfold.

Full of this strange sense of dread I moved back to my kinsmen and friends.

II

We arrived at Farinmael's camp to be met with a great show of respect, as was fitting for men with the status of my uncle and brother. Even if they did not know of Cormac's status, men still stood up from their fires as the giant strode through the camp. I swear that I could hear a low roar of voices, like the sound of a mountain breeze passing over an upland lake at night, gather over the camp as the news spread that Cormac, Farinmael's champion, the giant, was amongst them. Perhaps hearing this, the white muslin cloth entrance to the largest tent, flying the red and gold standards of Corinium, was thrown back and Farinmael himself came out to greet us, flanked by his kinsmen and chief warriors. It was right and proper that he should greet Gavin first, old friends that they were.

"Gavin! How does life go with you? You look fatter, you have grown lazy on that farm of yours! Is Dorianna still as beautiful as ever? How she could ignore me for your ugly mug I shall never know!"

"And you Farinmael, you have grown old and grey, the cares of leadership have done for you! Dorianna is strong and well. She has asked me to tell you that she thinks of you often, in fact very often, and wonders always what the life of a queen might have been, instead of that of a fat farmer's wife! And I too sometimes think of how peaceful my life might have been, had she chosen you and not me!"

The two men, good friends, bonds long ago forged in the frenzied heat of battle, laughed a true laugh, and reached forward to clasp each other in a bear hug, both men rocking from side to side. Men on each side laughed and shook hands.

Presently Farinmael stood back from Gavin. It was the first time I had met him. He was of middle height only, which surprised me, but there was no mistaking the strength of his shoulders and arms, and the large head stood proud on a bull neck. A few slivers of grey hair could be seen in the long black hair that was swept back from his proud forehead.

He looked up at Cormac.

"By all the gods in heaven, I swear that you have grown again since I last saw you! How are you Cormac, is your appetite still what it was? Men, kill another cow, for this man will eat it for himself!"

I knew that Cormac hated these rituals. Out of battle, in those times before Deorham, he was a shy man. In battle, he was not shy. No, in battle he was not shy at all.

Farinmael's chiefs and fellow warriors waited to see how he would respond to the words of the chief. Some, who had never seen him before, stared in stupefied awe at the sheer size of my brother, this man who was already Farinmael's champion. Perhaps they were surprised by his youth, for my brother was but five full winters older than me. Cormac looked down at Farinmael, thinking of the right words. A light came into his eyes and his face reddened slightly.

"My appetite is well, Chief. My mother tells me that she despairs of feeding me. But may I ask of you, is Gwen well?"

A light-hearted muttering went around the group of warriors. Farinmael's daughter was a beauty, and she had given Cormac her amulet when they had last met.

Farinmael raised an eyebrow with laughter in his face, and slapped Cormac on the shoulder, glancing at my uncle as he did so. It was not really the right question to ask, to talk of Gwendolyne here in front of Farinmael's warriors, but age would teach Cormac the right ways, if the gods were kind. "Gwendolyne thrives, Cormac, and I know that she thinks warmly of you. Gavin, tell me, the wife of my great friend Advil – may the gods give him eternal victory – is she well?"

Gavin, quick to cover the inexperience of his nephew, answered swiftly:

"Ethna is also well, Farinmael, and prays to her god for your success on the field of battle tomorrow."

In those times, before the coming of the holy man sent by Rome, there was a great mixture of belief in the world. Some men followed the old gods of the elements, of the trees and the winds, of the rivers and the mountains. Some men followed the warrior-gods; some men followed the eastern cult of the bull; some men followed the Christian God of the Romans and the Irish, as did my mother. Most men of fighting age perhaps favoured all of the gods at some time, depending on what was in front of them on a particular day.

A shadow crossed over Farinmael's features.

"Ethna's prayers are welcome. We may need all of the help we can get, even that of her peace-loving god. The reports are that the Saes kings have gathered an army bigger than any they have put together before, reinforced by many new boats arriving over the last few months. They have sent emissaries to me and to Conmael. They mean to avenge their great loss to our grandfathers at Mount Badon, and unless we surrender Bath, Corinium and Gloucester, those cities will be taken by force, and no-one, man, woman or child, shall be spared."

A hush came over the gathered fighting men. Farinmael spat on the ground in front of him.

"We shall send them back to their heathen hells!"

Real fury passed through his eyes. He shook his head.

"But enough of this for now. We have much to discuss this night."

He caught sight of me on the edge of the group and lifted his arms.

"By all of the gods of the forests and the lakes, but that is Advil I see in front of me! Gavin, who is this apparition?"

"Lord Farinmael, this is Rhuadrac, son of Advil, brother of Cormac, and my nephew."

Farinmael grasped me by the arm and hand.

"Then you are a friend of mine Rhuadrac! But your brother must have eaten all of the meat in your family's pot, for you are no taller than me!"

"That is true . . ." said I, ferociously, ". . . but I am twice as fast as the big lump, as you shall all see tomorrow when I prove myself on the field of battle!"

Farinmael and Gavin laughed at my enthusiasm; I was but a boy at this time. The chief slapped me on the back then looked at Cadolan, for the first time noting the cut in his forehead.

"But holy father, you are hurt! What has happened here?"

Gavin answered:

"A skirmish with heathen outriders, not two furlongs from here. The monk was lucky – we got to him before they could finish him off."

Cadolan brushed it away.

"I thought that my time had come, but no, not this time. Already my spirit revives."

Farinmael looked at Cadolan quizzically, with a smile in his eyes:

"So now, holy father, you have come to pray for all of our souls on this battle eve?"

Cadolan looked at the chief with a doleful countenance, the firewater now having its full effect.

"But of course, mighty Chief. To pray for all of our souls in this terrifying world. But also, if God but wills it, I also hope to sample some of the fine roasted meats I see on the spits of the fires around me, and perhaps a little also of the Frankish wine which I see in the clawed beakers on the tables over there, if it so pleases the Lord."

Farinmael laughed.

"Eat and drink, all of you, but do not drink too much. A well-fed warrior with a sore head is half a warrior only. We will need all of our strength tomorrow."

So saying, the chieftain himself led the way the short distance from the high central plain on which the camp had been set out, passed on downhill through a small copse, and arrived at the central hearth which had been set up on an open slope below the plain on which the main camp had been pitched. As Cadolan had typically been first to notice, huge spits of roasted meat were being turned slowly over the wood and coals, and great wooden mead-tables were loaded with beer and wine.

Soon our meat-plates were empty and we had each drained a couple of wine claw-beakers and there was much high spirits around the central hearth. Just then we all turned at the sound of a low melodious singing note from a few paces away. Little Fintan immediately stood up from the stone he sat on, untied his lyre from his back, and began to pluck a few notes in tune with the singing voice that we could hear. It was Oisin who was singing, and Fintan, that quiet man, always loved to play in tune whenever he heard Oisin's voice.

It was then that Oisin hit his first full note; the effect on those around us was marked. The heads of many men jerked back and others stood up to see who it was singing, for Oisin had a strong and beautiful voice, and he never sang better than that night on the eve of Deorham. His voice was somewhere between deep and light, with a perfect pitch; he sang one of the favourite West Briton songs:

". . . the long rugged coasts of Alba
The green central plains,
The rivers that run down
To the sea . . ."

That voice rose and fell with almost a phantom air; it faded, swooped, questioned, then held to the long notes like a bridge of oak as he sang:

"Our valley homes in the mountains,
Our women we leave behind there
When the battle cry comes . . ."

So then it was that the warriors assembled there stared at the ground, or at the fading outline of the hills around them, or at the great blackness to the south. There was an unsettled sadness in their eyes as they stood there amidst the hills of West Britain, and their faces grew sombre as Oisin's voice soared up to a crescendo:

". . . to lay in shade at last with those we love . . ."

Then the voice slowly faded away on the final trembling note from the lyre.

Farinmael's face was sombre too. It was time for him to address the task in front of us. He saw that these West Britons, restless men facing a battle that would determine their future, had all turned their eyes towards him. He stood there at the head of the slope, just ten steps to my left. The great black void of the now night-darkened central plain of the lower Severn Valley met his eyes too as he looked out over the heads of his assembled army. No doubt he sensed then that a moment of truth had come for those men in the camp that night.

He looked around him; the camp had been struck in the largest clearing at the head of the valley, and the clearing was ringed with high hills, as if the hoof of some colossal horse of the gods had left its imprint there, so forming almost a natural theatre in the old Roman style. The tents and the horse paddock were placed at the top of the camp, fifty paces or so back up on the high plain, so that this sloped clearing was a great open space. Many fires lit the clearing, and hundreds of men formed small clusters around their own fires, still in their war-bands.

A full moon – it seemed gigantic to me that night – bathed the clearing with an almost spectral light. And a strange and wondrous thought occurred to me at that moment, just on the closing of Oisin's song and before our king began to speak: it was as if we were all ghosts, arrayed there in our cloaks and tunics, all hushed, waiting for our mighty chieftain to speak in that space amongst the hills and plains of middle Britain.

Although we were at most just seven or eight hundred men, it seemed to me just then that we were many thousands more, as if the spirits of all those who had fought for this land before us were near, and pressed close to us, and threw their arms around our shoulders, as if they too listened for the voice of our king.

As Farinmael began to speak, the breeze seemed to carry his deep, deliberate voice, so that it rang around the clearing, and the separate clusters of men began to move forward, began to congregate together around the central fire.

"Men of Corinium, West Britons, I will not lie to you. Tomorrow we face the greatest trial of all. We have reports that the Saes are reinforced, that the enemy we face tomorrow will be like nothing that we have faced before. Those of us who are older know this adversary. I tell you straight, expect no mercy from them. They will take no prisoners."

The great chief paused and looked around him. All were quiet, for they felt the weight of his words. With a barely perceptible movement he laid his right hand upon the hilt of his battle sword.

"There is much resting on us tomorrow. The three cities of Corinium, Bath and Gloucester, our cities, depend on us for their very survival. If we do not achieve victory tomorrow, the whole of West Britain as far as the western boundary of Gwent on the far banks of the Wye will lay open to the heathen hordes. We must not fail."

He paused again, then slowly drew his sword from its scabbard and placed its point in the ground before him, leaning his weight forward so that both hands rested on the hilt of his sword. The folds of the red-gold cloak of the great chieftain fell across the top of his shoulders; the breeze flicked forward his long black hair. He began to speak again in a quieter voice, but a voice that grew louder as he spoke. No other sound could be heard in the clearing. Those men on the outer circles around him moved closer to hear his words.

"These lives that we live here, brother amongst brother, tilling our fields, meeting our women, raising our children in this west British place. The planting of the crop, the nurturing of young shoots, the bringing-in time of the harvest. The death of the old season, the turn of the new. The bread broken with kinsmen around the evening hearth. Aye, all of that we consider to be our ways. If we wish the pattern of our lives to continue, brothers, then, no, we cannot fail."

By now all had drawn up close to hear the quiet words of our leader.

"And brothers, we shall not fail. Tomorrow we meet up with our allies. Now, even as we speak, to meet this challenge in front of us, out of the west, from Gloucester, comes King Conmael; up from the south, from Bath, comes King

Condidan; all gathered to meet the heathen invaders come up out of Wessex, all gathered here on the plains of the mighty Severn, to fight to keep the Saes from British soil! Let me tell you now what that means for the field of battle . . ."

His voice began to rise. There was iron in it:

". . . for each of Conmael's warriors that might fall, two of us will stand in front of him and protect his back. We shall raise him – we shall lift him back to his feet. If a man for Condidan shall be hacked down, three of us will fill the breach in the shieldwall, we shall stand shoulder to shoulder with Condidan's men! For tomorrow we are all kinsmen, and if the gods decree it, we shall fight and die together as kinsmen!"

He raised his sword in front of him, his voice still rising: the hilt with its bedded jewels struck red-green-blue in the light of many fires

"Tomorrow, we fight for the future of our land. Our names will be recorded in the annals – these were the men who finally defeated the barbarian hordes, these were the men who threw them back forever, these were the men who brought honour to themselves and to their families!"

He paused then, slowly bringing the sword back to the moist earth. With a double-handed thrust, he plunged the blade deep into the clay-heavy soil. Now he spoke quietly again, and all there pressed in to hear his words.

"In truth, when words have passed like smoke into the night air, only the gods can know and decree what might pass on the blood-field tomorrow. I ask you to believe only this – whether we stand or fall, live or die, I am proud to stand here tonight as the leader of West Britons, and tomorrow, if I should die, know that I died a proud man, a West Briton king."

There was silence in the clearing. The men assembled there watched their chief; they would not take their eyes from him as Farinmael turned, gestured to his shoulder-men, and then walked through their midst with his head held high, his kinsmen and chief warriors at his side. Our small war-band, with the giant Cormac, Farinmael's champion, at its head, strode out at his right shoulder and we moved through them all the way up the slope. A quiet murmur swelled up amongst the war-bands; men nodded their heads, clapping each other on the shoulder, and slowly the tightly formed circle broke up, dispersed.

I walked with old Cadolan who spoke quietly to himself, but as I walked next to him I could hear his words.

"Ah yes, fine words, a mighty chief, he spoke from the heart, it is true. But then, fine words never did feed a man's belly, and fine words will not protect the shieldwall from the Saxon hordes tomorrow, and fine words will not clothe and feed and protect the widows and children of those cut down in the field. But, fine words, fine words indeed, the true ring of history."

But then he noticed me standing next to him, and promptly stopped muttering to himself.

*

Before we left our chief that night, Farinmael drew me away from the rest of his warriors.

"Rhuadrac, I have work for you at first light tomorrow. I have words for King Conmael, and I need somebody I can trust to take them to him, alone, without escort, so as not to draw the attention of the Saxons."

He gave me a rolled-up parchment, tied with red cotton, and looked at me straight in the face.

"It is crucial that Conmael sees this tomorrow before the sun has climbed far into the sky. It tells him of my battle plans, and suggests how he might best support me. It is a big responsibility, Rhuadrac, but I trust the son of Advil with my life, with all of our lives. Keep this document with you tonight, stay near to the protection of your brother, and go to Conmael at first light."

Farinmael was a great king. I promised myself at that moment that I would fight five columns of the Saes to get the document to King Conmael.

That night I did not sleep well. I was plagued by strange dreams. In one of the dreams, troll-faced thieves stole into the tent during the night and stole the document whilst I was sleeping. When I awoke, but still in my dream, and discovered that the document was gone, I felt as if I was suffocating, as if the roof of the tent had collapsed and was crushing me.

I woke up in a sweat. The document was still in its place by my left side.

Cormac slept next to me. I prodded him with my elbow. "Brother, do you think that the Christ of our mother's belief looks down on us tonight? Do you think that there is such a god that preserves the souls of good men in the afterlife, who protects those souls from the evils abroad in this world and the Otherworld?"

But Cormac said nothing, and slept on.

I lay there not able to sleep for what seemed to me to be many hours, full of heavy thoughts. I finally joined Cormac in sleep, but my strange dreams did not leave me and the troll-faced creatures kept coming for my precious cargo during the night.

III

The next morning I awoke from my fitful sleep to discover at the first hour of dawn, though we were still in the warm months then, a storm-tossed day – a rumble of thunder rolled through the heavens and over our heads hung heavy rain-filled grey clouds that promised to break and cause holy hell to be let loose at any moment.

We washed and dressed quickly, Cormac and me, and soon enough we were in front of Farinmael's tent. Cormac turned to me.

"Brother, here we must part, for we both have duties to perform. Look out for me on the field of battle. And brother . . ."

He placed his giant hand on my left shoulder.

"Take this. Our mother gave it to me years ago, and I want you to have it today."

He held out a small bronze cross on a silver chain.

"It is a sign of our mother's faith. Believe in it."

I wondered if he had heard me talk to him on the previous night. I did not know that Cormac had any interest in our mother's faith. He usually kept his thoughts to himself. On his own neck I could see the amulet that Gwendolyne had given him, a dragon serpent breathing fire.

"Take care, Rhuadrac. Go to your business. Much rests on you today. Bring glory to our family."

With that he was gone into Farinmael's tent. One of the chief's men came out to meet me.

"I am ordered by Farinmael to give you his second-finest horse, Brindowen. Follow me."

Behind the tents was the makeshift paddock. The man led me to a fine white stallion, surely the finest creature on four legs that I have ever seen, before or since.

"We are informed that Conmael is less than two miles to the east, back towards the Fosse Way. But have great care, there may be Saes raiding parties in the area."

With that he was gone.

I stroked the head of magnificent Brindowen, muttered a few calm words to him, then leapt up onto his back. Within minutes we had left the camp behind and were at full gallop through the forest, densely thick on both sides of us. I made the crest of the hill and, turning east, headed in the direction of the Fosse Way.

Soon I was enveloped again by the dense foliage of the forest. The path ahead of me was marked well and I decided that I could make best progress if I kept to it. But, just then, I rounded a bend in the path and in front of me stood a band of men, on foot.

The blood jerked through my body with a jolt.

In the space of three heartbeats, I knew from their furs and their war-helmets and their spears that these men were Saxons, and that they would take my life without a second thought if I let them. Instantly I dug my heels into the flanks of Brindowen and charged them, drawing *Saesbane* with my right hand as I did so. In the next moment I was upon them, and with a sharp sweeping chop of my right arm brought *Saesbane* down on the head of the Saxon who stood in front of me, even as he half-drew the short sword at his left hip. He yelped in agony as *Saesbane* cut through the right side of his head, taking part of his right ear with it, and in the next moment I was through them, the guttural accents of their strange language ringing in my ears. I dug my heels into Brindowen and within ten heartbeats I was clear of them, their shouts now fading behind me.

Soon after, I allowed Brindowen to slow to a walk. My breathing came fast and the blood continued to pound through my body and my head pulsed with the shock of the encounter. I felt sick in the pit of my stomach. It had all happened in a blur, and even now I could not be sure that it had truly occurred. I dismounted at a stream and took a few mouthfuls of the cool, refreshing water, cleaning the blade of *Saesbane* with the wool cloth in my pocket. A few dispersed shafts of unsettled pale sunlight filtered through the forest canopy into the space around me. Here and there came the sweet song of some bird, doubly loud it seemed to me, and untroubled too. I pulled myself together, remounted Brindowen and pressed on through the forest. At the crest of the next hill, I allowed Brindowen to canter to a halt. I thought that I could hear something, something which at first I mistook for the thunder that still rolled through the sky. I listened hard for a minute or so. There it was again. Unmistakable. A steady beat, as if of drums, inexorable, perhaps a mile or so to the north. I nudged Brindowen on to the next crest. And what I saw there made the blood freeze in my veins.

From my vantage point I could see down the valley as it doubled back on itself about three furlongs from where I stood. To the west of that road, just two furlongs or so from me as the crow flies, I could see an army of men in ranks of six in line advance into a vast natural plateau set between the rolling hills. Straining my eyes, I could see that the road north behind them was covered with marching ranks of men for as far as my keen eyes could see. Further back still, over the crest of the next valley, I could see this army of men still unfolding, vast numbers of men pouring through that valley and making for the plateau which the lead soldiers had now reached.

This army was like none other I had ever seen or heard about. On their heads they wore helmets of metal, with side-panels protecting their cheeks and jaws, so that you could not see their faces. Each man had a long spear across his shoulders, and some of them had short swords at their hip. Over their shoulders hung heavy skins and furs. I realised now that I had seen the same helmets and clothing on the war-band I had encountered in the blurred skirmish last night and just now again in the forest. They carried banners with dragons and ghouls painted on them, and wolves-head crests, and pictures of their gods hurling thunder hammers and giant spears. They held great iron poles, and on these poles were the skulls of bulls, and stuffed eagles, and human skulls too and many other grisly marks of their march down the Fosse Way.

At the head of this army, the first six columns carried great wooden logs between them, held by a heavy leather belt around each of their necks. They beat time on these logs with iron staves, pounding out a relentless uniform rhythm that sent fear down to the marrow of my soul. And above this devil rhythm they sang a tuneless dirge of such guttural sounds that it seemed to me as if I had stumbled upon a scene out of hell, and I knew that this hell was to be unleashed upon me and my people.

Just at that moment great cries went out from the lead horsemen, who rode up and down the flanks of this army, and they each held up an outstretched arm. As one, the ranks of soldiers at the head of the column stopped marching, and the devil rhythm ceased abruptly. For a few moments there was complete silence.

Then I could hear orders being shouted in the same strange guttural language, unlike anything I had heard before, and the army began to fan out, and I knew that this place would be the battlefield that day.

I tell you that I knew fear then. And I knew fear because I could see, sitting there on the back of the magnificent white stallion Brindowen, as this devil army unfolded before me, that we were lost. Totally lost. Even if the kings Conmael and Condidan could match Farinmael's warriors in numbers, by my first guess we must have been outnumbered five times to one. We could not win. Even the finest warriors stood no chance against such odds.

In truth, there was no hope for us.

I thought of my brother Cormac, Farinmael's champion, and for the first time in my short life I feared for him. I thought of my uncle and friends, of Farinmael himself, and I lowered my head.

I stopped being a child, there, on that hill, on the back of the great white stallion Brindowen.

*

I wheeled Brindowen away from the crest of the hill and sped down into the next valley. Within five minutes I saw sentries, and they were dressed in the British style, so I knew that I had arrived at Conmael's camp. I explained my business and at the mention of Farinmael's name one of the sentries ran for his horse and beckoned me to follow him. A few minutes later we were in front of King Conmael's tent, and the king stood there himself with his chief warriors. Briefly the sentry explained who I was, then saluted, turned his horse and made back to his post.

Conmael was older than Farinmael and to my eyes he looked tired. No doubt he had been discussing the battle with his lieutenants throughout the night. No doubt too that his outriders had already seen what I had seen and he knew what awaited him that day.

He greeted me warmly. I told him my name and explained my business. I handed him the document I carried tucked into my belt. Without formality, he broke the seal and read the words set out there, which I could see were set down in the written language of the Romans.

"Rhuadrac, go back to Farinmael and tell him I understand his plan and that I will meet his requests. Let the first encounter with the enemy be his, we shall support him from the south flank after the first assault has been repulsed. Tell him too that his bravery is already known throughout these lands, and that this day will enhance his name in the annals of this place for as long as the stories continue to be told by our ancestors."

I thanked him. Before I left him, I began to explain what I had seen to the west of the Fosse Way. Conmael held up his hand to stop me.

"No need, Rhuadrac. My men have been tracking the Saxon army for the last two days. We know their numbers, and we know what is in front of us. Let us be brave, let us bring glory to our families, let us place trust in the Lord our God. Good luck to you this day."

I raised my arm, tugging on the leather rein to turn Brindowen's head about, and made my way back to my people, reflecting as I did so that Conmael followed the Christian God of my mother. I realised also that Farinmael's scouts too must have been aware of the strength of the Saxon army for some time. His address to his men last night had been spoken in the full knowledge of what lay before him.

I wept then for my proud king, and pledged to die fighting at his side.

IV

The two opposing armies faced each other on the open plain.

Farinmael stood in the centre of the three armies that made up our ranks, as had been agreed between the three kings. To Farinmael's right and rear, perhaps a furlong behind him, stood King Conmael's army, and I was pleased to see the proof of the success of my lone expedition. On Farinmael's left and rear was Condidan's army, and I knew that he too had agreed to follow Conmael into the fray, in the hope that by then some success had been achieved in driving the Saes back.

I sat on Brindowen in Farinmael's lead rank, and my pride was as great as my fear as I sat there. The grim reality of our task must by now have been clear to all on the West Briton side. The size of the Saxon army was colossal, and for as far as the eye could see it spread across the plain in front of us. For some time now a devil rhythm from the Saxon drums had been echoing across the plain; it was not the inexorable marching beat I had heard that morning. This was different, a much slower beat, as if they were marking time before they descended upon us.

I had met with Cormac briefly on my return from Conmael's camp. I barely recognised him, made up as he was in full battle rig. He had on the gold helmet of our father, and his mail shirt gleamed, and the wide gold belt buckle of our father was wrapped around his waist. In his hands he held the battle-axe called *Gaeallon*. Black and red streaks of dye covered his face. I knew better than to try to talk to him now. He left me at these moments. He seemed to be in his own world. All of his childlike qualities went from him, and they were replaced by an eagle stare, by monosyllabic grunts, by a facial expression that I knew only too well. This was his place, and his place alone, for I had come to understand that my brother was born for battle, that in battle he was his true self.

Many seasons before, I had found Cormac alone in a field by the stream near our home. He would hardly speak to me.

Finally he told me that a much older boy, a bully from the next village that we all knew and hated, had insulted our family in some way in his presence. He sat on a tree stump, staring into the stream, and then he looked at me in a way that I have never forgotten and he said to me, in a very calm voice:

"I am going to go back to the village, I am going to find him, and I am going to make sure that he never insults our family again."

With that, he had left me. I never knew what really happened in the village that afternoon, but I do know that the bully was found with his back broken, and he did not walk again. There was no outcry from the village, because the bully's ways had long been suspected. It was the start of Cormac's reputation and it had led us all the way to this field, and now he stood at the right shoulder of Farinmael as his champion.

We watched as three or four horses broke out from the opposing army and raced towards us, their wolf's head standard streaming behind them. They stopped in the middle of the space between us. Farinmael kicked his horse forward and with Cormac and Gavin he rode out to meet them. We all watched as Cormac dismounted. Presently, Farinmael and Gavin came back to us, holding Cormac's horse by its leather rein, and Farinmael indicated that the warriors were to move forward. The Saxons had called out our champion to meet theirs in a trial of strength, as was their custom.

Cormac stood there calmly, waiting for his opponent. From out of the first rank of the Saes strode a warrior, dressed from head to toe in black, with a black shield and the short sword favoured by the Saxons. I could see long blonde hair stream out from under his black battle-helmet, and I learned later that he was a mercenary from the far northern land and had built up a fearsome reputation as a destroyer of men in that land.

Both armies had slowly moved forward, so that we could now clearly see the two champions.

We watched as Cormac held up *Gaeallon* and threw it to his right, drawing his sword from his belt. He would meet the Saxon on equal terms.

The two warriors circled each other, sizing each other, seeing what the other had to offer. It must then have struck the Saxon champion that he was facing an opponent like no other he had met, for, although he was a big man, he was dwarfed by my brother.

Suddenly Cormac sprang forward and knocked the Saxon's sword spinning from his hand. In the same moment he reached with his other hand for the face of his opponent, knocking off the black battle-helmet as he did so. Cormac held the Saxon full by the face in an iron grip with his one hand, holding him still, and threw his own sword away from his other hand. I saw the Saxon's knees buckle. With a deliberate movement, with his second hand now under the ribs of his opponent, Cormac lifted the Saxon bodily from the floor, hurling him into the air, and he dropped him and caught him with his arms locked around the top of the haunches of the other man, wrapped around the small of his back, and with deliberate leverage, he clasped his own left wrist with his right hand and he crushed the life out of his opponent. I have never seen a look of more despair on the face of any man than I saw that day in the face of the Saxon champion as the top half of his back arched backwards away from Cormac. He knew that he was pinned by this behemoth of almost superhuman strength. It was as if he was being crushed between slabs of rock, and he knew that he was done for. There was a scream and a loud crack as the hasp of the Saxon's back disintegrated, and then the life went out of him. Cormac threw the broken body aside like a rag doll, and it lay motionless in the soil.

Cormac stooped to pick up *Gaeallon*, and shook it at the Saxon hordes.

"Who else do you have?" he roared.

"Bring him out to me you filthy heathens. Bring him out to me now if you dare!"

There was an unreal silence for about thirty quick beats, which was broken by a deep roar from our warriors, and they waved their swords and spears in the air, and jeered at the Saes ranks, for the Saxons began to back away, and back away, until they stood about seventy-five paces from us.

The first small victory was ours, but we knew it could not last. Farinmael and Gavin rode out to Cormac with his horse, and I saw Farinmael clasp Cormac's shoulder and hand as he helped Cormac up onto it. They galloped back the short distance to our ranks.

"Set free the horses, close the ranks, prepare, form three shieldwalls at twenty paces apart, they will soon be upon us!" roared Farinmael.

As he did so the warriors in the second and third lines stepped forward to the first, their shields all overlapping, so that a tight shell was formed. The spearmen fell into place behind them. The warriors in the first two ranks at the end of each line also turned about, and overlapped their shields, and the spearmen stood behind them. In this way the first shieldwall was formed. Behind the first, a second was formed, then a third, as Farinmael had ordered.

The devil drummers continued to beat their drums, but now the beats began to increase, now the tempo of the drums grew faster, then grew faster still. I understood then that the beat of the drums matched the beating of my own heart, because the battle-spirit began to flow through me and I knew that the devils would be soon upon us.

I looked at my uncle, Gavin, veteran of many battles, and I saw him swallow hard. He looked at me and nodded, as if asking a question of me. I looked at him and slowly nodded my head slightly too, and straightened my shoulders. My uncle smiled then, an old smile, for he knew that I would face this battle by his side, and likely too we would die here together.

Now the drums were almost one long drone, their beats matching my own now racing heart.

Suddenly, with a great howl, the Saes ranks burst towards us, and their shouts and screams filled the sky, and their spears and knives cleft the air, and it was as if the gates of hell had burst asunder and the worse ghouls and monsters of the underworld had been unleashed and they were coming to claim us.

"Stay still!" roared Farinmael.

They were forty paces from us and it was as if my heart would burst through my chest, and the blood roared through my head as if it was fit to burst.

"Stay still!"

They were twenty paces from us and I could see their painted faces and I knew then they were not monsters, but old men and young men like me, and some like me were scared, but all were filled with the battle-spirit, and I knew too that now all of our fates were in the hands of the gods, and none of us could know the outcome.

"We fight for our British soil!" roared Farinmael.

Then the first wave of the heathen was upon us and in amongst us and I saw in the same moment the thickset form of Gavin instantly swept backwards by five men and Fintan fall under the feet of the hordes and Oisin bent in half by a spear thrust in his gut and I was fighting for my life in a frenzy of sweeps and cuts and chops of *Saesbane* and I ducked and I weaved and I kept moving as men fell around me and on top of me and blood spattered my clothes and my face and the ground around me and the wild clamour of human voices and the smell of struck iron thick in the air as men screamed and howled and shouted and there was no time to stop and think only to cut and to stab and to block and to parry and I have no memory of any one face just a blur of painted faces and already the shield-wall was broken and they were through us and on to the second shield-wall.

I gasped for breath, exhausted, and we had been fighting for no more than five minutes. I caught sight of Farinmael and Cormac in front of me as they fought and stabbed and hacked, and Cormac wielded *Gaeallon* in great scything double-handed movements and whole ranks of the Saes fell under it. Already the Saxon bodies lay mutilated in great heaps before him, and there were body parts all around and I saw other sights too that I will not record out of respect for the proud warriors who fell silent that day.

I reeled as a stinging blow hit my head and a myriad of yellow lights clouded my sight. I was down and the smell of cold black mud was thick in my nose and I knew for sure that my moment had come. But nothing. The final blow did not fall. I looked up and Cormac and Farinmael were there, and Cormac held a Saxon by the throat and crushed his windpipe, before flinging him aside.

"You will never take my brother's soul while I still live!" he roared.

But the shape of the battle had already changed. There was a strange lull in the fighting in the place where we were, for their first wave had ripped straight through our sector, even though the fight went on all around us. But in truth the damage to our ranks in that first collision was already devastating. The first two shieldwalls were already broken and our army was already splintered, for the remnants of the Saes first wave had rolled on to our third shieldwall and vicious fighting whirled about us. Every British warrior fought bravely, but there were too many of the Saxons. For every one of the enemy that we cut down, three more took his place, and still their waves rolled through us.

"The shieldwall is breached, fall back, fall back!" cried Farinmael.

As we fell back, we could see and hear that the next Saxon wave was already almost upon us, now no more than fifty paces from us, and I saw the jaw clench in Farinmael's face, for he knew what this next charge must bring.

At that moment, we heard a great clamour from our right and we saw that Conmael's men had come into the field, and had hit the Saxon forces from their left, and their momentum was momentarily checked. Seeing this, Farinmael turned to his warriors and shouted:

"Forget the shieldwall, men. There are too many of them. Every man for himself, and I will see you all at the feast on the other side!"

With those words he roared at the sky, lifted his sword and charged at the Saxons with Cormac at his side. They reached a small mound in the battlefield, and they stood there side by side. They hacked down Saxons on all sides, and still the heathens came at them. Cormac heft *Gaeallon* at chest height in great sweeping arcs, and the Saxons fell all around him, and Farinmael then too was true to his nickname, which was Battle-serpent, and together they fought shoulder to shoulder.

Then the next wave reached me and I continued to stab and to cut and to chop at everything Saxon in front of me, be it face, or arm or fur or leg, and I kept moving and bending and crouching. Slowly I worked my way over to Farinmael and my brother. Suddenly I was struck by the fact that all around me in our sector the fighting seemed to have paused and men on both sides had fallen back slightly. All were watching Farinmael and Cormac and their assailants, now just ten or twelve Saxons still standing, all of whom had a wolf's head on their shields, and it seemed to me that they were part of a special war-band. Elsewhere, the battle waged freely, as Conmael's men joined the fray over on the left flank, engaging with yet another wave of Saxons, but in our immediate sector at least there was a pause. For now all there understood that a great king was in his last moments, and his warriors knew that there was nothing they could do to help him for he would be finished by the time they could get to him. I understood too that it was only a matter of time. All around me men lay two and three deep, and wailed or cried out, as they began to feel their wounds. I could not see my kinsmen; they too must be buried amongst the heaps of groaning men all about me.

Then, in the midst of this hell, I had a clear thought. I would get to my brother and my proud king's side. This is what I would do. Nothing else was of concern to me. I would get to my brother's side. I ran to the mound, and I fought to get next to them, because I had made a promise to myself that I would die at Farinmael's side, next to his champion, my brother, the giant Cormac, and I would be true to my word.

And then the dark moment came. Already the Saxons were behind the king and my brother, and other Saxons were inside the arc of *Gaeallon*, and now several heathens were about the shoulders of Cormac. Still he threw them off, still the champion strove to protect his king. I got to his side, and I saw that he recognised me in that great crisis, for he smiled, and I understood that he was pleased that his brother would be with him at the end. It was then that Farinmael fell. Already wounded, with blood pouring from strikes to his head and to his side, a Saxon warrior – a brave man too, for he had been twice hit glancing blows by *Gaeallon* – got through with the fatal blow, his short sword finding the weak spot in the stretched links of Farinmael's mail shirt and driving up and through into Farinmael's ribcage, just below the heart.

Cormac roared and fell on one knee and the Saxons were at him like mad dogs on a wounded bear, striking at him from all angles. I cut, and I chopped, and I wielded *Saesbane* with all the remaining strength left to me to save my brother.

Then something strange happened on that battlefield.

A shout went up, and the Saxon warriors immediately fell back from my brother and from me too. I stopped laying about me and gasped for breath, and bent forward at my knees, not really believing that I was still alive. Sweat ran into my eyes, and I could barely stand. By some miracle, I had sustained no serious wounds, but I was bloodied and badly bruised. I looked up, and saw a great tall warrior stride through the Saxon ranks, and they cleared a path for him, and at his side walked two shoulder-men, they too bearing the wolf's head on their shields. It struck me that this must be the Gevissa king. He wore a magnificent mail shirt, which too had the wolf's head crest upon it, a silhouette in black outline. This shirt and his battle-helmet and his shield were inlaid with gold and the rare mixed metal called *niello*, and I understood that this was a sign of their kings, for no other of the Saxons were allowed at that time to use armour inlaid with these metals on the field of battle.

Their king came up to where I stood, next to my brother, who lay barely alive at my side. He looked at me and my brother, placed a hand on my shoulder as if he knew that I would not strike at him (and for reasons I have never understood since, he was right) and said something to his warriors in his strange language.

Then he moved through to Farinmael, and, removing his own great battle-helmet which he laid on the ground next to him, he knelt by Farinmael's side. I could see that he had a lean and lined face, his jaw was clean-shaven, and the short hair on his scalp was mostly white, and it seemed to me to be the face of a learned man, not that of a warrior. I realised that Farinmael was not yet dead, for the Saxon king stooped over him, as if listening to Farinmael's words. Then I too heard Farinmael's quiet voice and they talked to each other for a few moments in the Saxon's strange language, which I had not known Farinmael could speak, but I know not what it was that they said to each other. Then the Saxon king lifted his arm, and slowly clasped Farinmael's hand in his own, as if they too were brothers. Then, taking his knife from its sheath, he dealt Farinmael the final death blow, in the way that was most fitting for a great warrior, and the soul of our great king left this world then for the Otherworld.

The Saxon king stood up, but his head was bowed. Speaking quietly, he uttered a few words over his fallen enemy, then turned to his men. He spoke quickly in short sentences, gesturing with his arms. Six of them came to Farinmael, and they lifted him up onto their shoulders, and they carried him in this way from the field, a path opening up in the Saxons ranks to make way for them. The Saxon king watched, then looked across to where I stood with my brother (alive or dead, I knew not) by my side. Again he barked out short, sharp orders. I breathed deeply and prepared for my death, for I had already decided that I would only leave this field with my king and my brother, and that I would never be taken prisoner, even if the Saxons should offer that path to me.

But I remember no more, for just then a great blow struck the back of my head, and all was dark.

V

O dark, dark, dark seemed that day in the history of the British people, when the Battle of Deorham was fought and lost to the Saxon invaders.

For the warrior-king, Farinmael, was dead, and from that day his name would pass into legend, and the verse-makers would sing of his deeds and his honour. As I was to learn in the days after the battle, the kings Conmael and Condidan also fell that day, earning great glory by honouring to the full the pact they had made with Farinmael, for they followed him into the fray against overwhelming odds without hesitation when they saw that the shieldwalls were breached. The Britons were completely routed from the field, and not more than one hundred men made the journey back to their homes, all wounded but saved from a certain death by the particular vigour of their fighting (for I came to learn that the Saxons respected this), which was all that was left from a combined fighting force of some eighteen hundred warriors.

The Saxon victory was complete, for now there was nothing to stop them taking the cities of Corinium, and Gloucester and Bath, which they duly did. There was nothing between them and the western marches as far as the west banks of the Wye and the Gwent border, and so in this way Farinmael's grim prediction on the eve of battle came to pass.

My uncle, Gavin, was lost that day. Oisin, called also Singer-of-Songs, and Fintan the slingsman and lyre player, also perished, as did many others whose names the annals do not record, but they were all proud men, and warriors to the last. There is no record of even one man fleeing the field from the ranks of Farinmael's army, and I believe that was because of those few words of our king on the eve of battle. A bond had been made between men at that moment.

As for me and Cormac, well, it was the beginning of a new life for both of us, one which ill-fitted us at first, and a life that initially threatened a great rupture between us, but that is the next part of my story.

*

PART II

Aftermath of Deorham

I

When I opened my eyes I thought myself to be in the banqueting hall of the warrior-gods, for I knew not where I was. A dull ache pounded behind my eyes and my mouth was so dry that I cried out for water, not thinking if there was anyone to hear me.

A gentle hand raised my head, and I could smell a sweet perfume, and I thought that perhaps I had left the real world and that I was now started upon some great adventure, the like of which no man had before experienced. A clawed pot was raised to my lips, and I tasted as cold and as fresh a sip of water as a man has ever tasted.

A woman's voice was talking to me and it seemed to me in my dazed condition that the voice spoke the language of the Britons, which surprised me, for I did not expect it.

"You must not move . . ." said the sweet female voice, ". . . you must not move or the consequences will be bad for you."

I opened my eyes fully for the first time and I knew myself then to be in the warrior's heaven.

My memory of this moment is as clear to me now as I record this as it was on the day it happened, even though more than forty winters have gone around since the woman whom my mind beholds in glory first appeared before my eyes. I say a woman, but in truth she was no more than my age, and she held my head in her arms. Her long and plaited hair was dark, and her eyes were blue-grey, though the outer rims were green, and her skin was a light-golden colour the like of which I had never before seen. She wore a royal-purple gown, and around her neck was a gold necklace. In the centre of this necklace was a triangular pendant with a dark-blue stone at its centre, set in gold, and this dark stone was hung from a chain made of spun gold beads, and each bead was followed with oval and triangular dark stones set into each link.

"No need to talk," she said, still in the language of the Britons, but with a strange accent, for although I could understand her, some of the words had a strange inflection, and it was clear to me that she was not a Briton.

"Now you must rest again, then I will arrange for food to be brought to you when you next awake."

And then this vision left me and I slept, neither knowing where I was nor who it was that tended to me.

I had terrible dreams that plagued me and caused me to wake in sweat, for in my dreams wild hordes with animal faces burst at me, wave after wave, and I hacked and chopped at these animal faces in frenzy and still they came at me. I would wake and my blood would be pounding through my body and I felt somehow ashamed that I had been a part of this frenzy. Slowly, my senses would come back to me and I remembered that with my own clear-thinking mind in the middle of this madness I had decided my own course of action; I had chosen to get next to my king and my brother.

In this way I managed to slowly overcome my terrible dreams, and they grew less, but did not completely go away for many months after my first taste of battle.

So I learnt that it is one matter to survive the battle itself; it is a second matter to survive the aftermath of battle.

*

Over the next few days the story became clearer to me. I fell in and out of a stupor, and in that time I saw several women come to tend me, and occasionally I saw this young beauty, and I was best pleased when it was her that attended me. At first she did so in the company of an older woman, but after a few days, when it became clear that I meant her no harm, she would dismiss the older woman with a curt command and she would leave us, but not without some concern. I discovered that the beauty's name was Ulla, and she was a Saxon, but she was no ordinary Saxon. She was the daughter of Ceawlin, King of the Gevissas in Wessex, for it was he who had spared my life.

Ulla told me, with great reservation at first, for she had had few dealings with the men of West Britain before she met me, that her father, a veteran of many battles, had at first watched the battle from the crest of a nearby hill, for he had wanted to gauge the strength of our armies. He had been astounded by the prowess of the giant, Farinmael's champion. He had decided to come on to the field himself, to see if this giant could be in some way preserved, for he had work for him in his own armies. Once on the field, he had witnessed for himself the glory of Farinmael, and had resolved that such bravery should be honoured. He had managed to talk to our king before he died, but Ulla herself had not been told of what was said, which did not surprise me, for such matters are for the ears of the participants alone, and that is the right way.

It was now that I learned that the Britons had been routed, that Conmael and Condidan had both perished on the field of battle – "with great honour" – and that her people were now in control of the whole of the lower Severn Valley as far as the borders with the land of Mercia. My face clouded at this, but it did not surprise me, for I had known when I first set sight on the Saxon army that this outcome was inevitable. I lay back on the bed in which I had been placed, and my mind was troubled. I had not expected to survive the battle, yet here I was, and already the shape of my world was changing in ways that I could not have anticipated.

I had by now become accustomed to the room in which I lay, which seemed to me to be more like a small hall, rather than a bedroom. It was of timber construction, with great crossbeams below the centre of its roof and ornate and sculpted corner-pieces of wood. But otherwise I knew little of my circumstances. Where was I? Why was this woman, a king's daughter, attending me? Where was my brother, Cormac? Was he dead?

"I shall try my best to answer you," she said to me when I began to ask her some of these questions.

"Your skull was almost split with the blow that felled you, for my father understood that you would not leave the field unless you were carried from it. But he also saw that you are in some way connected with the giant, for you fought together and were prepared to die together, saw also that you have the fighting heart of a wolf-leader, so he decided that you too should be spared, and brought here."

She looked at me and smiled in a manner that was full of mischief, and it beguiled me.

"As for why I am attending you – well then, I like the shape of your face, and the way that you are made, and I thought that I might speak with you."

At that time in my life, I knew nothing of the ways of women, although several of the older village girls had by then long since took it upon themselves to educate me in the delights of physical love between a man and a woman, and like most young men I was more than keen at that time to continue my education at every opportunity.

I was completely spellbound by this lady. I had begun to notice that, although her figure was slender, it was full, and womanly. I could watch for minutes in silence as she walked around the room, the curves of her body creating delightful full shapes in her gown. Once or twice she noticed me do this and would look at me and I would meet her eyes steadily and some knowledge passed silently between us then.

But not only was she a gorgeous creature; it was as if I had already known her in some way for all of my short life. Somehow, it seemed as if it was only right that she should care for me, because she was the greatest friend I had always had in my life, which was the right and correct order of things and we had not been together in the same room before now merely because of the mysterious workings of some arbitrary fate.

I was totally bewildered by these thoughts, but I swear on my life that is what I thought when I first met Ulla, the daughter of Ceawlin, the Gevissa king.

"There is some good news for you today . . ." Ulla continued,

". . . for your friend, the giant, is still alive, and though he is fighting for his life, our physicians, who are astonished that he survived the blows he received in the battle, think that he is through the worst . . ."

"He is not my friend, he is my one true brother, and I am proud of it," I growled, much too ferociously, for she backed away from me, and she looked worried, and half made to reach for a rope hanging next to the bed. I later learned that the rope was attached to a bell in the corridor outside, in which stood three of the king's personal guard, who had clear instructions to despatch me without mercy if I should attempt to attack Ulla.

But I immediately regretted my response, for this beautiful girl had shown me nothing but kindness since I had revived. Also, she had just given me the best news I had received in days, and, in any case, she fascinated me, and I wanted her to stay with me. I made it clear that I had no wish to alarm her, and that I was grateful for her kindness, but most of the news that she brought me made me sad, so she must expect some reaction to it.

"At least Cormac is alive then," I muttered more to myself than to Ulla.

"Cormac? Is that the giant's name?"

"It is, and mine is Rhuadrac, and our uncle, Gavin, like our dead father before him, is right-hand man to King Farinmael."

Even as I said the words I groaned for my dead king, and the thought struck me that Gavin too was probably dead, and I fell back in the bed and a shadow must have crossed my face once more, for Ulla quickly changed the subject.

"But those are not British names."

"No, my mother comes from across the western sea. She is Irish, and it was she who named my brother and me."

"Rhu-ad-rac." She repeated, emphasising the syllables.

"I like that name. Yes, Rhuadrac, it suits you. What did you say your mother's name was?"

"I did not say, but it is Ethna, and I have a sister, Aisha."

"Ethna and Aisha . . ." she repeated, as if committing their names to her memory, but I could not think why she would want to do this. She then looked at my neck, for I still wore the bronze cross that Cormac had given me before Deorham.

"Are you of the Christ faith?"

"My mother is, and my brother gave me this before the battle."

"I persuaded my father to allow you to keep it during the high point of your illness, for I know of this faith and its powers through my mother. My father says it is no faith for warriors, and forbids any outward show of it. His one stipulation is that you do not wear it in front of his warriors, although you may keep it hidden about your person."

It was not a matter of importance to me that I should declare to the world what I believed, for I believed many things. I was young and much moved by the warrior spirit, so I removed the cross from my neck.

"Now rest, we shall talk again soon enough, that is, if you should wish to talk with me again?"

She looked at me sideways, and I felt as if I was being tested in some way, but I had no idea why, or in what way. Frankly, the question baffled me. Why would I not wish to see her? She was the only person I knew in this world, the world of the Saxons. As I say, the ways of women were a complete mystery to me at that time.

"Yes, as well to see you as any other person in our current condition." I said.

I had Cormac in mind when I said this, but for some reason this statement proved to be a mistake, for a look of fury passed through her eyes and a tiny frown appeared in the middle of her forehead and she turned from me abruptly, and I did not see her again for the next five days, each moment of which I counted.

II

By the end of the third week I began to feel stronger. They would not allow me to see my brother, which angered me, but one day I received a visit from the older woman who had first attended to me with Ulla.

This lady had seen maybe thirty and more winters. She was big-boned, and the sleeves of her working tunic were rolled up, revealing thick arms, and she had a big flushed red face with large blue eyes. She now fussed about the room, tidying things up here and there.

Soon enough she drew closer to my side of the room, but would not venture too near to where I lay. Then she took a deep breath and fixed me with a cautious stare, that somehow failed to disguise the natural good-natured set of her features, for her big face looked as if it might break into laughter at any moment.

"Now mind that you don't go messing about with the lady, young fellow-me-lad."

She spoke in the British tongue, and I was astonished to realise that she was a Briton like me.

"Aye, I'm a Briton, just like you. My name is Peg. I've been part of this king's family since he met my lady, the Queen Acha. She's a Briton too, and between us we've made sure that her daughter understands our ways of doin' things, even though she's one o' them, and she's none the worse for it."

The mother of Ulla was British? I was astonished by this news. This woman, Peg, lived at the Saxon hall? How could this be? The Saxons were deadly enemies of the British; they were taking our land from us. What caused these women to desert their own people?

"There's many a British woman who's taken a Saxon husband. And why not? They're good men, good fathers, they know how to farm the land."

"But they are our enemy. How could these women do such a thing?"

"One day, boy, you might learn that there are many mysteries in this life, and that's one o' them. Men were born to fight and make big statements – women were born to love and get things done. That's the start and the finish of it. These Saxons are not bad people when you get to know them. They think as we think, do as we do, dream as we dream. Their customs are different to ours, but deep down they're just the same as us."

Now Peg stopped talking and fixed me with her stare again, then prodded her thick first finger at me.

"But I've not come to talk about the Saxons. You mind that you treat the young lady well. She's sensitive, is Ulla, and she has taken some great liking to that handsome mug of yours, so you mind you treat her properly, or you will have me to answer to for it!"

"Have no fear, Briton Peg, she has captured my heart already, and I miss her more by the day."

As I said this, Peg's face cracked into a great beaming smile that displayed a couple of missing teeth.

"Good boy! You seem like a right 'un to me, but I'll be watching you, mark my words!"

With this, she left me. A British woman, waiting attendance on a Saxon princess, who was herself the daughter of a British woman? I could not understand any of it.

The visits of Ulla soon resumed.

She confirmed that she had learnt our British language from her mother and Peg. I told her all that Peg had said to me. Ulla looked at me watchfully, then, as if making up her mind on some question that she had asked herself, decided to share her thoughts with me

"It is true. There are also many other British wives of Saxons in my father's hall, and throughout his lands. The numbers grow monthly, for everywhere there is a move towards settlement. Some of the people are growing tired of battles. Some want to work the land they have won, and put down roots, and see no need to continue the move north and west from the first settlements. The land they have is fertile, why then look for more? But my father knows that his work is only half done. If he does not look to expand his borders, then others will come to threaten his own lands, and the peace that the people have now will one day be taken from them."

She stopped, seeing that I frowned at these words. Her father's future peace was being bought at the expense of my people.

"I have a brother, too, called Cutha, who is down on the Saxon Shore looking after my father's interests there. He is noble, like my father, and perhaps you will meet him one day. He is just two winters older than me. You remind me of him in some ways."

Then Ulla coloured slightly.

Perhaps you will meet with Crida too, who is Cutha's great friend, and my friend too."

I looked at her then; she seemed somehow agitated, but I decided to say nothing.

Ulla explained to me that her great grandfather, who had come to the British shores many winters ago, had first come "with others on three boats" to fight in the British wars as a mercenary, and he had thrived in that way. His kingdom had been won by battle in the southern lands of Britannia, and now her father was king over a great kingdom.

"My father has led my people now for some seventeen winters. His victories are already sung by the verse-makers – his story is a fine story. He likes this land: he knew that the encroachment of the sea had much reduced the coastal areas of his own homeland, and the shortage of land there had forced his grandfather to abandon his own land, and he became minded to stay in this fertile land. There is a future to be had here."

"Aye, and at the expense of my people," I said, and I could see that these words angered her, but they were true, and I did not regret saying them.

"What have the British done with it? You do nothing but fight amongst yourselves, your weak kings seeking nothing but gold and power for themselves, and when they prove too weak, turn to my people to fight their wars for them. The Romans themselves could make nothing of you Britons! Even now the great cities they built lay in ruins, because there were none in these lands with the strength to maintain them, and rebuild them, and make your country a part of the civilised world. Now there are others who will take their chance. This is a great land, and surely there is room for us all?"

I looked at her then with some bemusement in my face. It was a notion that had never crossed my mind before. Britain belonged to the British; it was our land and had been so for as long as the lays and verses had been spoken. There was no other race in Britain before the British, and this is well known in all lands to this day. Why should we share it? Truly the Romans had established their garrisons here, and had built walled cities and had left us their customs and their language which we write and sometimes speak, but even they had come and gone, leaving Britain to the British once more.

Already in the last few weeks all of my expectations had been utterly confounded. I had been told that the Saxons were heathen hordes, that they were monsters, and the stories of their cruelty stretched the length of the land in which I lived. I had cause to believe that these stories were true, for the people who told those stories were honest men, and I had no reason to doubt them. But then I remembered the faces of those warriors who had attacked us in the first wave at Deorham; those men were not monsters, they were flesh and blood men like me, and they lived the joys and the sufferings of this life as we all do, and so much had been clear to me in the few moments before we joined in combat on the field of battle.

But more than that, there was the fact of Ulla herself. She was my friend. I cannot say more than that. It was already beyond dispute. She was my friend; I had barely met her, yet it seemed to me that I had known her all of my life. I might be wrong, but it seemed to me that she thought this too, that we were friends, and it was right that we should be with each other.

But she was a Saxon woman.

I did not know what to make of this dilemma. I looked forward to the day when I could speak with Cormac, and take his counsel, for Cormac was older than me, had sometimes sat at the elders' table, and he knew more than me about such matters.

At the beginning of the fourth week, Ulla told me that I was now well enough to receive her father. This news did not impress me, for the man might be a king, but he was my enemy, and at that time he represented everything that I hated – but for her – although I did not express any of this to her, for fear that I might distress her.

But I had little time to reflect on it, for the door to my room was thrown back and Ceawlin stood there. He now looked much changed from when I had last seen him at Deorham. He was a very tall man, not as tall as Cormac, who was beyond tall, was indeed a giant, but nonetheless a very tall man. I was struck again by the noble cast of his head and face, and again I thought of a learned man, a scholar or monk, not a warrior. There was none of the heaviness of a typical older warrior about him, none of the excess caused by feasting and wine that I had already seen so many warriors succumb to in their later years. His lean and etched face, which remained clean-shaven, was as if full of profound thought. I have come to learn that the correct word to describe him was ascetic; he looked like an ascetic man, like one who fights battles of the soul, as much as he fights battles of the sword. Whether in fact this was his true character I could not at that time say, but I well remember how strongly these thoughts struck me. He could not have been less like the image of a Saxon that had been drawn for me by my elders all through my childhood.

He exchanged words in the Saxon tongue with Ulla, and I noticed that there was a warm tone to his voice when he addressed her. I saw with relief that she would stay in the room, for it became clear that although Ceawlin had some knowledge of our language, he preferred to speak in his own tongue, and so Ulla would translate between us. Peg was allowed to stay in the room too, and fussed backwards and forwards behind Ulla, clearly listening to every word that was said.

Ceawlin began to speak; I noticed immediately that the warm tone of his voice when he addressed his daughter had disappeared and his words were clipped, short and measured.

"My father is pleased that you are recovering well, for he has work for you when you are fully well again."

I had resolved to be sullen, as was befitting the son of Advil, brother of Cormac, and a proud warrior of King Farinmael.

"I have no interest in working for your father, who is my enemy."

Ulla looked at me curiously and said something in Saxon to her father, which did not produce the response that I had expected from Ceawlin.

The Saxon king then launched into a long formal speech, which Ulla proceeded to translate in short bursts, though I had the impression that she was not telling me all that he said, nor giving me a full translation of all of the phrases that he used.

"My father saved you and your brother, the one you call Cormac, the giant, for two reasons: firstly, you fought well and proudly, like true warriors, and he was impressed by the prowess of the giant . . . but yours too also. Secondly, he has work for the giant, and he thinks that the giant will work better if his brother is with him. He does not propose that you fight against your own people, the West Britons, for he knows that you are both proud warriors and that you would die before doing so. Therefore he makes two alternative proposals. He has alliances with other Germans in the east of this land of Alba, the Jutes in Kent, and they wage war against other Aenglish and the Britons in the north-east of your land. Warriors with the skills of the giant . . . and you too . . . could be of use to his Kent allies. The alternative is this – if you do not wish to fight with the Kentish men, against those who share your language and your ways, then he has other alliances and arrangements in the Frankish kingdoms and if you both agree to work in the land of the Gauls, you will be allowed to earn much gold, most of which you may keep."

My face had clouded as I listened to the content of these proposals. I had a mother and sister, who even now may have suffered some terrible fate at the hands of the victorious invaders, a thought that had begun to trouble me greatly as I had started to recover from my injuries. Ceawlin, with his long, lean face studied my youthful features closely and began to speak again, although somehow his tone seemed softer. Ulla listened to him and then began again to translate, colouring a little as she did so:

"It is only natural that, in the face of a proposal to travel and fight overseas, you might want to think of your close kin who depend on you at these moments, and you might have concerns as to their present safety. From the information that you provided to my daughter . . ."

I looked at Ulla sharply when she said this, and I saw a light redness run through her face. So, she was a spy for her father, and I had fallen for her ruses. I looked at her angrily as she continued.

". . . we have searched for the Irish mother of the giant Cormac and his brother Rhuadrac, and she, the woman called Ethna and her daughter, called Aisha, have both been found safe and well, travelling west together with a fat white-haired old monk who sought to protect them from my father's war-band with only his staff . . ."

May my mother's god help me, I was so relieved by the news of my mother and sister that I almost laughed at this unexpected but most accurate description of Cadolan, whose own survival pleased me greatly. I stopped myself and instead tears sprang to my eyes at the words that Ulla used, but I knew not why. And I saw that Ulla herself was, for some reason, delighted by my reaction to this news.

". . . and they are now all under my protection. I pledge that no harm will come to your mother, nor to your sister, not even to the monk if you so wish it, for so long as you and your brother remain protected by me."

Ceawlin now reverted to the formal tone he had previously used. Ulla continued to translate:

"The kings of Corinium, Bath and Gloucester are all dead. They died good and true warriors, especially the one you called Farinmael. He was a great king. I wish you to know that he was sent to the warrior-land in the Otherworld with all honours, a funeral befitting even the greatest Saxon warriors. With his dying words, amongst other matters, he asked me to grant protection to you and your brother. Whether you decide to work for my armies or not, I will do this, but only for so long as you agree not to engage in war against me. The choice is yours. Think on my proposals, discuss them with your brother when he is well enough, and let me know your decision then."

The Saxon king paused as his daughter relayed these words to me. Then he took up his theme again, his voice lighter:

"I will say only this to you by way of persuasion. You are both warriors, I have seen you both on the battlefield. Your brother may very well be the greatest warrior I have yet seen in battle. You are both young, healthy and strong, and you have many good fighting years in front of you. So, think on this – warriors who do not fight grow old and fat, and restless, and their thoughts grow lazy. It will be better for you both if you decide to take up one of my proposals."

With this last comment, he looked at me intently, nodded his head in a short, sharp movement, said something to Ulla, kissed her lightly on the forehead and left the room.

I had much to think about. But first I needed to know something.

"So, you are just a spy for your father then?"

Ulla's eyes flashed with fury.

"You are a stupid man! I have been working for your best interests since the moment I first saw you! I told you, for some reason that is not clear to me I . . . took an affection to you . . . when you were first brought here. I could see, even if you could not, that if you had a family then they were in mortal danger after the complete destruction of your forces at Deorham and steps had to be taken to protect them. That was why I had to know some facts. You are a stupid fool, and I wish that I had never set eyes on you!"

With that, her face flushed a deeper red and she clenched her fists and turned away from me and rushed out of the room.

Now Peg came forward, a furious look on her big red face.

"You're a stupid boy, you are! Goodness me, can you not see that she was trying to save the womenfolk in your family? There has been a great massacre, you idiot. Ulla has saved your people!"

With that she threw me a final withering look, shook her head, then she too left the room.

I could see that there was much that I had to learn about this woman called Ulla, daughter of Ceawlin, King of the Saxons. She had a woman's insight into matters that I did not have and I realised that I had offended her deeply with my stupid remarks. I would find a way to thank her, for I was sure that I would see her again.

*

So, a new world was now opening up to me. To stay in West Britain, perhaps as a farmer and a tribute-paying puppet of the Saxons, or to fight in the eastern lands of Alba or the land of the Franks, and to grow rich there or perhaps to die there, over the sea and away from my family. I needed to talk to Cormac and I had much to think about.

But, in truth, mostly I thought about Ulla and the thought of this woman refused to leave my mind.

III

I had been in the Saxon hall for perhaps sixty days.

I had seen Peg on a regular basis, every day, and learned much of the Saxon ways from her. I had taken a great liking to her, for she spoke in plain language always, and said straight what came into her wise and comic mind. Thanks largely to her wiles, for it seemed that Peg also, for some reason, had taken an affection for me, Ulla had resumed her visits to me after a gap of seven days. She eventually began to talk to me again in the open fashion that was natural to her.

She mentioned to me that her father had requested that I attend a feast in the hall at the time that the moon grew full again. I had by then managed to walk outside in the grounds of the hall on occasion, for the head sickness that caused my body to lose its balance when I tried to stand was by now much less.

"Uthwine and his warriors are coming to see my father at that time, and they will bring their women with them. There is to be a feast, in honour of our mighty victory over your people, but in truth my father and Uthwine need to speak, to see how the land is to be divided between them."

I had no interest in sitting at a feast that celebrated the defeat of my people, and I told Ulla that.

"There are reasons why my father wishes you to be there. It is lucky for you and your brother that it was my father's warriors who first engaged with you. Uthwine is a thug and a bully, and he is a disgrace to the Aenglish."

I had not heard this word "Aenglish" before arriving at Ceawlin's Hall. It was a strange word, and I repeated it.

"Aenglish."

It had a resonance to it and I asked Ulla what was meant by it.

"Why, the German people are split into many regions – my father and I are Saxon, Uthwine and his people are Engles, the Germans who fight in the Kentish east of Britain are called Jutes, all over there are Frisians with their strange dialects. But many winters ago we were all originally from the lands north and east of the Frankish lands and since we came to this land we know ourselves as Aenglish, not German. We are all together Aenglish, for that is what we call our mingled language in this land and that is how we see ourselves."

I had thought the Saes were all Saxons, and I did not know that there were differences amongst them.

"Huge differences, and then further differences in the character of men, for my father and Uthwine are as different in character as it is possible to be. You will perhaps have noticed . . ."

Here Ulla looked at me very directly, as if she tested me again:

". . . that my father is a learned man, a thoughtful man, a warrior who wields the sword in battle, it is true, but only for reasons that he has long before considered, reasons that are part of a greater design in the interests of my people. He has learnt the duties of kingship from the sagas and verses, and he thinks of it as a sacred duty, the leadership of his people, for he feels that a great office has been laid upon him."

She paused, searching for my response. I said nothing. Her face coloured again:

"But Uthwine! Uthwine is a brute, a pig, a lecher, a man who takes a life for the fun of it, who thinks only of land and gold. Gold has corrupted that man's mind, and I hate him!"

These shows of temper from Ulla had by now become familiar to me. She had definite opinions in life, and was not afraid to voice them. I must confess that I found this spirit in her just one more part of her overwhelming attraction for me. But, in truth, I was also fascinated to learn of these differences between the Saxons, or, I should now say, Aenglish, for it was information that might have served Farinmael well if we had known of it before Deorham, but now all was lost for us West Britons.

"Why then does your father want me to attend this feast?"

"If you and your brother take up his proposal to fight in the land of the Franks, then it is with Uthwine's army that you will travel as my father's representatives. My father wishes you to report on the actions of Uthwine, of the alliances he makes with the long-hair kings in Gaul, and he wants you to ensure that his interests are best served."

Ulla had reddened a little as she said this, and I could see that these words were not easy for her. She shrugged her shoulders.

"It is the way that our alliances work. There is very little that is straightforward when you are a king, for you cannot drop your guard for a moment, otherwise your power and authority will be gone, and the people will be in the hands of men like Uthwine."

I told Ulla that I would think it through and talk to my brother about it. I asked her again, as I did every day, when I would be allowed to see Cormac.

Her words were guarded and it seemed to me that something troubled her.

"Why do you not look at me when I ask you about him?"

"I am amazed that he is your brother! He is a brutal man, a barbarian, and I am shocked to hear the reports of what he says to my father."

I looked at Ulla, and I was perplexed. That was not my brother she described. As the sons of Advil, and nephews of Gavin, we had been close to kings, and we understood that a respect was due to them, even to enemy kings, and that there were certain rules to be observed. Surely Cormac had not forgotten his upbringing?

"You amaze me, for the man you describe does not sound like my brother. He is a warrior, perhaps, to use your own father's words, the finest of all, but he lives for the battle only, and once out of the battle my brother is a quiet man. We have been taught to respect kings and the authority they have."

"Then your brother needs to learn his lessons again, for his behaviour towards my father is unacceptable, and he needs to learn respect, or things may not go well for him!"

With that, she left, and none of it made sense to me.

After that, I was determined to see my bother and my requests to do so became insistent, so much so that they were finally granted. A couple of days after she had told me of the feast, Ulla led me down corridors in the king's hall to a bolted door outside of which stood perhaps ten men, all armed, all of whom bowed their head briefly at the appearance of Ulla.

"My father has agreed that the Briton be allowed to see his brother."

The lead warrior took a heavy two-handed iron key from the wall, and said to me, in my language, which surprised me: "Very well. We will open the door and let you in, but we shall not come in with you."

With a deft movement, he unlocked the door and stood back, shoved me through it, and as deftly locked the door behind me.

It was another small hall, larger but otherwise not unlike the room I stayed in, with similar timber crossbeams and ornate woodwork underpinning each corner. The difference was that a huge window dominated the centre of the room, and in front of me, sat on a chair placed in front of the window, I could see the bowed back of my brother.

"Cormac!"

I shouted with delight, and rushed over to him.

Cormac did not leap up. He continued to look out of the window.

I reached him and he turned his face to me. I stood back with the shock of it. Great vivid red scars lined his cheeks and forehead, and one of his eyes was half-closed. I could see that parts of his scalp had been exposed, where his hair had been shorn to allow for wounds there to heal, but there would be more scars there too. He had lost much weight, but the bull neck still bulged with power.

He lifted his arm weakly when he heard my voice, and he smiled.

"Good brother Rhuadrac, how good it is to hear your voice. You fought like a true warrior at Deorham, and you brought honour to our family."

He spoke very quietly, and it was then that I realised fully for the first time just how close he had come to death, and how great a struggle it had been for even his titanic spirit to pull through.

"Cormac, it saddens me to see you like this."

"Brother, I get better every day, for it was not until seven nights ago that I could sit in this chair. I have fought with the spirit-world brother. It wanted to take me to it, but I was not ready to go to it just yet."

He smiled weakly, and I threw my arm gently around his massive shoulders.

"Brother, we are alive, and they tell me that our mother, and Aisha, and even Cadolan, are safe and well."

Cormac's eyes flickered at the good news of our womenfolk. But then his face darkened, and he bowed his head, and a great cry went out from him, and he put his face into his hands and sobbed.

"But Farinmael is dead. Our king is dead. I was his champion, but I could not save him."

It distressed me to see my brother like this. I had never seen it before. It was clear that the fight he had fought to survive had taken much from him. He still had to learn how to survive the aftermath of battle.

"Brother, no man could have done more to save him. Look at you, you were cut to pieces. No man else could have survived what you endured."

"But it was not enough."

And then something came into Cormac's eyes, something that troubled me, something I had never seen before. It was a look of cruelty, and it disfigured further his already scarred face. I briefly wondered if the Saxon champion before Deorham had seen this look in the last moments before his demise.

"The Saxons will pay for this disgrace. I will not rest until I have wiped the Saxons from the face of this land."

"But brother, the Saxon king, Ceawlin, is a noble man. He had words with Farinmael before he died, and he treated Farinmael in the right and true way, and Farinmael died as a great warrior should, on the field of battle, with great glory. I saw this with my own eyes. The Saxon king told me that it was Farinmael himself who had requested before he died that Ceawlin should offer us his own protection."

Cormac looked at me then in a way that he had never looked at me before.

"What did you say?" he said, and his voice sounded distant from me.

I repeated what I had said, for I believed every word of it.

"You have gone mad. Why do you believe that rubbish? The Saxon king has his own designs upon us, for Farinmael would never have requested such a thing."

He turned away from me.

"They have warped your mind in some way. Leave me now, brother, for I grow tired."

I began to say something, but stopped. He had lowered his huge head into his gigantic arms, and turned his back from me.

"We will talk again, brother, when you are more recovered."

Cormac said nothing.

I knocked on the door of the room, which opened quickly, and the sentry pulled me out of the room, and locked it again with haste. Cormac's reputation had followed him from the field of Deorham and they were taking no chances.

Ulla still stood there. She saw from my face that something troubled me.

"He is not himself. He needs rest, and then his natural spirit will return to him."

That was all that I said, for I could not bring myself to talk even to Ulla about our meeting, and I asked that I might return to my room alone.

I lay there for long hours during the day and night. The person I had met in that room was not the Cormac that I knew. The cruelty I had seen in his face had shocked me. But perhaps he was right, and it was me that had changed. I was here in the Saxon camp, and I had taken their food and their drink, had lain in a Saxon bed and had recovered under their roof. Ulla was the daughter of a Saxon king, and already it did not seem possible to me that I could lead my life without her. Yet I knew that there were intrigues in this king's hall; why should my brother and I not be part of those intrigues? And if there were such intrigues, what part did Ulla play in them?

My head pounded, and I did not sleep for many hours that night.

IV

I then had many days that were days of anguish for me. For it seemed that my brother was estranged from me, and I could not be sure who to trust any more, and some of the delight was gone from my talks with Ulla. She noticed this, and it saddened her, for one day, as was her manner, she asked me straight out what it was that made me go distant from her.

I looked at her. Her dark hair was well brushed that day and had been braided. Where it was tight on her scalp, it shone. She wore a pale-gold gown which favoured the honey-gold of her skin. The gown was held by a simple light-blue brooch at each shoulder, and at her neck she wore a gold necklace, with spun gold beads, and from each bead there fell an oval stone, of the type which I think is called garnet. I already knew, but I could not say how I knew, that I wanted to be with this woman for the rest of my days. I would tell her what troubled me, and if she was playing me false, well, I needed to know that now, for otherwise there was no hope for us.

I told her about my meeting with my brother, and of his suspicions that her father was playing his strategic games with us, and that Farinmael had not asked that Ceawlin give us his protection and that I was being used to win over my brother to the Saxons.

Ulla did not fly into the rage that I had expected. Her face became pale, but she did not rage at me. A strange and vulnerable look came into her face and I could see that she wrestled with her thoughts. She looked at me then and walked over to the window that opened like a door into the meadow.

"I suppose it is only natural for you and your brother to doubt my words and those of my father. After all, we have been enemies, and such matters are not forgotten easily."

She lifted the iron latch of the window-door and looked at me over her shoulder.

"Come and walk with me, Rhuadrac."

She stepped out into the garden. It was a warm day, and a clear and gentle breeze stirred the red and purple blooms set into the beds. Ceawlin's timber hall had been built in a clearing in a forest, and the small garden area in which we walked was ringed up-close with trees. The winter had not yet come, and the trees still had most of their leaves, but they were no longer green, and had turned gold, and red, so that the garden we walked in was as if curtained. A stone path had been set into the meadow, and we walked along this stone path. I remember that our voices were as if amplified to each other, like when we talk in a cave.

Ulla walked slowly next to me, and her perfume fell over me and her hand touched mine. It was as if I had touched blue fire, for the thrill of it shot through my arm and made my heart thud.

"It is true that there are intrigues at this court, but my father tells me that there is no other way. He says it is in the very nature of power – for men will scheme, and make designs, and it is a rare king who can say what he means, and do what he plans, without intrigue."

I walked next to her. I could still feel the touch of her hand on mine.

"It is true that my father has plans to break the power of Uthwine. He has decided that Uthwine cannot further the cause of the Aenglish in this land, and he will break his power. He is hopeful that you and your brother may play some part in that, and in this way too he can honour his pact with your dead king."

She looked across at me, and her gaze flickered over my face, from my lips to my hair. She then looked deep down into my eyes. I saw that her eyes were black that day.

"I ask you to believe only this of me and my father: what he said to you was the truth, and Farinmael did ask that you be protected, for that part my father reported to me straight the day that you were brought here. Why would he lie to you about this? Your brother is a great warrior, but in truth, as my father has told me himself, what power the West Britons had is now broken, and you and your brother have little or no strategic value in the Aenglish world."

Ulla was truly a king's daughter, and what she said made perfect sense to me.

She stopped on the stone path.

"There are reasons that I am telling you this, Rhuadrac, proud warrior of Farinmael's army. There are reasons why I hope that you might consider very seriously my father's proposals. I have hopes that you might become a thegn to my father."

Ulla noticed my confusion at the mention of this word.

"You do not understand our word 'thegn'? A thegn is a young warrior who chooses and is chosen by a Saxon chief. The thegn gives unquestioning loyalty to the chief. In return, when he has proven his loyalty and his prowess in battle, the thegn receives gold and rings from the chief, and in this way his loyalty to the chief is rewarded. You should know . . ."

Here she gave me a sideways glance, and hesitated slightly.

". . . in my father's world, all warriors must have a strategic value if they are to play a role in his family. The daughter of a king can make powerful alliances when she marries, and no king, particularly an Aenglish king in these days of conquest, can easily allow his daughter to be with one who has no power or strategic value. If you become my father's thegn, then one day you may become a gesithas, or, as you Britons might say, companion, of my father. Companions are next in power to the chief, and few thegns become companions, but it is my hope that you one day become a gesithas to my father, and in this way will receive much power, much gold, and much land, and may even be seen as a man who might one day . . ."

Her words had become hurried; she again paused. I could see that now she hesitated to say what she wanted to say.

I took her hands in mine and she looked at me and she said these words to me:

"It is madness, I fear, for we are barely met, but since the day that my father brought you to this place I knew that you would have a special place in my life. It is as if I have known you all of my life, that we are born to be together. I cannot stop thinking of you, Rhuadrac of the West Britons, and it is my wish that we shall be together all of our days, and that we shall die together too, if the god of my mother should allow for it."

And she looked at me with those eyes of hers which now held some fear, for, in a way that was always natural to her, she had declared herself directly and openly to me and I held all of her hopes in my hands.

I kissed her and I told her that this too was my greatest hope, my only hope, and we laughed then, and cried too, and our hearts sang, for we knew that something wondrous and good and powerful had happened between us, and it would lead us we knew not where.

For in truth in these matters we were still but children at that time.

V

I had by now almost fully recovered, and I began to wonder what fate had in store for us all, for me and Ulla, the daughter of Ceawlin, King of the Gevissas, and for my brother, the giant warrior, Cormac.

I had deliberately not asked to see Cormac, for I wanted him to regain his strength before I saw him again, in the hope that his natural spirit might be restored. But it was the day of the feast, and I understood that Cormac was being made ready, and that he too would be at the feast, so I wanted to see him, for I feared that some calamity might occur.

Ulla took me to his room. We had determined that none should know of our pact, for we could not be sure how Ceawlin might react, and there was much that we had to plan and do if we were to be together.

I was let into the locked room as before, the sentry pushing me in and stepping back abruptly, locking it behind me.

Cormac stood at the window and turned as I came into the room. I saw with real pleasure in my heart that he was much recovered, but not completely, for his left eye was still half-closed and he was slightly bowed and it was clear to me that his face would be forever disfigured because of the blows he had sustained at Deorham. Even so, his giant frame still blocked out much of the light that came through the window space.

He greeted me warmly, which was a huge relief to me, and wrapped his arms around me.

"Gently, brother. You are still recovering I know, but you could crush me and not know that you have done it."

He stood back and laughed. It was good to hear that laugh, for I thought that the old Cormac was restored, but I was wrong.

"How are you brother? I have thought a lot about our talk the other day. Are you still convinced of the nobility of these Saxon swine?"

I could see that he was still of the same mind. Ulla's people were his enemy, and that would never change. I looked at my brother then, and I knew that the old days were gone, and that they would never come back. In truth, the Battle of Deorham had destroyed many things.

"Cormac, you are my brother, and I will be straight with you. I do not believe that King Ceawlin is anything other than a noble man. I have talked with him and his daughter . . ."

Cormac raised his eyebrow at the mention of a daughter, and I did not meet his eye.

". . . I believe him to be a good king, even a great king, and a great warrior. You did not see his actions at Deorham. I believe that if you had, you would have a very different opinion of him."

"Rhuadrac, on this point we shall never agree. The Saes are my enemies, and they will always be my enemies."

He turned back to the window. I could see through the thin white tunic that he wore that his back was red with scars, almost as if he had been flayed. I thought again of the crisis that he had been through and it was not difficult to see why he thought as he did. Nor did he have the complication of Ulla to colour his mind.

He turned back to me.

"You are my brother, and probably my greatest friend, too. We are brothers, and we will always be brothers, but on this matter I will never agree with you."

He reached out his hand, and I clasped it.

"We must hope, brother, that our disagreement does not come to haunt us."

He looked hard at me, then his face broke into a smile.

"Now, we must talk. Tell me more about this protection that we are offered by the Saxon king."

I then told him about Ceawlin's proposals, and it was the first that he had heard of them, for he had refused to see Ceawlin, and on the one occasion that they had met he had hurled a table at him.

"So, what do you make of these proposals?" he said, "I will never fight for the Saxons."

"I am minded to. I am no farmer, and I have an urge to see something of the world."

I said nothing about what had passed between Ulla and me, and how I might win her.

He looked away to the window:

"Then, brother, our paths will part, for I am going home, and I am not finished with these Saxons yet. I am minded to accept this kind offer, if only to regain my full strength. Then we shall see."

That look of cruelty flickered across Cormac's disfigured face again, and I did not care for it.

"This feast tonight, what do you know about it? I have been told that I am to be paraded like a bear. I have not yet decided whether I shall refuse to go, and cause a drama and destroy a few of the Saxon dogs should they try to force me."

I told him about what I knew about Uthwine, and of Ulla's opinion of him, and that he was not a Saxon, but an Engle, even though all were Aenglish, which was a word new to my brother also. But I did not tell my brother what Ulla had told me about Ceawlin's designs regarding Uthwine. Already a curtain was descending between my brother and me on these matters.

"You are well informed, brother. How is this, in a Saxon hall, where we know nobody and they do not speak in our tongue?"

I told him about Ulla and about her mother being British, which surprised him.

"And this Ulla, what of her then?"

He stared down at me from his great height, and waited for my response. This was a new Cormac, for the first time I felt all of the five winters that separated us. He was now my elder brother for sure. I marvelled at the changes wrought in him – it was as if all of his childlike ways had never existed, and a man much more like our father in attitude addressed me.

"She is my friend."

"Oh? What is the nature of this friendship?"

"It is the same as you and Gwen."

I knew that the mention of Farinmael's daughter would tell him all that he needed to know in the matter.

"Ah."

He looked out of the wood-framed window, then walked over to it. He stood there for some time, before turning back to me.

"I see your dilemma, brother, and I see how they have turned your mind. Well, she is half-British at least." His words irritated me.

"My mind has not been turned. My views on Ceawlin are my own, formed by what I have seen with my own eyes and by my own thinking on the matter. Whether Ulla is British or Saxon is no longer of any concern to me. She is Ulla, we are pledged to each other and we will spend our lives together."

Cormac laughed, but it seemed to me a cruel laugh, and he said to me:

"Do not be angry with me brother. Our paths in life may separate from here, at least for as far as we can see into the future, but we are still brothers. I will agree to go to this feast tonight, so that I can formally meet with my protector . . ."

A cruel sneer passed over his face

". . . and we will meet with this Uthwine, for if nothing else, he sounds like an authentic Saxon dog, and, even as I am now, I might still find a way to kill him."

VI

The hall was lit with a yellow flickering light from the fires and the countless torches set in their rope-coil beckets high up in the walls. No window had drapes, so that it was as if there were huge black holes cut out of the timber. Great wood fires burned in the two hearths, one at the head of the hall, another set into the centre of the lower end of the two side wings that streamed out from the rough-hewn top table. The walls of the hall were lined with animal skins of all kinds, and standards. Prominent amongst them was the wolf head standard of Ceawlin. As I looked about me I knew beyond doubt that I was in a Saxon feasting hall. I marvelled at the changes that had been wrought in my life since Deorham.

The great tables were laden with food, and I could see all kinds of roast meats there – wild boar, steaks, venison, lamb, whole pigs. A spit had been set up at one corner of the great hearth at the top end of the hall, where slaves ran backwards and forwards with dishes of all colours, and smaller dishes of many hues were set out at each place on the table. Musicians played sweet melodies on harps and lyres. I could see huge bowls of fruits, and giant loaves from the ovens in the kitchen. There was a separate mead-table on which were stacked barrels of beer and mead and casks of wine, which I was told came from the south-east of the Frankish lands, from the Mediterranean Sea.

There was a great hubbub of men and women talking, and it was a grating sound to my ears, for this Aenglish, as I was learning to call it, had terrible abrupt stops in it, and drags, and bungling rhythms; it was as if everything was "brggg" or "gnnng" or "umpdngbggg". It was such an ugly sound to my ears, I longed for a time when the beautiful cadences of my own flowing language could be heard once more.

I could see Ceawlin and Ulla as they entered amidst much ceremony, and bowing, and cheers from the warriors and their wives who were already in the hall. I could see Peg and another, older woman with them, and she moved forward to catch Ulla's sleeve and then talk to Ulla. I realised that this woman must be Ulla's mother, a Briton as I was.

I saw Ulla look around the hall and then point towards me.

The older woman talked to Ceawlin and he nodded, and then Ulla, her mother and Peg came over to the part of the hall where I stood flanked by a guard of Ceawlin's warriors. By then I understood that those guarding me were sure that I would not try anything, for in fact I was on nodding terms with several of them. One or two could even speak some basic British in a strange accent, learnt, they said, when they had worked as paid mercenaries in the north.

I could see a glow pass over Ulla's face as she came towards me, and I smiled as she came up to me. She was wearing a deep-purple gown, pinned by two deep-blue brooches at her shoulders. She wore pale-red sandals, and at her neck she wore the necklace she had worn when I first woke up after Deorham, with the dark-blue stone set in its triangular pendant perfectly matching her gown. I was astonished by her beauty, and I could not take my eyes off her.

Ulla too seemed a little breathless for some reason, but managed to say:

"Rhuadrac, this is my mother, Queen Acha."

I managed to tear my eyes away from Ulla to look at a lady who was much like her, although her figure was fuller but very comely. There were swathes of white in her black hair, and her eyes were much darker than her daughter's eyes, and a fine web of delicate lines, like the filigree created by a master-artist, cascaded out from those eyes when she smiled, as she did now. She regarded me with great kindness, and no little amusement. She looked then at Ulla, whose high cheekbones glowed red, then her knowing eyes came back to mine. She paused for a moment, raised one shaped eyebrow, then said, in my own language:

"Well, Rhuadrac, you live up to the reports that my daughter has been insisting on providing to me every day. You are an extremely handsome man, with a fine physique, and you do your family proud."

Now it was my turn to colour up, and I felt my face burning. Out of the corner of my eye I saw that Peg clapped her hands together, and was laughing quietly to herself. Amongst men it was my giant brother who received all the praise. I could see clearly from whom Ulla had taken her habit of directly speaking her mind. In truth, I was more used to the company of men, and I struggled to think of a proper reply to this lady, who was a queen. I was saved by the blowing of a horn, which made all in the hall look around, and just after this a band of warriors swept into the hall.

I have never before seen in one place such a collection of cut-throats and robbers. The man at their head was a big heavy man with a shaved head, and a flabby face and red-rimmed eyes that spoke much of his acquaintance with the mead-table. He had iron serpent rings fastened into each ear lobe, something else which I had not seen before that night. Aggression spat out of him. I could see the leer on his face as he swept past me and bowed perfunctorily to Queen Acha. Her bow in response was equally curt. Peg had stood back from this man, and looked frightened, watchful. It was plain to me that these people hated each other, and I could see Ulla grow tense as he bent and kissed her hand. She was about to say something when her mother cut across her, and said something to the man in his language which included a word that sounded like Uthwine. She then swept around to indicate where Ceawlin stood at the far end of the hall, talking to his chief warriors.

Uthwine – for I was sure that it was he – took a couple of steps in that direction, then stopped, and turned back to me. He came right up to my face and stared at me and then said something in a questioning tone to Acha that included the word "Briton." She nodded and replied calmly. Suddenly he turned back to me in a fury, and moved as if to draw his short sword from its scabbard and the other men in his war-band did the same. I stepped back, as did they, and just then I heard Ceawlin's voice.

Uthwine looked up to see the Saxon king towering over him. They talked in their language. Whatever was being said, Ceawlin was insisting, and Uthwine was refusing.

Ulla took me to one side.

"Uthwine has objected to the presence of a male Briton of fighting age in the hall. My father has explained that you and your brother, who we might see later, are under his protection, and no harm will come to you in his hall. He is now insisting that Uthwine and his men leave their swords outside. Be calm, my father will prevail."

Their argument proceeded from discussion to shouting until Ceawlin stared at Uthwine with anger in his eyes, and it seemed to me that a full-blooded fight might start, for several of Ceawlin's warriors had come to stand next to their king. The music players had stopped, and there was a tension in the hall.

Uthwine's tone suddenly changed, and he laughed a laugh that was without mirth. He placed his hand on Ceawlin's shoulder, but Ceawlin promptly removed it, and barked a curt command at his fellow king. Slowly, with great reluctance, Uthwine unbuckled his great sword belt, and indicated to his band that they should do the same. He stared at me as he walked past me and muttered something in his own language.

Ceawlin gave a signal to the harpists to resume, which they did, and it seemed that the crisis moment had passed.

I was placed at the left wing of the top table, and saw that Ulla and Acha sat on the left of Ceawlin at the centre of my table, with Uthwine on his right with two or three of his own warriors.

The harpists struck up a slow marching tone. Queen Acha and Ulla stood up from the table. Serving girls brought cups of mead to them and to several other women, including Peg. These now formed a paired column behind Queen Acha and Ulla.

Slowly, in time with the slow march created by the harps, all done with a formal elegance and cadence, Acha and Ulla led the column of women around the hall, their gifts held high above their heads. The queen presented the first mead-cup to Uthwine, then each of his shoulder-men was similarly treated. Soon, all of Uthwine's warriors had each been served a mead-cup in this way, to much cheering and banging of mugs from the benches. The women then returned to their places.

In this way, Ceawlin paid formal respect to his battle ally in his own hall, which I later learned was a custom amongst the Saxons.

I felt ill at ease throughout the feast. This was not my place, and I remembered well the last time I had sat with other warriors, my own friends, on the eve of Deorham. Now all was changed, and I wondered again how it was that I found myself in a Saxon hall. Just how I could have any influence on the Saxons' intrigues was beyond me at that time, for working in Uthwine's forces seemed impossible to me then.

There was a loud clapping, then a stout squat fellow stood up, and made some sort of declaration to the hall. He spoke in short phrases, pausing at the end of each, as if asking a question. Occasionally somebody would shout out, but he would shake his head and continue with his short chopped verses. Everybody in the hall would shake their heads, and talk amongst themselves quietly as he continued to declaim. Then he stopped, and again asked a question, arms outstretched, and palms to the roof. Now Ulla stood up and confidently gave an answer, and the verse-master looked pained, but clapped his hands and, laughing ruefully, nodded his head. Then all in the hall laughed, and they too nodded their heads, and it was plain to me that he had set out some sort of riddle, and that

Ulla had solved it. The verse-master was not a young man, and his battered face made me think that he was a time-served warrior. I was therefore surprised when he started to declaim, in a deep and serious voice, some form of elaborate Saxon verse.

This man pointed to Ceawlin, and nodded to the benches, speaking words that to my ears sounded like this:

". . . thate vass goda cuninge . . .!"

His words had a doleful beat; sometimes the man would growl, and raise his arms in wonder as perhaps some great beast was described to the listening warriors. Or he would thrust his sword arm, or parry, and it was as if some battle was being fought in his verse. At other times his voice would grow sorrowful, and a lament went out from him. Then he turned to the top table, and looked directly at Ceawlin, and pronounced the word "Bretwalda". Again he took up the rhythmic beat of his verse; again he looked to the top table and looked directly at Ceawlin, then swept his arm towards the Gevissa king, finishing his line with the same word, "Bretwalda".

The reaction in the hall was strange. All of Ceawlin's men banged their mugs on the table, and cheered. But I noticed that Uthwine's men sat still, looking amongst themselves, then up at the face of Uthwine on the top table. His face was still, impassive. The Gevissa scop ceased his verse, and sat down. He was applauded by Ceawlin and his men beat their mugs on the benches. Uthwine's men sat silent, and it seemed to me that there was a tension in the hall. I told myself that I would ask Ulla what this word Bretwalda might mean.

The poet was followed by a young man, who stood up and began to sing. It was a fine song, and the youth had a good and powerful voice, but it served only to make me more miserable, for I was reminded of Oisin's song on the eve of Deorham, and now Oisin was no more.

The youth sat down, and a loud horn blast again swept through the hall. This must have been some prearranged signal, for the main doors of the hall were thrown back, and then they brought my brother in.

I had never been more proud of my brother than I was at that moment that night as he came through that door. He had his head held high, and he dwarfed the guards who walked with him. His head was still wrapped in bandages, and the livid red scars on his face and his arms seemed even more macabre under the yellow lights of the torches. I could see that his arms were wrapped in great chains. And I remembered then my brother when I had first seen him after Deorham in his sick-room in this king's hall. I remembered his despair, and his pain, and I was proud of my brother as he strode into the feasting hall, his head held high, and stared at his adversaries as he strode slowly past them.

Shocked cries went up in the hall, for they realised that Farinmael's champion was amongst them. One or two of Uthwine's bigger men stood up as Cormac was led past them, but immediately sat down again, for he made them look small. A loud banging started at the end of the lowest table as he strode past it and on up the hall, and it was maintained at every table as he passed by; Uthwine's men were hammering their beer mugs on the table, and the demented banging spread throughout the hall, wherever Uthwine's men were sitting. The din grew louder, as Cormac was led to a seat facing my own, and was told to sit down.

He smiled at me as he slowly sat down and raised his chained arms.

"This is a fine feast that you have led me to, brother," he shouted through the noise. "I gave the bastards something to think about before I left my room."

I threw my arm around one of his great shoulders, for I was proud to see him there, and I must confess that the battle-spirit swelled up in my heart too, and I would have fought any warrior in that hall if they had attacked my brother.

Suddenly all was quiet. Ceawlin had stood up and rapped out a curt command, and the table pounding ceased. He turned again to the musicians and told them to play on. Then he turned to his wife and daughter and said something to them, and they nodded and got up and left the hall. As they did so, the women at all the other tables began to get up and go out, and I saw the women who had arrived with Uthwine's men do likewise.

It was a sensible move by Ceawlin, for the mood in the hall had grown ugly.

Uthwine had turned to Ceawlin and continued to drum his fist on the table. Ceawlin looked over towards me and indicated that he wished to speak to me. I got up and went to meet him, and he came to meet me and we met halfway.

"Can your brother fight?" he said, in my language.

I shook my head, for although Cormac was much recovered, he was far from his full fighting self, and would be so for a full season-cycle at least.

"He cannot fight yet."

But just then I noticed that Ceawlin had raised up his eyes, and he was looking up at something over my right shoulder.

Cormac stood there.

"No need to worry about me, little brother, I will fight any Saxon, or Aenglish, or whatever they now call themselves, if they dare to face me, but I want to fight with this Uthwine's dogs."

I looked at him, and I knew that he had gone beyond me again, but I also knew that he was protecting my friendship with Ceawlin's daughter by challenging Uthwine's men, and I was grateful to him.

Ceawlin understood enough of our language to know that Cormac had accepted the challenge, and that Uthwine's men were being called out to meet him.

Cormac was led from me, the musicians were dismissed, and a space was cleared in front of the top table. A great hum flowed around the hall when they saw that my brother's chains were being removed, for this is what warriors lived for, and the battle-spirit rose up to the rafters of that great hall. Ceawlin stood up and said something in their language to them and pointed at my brother and I knew that he was repeating Cormac's challenge to Uthwine's men in the hall.

There was a silence. They had witnessed Cormac in action before the battle at Deorham and I believe that those proud men were afraid, and I could not blame them, for he had dealt with their own champion brutally, and in moments. It had been no contest.

Cormac looked at Uthwine and laughed mockingly. He held up three of his fingers.

Uthwine leapt to his feet and shouted angrily at his men, and pointed at three of the tables, barking out three names as he did so, then sat back again, deep anger pulsing from him.

Slowly, the three nominated warriors moved up the aisles to where Cormac stood.

Swords were brought up from the back of the hall, and all crowded in towards the top table.

Cormac stripped off his white tunic, and shouts of amazement went up from the assembled warriors, for they could see for the first time the red livid scars of the still-healing wounds all over Cormac's massive back. They realised that it was some sort of gift from the warrior-gods that any man could withstand such an assault and still live.

Cormac crouched and made ready to fight, half-sheathing his sword in his leather belt as he did so, his face taking on that brutal stare that I knew so well, but now intensified by the disfigurement to his face caused by Deorham.

I looked at his opponents, all big men. I could see one lick his lips and there was no doubt that he was worried, for he knew the strength of Farinmael's champion. With a lunge, he leapt at Cormac, and Cormac knocked the man's sword from his grasp and, his weight perfectly balanced on his feet, he cupped his left hand behind the man's head and then there was a sharp crack! crack! crack!, one-two-three as Cormac, with a short movement of his arm, drove his right fist into his opponents face, who promptly collapsed to the floor, unconscious.

The other two warriors circled the giant cautiously. They had seen enough not to leap in. Cormac crouched and they circled each other; then suddenly Cormac pounced with a speed that belied his bulk. He seized the bigger of his two remaining opponents by the throat, and butted him with his head, and turned him over and drove his head into the stone floor.

The fellow was unconscious, or dead, and lay there motionless.

The last man charged in, sweeping with his sword, knowing that he had to catch the giant off-balance, but Cormac was too quick for him, for he whirled around and in one movement swept the blade of his sword from his leather belt across the throat of the third warrior, who spun round, blood gurgling and spitting from his neck, and fell to the floor, writhing, but silent.

All was then deathly quiet in the hall.

Cormac staggered back against the top table. I could see that he was exhausted from his exertions, for he was not at full strength, and his energy was almost spent. The warriors in the hall kept silent, for they knew that they had seen no ordinary man in action this night.

Cormac stood up to his full height, and looked across the table at Uthwine who had risen to his feet and stood opposite him. Ceawlin shouted an order to his men, but he was too late.

Cormac leapt at Uthwine and grabbed the Engle warlord's leather jerkin, dragging him bodily across the table. In one movement he lifted him up into the air and caught him, and I knew then what was in his mind.

In that split second I knew that if Uthwine died at the hands of my brother, Ceawlin would be dishonoured in his own hall. My plans to win Ulla would come to naught.

His arm clasp had already closed around the small of Uthwine's back when I ran up to my brother and I shouted at him to drop the Aenglish warlord.

My brother heard my voice. He looked at me with great cruelty in his stare. Then, as he saw me, it faded. Slowly he released Uthwine.

The Engle chief's face had turned white, such was the shock and the speed of Cormac's move. The warlord had begun to understand the terrifying power of my brother.

Cormac dropped Uthwine to the floor, where he lay motionless.

Ceawlin's warriors then swept past me and leapt on Cormac and managed to chain him again. But in truth he had stopped fighting. He allowed himself to be led away, staring at me all the way down the length of the central isle, his gigantic shadow dominating the timber walls as he was led out of the Great Hall of Ceawlin, King of the Gevissas.

VII

I was allowed to see Cormac just once, briefly, three days following the night of the feast in Ceawlin's Hall.

I was to leave British shores later that day. The speed of my departure had something to do with Queen Acha. She had seen the truth of what was between me and her daughter, and thought it wise to tell Ceawlin to get me abroad for a while, in the best interests of their family.

I stood in the small hall that had served as my bedroom during my stay with the Saxons. I had packed two canvas sacks with my possessions, which included all of my battle kit which had been restored to me, including *Saesbane*, and additional clothing provided by Ceawlin's men. Now I held *Saesbane* in my hand, marvelling at the craftsmanship of old Dermot, once again noting with a quiet pleasure the bronze inlay around the pommel, a series of concentric rings typical of the patterns wrought by the metalsmiths of my mother's country. Dermot was a kinsman of my mother, and had travelled across the western sea with her when she had followed my father to seek her future with him in West Britain. Where was she now? Where was Aisha? Cadolan? What news did they have of us? Did they know that we were in Ceawlin's Hall? Did they know that we were still alive? Later this day I would leave the land of my birth. Would I even see them again?

The previous night I had been summoned by Ceawlin to a small chamber. The Saxon king stood with his back to the smouldering hearth at the far end of the room; the smell of woodsmoke filled the room. To the king's left sat Willem, right-hand man to the king. To his right stood Ulla, and I understood that she would once more translate her father's words to me.

Ceawlin greeted me with some warmth. He placed his hand on my right shoulder and smiled at me; some decision had been made concerning my future, of that I was sure. He spoke firmly, and Ulla talked his words, her eyes searching deep into mine as she did so:

"The time has come for you to leave us, Briton. Tomorrow evening you will travel down to the sea, to the place of the white cliffs. From there you will meet with Uthwine and his men, and cross by boat to the Frankish lands."

A look of some concern must have passed across my face, for Ceawlin looked at me closely, then talked again through his daughter.

"Uthwine has, with some reluctance, accepted you as a traveller with his warband. In my eyes you saved his life on the night of the feast. He was in my hall, therefore he cannot refuse my request that you travel with him as my representative. You will be safe enough. Otherwise he will answer to me for his actions."

I nodded at Ceawlin; he had understood my concern. "When you arrive in Gaul, your task is to watch Uthwine at all times – see who he meets, the alliances he forms. I know that the advisers of the Jutish child-king has strong ties with the long-hairs, Aethelbert looks to become a sub-king to the Franks. Any information concerning this potential alliance will be of importance to me. Ulla tells me that you write in the Roman language – this is good. All information must come to me under protection of my personal seal."

I looked at Ulla, then nodded at her father.

"You will watch Uthwine at all times."

His eyes narrowed as he repeated those words.

"When the moment is right, I will strike against him, and you will be my instrument in this matter."

I looked into the iron eyes of the Gevissa king. I saw then how this man had become a king of his people, saw the ruthless will that had enabled him to hold onto and build up his power in Wessex. Now I would be a part of it. Ulla was watching me carefully; again I nodded. The king again placed his hand upon my shoulder.

"Briton, I thought that I had judged you correctly. You are a young man of sound good sense. Perform well in my service and the rewards for you will be great."

As she translated these words, Ulla smiled at me. These words of her father had been what she had wanted to hear.

So, in this way, my path had been decided. I had returned to my room full of thoughts. I would be a part of the intrigues of Ceawlin; so too would I play a part in the affairs of his family. It was precisely what Ulla and I had hoped for, yet some part of me was uneasy. I was not Saxon; these were Saxon matters. Just a few short months ago I had been sure of who I was and what I would do with my life – a West Briton living in the lands of my father's family. Now a whole new journey opened up before me.

My eyes now came back to the intricate filigree work of my sword pommel, beautifully cut into the metal by old Dermot.

All of these tumbling thoughts were cut through abruptly by a rough knock, metal on wood, against the oak door, which was immediately thrown back. Several of Ceawlin's men entered the room, and my brother was with them, his wrists still chained.

I recognised the Saxon lead-man, one Adwulf, a man who knew the British tongue. He had shown me an occasional rough kindness during my stay in the Saxon hall. He walked up to me now.

"Talk to your brother. Ten minutes only. We are outside of the door. Tell him that if he tries anything more whilst in this hall we have orders to finish him. Ceawlin's patience runs thin."

With that he and his men left us, slamming the heavy oak door behind them.

My brother looked at me now with a wary affection, his head thrown slightly backwards. He wore a green tunic that was too small for him, and the sleeves of the arms had been cut off at the elbow. Still the scars were livid on his face and arms, on his scalp where his black hair had been roughly shaved, and the chains binding his wrists caused him to hold his arms in front of his belly. I did not know when I would see him again after this day. I broke the long silence between us:

"So, Cormac, you heard them say that you must cause no more trouble, for the Gevissa king is at the end of his patience with you."

Cormac shrugged his massive shoulders, causing the chains at his wrists to jangle. He continued to stare at me.

"I leave today for the land of the Franks. I have no idea what my life holds for me from here on, but for now I have agreed to take Ceawlin as my chief and will do his work across the seas . . ."

"I could see that your mind was set when we last spoke."

Another silence. Cormac looked down at me from his great height, his face neutral. I could not gauge his thinking.

Eventually he spoke:

"Our paths must diverge from here then. I would never have thought that my brother . . ."

He checked himself, turning his face away from me. I could see that he wrestled with his own thoughts.

"Cormac, you should know that there is a reason for my actions. The Gevissa princess and I have made a pact. We wish to be together in this life. To be together

I must become something in the eyes of her father. She tells me there is no other way, and I believe her. Therefore I will take the sponsorship of the Gevissa king. I go to Gaul. I will learn the ways of the mercenary over there. Then we will see. But brother . . ."

Cormac turned back towards me.

". . . be sure of this. I will not fight for the Gevissa king against our people. I will do nothing that will cause dishonour to our family. And I plan to grow strong over the seas, I plan to learn something of these strategic arts from Ceawlin. Then we shall see where we stand, you and me."

My brother looked at me again. With some surprise I saw that there were tears in his eyes. We had been inseparable through our lives until this moment. He raised his chained hands and placed his left hand roughly on my shoulder, then rested his forehead against mine for a moment, then stood back, even as there came another loud rap at the door. He spoke quietly.

"Take care brother. Bring honour to the family. Never forget where you have come from."

With that he stepped back towards Adwulf and his men. Before he left the room he turned back once more and looked at me.

"Wear the chain I gave you. From our mother. Seek its protection in the foreign lands."

With that he was gone.

I did not see him again for seven winters.

Other visitors came to see me before I left. The light had begun to fade out of the day; I had already lit several candles in my room. There was a light tap at the door.

When I threw it open, Ulla and Peg stood there, and both stepped quickly and lightly into the room. Peg stood away from us, at the back of the room, and watched us with a sad and distant look upon her face. Ulla and I held no secrets from this lady. She knew how we felt for each other, and knew too of our plans.

Ulla wore a deep-purple gown which I had not seen before: her hair shone black and she wore at her neck the triangular pendant with the dark-blue stone at its centre, set in gold. I looked once more into the light-grey-blue-green of her eyes. A faint blush sat high on her cheekbones contrasting with the soft gentle light-gold of her skin. This picture of her I was to hold in my mind during all of the time I spent across the seas.

I held her hands in mine and looked into those eyes, now saddened by the moment of my leaving, but excited too, because this was our plan; my departure now in the service of her father was done so that we might remain together in the future.

We talked quietly about what this future might hold for us. I remembered to ask her a question that had been playing on my mind since the feast in the hall.

"The other day, when the poet spoke his verses at the feast, what was that word he used . . . Bret . . . Bretwalda . . ."

Ulla reddened a little more before responding to me.

"It is a new word, even for my own people. The poet translated it in his verse as 'overlord.' The poet said that after Deorham my father should now press on to become Bretwalda in this land. My father is much taken with this word, although it caused some hard words between him and Uthwine the day after the feast."

So then; the verse was some song of battle conquest, and I was again reminded that it was my people who had been defeated.

Ulla looked into my face.

"Rhuadrac, we must not let these matters between our people come between us. We must keep strong. We have made a pact to spend our future together, have we not?"

I looked at her then, this woman whose beauty would put Helen herself to shame, and I smiled. She looked back at me with that proud yet somehow vulnerable strength that had captured my soul.

"Yes, Gevissa princess, of the fiery temper and the straight stare, there is no doubt in my mind. Whatever obstacles stand before us, we will find a way to spend our lives together, or I will die in the attempt."

Again I held her.

Her eyes shone as she spoke to me:

"I know that you can write in the Roman language. I will write to you each month and tell you of events in this hall and in this land. You must write to me also. We may not see each other for some time, so in this way we will keep our pact strong."

"Yes."

"You will remember me over there in the land of the Franks?"

"Yes."

"You will find many women over there and you will forget me within weeks . . ."

Her eyes again flashed momentarily with the proud anger I knew so well by now. I put my finger to her lips gently, then kissed her, deeply.

Just then, Peg, who had wandered over to the door with her back to us, turned and whispered:

"That's enough you two. Somebody is coming!"

A knock on the door announced the arrival of the warrior who would go with me as part of the Saxon war-band to Gaul.

Ulla stepped hastily away from me. Whatever her mother had guessed of the true nature of our pact, neither of us had any reason to display it to the rest of the world, and only Peg had been taken into our confidence. Ceawlin's Hall was a place of secrets and intrigue, and I wished to play no part in those intrigues, at least until such time as I had gained some strength, some substance.

Now Peg came up to me.

"Take care of yourself, young 'un, and don't forget old Peg when you're over with them Franks."

I saw that she was sobbing gently, and I hugged her and kissed her cheek.

"Don't be silly woman, how could I forget such a beauty?"

Peg half chuckled, then turned away from me quickly.

Now Ulla lifted her lips to my ear:

"Take care of yourself, my love."

Those were her last words to me, spoken in barely a whisper.

The evening was well advanced when we were finally ready to leave the hall. Uthwine had already left, and I was to travel alone but for one man down to the Saxon Shore.

Ceawlin was there with his shoulder-man, old Willem, to see me leave.

"Remember, Briton, you act under my orders at all times. Observe Uthwine closely. When the time comes I will strike against him. Be prepared for that moment."

I nodded.

"I understand. Provided that you understand too, that I will never lift a finger in anger against my own people, then I am prepared to act as your representative in these matters."

"May Woden's power protect you in your travels."

I said nothing, but silently nodded and took the hand proffered by the Saxon king.

My last sight was of Ulla's slender form standing alone, slightly away from the small gathering that had formed to watch as the horses moved away from the hall. She raised her right arm slightly as I headed away from her father's hall. I felt her gaze upon me until I turned onto the path for the Saxon Shore, thence to Gaul, and forward into my new life.

*

PART III

Adventures in Gaul, New Friends, Called home

I

So began the next great season of my life.

My world changed completely. After the fracas at the feast in Ceawlin's Hall, I was seen to have saved Uthwine's life, after a fashion, so Uthwine could not refuse my presence in his war-bands, though he always resented me. I became a freebooter, which meant that I was a Saxon mercenary. But a mercenary with a sponsor, who was Ceawlin, which meant that I had authority in the field and I could keep close to Uthwine.

In the Frankish lands I prospered in every way, for I filled out, and grew more, and became a warrior of some repute in my own right, though not of the fame of my brother. And all of this time I was under the tutelage of Ceawlin, and I came to know him as a great man, or, to say it more correctly, a great man of strategy, for he was always two steps ahead of all others in these matters, and I learned much from him.

After two winters in the land of the Franks I was instructed in a letter from Ceawlin that I should now make a move against Uthwine. Like Ulla, I had no love for the Engle, nor he for me, so I had no remorse in carrying out Ceawlin's instructions to the letter.

At this time Uthwine's war-band had been assigned to guard Merovich, husband of Queen Brunhilde, that mad woman from the east of Gaul. This family was notorious throughout the Frankish lands for their many intrigues and plots, both against others and against themselves. Because of these countless intrigues and counter-intrigues, Uthwine's task to guard Merovich was no less than the most difficult work in Gaul at that time. Merovich was the son of King Chilperic, whose brother had been a previous husband of Brunhilde, so that Merovich had married his aunt. Such was the mixed-up and lawless state of this land.

Under Ceawlin's instruction, I sent anonymous letters provided to me by Ceawlin to King Chilperic. I learned later that these letters claimed that Uthwine had been bribed by Merovich to kill the king, so that Merovich himself could claim the throne.

All of this came out in the trial of the Bishop Praetextatus, and Ceawlin's anonymous letter implicating Uthwine was used in the trial of that good man, a matter that haunts my conscience still.

But the letters did their work for Ceawlin, for Uthwine was captured and killed by the Frankish king, and the bulk of his war-band broken up, most returning to the northern Saxon lands, a result that could only be good for Ceawlin.

So now I became more important still, for Ceawlin let it be known that I was his chief emissary in Gaul. Much more work came my way. The winters went by. I fought in campaigns in Lombardy, so too in the land of the Visigoths. I fought in many small battles all over the land of the Gauls, for in that land at that time there was much strife, and many minor kings, and they all fought each other.

I had won much gold, and I now had under my command an elite war-band numbering, with me, eight men, all of them mercenaries and freebooters from all the lands of the world – Gaul, or the Norse lands or the besieged homeland of the Romans, Syria too, and even the north African lands. These warriors, though few in number, were amongst the best at their respective warrior-arts in the whole of the land of the Franks, and my war-band came to be spoken of in the verses, such was their prowess.

During my time over the seas I had many times offered thanks to the gods of learning that Cadolan had taught me to write in the language of the Romans, for Ulla was true to her word, and I received regular letters from her. Those letters from Ulla whilst I was in the land of the Franks soothed my soul, for they reminded me always of the reason that I was there – namely, to win honour and status for Ceawlin, so that one day the Saxon princess and I would be together.

From these letters, I learnt that Cormac was returned to our people, and took up home again with what remained of my family. I heard that he lived the life of a farmer. I heard nothing about his further relationship with Gwen, Farinmael's daughter, and it would not have surprised me if Ceawlin had prevented any formal arrangement. A warrior of Cormac's status marrying the daughter of a great British king could only spell trouble for the Gevissa king. If this was Ceawlin's strategy, Ulla did not tell me, for reasons I could guess at, for such news would remind me of the divisions between our families.

Ceawlin was, however, true to his word, and my family continued to live under his protection. In fact, from the news that reached Ulla, it seemed that my family grew stronger, for there was no disgrace to Cormac amongst my people or even amongst the Saxons, for they too respected a great warrior, and already his name was being sung in the lays, and his fame added to the verses.

Ulla told me all of this in the wax-woods that came to me in all parts of the lands that I travelled through. She told me her hopes and wishes, told me of everyday matters, told me of her mother and father, and, sometimes, told me of the plans of her father.

One day I received a wax-wood from Ulla that much saddened me, for it spoke of the death in a riding accident of her mother, Acha, and there had been devastation in her household. Ceawlin's Hall had mourned for a full three months, so great was the bond between Ceawlin and Acha. Her father was in despair, and refused to see anybody, even Ulla herself, and would go out riding and not be seen for days.

Thereafter, the letters from Ulla grew more sombre. Though she herself was through the worst of her mourning, and could at least begin to plan again for the future, she told me that her father remained in despair, and he was much changed, and his decisions had grown erratic.

I had learnt long before now that Ceawlin was no ordinary Saxon king. He had by this time been victorious at the battles of Barbury Hill, and of Wibba's Don, and now Deorham. I had been told by Ulla that his power now stretched from the Saxon shores in the south of our land, up the eastern strip to the river Humber in the north, and from the foot of the Chiltern Hills to the lower valley of the Severn.

His power was now greater than all other of his fellow Aenglish invader kings and Ealdormen. Such was the overwhelming strength of his position at that time.

Ulla had told me that he had now, since the death of her mother, started to believe that one more great victory would secure for him a position never before achieved by the invaders. He had become obsessed with the new-coined word of the poet, *Bretwalda*, and he meant to become overlord in Britain, and he had begun to plan the way by which he might truly achieve that status.

It was at this time that I received another wax-wood from Ulla, but fastened with Ceawlin's own personal seal, which had been carried to me amidst great security by a war-band sent under the personal authority of Ceawlin himself.

The wax-wood in part said this:

> *'It is my father's wish that you now return home to us, my love, for he has designs to make war again near the region of your birth, and your knowledge and your kinships may prove to be of value to him. His plan is to press on to capture the upper reaches of the Severn Valley and to use the once-great Roman city of Uriconium as a strategic base for new conquests. If he should succeed in this plan, then he will advance on Chester itself, and victory there would surely give him the prize which he most desires, which is power over all of Aengland, for there can be no other power that might oppose him.'*

In the same pouch that carried this wax-wood, I received another, which carried Ulla's personal seal, and when I read it the sense of foreboding that had come over me whilst reading the first only increased.

'My love,

You must come home to us.

My father is much changed, and I fear that the death of my mother has unhinged his mind. He talks of nought but 'Aengland' and his rightful place as Bretwalda. He insists that you return, for your connections can only be of value to him.

We have reports that the wife of Farinmael has now died, and your brother has married Gwendolyne, her daughter, and together these events have stirred up your people, so that they seek to arm themselves and throw off the authority that my father has over them.

Your help is needed here.

My brother, Cutha, and my good friend Crida are worried about my father. They fear that in his present state of mind he will make mistakes – mistakes that could prove disastrous to the welfare of his kingdom.

Rhuadrac, I long for your presence, but you must take care when you return, my love, for all is intrigue in this place at this time.'

My mind was in turmoil when I finished reading these letters.

I had long since realised that all was potential conflict in front of me. I had refused to fight against the people of Britain, though all of my gains had come under the auspices of Ceawlin, and Ceawlin's power was based on his authority in my land. Now he was asking me to help him directly in the conflict with the British and even against the West Britons, my own people. And now too my brother was stirring up our people and Ceawlin was much changed. I knew that the time had come for me to work out my true allegiance, but I could not fathom my next move, and I sat staring at the two letters.

Something else in Ulla's words needled me. What were these words 'good friend?' This Crida had been mentioned several times in Ulla's letters. What role did he play in her life? Why mention him at all?

There was a loud banging at the door and, without a word from me, the door of the chamber in the white-stoned Roman villa in which I sat reading these letters was thrown back, crashing against the wall.

"Now then, Love-struck, what goes on in your life?"

Torquato stood there, and my cares fell away from me for a while, and I smiled.

He looked at me now with a look that was typical of him, which is to say, he looked like he might burst out laughing, for nothing could be so serious as to warrant the solemn look on my face. Then he said, in his native Roman language:

"By the gods, but the cub-general looks like he has left his sword out in the rain for two weeks, and it has rusted. Love-struck, you will learn, your sword is like your prick, it needs to be used all the time or it will rust and the blade will fall off . . ."

For all of my worries, I could not help but throw back my head and laugh momentarily, but I quickly recovered my composure. This man was in my command and I had to at least try to perform the ritual which we had long since perfected.

"Have a care, you Roman dog, for I am in charge here, and I will not stand for that sort of insolence."

A look of sham innocence came over Torquato's face.

"But it is true, for a physician told me so once."

"It has nothing to do with my sword, or whatever other nonsense you are spouting. I am to return to my country, for there is trouble brewing, and it concerns Ulla's father, and my brother, and I can see much trouble ahead."

"Ah, the very Saxon king's daughter, the lovely Ulla, the beauty to whom Love-struck has lost his heart to. General, as I was just telling you . . ."

Five winters previously I had been in the city of Tours, part of the war-band that was guarding Merovich. The day's work was done, and we had been relieved by the night guards. The evening was already well advanced. I took myself into the city to find a tavern. Soon enough I found myself in some dimly lit den, attracted by the laughter filtering through from a back room. There was much revelry in the place. Three small hearths threw a baleful light onto the enflamed faces, and I could see that much mead and wine had already been flowing.

Somewhere in the recesses a lyre was being played, and amongst the loud laughter I could hear the drunken strains of some soldier's lament. I grabbed a flagon of wine and made my way to the back room. It was lit by many candles and several flaming torches, but even so it was murky, and I winced as the smell of woodsmoke filled my nostrils and fumes stung my eyes.

A huge man stood in the centre of the room, and it was he that was singing. He wore a long black leather waistcoat, unbuttoned, over his simple white sleeveless tunic. Each of his red-blue arms was covered from wrist to shoulder in tattoos of naked women and coiled serpents. A woman held onto each of those arms as he threw his head back and wailed his lament, stopping every now and then to gulp more wine from his beaker and to turn to the women and roguishly kiss their necks, and laugh, his aquiline features splitting into huge creases as he did so. His singing voice was terrible, but it was of no concern to him. He continued to sing and shout his song, oblivious to everybody else in the room other than the women. Several ranks of men, mostly mercenaries or warriors, ringed the room, and all were laughing at the antics of this great clown.

Finally the giant threw his head back with his eyes closed, his bellowing voice straining to the final high note:

. . . and ever the soldier walks alone, his battle path un-ending

His song completed, he brought his head back, opening his eyes on the room, nodding his head furiously and laughing, evidently well pleased with his performance.

All in the room crashed their hands together and banged their mugs on the tables. With a slightly dazed and happy air, the rogue pushed through the room, a woman still on each arm. As he passed me, he staggered into me, almost pitching me from my stool. He slowly focused his red-rimmed eyes on mine.

"Get out of my way, you little pipsqueak, or I'll break your neck!"

I looked calmly at this great galoot.

"Do not abuse me."

"If I say you are a little pipsqueak, you are a pipsqueak."

He laughed, and looked arrogantly at the two women with him. I looked around me; in one movement I stepped back and drew *Saesbane*.

"Call me that again and I'll finish you."

People around us stopped speaking, and a hush descended on the room.

The two women slowly detached themselves from the arms of the giant. He laughed, and stood up to his full height, looking down at me. He leaned his head to one side and regarded me with great interest. For some reason I could see real affection in his eyes, and humour played around his face, which baffled me. He spoke to the whole room.

"Oh-oh. Now then, what do we have here? Why, we have a little general, I think. Tell me, Little General, why should I not finish you off right now?"

"Because, oaf, you are drunk, and it was you who barged into me. I have done nothing to provoke you. The contrary is true. And anyway, I have the drop on you, so make any such attempt and you're done for."

He weighed these words in silence, his lower jaw causing his mouth to pucker, his head nodding as if pondering the wisdom of my words. Then the great buffoon again threw back his head and laughed, his eyes disappearing into the great creases of his face, gold teeth gleaming in his mouth.

"Well then, what logic! I cannot fault it."

He turned again to the room, sweeping his right arm around in a great arc.

"All here take note. I have decided that this little pips . . . err . . . little general is my friend, and now he is going to get drunk with me! Ladies, more wine over here for the little general and me!"

All in the room burst into laughter, and the lyres started up again and people turned away from us. I slowly returned *Saesbane* to its scabbard.

So did I meet my friend Torquato, and that night I did get drunk, and we left that den as confirmed friends.

So now I looked at him stood in front of me; the gigantic frame, the shaved bullet head, the square shoulders, the tattooed arms – he was almost as big as my brother. He reminded me of my brother too, not in appearance, nor in manner – for Torquato was one of the funniest men I ever met in my life, with a humour that was, in truth, having by now survived many battles, much to my taste – but in some other quality I could not describe, a quality that I saw only in the white heat of battle, in the moments of greatest crisis, when his warrior spirit shone through, and he was his own true self.

He told me that he was a mercenary born in Rome. He was perhaps five or six winters older than me and was by now my right-hand shoulder-man. Over the several seasons since our first meeting I had learned that the big man was truly a great rascal and a rogue, with no sense at all of the proper way of doing things, for such matters bored him. He was alive, and one day he would be dead, and all the rest was battles, wine and women. He had a lust for life, and he was a man who women loved. When not in battle, he was forever in their company, whether they be old or young. They were all devoted to him and he broke many hearts. Other warriors learned not to introduce their women to him, for seemingly no woman could resist him, and I had to step in to resolve many a dispute.

On one occasion, at Ceawlin's written command, my war-band was sent to guard the Gaulish king, Chilperic. On our first meeting with that king, he had swept into the room, barely registering our presence, his long black hair hanging loose at his proud shoulders, men waiting on his every word.

From habit I had bowed my head as he came in. The king pointed to Torquato, who stood barely five paces from him, then speaking lazily, as if momentarily distracted:

"You, giant, why do you not incline your head at my entrance?"

Torquato had looked at this cruel tyrant with equanimity.

"Because I live by a simple rule. I believe myself better than no man. But then, so too do I believe that no man is better than me."

A silence descended on the court. Such insolence was unheard of in that place.

The king had looked at my friend, first in outrage, then with an increasing interest. Finally he nodded to his courtiers, and smiled a humourless smile, having come to some settlement with himself, no doubt too reckoning the distance between himself, Torquato and his nearest personal guards.

"Very well then, your pride will make you the best guard of my person. But do not try my patience further, mercenary."

Torquato had said nothing in response, just stared at the king, unruffled, as if the king's words were a matter of indifference to him, which in truth they were.

So he had survived, and in fact we flourished under the protection of Chilperic for a time. But never once had I witnessed my friend bow down to any man, not even a king.

Out of battle he was the worst-disciplined warrior I ever met. Yet, for all of that, he was no fool, and I loved the man like a brother.

This then was the fellow who now stood in front of me.

I held up my arm. Ulla was out of bounds to his wit, and he knew that and it was one of the few areas that he was not allowed to transgress with his profanities. He made to say more, but looked at me sideways, and thought better of it.

He decided to change course, to see if he could bait me in some other way.

"Well then, maybe I will get to meet this brother of yours, and take him down a peg or two."

"For that, Torquato, you might have to go into extra training, for he makes you look like Little Sigfeldt by comparison."

Little Sigfeldt was the smallest man in our band, a slingsman, and was a full half-arm's length shorter than Torquato.

A disgruntled look passed over Torquato's face, and I laughed to myself. I loved baiting him in this way. Doubting his prowess as the world's greatest warrior in battle was, in the words of the Roman poet taught to me by Cadolan, his *Achilles heel*, and I could always off-balance him when I played on it, and get him to where I wanted him. I played on it always; I told him that big as he was, he was but a midget compared to my brother, because Cormac was a true giant, all of which riled him greatly, as was my intent.

In truth I think now that this was a main source of our bond, for all other warriors were in awe of him, as he was truly a giant, and a great warrior too. But to me he was not the greatest warrior I had known – Cormac was that. I was never in awe of him, right from that first meeting. He had recognised this from the start, and in some way it allowed him to relax with me, to be open with me, and even, within limits, to accept me as his chief, a role I had never once sought in relation to him. *He* decided that *I* would be his chief. Once made, his decision was final. For reasons I never really understood, my first reaction to him had come to him as some sort of relief; it was as if some weight had been taken from him.

"Anyway, that is all nonsense, but I am coming with you, so the matter is settled. When do we leave?"

I was lifted in spirit by both his manner and the simple declaration of his bond to me. He was a mercenary, a freebooter, and his life was his own. Although at that time he owed his allegiance to me, it would have been a simple matter to settle up and divide the spoils we had built up in the Frankish lands, and for him to go his own way. By this simple declaration he had bound himself to me again, and I was glad of it, for I knew that Torquato would be needed in whatever business lay ahead.

I outlined to him the contents of Ulla's letters, but said nothing of the change in Ceawlin, for that struck me as family business, and Torquato did not need to know it.

He heard me out, then said:

"All the usual tripe then. Frankly, I could not give a monkey's toss for the whys and the wherefores of it. If I receive a regular full plate of food, and enough of the wine of my own people, and do not have to drink too much of that mead-piss you Britons drink, and can get in between some of these beauties that I keep hearing about, and earn gold – well then – I am a happy man. So, what next?"

"Get the men together, tell them that we are to leave for my country as soon as we can arrange for it, that we may be away for some time, and so find out how many wish to stay with us. See that they are all made aware of the facts, and that there may not be much gold in it for them."

Torquato stood back and sprang to attention, clicked his heels and lifted his arm in mock salutation.

"Yessir, Cub-General sir, it will be done, sir."

He left me then, and I smiled.

Then I picked up Ulla's letters, and my face grew solemn again, wondering what was in front of us, for I had long known that this conflict would come.

*

All of my war-band elected to come with us across the sea, which was a surprise to me, for these men were mercenaries. They lived by their earnings in battle, and they had been told that there may not be much prospect for gold in the Briton lands. But Veostan the Scandinavian, Scipio from Africa, Rama Bec from Syria, Little Sigfeldt, and young Gregor from east of the German lands would make the journey with us. Even that strange fellow Felix had committed himself, which surprised me, for this man's first and last priority was the earning of gold.

But these were all fine warriors and with Torquato we would be eight in total.

So it was that three days after receiving Ulla's letter, we set out from the city of Tours for my homeland. Seven of us rode next to the covered wagon, driven by Scipio, which carried our battle armour, and the chests in which we kept the spoils from our work in Gaul.

We rode hard for the north coast. Ceawlin had arranged for a Saxon boat to meet us there at first light on the last day of the first month in autumn, that is, October. We had made good time, and we could now see the sea stretch out beyond us on our left-hand side. We were within a couple of miles of the meeting point at the boat-place at Grannona.

Torquato drew alongside me.

"Now then, General, it's time we found a grog house. This is our last night on these shores before we leave for the barbarian lands, so we should make the most of it . . ."

I looked across at him. None of my war-band had been to the land of my birth; all were fascinated by the prospect, but the older warriors, Veostan, Scipio, Torquato and Felix had no great expectations. Even amongst the mercenary ranks, Britain was known as the land of the barbarians. It was a reputation that riled me. My land may not have had the splendour of some of the Frankish cities which still thrived under the old Roman influence, yet the people I had met in this place seemed to me no more civilised than my own people.

But then, as a mercenary, I had mixed only with those who knew power in this land.

"So be it. Do you know of anywhere near here?"

A mischievous grin crossed the great rascal's face.

"As it happens, I do. About thirty minutes ride from here, a place not known to many – only the best warriors get to know of it."

I did not take his bait.

"Tell me about it."

"An entire hut compound dedicated to wine, women and song. We can eat and drink, and choose a woman or two at the end of the night."

He fired a glance at me. He never failed to test my pact with Ulla, for such a view on life was unthinkable to him. I ignored him.

"How do you know of this place then?"

The Roman grinned at me.

"The man who runs it, one Scapthar, was once a great warrior, and a friend of mine. But we fell out over some woman or other. Some time later he sent word to tell me that he had walked away from the mercenary's life."

I raised my eyes at this sudden conversion. Torquato looked at me and laughed.

"Another shambles connected with some raven-haired beauty in Rouen apparently. Anyway, he had seen the light, he said. He wanted now only to live off the proceeds, and run this tavern-brothel of his, for those of his friends whom he respected after a long life in harness. Invitation only. I have visited him several times in this place. Believe me, the lads won't forget it in a hurry."

I thought about it. We would need to sleep one night before we reached Ceawlin's Hall once we had crossed over to the Saxon Shore. Time enough for a thick head to recover.

"So be it. They've earned it. But tell them to watch the excess. I want to cross over with this war-band in one piece, not with what's left of it."

"Yessir, General sir, it will be done."

He kicked on his horse and fell into step with the wagon, no doubt telling Scipio to prepare for the best night of his life, no holds barred.

A short time later, Torquato reined in at a crossroads. He indicated a narrow track to his left, which was just wide enough for the wagon to navigate in the skilful hands of Scipio. The track sloped down to the shore.

"Here is it. Let me go first. We don't want a full-scale fight on our hands. At least not until we've drunk the place dry."

With that he charged down the narrow lane, the rest of us following at a steady pace. After some five minutes or so, we came across a rough timber fence, and set into this fence was an entrance, really no more than two upright timbers with a crossbar at the top. The word *Paradiso* was chalked onto a slate hanging from the crossbar. Beyond this gate was a hut compound. We could see some five or six huts, and between these huts men and women walked freely, some with their arms around each other. Other men carried barrels, and casks, and went in and out of the largest of the huts, from which a steady stream of woodsmoke poured out through the well-thatched roof.

In front of this building we could see Torquato, and he rocked in the arms of a much older man. This fellow was of medium height, very heavy, thickset, with huge upper arms that bulged out of the red leather jerkin that he wore.

His chest was a bit fallen in; his belly sagged over his belt. We would have known that he was long past his best years as a warrior even if we had not seen the long unkempt grey hair that fell to his shoulders.

Torquato said something to this fellow as we slowly came up to them, with me at the front of my men.

The old warrior held out his arm to me and spoke in a curiously quiet voice, which was somehow laden with a sensitive good sense.

"So, he tells me that he has finally found a good chief, for once."

I fired a glance at Torquato, who looked away at the main hut.

"My name is Scapthar, and any friend of this rogue is a friend of mine."

"I am called Rhuadrac."

Scapthar stood back from me, looking me up and down. His face was a mass of wrinkles, like one who has found much to laugh at in the world, but some sadness was in that face too.

"Rhuadrac? A Briton? By the golden shield of Mars, do you have a brother, a giant, by the name of Cormac?"

I was astounded.

"It is true, I have a brother, his name is Cormac, and by any estimate he would be called a giant, bigger even than Torquato."

I glanced at Torquato, who frowned momentarily.

"By the gods, but that is amazing. Two weeks ago, in this very compound, a travelling band of Saxon mercenaries came through, led by an old friend of mine, Bangarth. He was a rogue that man, you know, could never keep his hands off another man's woman, but by the long-shadowed spear of Mars, he could fight, I'll give him that."

Scapthar's mind seemed to be wandering. He pulled himself together.

"Anyway, that is a different story. In that band of Saxons, they had a scop. That man could have charmed the birds down from the trees with his verses."

Scapthar seemed lost for a moment in his memory of the verses of the unknown Saxon verseman who had passed through his camp.

"Anyway, this is the point. His best verse of all was saved for the last. He talked of a black-haired softly spoken giant, Cormac of the Britons, who was Farinmael's champion. This man had fought like some fabled hero at the Battle of Deorham Field, seven winters ago. He had crushed Dragarth, the Scandic destroyer, in moments. He had fought against overwhelming odds to protect his king. He had finally failed, for there was no hope of victory, but had to be carried from the field with his brother, Rhuadrac. Both of these great warriors had fought till they dropped, having taken many of Bangarth's best men with them."

I had listened to all of this in silence. My brother was now spoken of in the verses; even I, in my small way, had been mentioned. I spoke quietly to Scapthar.

"Well then, friend of my friend, it is all true. At least about my brother, that is. I hope that I do not disappoint you in the flesh?"

"It is a great pleasure, Briton. Never before have I played host to a real true hero, one who is spoken about in the verses. Tonight we will drink till the stars fall in on us! Bagotin! Bagotin?"

He shouted out to the air.

A small thin man appeared out of the central hut.

"Go and get the lyre players. And the harpists. Get the verse men too. We have a real hero in our midst!"

He looked back to me.

"And women maybe? There are enough women here for all! Take your pick!"

And so we were swept into the high-roofed hut. I just had time to smile at Torquato as I was rushed past him. I saw that he stared at the ground and that his face was like thunder, but then he too lifted his head and smiled, and I knew that I had won at least this round of our game.

*

As evening came on, many cups of beer had been drunk, the wine was still flowing, and the fire still burned strongly in the centre hearth of the main hut, the smoke and sparks cascading out through the open roof flap.

Much laughter and shouting rang around the hut, for these were all men of fighting age, and for now there was no fighting to be done. Frequently some soldier's song would strike up, and many voices would join in, and the smoke-blackened timbers would shake with the lusty joy of it. Now and then some fight would break out, but Scapthar's men, several burly warriors armed with clubs, would quickly close in on it, and the miscreants would be carried out of the central hut, to sleep it off in one of the many side huts.

Scapthar sat on a high stool at the far end of the hut, his huge arms folded, the grin on his face stretching from ear to ear. He soaked everything up: the songs, the laughter, the fights, the smoke rising from the hearth. This was his world, he understood it, and he was happy here. Two or three women were sat around him, and I could see that he took pleasure just sitting there, watching the antics of my warriors before him, nodding and smiling to himself every now and then.

A few other war-bands stood around or sat in the hut, all of which added to the hubbub, but the area around the central hearth was for us that night.

Now was the time to tell tales and to break bread. Men and women ran here and there, filling up our cup or beaker even as we finished the last one. The harps and lyres played; women would move out in front of the hearth and dance in strange, sensuous movements to the simple rhythms.

I sat next to Scipio, expert with the trident and net.

He came from the far southern lands, from the country south of the land of the Visigoths, across the Mediterranean Sea. I knew Scipio to be a quiet man, not given to excess, always controlled in his words and manner. Even so, he laughed long and hard when something amused him, and then the eyes lit up in his ebony black face and he laughed a deep long laugh. I liked this laughter that boomed out of him, for the very sound of it caused me to laugh too, and to feel at peace with the world somehow. He looked at me now with honest eyes:

"Now tell me again, Chief. This Saxon king, Ceawlin, this man in whose name we work. What is he like?"

He talked to me in the Roman language, which was the core language of my band, for all had served time in the land of the long-haired kings, and the Roman language was widespread in that land.

So I told him then about the Gevissa king; how he had come onto the field at Deorham, and the respect with which he had treated Farinmael. Scipio was impressed, and he leaned towards me.

"Then he is an unusual king, for not one of those that I have met in the land of the Franks would have been capable of such nobility."

I said nothing. I led these men; it was not for me to pass opinions on those who paid us in gold. But I agreed with him.

Both Scipio and Veostan were men whose curiosity was easily aroused, so that they asked many questions, and enquired always as to the motives of men. Veos would ponder on the answers he got to his many questions. When Scipio found out the answer to a question, he would nearly always laugh, as if the ways of this world were a constant source of amusement to him, once he understood the reasons for events and the strange motivations of men.

Two big-hipped women strolled in front of us. Scipio looked at me.

"So, now we go to your homeland. Do you have a woman there?"

It was unusual for Scipio to be so outspoken. I nodded quietly. He was a man I could trust.

"Yes. We have a pact. But there are difficulties there."

"She belongs to another?"

"Not that. At least, not when I last saw her. Her family is a Saxon family – not British – it is of some power in my land."

Scipio nodded silently, but said no more.

We drank in silence for a few minutes.

Around us, Torquato and Veostan arm-wrestled at a nearby table, the Roman finally forcing down the thick arm of his opponent. Veos leapt up and howled with disgust.

"Drink it!"

Several warriors in my war-band joined in the chant.

"Drink it! Drink it!"

Veos cursed and lifted a heavy beer mug to his lips, drained the contents, then wiped away the spillage from his blonde beard, raising his smiling face to his comrades as he did so. His short powerful frame shook with laughter as another drink was poured for him. With his right hand he threw back the long blonde hair from his battered and good-natured face, then again sat down opposite Torquato.

"Now then, Roman, enough toying with you, let's do this for real!"

So saying, they locked arms, looking directly into each other's eyes, scowling, the veins standing out in their foreheads, the blood pulsing through their reddened necks.

Scipio turned to me again.

"What is this Britain like?"

"It is a green and fertile land – you will be surprised by it. True, its cities may not be as marbled and columned as some of those in this land, but there is a strange and powerful beauty there, as you will see."

We talked for a while longer about Britain, and I told him that my people were sore oppressed by the Saxon invaders, who sought to spread their ways everywhere to the cost of my people. Then I stopped and looked at him.

"But in truth, I am not sure myself that I really believe what I have just said."

Scipio looked at me calmly.

"How so?"

"It seems to me that there is a new way being born in my land, which is neither Saxon, nor Briton. Some new thing."

Scipio said nothing, just drained his wine cup. Then he turned to me, fixing me with his honest dark eyes.

"Chief, this will be my last campaign."

I looked into his strong black face. He was neither young nor old, so I was surprised by his words.

"I have made nearly enough gold to make my family strong."

He paused. We both watched the slowly swaying hips of a black-haired dancer, her right hand gently fondling her own outstretched left arm.

"My woman Mounira: she is the most beautiful woman in the place where I live. It is a city too: Constantine, the city in the ravine, in the north-east of my land. We have four children. My eldest boy, Scipion – one day he too will be a fighter, but maybe not a mercenary."

I understood his words. To be a mercenary was to live the life of one who was rootless, who had no home, no family, no community.

"My wife and I – we agreed. I would take the mercenary path to make our family strong. Now there is almost enough of my share of the gold in the wagon chests to make a difference to our lives. My hope is that Scipion will grow strong as a commander in the armies of my own people. So – this will be my last campaign. After this I go home to Mounira and my family."

He said no more. I poured him a fresh beaker of wine, and myself too; together we drank in silence. I looked around the hut; several women mingled with the warriors of my war-band, gorgeous women, well kept, with full bodies.

Felix stood on the edge of the room. He was a Gaul. He was also a dart-carrier, who lived or died by that strange and solitary skill of his. In battle he carried these deadly weapons in a leather pouch on his back. Sometimes called *martiobarbuli*, the lead-weighted darts, like giant arrows, were used against the chief cavalry warriors of the enemy. His strategic role in my war-band was to finish off the right-shoulder-men of the opposing chiefs, and our job was to get him into sufficient range to be able to do it. Felix was the best exponent of this strange art that I had yet met, and on many occasions his dark skills had enabled us to win battles, for an enemy shorn of its chief warriors is an easily defeated foe.

But away from battle he was an arrogant man, and I found little to like in him, for he talked only of himself at all times. He was always preening himself, a man who spent little time with the rest of us, and spent long periods on his own, sharpening his darts or practising with them. Many a time I had to prevent men in my war-band venturing through his line-sights during practise. He would have despatched them without much thought. He was a cold man, with cold manners. He had no religion or creed save one, which was the accumulation of gold. This creed he lived by, and it provided the motive force of his every action.

Now he leaned with his back to the wall of the hut, watching events unfold around him, a bored look on his face. Occasionally a woman would approach him, and they would talk for a little while. Then the woman would draw back, as if shocked, and she would find another man to talk to.

Just then, a warrior from one of the other war-bands stood up. The room again became quiet.

"We issue a challenge to the mercenaries led by the Briton."

All looked at me. I stood up.

"We are happy to accept any challenge that you propose. But have a care! We are much . . . grizzled by the ale. Make it something gentle, eh? Tonight we play – tomorrow we start a new campaign."

A good-natured low groan went up in the hut. Scapthar frowned; this was no way for a hero to accept a challenge! But I laughed, and took my place again.

The warrior who had first spoken rose again. He was of middle size, with short hair in the Roman style.

"Well then – a knife throwing contest?"

Scapthar stood up.

"Too much ale and wine has been taken. No weapons to be used here tonight."

He sat down again. Nobody argued; it was his brothel.

I stood up again.

"Look, we have all been drinking and singing here tonight. Get the storytellers up – let us see if they can entertain us!"

There was another discussion, then it was agreed, grudgingly by some, that the storytellers should be given the chance to tell their tales.

The war-band of the warrior who had issued the challenge began to prod one of their comrades, who seemed reluctant to stand up at first. After much coaxing, he got to his feet.

He was a young, slight man with red hair, and the beard had barely started to grow on his chin. He collected himself for a few moments, recalling his tale. Then he climbed onto a stool and began to speak. Although he spoke in the Roman tongue favoured by freebooters in those times, he had a strong German accent, and I guessed that he came from the northern lands. He had a deep resonant voice that seemed as if it belonged to somebody else:

"Once, a few years ago, a verseman from my home lands travelled to the British shores. The poet's name was Gundar. He went to see King Aethelbert, who was then a very young man. As we all know, this king is a good man, if only because he has just married a Frankish queen . . ."

The Gauls in the room cheered, though others booed and hissed. I knew this queen, Bertha, for we had been guard to her in Gaul for a time. It had been a matter of great importance to Ceawlin that the Kentish king should make this alliance; he knew all about it from my reports, and he had been impressed when my war-band and I had become personal guards to the woman who was now Aethelbert's queen; such connections could be of some value to the Wessex king.

"Well anyway, this Gundar was asked by the king why he had gone to see him.

'Well, good king, I have written a poem about you, for your fame has already spread far and wide. Now I wish to read you my poem,'"

Again, more boos and hisses rang around the room. Veos shouted out

"What a brown-noser!"

The room rocked with laughter.

The speaker, now a little deterred, took up his story again.

"Well anyway, the poet read his poem to the king. It told of many brave deeds by the king, and each verse of the poem finished with the words:

'The whole army is cowed
By the great Kentish king, as are the gods
At Aethelbert's feet all bow down
All men and warriors too'"

A great groan went up from the floor.

"By the gods, this poet is so far up the king's arse they will have to pull the bastard out by his ankles!"

Now this from Torquato, who had got to his feet, swaying slightly, and again laughter spilled around the smoke-filled room. The young verseman pressed on with his verse, now quickening his pace:

"Anyway, the king liked the verses. He rewarded the poet with many gifts, and made him one of his warriors. He gave him a ring."

"Aye, I'll bet he did. We know all about these kings in Britain."

More laughter. My face was stone when my friend looked across at me, grinning from ear to ear.

"But now I come to the main part of my story. One day, as Gundar walked down the street, he was met by three men. Their leader was named Thorm. He was a thug, and never said please or thank you to anybody."

This part was met with stony silence, and puzzled shaking of heads. What sort of a description of a thug was that? The lad rushed on with his tale.

"Anyway, this Thorm said to Gundar: 'Let me have some gold, and I will give it back to you in three days time.' Gundar thought about this, because it is never a good idea to give strangers gold . . ."

Now one or two warriors shook their heads again, and started to clap their hands slowly.

"Sit down! Learn how to tell a tale."

"But Gundar decided to risk it and gave Thorm the gold. He went back and told the king what he had done. The king said to him: 'Now you've put your foot in it. That man is a thug and a master warrior. He can blunt a sword just by looking at it.'"

A few laughs sputtered around the hut.

"Well then, Gundar went back for his gold, but Thorm told him that he would never return it. So Gundar returned to the king, and told him what Thorm had said. The king told him that he had a plan: Gundar should go back to Thorm and show him the rusting old blunt sword that he had, and challenge him to a duel. But for the real duel, the king would give Gundar the magical sword of the Cantawwa, the cleaver of legend."

A few cheers went up, largely from the warriors in the poet's own band.

"So Gundar met with Thorm in a duel. Thorm, seeing the old rusted sword, rushed in at Gundar, leaving himself open. Gundar immediately dealt him the death blow with the magical sword of the Cantawwa, which he had hidden in his cloak. The king thanked him for his services in killing this thug, and Gundar's fame spread throughout the land of Aethelbert."

The storyteller stopped at this point. He had rushed the end of his tale, because it had not been too well received.

Somebody shouted: "What, is that it?"

A few warriors banged their mugs on the table, but most thought that the story was a bit thin.

Scapthar stood up.

"Now then, don't give the lad a hard time. At least he had the balls to get up and try. Mind you, that Thorm must have been a real nasty bastard if he didn't say please and thank you to anybody, and no mistake!"

Wine-fuelled laughter rolled loudly around the hut.

"So. Who is to reply from the hero's team?"

Rama Bec got to his feet, and immediately my warriors pounded their cups and beakers on the table and made a great clamour.

Rama Bec was a Syrian, a handsome man by any standard; his face and physique were lean, and he was nothing like a warrior to look at. I might have thought him a physician, or a lyre player, for he had fine hands. He was a thoughtful man, not given to displays of emotion of any kind. He was always self-possessed and calm, like one who plays the wooden war-piece game, but who plays it slowly, making his next move only after much deep thought.

He was a specialist with the mace and chain, a brutal weapon that I always thought was unsuited to his appearance. Until, that is, I saw him use it in battle. Many a warrior felt the full force of that cruel device, and none had to be hit a second time.

Torquato stood up and called for silence; the hut slowly quietened down, and all looked at this lean graceful man from the eastern lands. Torquato sat down next to Veos, and each pulled down a woman onto his knees, the women laughing with delight as they did so.

Rama Bec looked around his audience with great calm, then smiled, and started to speak in a quiet voice, light-timbered:

"I speak of a time long ago, in a land far away. Here, all life was abundant. The sun lit the land, the rivers flowed freely through green pastures and the birds sang gaily from the lofty trees. Man and woman too loved each other passionately, bringing forth new life into the world. All was harmony in this faraway land.

"Young King Tammuz lived with Ishtar in the palace. Their love was legend. Mighty was their lustful passion. The motion of the stars and wandering planets was bound up in it. If one hour would pass and they were apart, the other would grow restless, and fret.

"One day, Tammuz left the ravished bed that he shared with Ishtar. From the window of their bedroom he looked out upon the land.

"'The leaves begin to fall from the trees. Soon it will be winter.'

"He did not know it, but these words caused much distress to his lover, Ishtar. For Ishtar was, in truth, the great mother goddess herself – she whose loving embrace enables the sap to drive through the flowers and the trees, she who makes green the fields, she who fires the great love passion between man and woman.

"Ishtar knew that the falling of the leaves from the trees signalled the death of Tammuz, and the start of his journey to the dark underworld, where light gives no relief and the dead men lose their bones.

"And so it proved. From that day, Tammuz began to grow weak, the land grew dark, the flowers faded.

"Then the dread day came when Tammuz died. Ishtar sent up her lament to the very gates of heaven itself.

"The land grew cold, the rivers froze over, the flowers were all gone. The bare branches of the trees swayed in the cold winds.

"Ishtar knew no consolation. At the peak of her despair, she knew what she must do.

"'I will follow Tammuz. I will seek him out in the dark lands.'

"So she did.

"But while she was gone, all life in the land was suspended. No sun lit up the land. The grass grew grey and died. No birds sang. The trees became withered. The beasts in the field grew thin. Man and woman kept apart. The land and the rivers became frozen over.

"Seeing this, the mighty warrior-god Ea was sent from the heavens into the dark lands, the subterranean lands, to seek out Ishtar, and to restore her to the dead land.

"But Allatu, queen of this dark land, was not happy.

"She said this to the warrior-god Ea: 'You know that none should return from these lands. Why should I make an exception for this woman?'

"Ea was a resourceful god, and answered her thus: 'Dark queen of the underworld! Do you not see? In the land where Ishtar reigns, all is frozen over. There is no new life, for it is Ishtar brings life to this land. If there is no new life, who then will replenish your realm in the times to come?'

"Allatu thought on this and saw that it made sense. So she called for Ishtar. They met in a dark hall, where the torches burned with a barely visible flame, ash stood in the dead hearth, and the dust piled deep on all the surfaces.

"'Mother Goddess! Your land grows dark and frozen. It needs you. Therefore I will sprinkle you with the water of life, so that you might return to the upper world.'

"But Ishtar cried out: 'Not so fast, dark queen! I will only go from this grey place with Tammuz, for life in the other place will be unbearable without him!'

"Allatu thought on this. Ishtar needed to be returned to the upper land. She would not go without Tammuz. A bargain needed to be struck.

"'Very well then, queen of life. Your consort too shall return. But on one condition. Each year, after the falling of the leaves, he must die and return to me. You must come for him and spend time in this dread region. Then you may both return. Only you will know of this condition.'

"Ishtar agreed.

"Allatu bathed Ishtar and Tammuz with the water of life. They returned to the upper world, rejoicing.

"Soon, all life was abundant again. The sun lit the land, the rivers flowed freely through green pastures and the birds sang gaily from the lofty trees. So too did man and woman love each other passionately, bringing forth new life into the world. All again was harmony in this faraway land.

"In the palace, the two lovers were entwined in passion. The motion of the stars and wandering planets was bound up in it. Ishtar delighted in their ecstasy. She had only one dread.

"The day when Tammuz would move to the window, and announce: 'The leaves have begun falling from the trees.'"

Rama Bec stopped speaking. All had been rapt with attention as he spoke. There had been quiet cheers at the description of the lovers, and nods of approval when the warrior-god argued with Allatu; that was a deep thought, and all there understood it.

I looked around me at these silent, battle-scarred men; the challenge had been forgotten, for Rama Bec's story had moved them. The women too looked at Rama Bec with shining eyes, as if for the first time they had heard a story that told something true of their lives.

Then Rama Bec bowed, a low bow, and smiled, and the pounding of the tables started then, and even the red-haired youth banged his cup on the table, because he knew that he had just heard a good story.

Scapthar stood up. He stood there for a few moments, nodding and scratching his head, looking a little flustered for some reason. Then he raised his arms, saluted Rama Bec, and then turned to all sides of the room:

"Bravo Levantine! Another hero – that's two in one night! Well done, lad, you win hands down! Now, Bagotin! Bagotin? Where is that man when I need him? There you are! Go and fill that man's cup with the best wine. Now – strike up the harp, let's have the drums! Bring on the dancers again . . .!"

Rama Bec bowed once more. He took his place next to Little Sigfeldt, who talked animatedly to him now, and he listened quietly with great attention to whatever it was his friend said to him.

*

The night was drawing to its close. All had drunk too much, and eaten too much, but there had been no trouble for my war-band. A crescent moon was high; the night was clear. There was enough light in the compound from several flickering boughs for me to make out the faces of those in my band.

Scapthar now walked across to where we stood, in the yard just outside the entrance to the main hut.

"Well, heroes and warriors! A good night, eh? Now then, it is time for bed, and perhaps your thoughts turn to love?"

Several women had followed him from the hut. All were attractive, big-bodied women. Torquato and Veos immediately linked arms with the women they had been talking to all night, and walked over to one of the small side huts. Rama Bec and Little Sigfeldt did likewise. Loud and good-natured raucous laughter spilled over the compound as they all moved away to the small side huts. Then Felix too made his choice, leaving Scipio, Gregor and me in the compound.

Scapthar looked at Scipio.

"Can you see anything that interests you?"

"All of the women are beautiful. But I will preserve my energy tonight."

"But you are a strong and powerful man!"

Scipio looked at the old rogue and smiled.

"I do not talk of physical energy. Something else."

Scapthar looked at Scipio; then he too smiled and his eyes lit up. I remembered Torquato's words that this man seemed always disappointed in matters of love.

"I understand you. You have a special woman somewhere. You do not seek to break the spirit-energy of your bond!"

Scipio thought on these words, then smiled again, but said nothing.

Scapthar then looked at me.

"So, hero, are you not tempted?"

"I think like Scipio."

Scapthar again smiled, but I had the impression that this time it was a forced smile. It occurred to me that perhaps his belief in heroes had once again been shaken, somehow. I smiled to myself; perhaps there are many types of hero in this life.

This left only Gregor of my warriors left in the compound. I looked at him now. He had seen perhaps five or six winters less than me. He was above middle height, lean, with fair hair grown long, but had curiously dark eyes, which somehow did not match his hair. Although young, or perhaps because of it, he had a quick temper, and either Torquato or I were always pulling him out of some scrape or another. For all of that he was light-hearted, and never held a grudge, so that once the temper had vanished so did his ill-feeling towards those who had caused it. He was straight-talking and laughed a lot, and it was this aspect of his character that appealed to me most, for I talked to him often, and was always pleased when I could make him laugh. Of his skills as a swordsman there was no doubt, and of all in my war-band, only Torquato could match him in the sword skill-trials.

"So, Gregor, how do you see it?"

"I'm like you and Scipio – I'm saving myself for some special woman."

Scapthar, Scipio and I burst out laughing. These words had been said so earnestly, without defence, we had no choice. Gregor's temper flared up, but we calmed him down, and explained that we well understood his words, and he had been brave to state them.

"I've tried this stuff once or twice you know, and it left me cold – there was no love in it."

A smile flickered around my lips again. The lad flushed.

"You are all barbarians! None of you know anything!"

I burst into strangled laughter, and Scipio did too. Scapthar began to bellow in a slow deep voice – hoo-hoo-hoo – and that started me laughing even more.

Gregor looked at us angrily.

I managed to calm my laughter.

"Gregor, you misunderstand us. We all sympathise with you. It is just that there are certain things that no man can say to another with impunity. What you have just said is one of them."

Gregor stalked off towards the hut that had been shown to him earlier, shouting over his shoulder:

"You know nothing!"

He left us there, three drunken grown men laughing helplessly in the compound of a tavern-brothel, as the shadows cast by the flaming boughs lengthened around us.

*

Next day it was a sorry and bedraggled bunch of warriors that reached the boat that Ceawlin had arranged to be made ready for us.

The captain of it, a near silent man called Rathgere, had gruffly welcomed us on board his ship at the sight of Ceawlin's personal letter, and the wolf's head pennant that I had shown to him.

The boat was moored to two thick stakes set into the sloping half-grass, half-sand. The day had closed in after the clear night and was now grey and overcast; heavy white-crested waves chased each other into the land and pounded the shore, causing the boat to lift and fall at its moorings. Great groans went out from its timbers.

It seemed to me that Torquato had become very quiet, and his face paler than it had been. He looked with some alarm at the pitching boat, cursing under his breath.

"Damn these things. By the trident of the sea-god himself, we were never meant to travel over the waters. We have arms, not flippers . . ."

But he had no choice, and like the rest of us he boarded the boat, giving fearful glances over the stern, walking like a child amidst its timbers, deeply mistrustful of its seaworthiness.

The boat was about thirty full paces in length, and, in its mid-section, about four strides in width. The timbers reared up at its bow and stern, and at the bow some great pagan figure had been carved out of wood, coloured blue, and fixed there. A mast stood about two-thirds down the length of the boat, and the sail canvas was lashed tightly around it. I could see that the floor of the boat was comprised of overlapping planks.

Great wooden oars were set into the timbers, I counted twenty each side. Men of all ages and shapes took up an oar each as we came on board, Rathgere taking his place at the rudder in the stern. Immediately Veostan took a place next to him, and began to ask him questions about the construction of the boat, and the state of the seas, and the course we would be taking to the land of the Britons.

Soon enough we were away from the land, and the floor rolled under us, as we pitched high up and back down the rolling waves. The Saxon warriors pulled hard at the oars; I marvelled at the rhythm of their movement as they caught each wave at the sweet point with each collective surge, so that the boat flew through the churning sea.

Very quickly Torquato had grown paler, then grey. Soon he was leant over the bow of the boat, cursing at its every dip. In truth, I had little opportunity to laugh; my guts too very soon began to lurch and my head grew dizzy. My warriors sat on each side of me, a troubled expression on their pale faces; to a man they regretted their excesses of the previous night. These were men who fought for their living, but they did not trust boats, for there was nothing here that they could control.

At one point Torquato came back to where we sat; his face was now nearer green than grey, his eyes sunken. He blew air into his cheeks as he pitched up to us. He swallowed hard, and looked as if he would kill me if he had the chance, for he had undertaken this expedition at my request. I was not inclined to fool with him at that moment. Only Veostan seemed unaffected by it all. He had by now rejoined us, and looked up at the giant Roman, laughter in his eyes:

"Oi, Neptune, get back to the bow, or take a turn on the rudder, make yourself useful!"

Torquato curled up his huge fist under the jaw of the Scandic warrior, and looked as if he might kill him too. Just then the boat again gave another mighty lurch, and the Roman bent forward at the waist, turning back immediately to the bow. A great cheer went up from my fellow warriors, and on another day I would have laughed myself, but just then I too had to run forward to the bow, amidst more cheers from the warriors in my band.

All around me the sea plunged and reared, plunged and reared, amongst the heavy grey day. My legs had lost their bones; the sea-salt wind lashed into my cold sweat-laden face. I prayed to my mother's god for some sight of land.

But by some miracle the malady passed. The sea grew calmer. After a couple of hours my head cleared, my stomach ceased to churn. I saw too that Torquato was much recovered, and that Veos made a point of keeping the length of the boat between them. The sail was unfurled; it sat full with the breeze, we leapt forward through the waves. By now the oarsmen worked in shifts; ten men on each side for thirty minutes, rest, turn about.

A light fog lay over the waters at distance, but not so dense that it prevented the rudderman take his bearings from the land behind him. Even as the retreating scene began to grow hazy and dim, so then did the vague outline of land before us begin to take shape.

I was strangely moved by the slow forming shape of the land before me. I had not seen it for seven full winters. Much had happened to me during that time; I had prospered, I could not deny it. But still the best part of me was in this place, and soon enough I would see her again.

I leant forward at the bow. I could now see land away to my left, and I took this to be the island of Vente, peopled by the Wihte tribes. I had been told that we headed for landfall at a place called Cymeo Ora, near the town of Belgae, called Cissanceaster in the Saxon tongue.

When I had left this land, we had departed from the place of the great white cliffs, which marked the shortest point between Britain and Gaul. Here, I could see that the land was flatter and much cut into by the sea.

So now my land loomed up before me, and soon we would draw fresh horses, find a new covered wagon, and before long my war-band and I would be in Ceawlin's Hall.

Just then, I heard a great commotion at the stern of the boat, then a great shout went up as something hit the water. I looked to the back of the boat; all were looking overboard, at something in the sea. The oarsmen had stopped their rhythmic stroke. As I reached the stern I saw that my men were laughing.

Torquato stood there, and I heard him say:

"I'll give you Neptune, you Swedish bastard!"

I looked over the stern, to see Veos bobbing up and down in the water, gesturing wildly with his arms. "Help me!"

Then he disappeared altogether.

Long moments passed. We began to cast glances amongst ourselves. More moments passed. Even Torquato began to frown.

Then Veos broke surface, and laughed at us. In a simple graceful movement, he began to swim with powerful strokes towards the nearby shore.

Torquato breathed hard, then he too laughed.

On balance, both sides equal.

This was how my band of fine warriors, those rascals, arrived in the land of my birth.

*

Horses and a wagon were waiting for us as we left the boat.

We rode hard and made good progress. By the end of the first day we were south of Winche, and would be at Ceawlin's Hall before noon of the following day. We had by now left the flatlands by the Saxon Shore and were amongst the rolling hills of the southern downs. I could see that my warriors were amazed by what they saw. Although it was the beginning of the winter months, and the cold season had come early that year, the quiet beauty of my land was plain to them.

In truth, my heart leapt to see it again. Soon I would see Ulla after too many years apart; her father's work had kept me busy in all regions of the Frankish lands, and it had not been feasible to return. Whether this was a deliberate design on Ceawlin's part, I could not say. Our letters had sustained us, or so I hoped, but all would be made clear when I saw her tomorrow.

We struck camp within sight of the torchlights of Gwenta. We had found a small circle of stones halfway up a low hill, just off the main road. Soon enough the fire was burning, the beans in the pan were heating, and we tore huge chunks from the loaves of bread provided to us by Rathgere the boatman. Into these, we placed strips of cheese and dry salted beef. Two flagons of wine had already been passed around, and the sore heads of the morning were already a forgotten memory.

Little Sigfeldt was speaking.

"So, Chief, tell us more about this brother of yours that Scapthar mentioned. He seems like a great warrior. Did Scapthar say that he was champion to a king?"

I looked at Sigfeldt now. He seemed to be nothing like his great friend Rama Bec in character, which made their friendship all the more puzzling.

He was a slight, lean man, always moving, and even when he was not walking or running, his limbs still moved, or twitched. All was agitation in the man. He was always pacing up and down, or fumbling with something, or scratching his head, or his leg, which had then the effect of starting the rest of us twitching and scratching. But for all of his nervous energy, he was a humorous man, full of cheek, and few people could match his quick-fire wit.

He was also an expert with the short sword or dagger, and his speed in battle was frightening to behold. On the field of battle many a bigger man had had cause to momentarily regret the wasp-like speed of this man, before they breathed no more. Like Scipio, Sigfeldt had a family somewhere, but we could never find out where he came from. Also like Scipio, he believed that this would be his last expedition, for he meant to go home, and grow his family strong on the gold that he had won over the seas.

"Aye, Sigfeldt, that he was. Champion to Farinmael, proud king of Corinium, who was lost at Deorham. I fought at the side of my brother at that battle. It was his mighty prowess that won me the sponsorship of Ceawlin."

I said no more; I respected these men, but in my time abroad I had learned that the best chief was one who kept himself slightly apart.

"I'll bet he was a greater warrior than the Roman then? That big lump over there never stops boasting of his prowess."

Torquato did not look up from his task. He was sewing a button onto his tunic, peering hard at the tiny needle in his hand.

Sigfeldt pressed on.

"A real giant too, then, your brother?"

"Aye, that he is."

"Much bigger than the Roman, I think that you said?"

"Yes, he is bigger."

Torquato now looked up from his handiwork.

"Does anybody else hear an insect buzzing around here? Strange that, in this cold climate."

He resumed his sewing.

Rama Bec laughed at the unperturbed look on the Roman's face.

"Speaking of giants, I remember a tale somebody told me once of the greatest warrior he ever saw."

We all looked over to the Syrian as I passed the jug of wine onto Veos, who spoke now to Rama Bec.

"What tale was that then? Who told it to you?"

"The man who told me this tale was an old man. He had seen many battles."

"Go on then, let's hear it. Is Ishtar in it?"

Rama Bec laughed gently, and then shook his head:

"Ishtar appears only in the best tales. This tale is only about battles, and giants, and heroes."

He started on his tale:

"It was the time of Agila's reign in the land of the Visigoths. Emperor Justinian sent an army there under Liberius on account of Agila's oppression of his people. The emperor was successful and he captured many cities. During the siege of each of these cities, a great champion was brought forth by Liberius. His name was Dragolan, the greatest warrior of the Lombards. He was a brute of a man, and carried all before him when the champions were called out at the commencement of battle, as is the custom."

Veos passed the jug of wine over to Scipio, who took a long draught from it.

"Soon Agila was assassinated. He was replaced by Athanagild. This man was no fool. He had seen the success of the champion of Liberius, and knew that it sapped the confidence of the city dwellers before the siege. He was determined to do something about it, and made his plans.

"Soon enough, Liberius arrived at the gates of the city now defended by Athanagild. The emperor sent out his champion, Dragolan, and this mighty man bellowed at the walls of the city.

"'If there is one man bold enough to meet me, send him out now!'

"The great wooden gate of the city creaked open . . ."

Torquato made to take hold of the jug without looking, so intent was he on the Syrian's tale, but he missed it, and had to look away from Rama Bec to grab it properly.

". . . into the sight of first Dragolan and then the rest of Justinian's army came a warrior the like of which no man had seen before. Standing over seven feet tall, he had the arms and thighs of a leviathan. He strode with heavy purposeful steps towards the mighty champion of the Lombards.

"But now Dragolan knew fear, for he saw that it was a true giant from the High Mountains, no less than the Chinaman of the legends."

Nobody spoke in the ring of stones in which we sat. We had all heard of these legendary warriors, these Chinamen, but that name was talked of in awed whispers, and no-one knew if they really existed. Here seemed proof that they did. No man could resist the strength of these behemoths, and it was rumoured that they belonged to some sub-race of gods, such was their power in battle.

Torquato passed on the jug to Sigfeldt.

"The mighty man of the Lombards hit the giant with his sword, but it broke at the first strike. He drew his dagger, but his rival knocked it from his hand in one blow. With one strike, the Chinaman brought Dragolan to his knees. With his next he swept the head from the Lombard's shoulders."

All were silent around the fire. The mighty Lombard champion had been destroyed in two blows. Sigfeldt nervously touched the back of his neck.

"The Chinaman dragged the headless body by the ankle before the front wall of the city, then lugged it backwards and forwards several times. No sign of emotion showed on the monster's face.

"Great shouts went up from the city dwellers, though in truth they too were fearful of what they had witnessed. But the dreaded champion of Justinian was vanquished. The city dwellers became strong. They resisted the emperor, and his forces were thrown back.

"Athanagild grew in confidence. He won back the cities taken by Justinian. At each campaign, the Chinaman swept all before him.

"Then one day he was gone, and nobody saw nor heard of the giant from the High Mountains again."

Rama Bec had finished his story.

Slowly our senses filtered back to us. The cold night breeze blew into our faces; the flames flared up in the hearth. In the distance a pair of owls softly threw out their two note call.

Torquato cursed and spat into the fire.

"These giants are the stuff of legend only. Let one of them ever get in my way, that's all. Let one of them get in my way. Then we'll see, for sure!"

We talked for a little while longer, and tired laughter spilt around our makeshift camp.

Then we pulled up our travel blankets, and soon no sound but snores were heard on that hillside as we slept by the still flickering fire, the rest perhaps, like me, dreaming about combat with the fabled giant of the High Mountains.

*

So it was that, a little before noon of the following day, my war-band arrived at Ceawlin's Hall.

The leaves were all off the trees, so that the mead-hall and its surroundings looked different to me somehow. There was a cold chill in the air, and our breath came as smoke. I could see from Torquato's face that our British climate was not at all to his liking, for he had wrapped a great fur around his shoulders, and a sheepskin around his head, yet his nose was still blue with the cold.

As we dismounted in front of the hall we were met with some formality by Ceawlin himself, for my status had much grown whilst I had been away, and I was now of strategic importance to him. Several of his generals came with him. At his side was an older man, the chief warrior I knew from before, his shoulder-man called Willem, a time-served man who was of similar age to the Gevissa king himself. There were also two other men who stood in the first rank with Ceawlin, much younger than Willem, and more my age.

I was surprised by my first sight of the Saxon king in so many years, for he had changed. The strain in his face that had always been a feature had grown more marked. The lines on his forehead had become deep ruts. In his eyes there seemed to me a strange light, and he seemed distracted, as if he was in some other place even whilst still with us. Even if I had not received Ulla's letter, I would have thought that there was some sickness in him.

After we had greeted each other with all of the usual formalities that were right for the occasion, including my expression of sadness on the loss of Queen

Acha, – which was entirely truthful, for, though we had met but briefly, I had warmed greatly to the lady – he turned to the two young men next to him.

"This is my brother's son, my nephew, Olric."

These words were said coldly, without any sign of warmth or affection.

Olric held out a limp hand towards me, which was bony and thin, not meeting my eyes as I took it.

He used the Latin tongue, which surprised me.

"Charmed to meet you, I'm sure."

Even his voice was thin. I glanced at Torquato, who stood silent and watchful beside me, and his face was stone.

This Olric had a thin face, and thin pursed lips, was in fact all thin, from the top of his thin head down to the balls of his thin feet. He had the look of one who reads the words three times before signing a paper. I did not like the look of him, for he immediately struck me as a schemer.

"And this is Crida."

Ah, the good friend.

I looked into the face of this man. He was nothing like Olric. He had wild black hair, and big shoulders, though his face and frame were both lean. His clean-shaven face was handsome, there was no denying it. But somehow there was a subdued fury, a wildness, about him also; his eyes were dark, and his nature watchful, as if he was a man who preferred to walk his path through life alone.

He held out his large hand to me now.

"I have heard much about you."

I took his hand, and his grip was like rock.

"Yes, and I of you."

He nodded, but said no more.

Ceawlin looked across at me.

"Tell your men to billet themselves in the grounds. You and your shoulder-man are welcome into the rooms of the hall itself, and all of your men shall come into the mead-hall for a feast tonight, in honour of your return. There you will meet my son, Cutha."

Ulla had talked much about her brother. Tonight, then, I would meet him too for the first time.

Torquato gave the orders to my men, who began to fan out in the grounds.

But I saw nothing of Ulla, which surprised me, for I had expected her to be there to meet me.

*

The meal had gone well, there had been no trouble, and now Ceawlin had asked us to go with him to the side chamber, so that we might talk strategy. Torquato, who had spent much of the meal talking to a big country-girl slave who served at the mead-table, came with us, as did Olric.

Two tall young warriors were already stood in the small chamber set to one side of the main hall. One I recognised as Crida. The other I had not seen before.

"Briton, this is my son, Cutha."

This fellow looked to be two winters older than me. He was tall, slightly taller than Ceawlin, and much resembled him in appearance and physique, with the same lean features. His curled hair was black, though. Nor did his face hold any of the strain that was so obvious a feature in his father. His eyes, which somehow reminded me of his sister, were humorous, as if he found much to laugh at in life. So too was his manner full of courtesy as he quietly greeted me.

"I have heard much about you, Rhuadrac of the Britons. My sister speaks often of you."

I looked at him closely, but he said no more, and I was grateful of it. He nodded towards Torquato by way of greeting. I noticed with interest that he barely acknowledged Olric, and it seemed to me that there was some hidden animosity between them. Cutha then suggested that we relax a little, as a slave entered the room carrying a flagon of wine.

Ceawlin, Olric and I sat down in the leather chairs, whilst Torquato sat on a wooden bench set into a recess near the heavy oak door. Cutha and Crida stepped back and leant against the timber wall. A royal indigo drape covered the far end of the room, and a red rug was set out on the timber floor. A quiet fire burned in the open hearth. A little wine was poured into a cup for each of us and we drank in silence for a few moments.

Cutha then looked cautiously at his father.

"Perhaps, Father, you want to explain to Rhuadrac what your thoughts are on . . . certain matters?"

Ceawlin got up and began to pace the room. His command of my language was by now much improved, for no doubt he had thought it politic to master it.

"You will have seen in my letter sent to you through my daughter that I consider it time to make the next move forward on my march across this land?"

I nodded and he continued, in a strangely intense manner.

". . . I have thought for some time that a decisive move into the Upper Severn Valley will put the final prize of Chester within my grasp. Therefore I intend to move against the eastern boundaries of Brocmael, King of Powys, and those lands of his son, Chief Kynon, they who reside at Penwyrn. For I have plans for the strategic town of Uriconium, that place that your people call the City of the White Stones. But you should know that your people barely pose a problem to me any more . . ."

I bridled at this insult, but did not show it. I was aware that Cutha was looking at me closely at that moment.

". . . no, it is my own people, the Aenglish, who now stand in my way, and if I am to take my rightful place as the overlord of this land I must act fast."

The veins stood out in his forehead, and he talked quickly. Cutha stood quietly at the back of the room, scrutinising his father closely, a look of concern in his eyes. As Ceawlin continued to speak, from time to time I noticed that Cutha would look at me, perhaps trying to gauge my response to his father's words.

"For if I take Chester, your people will be finally crushed for sure, but more importantly, I will cut off the north-east of this island from the west, just as surely as Deorham cut off the south-west from the rest. Once thus broken into three districts, it will be the final solution to the problem that your people present to me. My borders would then stretch from the east of this land called Alba to the lower reaches of the river that you call the Trent. My power will be irresistible to my fellow Aenglish, for already my opponents exhaust themselves in pointless conflicts in the north-east of your country, in the regions of Deira and Bernicia. Only Aethelbert in Kent would stand in my way, and he is not strong enough to resist me."

I looked at him then, and there was a light sweat formed on his brow, and his speech came still more quickly.

"And they will not resist me, for this is where you can help me. Your brother has disobeyed me and has married the daughter of Farinmael. In itself, this has caused an unfortunate . . . enthusiasm amongst your fellow West Britons. I had to send Olric to warn him that if he did not put Farinmael's daughter aside, then my protection for him is over, for he has broken the terms of my pact with your dead king. But your brother humiliated Olric, and turned him out, and he defies me still."

Olric looked down at the floor, but I could see that a cruel and dangerous look crossed over his face. Cutha continued to observe his father quietly from the back of the room, the look of concern never leaving his face.

Ceawlin looked down at me now.

"I do not need the inconvenience of an uprising from amongst the West Britons at this time. If they were to seek alliances with Brocmael and Kynon, and seek to strengthen their hand in the lower Severn Valley, then it will not be tolerated. It is a distraction to my greater plans. I am making the arrangements as we speak, for you must go to your brother, and you must tell him that any such move would be disastrous for him . . . and for your family."

He looked at me stonily, and I was not sure who might be included in this threat.

"You can tell him that he is not required to join me in my march through the upper Severn, but that any resistance to my army will be dealt with ruthlessly. You must persuade him that he must bend to my will, for resistance is pointless. For I will tell you, as I have told Olric before you . . ."

At this, Olric shifted in his chair uncomfortably, and I had the impression that he was not convinced that what he had been told was worth knowing. Cutha made as if to step forward towards his father, and say something, raising his right arm as he did so, but he then stopped, and stepped back into the shadows of the room.

Ceawlin lifted his arms as he spoke next, and it was disconcerting to watch.

". . . that I have had a dream vision of this land, Rhuadrac of the Britons. And in my dream I saw a mighty city on a river, and the river curved like a snake, and on each side of that river sat stone buildings of many towers, and down the middle of that river sailed gigantic ships with many sails, all carrying the wolf's head standard, heading for the open waters. And this land was called Aengland, and its fame had spread over the world, and all had come to understand the role of Ceawlin, King of the Gevissas, as *Bretwalda* in the creation of this great land!"

As he finished speaking a slave had come into the room.

Ceawlin turned on this man now in a sudden rage.

"You imbecile! Did you not see that I was speaking to my commanders?"

He walked up to the man, and began striking him about the head.

"Imbecile!"

He continued to strike this poor unfortunate, who backed out of the room, finally helped in this by a kick from the Gevissa king.

He turned back to us in the room; we had all sat watching this strange display, stunned by the lack of connection in his actions.

"I am surrounded by imbeciles! Does nobody understand me? If only Acha had been here to share it with me . . ."

He lowered his head, his voice had trailed away on the last words and I could see that his mouth still worked feverishly. The veins stood out on his brow, and the light layer of sweat glistened at his temples.

I was deeply saddened, for I could see that something had broken in this once noble warrior; the death of his wife had hit him hard and I realised then that the pain it had caused might never be repaired. I looked at Olric, who looked away to the hearth, and it seemed to me that there was a terrible sneer on his face. I glanced then at Cutha, who had now stepped towards the centre of the room.

"Father, it has been a long and trying day for us all, and Rhuadrac and his men have travelled many miles to get to us. Perhaps we should . . ."

But Ceawlin held up his arm.

"Not yet Cutha, I want to hear the Briton's reply."

I looked at Ceawlin.

"I appreciate the fact that you have taken me into your confidence. You should know that I have no interest in any step that might endanger the fate of my family. I am happy to meet with my brother and explain to him your thinking in this matter. More than that I cannot promise, for my brother is his own man, and I am not his keeper."

"Very well, then, Briton, for now I ask nothing more of you than to meet with your brother and explain to him that I will not tolerate any alliances with Brocmael or any of his chiefs at this time. If he should promise me this, and complete neutrality in any further conflict that might arise in the upper Severn, then I will consider maintaining my protection of your family. I may even allow him to live openly with the daughter of Farinmael."

I nodded and bowed slightly to the Saxon chiefs, Olric refusing to meet my gaze. Cutha took my arm and shook it warmly.

"Perhaps we may have the chance to talk of other things soon, Rhuadrac, in more detail, for there is much I would like to know about the land of the Franks."

"Perhaps when I return from this mission to my brother, then we can talk more freely? I will look forward to it."

I meant these words. There was something in this brother of Ulla that I liked, and I would be happy to get to know him better.

Torquato and I then left the chamber, Ceawlin having told me that it was likely that we should set out tomorrow, but that all would be confirmed in the morning.

Torquato walked next to me and said nothing for a couple of minutes, then looked at me sideways and said:

"Can I speak again now?"

I had sworn him to silence for the meeting, for I knew that wrong words would not be tolerated.

I waved my hand dismissively; I knew that he was chiding me.

"Well, I can see from the look of him that this fellow might once have been a great warrior, but frankly, even though I could not understand all of what he said, judging from his look and his behaviour, I would say that bugger was now as mad as a sack of frogs thrown onto an open fire."

I said nothing, but silently I agreed with my friend.

*

I was taken by a slave back to the room that I had first occupied when I was carried back from the field at Deorham. It was as it had been at that time, nothing had changed; in truth, it had been only a few short years, yet I had changed, and my life had taken a direction that I could not have predicted when I first revived and I saw Ulla for the first time.

Ulla. Where was she? Why had she not been there to meet me? She had been a constant presence in my mind in the seven winters I had been in the Frankish lands, for indeed her image had not for one minute left me, yet she had not been there to meet me. I could not understand it.

There was a light tap at the door. Pulling my robe around me, I opened it, and Ulla was there.

She had on a green cloak, with a hood, which she removed immediately, to allow her long black hair to fall down past her shoulders and I could see that she had on but a white slip, tied at the shoulders. I could not speak and my eyes near failed me, for she was even more beautiful than when I had last seen her, and she was now fully a woman.

I looked at her now as she stood with her back to the closed door, felt her greedy hands pull open my robe and saw her black eyes flick over my face, my head, my lips, my hair, my shoulders, my whole body, and her eyes were wide and black and her breath came quickly and there was a high colour to her light-golden skin. I kissed her then, and lifted her, and I carried her to the bed and tore her slip from her. She was soft, and full, and strong, and she was lithe too. All of my senses were assailed by the perfect scent of her, by the full touch of her flesh, by the beautiful set of her eyes, by the urgent demand of her soft lips. I could see in her black eyes that her hunger for my body matched my own greed for the full sweet touch of her flesh, her great black eyes enveloping me, beseeching me, and her long fingernails dug into my flesh, and she pulled me into her body, urgently, more urgently still and my world was full of her scent and her perfume and her flesh and her female body and her eyes closed and I heard her whisper some secret words and I saw her gorgeous mouth open wide in ecstasy and it was as if all of the heavens and the seas rolled open before us and great long cries went out from us both then, our meshed spirit soaring up, dissolving through those rushing unfolding heavens and seas.

We finally fell asunder, our still-linked bodies drenched in sweat.

A silent peace and joy swept through my senses then. Next to me Ulla cried gently with a quiet joy and held on to me as if I was her one fixed point in a vanished world. I have never known a greater peace in my life. We had each given ourselves to the other completely and it was the most amazing gift anybody has ever given me. And in those moments, I knew with certain knowledge for the first time how little I understood about this world and this life, knew with an absolute calm and uplifting certainty how little I understood the eternal mysteries of this existence we all share.

I was taught many things in my life by Ulla, Gevissa princess, but what she taught me that night was the greatest lesson of all, for she taught me the sacred power of love.

*

We made love all through that night, the frenzied delight of that first time repeated many times with greater care but no less passion.

We talked of the past – of my life in the land of the Franks, the people I had met, my war-band.

"They are a rough lot, to be sure. But they are good, honest men at root, though maybe not the Gaul . . . anyway, I am proud to be their chief."

She told me about her life; she had many suitors, many men who would be son-by-marriage to the king. She had rejected them all.

"Only two weeks ago we had a visit from the Jutes in Kent. A young prince, handsome to be sure . . ."

Here she glanced at me to gauge my reaction:

". . . was sent here as a prospective husband. I was polite, but could not encourage him. Last year it was a cousin of the king of the Bernicians. It has been non-stop, let me tell you."

I could see that she was testing me, and a mischievous light played in her eyes as she did so.

"You mention this warrior Crida much in your letters. He seems something of a wild fellow."

I thought I sensed Ulla tense slightly next to me.

"I have told you about him before. He is Cutha's greatest friend. He is also my friend. Why do you ask?"

"You mention him often in your letters. Just how good a friend is he?"

"Why, I have known him all of my life, since I was a girl."

I said nothing. She was a beautiful woman. Like me she sought raw life and all that it could offer her; this she had just proved to me. We had been several years separated. There must have been many men seeking to know her during that time.

She looked at me.

"Briton, we have been apart a long time. You too have been a man alone in a foreign land. Let us not spoil our first night together after so many years with weak thoughts."

The old colour rose in her face. She had not changed; she spoke wisely.

I said no more.

We talked then of our future, of the death of her mother, and the effect of that on her father. Ulla told me her greatest fear, now that she understood that I was safe and well and that our pledge to each other was all intact:

"My father is much impressed with your work in Gaul."

I nodded; Ceawlin had already made this clear to me.

Ulla hesitated briefly, then looked at me; there was some terror in those honest eyes.

"I have fears that my father may no longer be in his right mind. He is not a young man. Kingship weighs heavily on his shoulders. All about him there are plots, and others seek his power. He has not been the same man since my mother died."

"We must see how matters work through, Ulla. Perhaps your father will revive in his spirit soon enough."

But in truth I understood her disquiet, for the man I had listened to in the chamber that night was not the same man who had talked with Farinmael after Deorham, and I could see that much strife might result from it.

"What will become of us, Briton?"

"I know not, Ulla, but we shall prevail, somehow."

It was just before first light that she left me.

I prepared for the day ahead, feeling somehow changed by the experience of the night just passed, but I could not say in which way.

*

I met first with Torquato in the great hall. He sat alone at a side table and tore huge chunks of bread from the loaf in front of him, and wedged slices of cheese and wild boar into his mouth.

He looked at me as I slumped down next to him, for I fear that my dishevelled state must have aroused his curiosity. He stared at me and rubbed his chin, and narrowed one eye at me. But he said nothing, and continued to eat his bread in what to me appeared to be a very coarse manner that morning.

We were alone, so he indulged in his insolence.

"How are you this morning, Cub-General?"

"I have told you many times not to call me by that stupid name. As it happens, I am fine, you insolent cur, why do you ask?"

"Oh, nothing, just a passing interest, that's all."

He continued to eat his bread, munching innocently, and helping himself to the mug of mead that sat on the table in front of him.

"By the gods, but it was cold last night. Do you not think so?"

"I did not really notice."

This was true, I had not noticed at all.

"But it was freezing. My feet were stuck out of these puny Saxon beds at least a hand's length, and they were blue with the cold. How did you not notice?"

"Perhaps my room is warmer than your room. Perhaps the hot-pans had been in my bed for longer."

"Ah, maybe so, maybe so. Yes, that might be it."

He continued to eat his breakfast, dipping the remnants of the loaf into the mead-cup.

"What I could really have done with last night was that tart with the big paps serving the mead-cups during the meal. Now, if she had done as I had asked her, and come to my room in the middle of the night, slipped into my bed and smothered me with those great paps of hers, and warmed me up with those big full hips, then slid her long cool hand down and took hold of my –"

"Have a care, you elongated ape, I am not in the mood for your coarse fantasies today."

"Oh, I see, right then, that's the way of it."

He continued to eat, still deliberately and slowly plunging a large hunk of bread into the mead-cup in front of him.

"Now then, let me see if I can work this out. I spend years with the cub-general in the Frankish lands, bedding every woman I can lay my hands on the length and breadth of that land, whilst cub-general here walks around with his tongue hanging out like a dog in the desert, because the love of his life is not there."

He rubbed his chin studiously.

"Then, we find ourselves here in Wessex in this godforsaken place, in the mead-hall of a great king, whose daughter just happens to be the very same lady, namely, the love of the cub-general's life."

He gazed innocently up at the great timber beams set into the roof of the hall, as if trying to work something out.

"Next, he turns up at first light the next morning, with a moonstruck face, and stares into space for whole minutes. His strength has left him – it is as if he is the Greek that ran to Marathon over the mountains, that hero we learn about in the Greek verses. He tells me that he has not even noticed the coldest night that I have ever spent in my life. He cuts me off at the knees when I try to share a good honest earthy fantasy of lust with him, for it is beneath his dignity."

He looked down at the table in front of him, still shaking his head.

"This is a curious riddle, for what could a man be doing during the night in the hall of a king whose daughter he loves, that makes him invulnerable to cold, exhausts him, gives him the dream-face, and causes him to place himself on a pedestal above his fellow man?"

He still dipped each fresh thick chunk of bread into the mead-cup, but now with a faster rhythm.

Suddenly he struck his forehead with his free hand.

"Wait, I may suddenly have understood it."

I looked wearily at the trickster, waiting for the axe to fall:

"The general has been pleasuring the princess all night!"

The dog had understood all from the first moment I had stepped into the hall.

I exploded with mock rage, and swung a punch at him, and he stepped back, parried my blow, then wrapped his arms around me and laughed.

"By the gods, but it is about time too, for the tension was killing me!"

And he laughed, and I laughed too, for I knew that he was pleased for me; somewhere in that black soul of his he could sense that something profound and good had happened to me during the night.

I waved my finger in his face.

"I confess nothing to you, you Roman devil, but do not go spreading your rumours around this place, for there is much intrigue here, and your thoughts must stay with you. Understood?"

"What thoughts?"

I could say no more, for at that moment Ceawlin and his chief warriors came through into the hall, and took places opposite to us. Ceawlin seemed more himself this morning, more the man I had known before I left for the Frankish lands. Neither Cutha nor Olric was with him, though Crida sat on his right. I thought that the young thegn stared hard at me when he first sat down. Ceawlin talked plain:

"It is all arranged. The meeting has been set up in the Hwicca country, up near Deorham, in two days hence, so you will leave immediately. You are to meet with your brother with no more than five men each side. My men asked for safe passage for you, but your brother's emissary, an old monk, said that this matter was understood, and did not need discussion. He said that you are his chief's brother, and his closest kinsman, so it would appear that you're well placed to succeed in your mission."

My spirit gladdened. I was sure that the old monk was Cadolan. But I was irritated too that the question had even been raised, for Ceawlin presumed that I was all in his allegiance, and he was wrong to think that. My brother and my people were strong in my mind, and I was still undecided as to how the future might unravel for us all. It was a mistake that the Ceawlin I had known at Deorham would not have made.

A short time later, I was sat on my horse in front of the great hall. With me was Torquato only, for I had decided that I needed only him with me for the task at hand. Ceawlin had come to wish us good fortune, and again Crida stood at his right-hand side.

"I will be away on the Saxon Shore for the next few days, for Cutha and I have arrangements to make with the arrivals on the new boats. When I return you will provide me with a full report of what your brother had to say, and what it is he plans to do next."

Just as we were leaving, Ulla came out too, and briefly laid her hand on my arm and quietly told me to take much care on my mission. I saw the muscles tense in Crida's jaw as she did so.

Next to me Torquato said nothing, his face remained a stone mask, though I saw his eyes blink two or three times in rapid succession when Ulla first came out to us.

Later, when we were clear of the hall, he rode next to me and said, whilst still staring straight ahead:

"I can almost see why you waited. That lady is the bullseye and no mistake, you lucky dog."

And he smiled across at me then and whipped on his horse and moved ahead.

II

Cormac had well chosen the meeting ground, for it was the site of Farinmael's camp the night before Deorham, and we reached it in the late afternoon on the second day of travelling. As we rode into the clearing, I could not fail to think of that night seven winters ago when the great chief, in the full knowledge of his fate the following day, had addressed his men before battle.

I dismounted, and walked over to the centre of the clearing. I felt the great spirit of the warrior-king, and that of Gavin and Oisin and Fintan and all of those other brave warriors by my side, as if they were all near to me. It was a sombre moment.

I had often told Torquato of that night, and he came and stood by me and placed his hand on my shoulder. He was silent too, for my tale had moved him. Tales that talked of great warriors were a serious business for him, and he would not make light of such matters.

As we stood there in silence, we heard horses approach from the west, and soon enough five horses came into view. I was surprised, for I could make out four men and a woman. As they came closer I could see that it was my brother, and Cadolan and two others I did not know, and my sister Aisha was with them too. My heart leapt when I saw them, for it had been a long time since we had been together.

As they dismounted, I glanced across at Torquato, for he was sizing up my brother closely. Then he pursed his lips, looked at me sideways and nodded with approval.

"Now *that* is one great big monstrous bastard!"

I had not seen my brother in seven years and even I was slightly awestruck by his appearance, for he had grown heavier, though was not fat. I could see that his damaged left eye had never fully recovered from Deorham, for he wore a patch over it, and although the scars of that battle were less vivid, his face still bore much evidence of that conflict. His hair had grown longer, and even then there were the first flecks of white in it. I stood stock still, for I too was a warrior of standing now. I turned to Torquato.

"Stand away a little distance from me, for my brother does not know you, and he may regard you as one of Ceawlin's warriors."

Torquato walked away perhaps ten paces, but no more than that.

Aisha ran to me, with Cadolan moving quickly behind her, and they held out their arms to me.

Cormac stayed by his horse, and did not move.

I threw my arms around Aisha and my old teacher, for it had been too long since I had seen them last. Aisha was a woman now, and a true beauty in her own right. Cadolan looked older, and if anything, he too was heavier than I had last seen him. But there was no mistaking the genuine joy in their greeting, and my teacher rocked me in his arms, then stood back from me.

"Well, warrior of the family, you have grown. Look at you! Do not let my appearance fool you, for I am as mean and as strong as I have always been, so do not provoke me!"

"Cadolan, I will never doubt your strength, for I heard the tale of how you protected the womenfolk after Deorham . . ."

At this, the face of my old teacher beamed and I saw him puff out his chest slightly.

". . . How is life with you? And Aisha! I do not know you, sister. You are now a beautiful woman. Cadolan, are you still the stoic? Is that your halo I still see before me?"

Cadolan made to strike at me and we all three laughed, for it was suddenly as if we had never been apart

"Stoic, Rhuadrac, stoic? But I am no stoic. I am merely a failed monk and I continue to get by as the Good Lord allows me, so none of your haloes if you please!"

He looked over at my brother.

"The giant hero is late for the homecoming. Aisha, we must bring these two idiots together, or we shall be here till the moon rises."

So saying, he walked across to Cormac, and moved him towards me, and my sister did the same with me. We met in the middle of the clearing.

Cormac talked first.

"How are you, brother? You are much changed, and for the better, for you are a man now. Has life been fair to you since last we met?"

His voice was warm, but guarded.

I looked up into the huge and disfigured face, and my spirit soared, for this great warrior was my one true brother, and let all of the politics of the world rot and fall away.

I threw my arms around him, and rocked him, and I said to him:

"Cormac, it has been fair with me, but I fear that hard times are upon us."

And he rocked me too, and I knew that he was pleased to see me.

As we stood there embracing, Torquato had come over to us. It seemed to me as if he walked with an unusually straight back and with his chin jutted slightly upwards, so that he was stretched to his full height. He walked around my brother, looking him up and down, and in truth he was not quite as big as my brother, for there may have been the width of a large hand between them.

Still the Roman walked around us. My brother looked sideways at Torquato and, noting his form of dress and the position of his sword-scabbard, said, in the Roman language:

"So, who then are you and what are you looking at?"

"Oh, nothing much, unless I miss my guess."

I stepped between them and talked to my brother in our own language.

"Cormac, do not take offence, for this man is my greatest friend beyond my family and he is a great warrior, a man who can be relied upon. We have broken bread together before and after battles, so do not be offended by his foolish ways – you will get to know him."

Cormac slowly looked away from Torquato, slapped me on the shoulder and said to me, in the Roman tongue, glancing back at Torquato as he did so:

"I will take your word for it, Rhuadrac, but he should not try me too much, for I do not much like this bantering style, it angers me."

I quickly led him away from the centre of the clearing, and we all sat down between rocks.

"How is our mother, Cormac?"

"She is well, brother. She spends much time at her masses these days, and I know that she is desperate to see you."

Cormac told me then of some of his life since I had last seen him.

The few reports I had received were true.

"They let me go back to our father's land, which surprised me. All the talk of our elders had always been that these heathens just massacred or drove out all those that they conquered. This has not happened in the lower Severn. Those Saxons who came into our land call themselves Hwiccas. They are largely for settlement, because they know farming – that is what they knew in their homeland."

Cormac looked at me then, and it seemed to me that his idea of the nature of the Saxon was not now as set as it had once been. He glanced at the two men who had travelled with him.

"Maybe some of the old tales were exaggerated. Or maybe these Hwiccas are not typical Saxons. Anyway, their leaders encouraged those of our people who survived after Deorham to stay on in their farms, and even to increase production. They welcomed the trade that would follow the creation of new yields. The Hwiccas themselves took over the farmsteads of those who had died at Deorham, even in some cases the widows of the warriors who had died . . ."

Here Cormac spat in the ground, and cursed viciously.

"Not all of our family had such a good time of it though. Gavin, Oisin, Fintan – all perished at Deorham. Dorianna too – she lost her life in the sack of Corinium that followed soon after the battle, before our family could reach her."

This last information was news to me. In my freebooter life it had been almost too easy to forget the tragedy that had overwhelmed my people.

Cormac paused in his tale, then continued:

"So, you will see very little difference in our lands if you ever return there. It is as it was before. Few new farms were started, the existing places were either worked as they had been before or have been taken over by Saxon settlers."

He looked across at Cadolan.

"But there have been other, less obvious changes. This Aenglish language is becoming strong, for it is the language of those who now rule in our land. Our language is already everywhere under threat, and a man has to go far to the west to be clear of this Aenglish, which is a powerful language. It is a cunning language too, for there is something in it that makes it easy for men to learn."

Cormac stopped talking for a couple of minutes. The sun had gone down by now, and a gentle cold breeze stirred the fire in the hearth. Aisha spread out her travel blanket across her legs.

Cormac told me then of his own life, and of his dealings with the Gevissa king.

"At first they more or less left me in peace. But they set one rule that caused me to hate them, for they forbid me to marry Gwen. They told me that it would stir up the people against Ceawlin."

So my guess had been correct. I took notice that Cormac did not say that Ceawlin was wrong in his thinking.

"There was nothing much I could do about it – Ceawlin's spies were everywhere – so even if I had been minded to ignore this edict, then this noble king of yours would have got to know about it."

My brother would not look at me when he said this, but I knew that his wish for my own prosperity was the reason for this behaviour, for it was not his usual character.

"After three years I could bear it no more, and me and Gwen were married."

Aisha lifted her head then:

"Brother, you should have been there to see the local rejoicing at this union! Our people saw that the daughter of Farinmael and Farinmael's champion were together, and it pleased them, and caused them to raise their heads with dignity once more."

Cormac looked at me with a question in his face and then repeated the part of the story that I had already learned from Ceawlin himself.

"But Ceawlin had got word of it and sent his nephew, that Saxon dog, Olric himself, to tell me that if Gwen and I did not live apart again, then I could no longer count on his protection. As far as Ceawlin was concerned, his promise to Farinmael would be at an end. So, brother, I threw that miserable little shopkeeper out on his arse, and he was lucky to escape with his life, for no man will keep me and my woman apart."

I said nothing, refusing to be drawn out on my current thinking.

A few of the old embers began to glow in his face and I saw that hard and cruel look pass over it.

"But, brother, this is where the story gets interesting, for I understand that Ceawlin has designs on the upper Severn Valley and Uriconium, and then Chester itself. I need to know, now, what you know and where you stand."

Torquato could sense that there had been a change in the tone of our conversation. I saw him quietly shift his position and move his right hand towards his sword-scabbard.

I looked around me. Cormac and Cadolan, my great friend Torquato, my sister Aisha, all gathered in that place. Already the full moon was up, and the late afternoon light was well faded. It had grown colder, for a light breeze stirred the leafless branches of the trees behind us, so that a low moaning went out through the clearing. Aisha had now draped over her shoulders the deep fur she had thrown over her legs as we talked.

"Well, brother, you have talked openly with me as I know is your natural character, so I will do likewise with you."

I stood up and paced a few steps in the clearing.

"I face a great dilemma, and what we both foresaw after Deorham has come to pass. I have earned some riches from my successes in the Frankish lands, and I now have my own war-band, and much gold. All of that was built up under the authority of Ceawlin, though at no time would I break my own principle and fight against a British man, for the Britons are my people."

My brother nodded.

"All this is as I have heard, Rhuadrac, and your adventures, if not your sponsor, do our family proud."

I continued:

"But my dilemma now grows acute. I well understand your words concerning Gwen, for I am absolutely pledged to Ulla, Ceawlin's daughter, and nothing will change my mind on that matter."

A fleeting image of my night with Ulla flew across my mind.

"I have been sent here by the Saxon king as your brother and to ask you to see sense, and to abide by his demands, for he states no good will come to this land if you do not do this."

"What are those demands?"

"That you seek no alliances with fellow Britons in our part of this land, especially King Brocmael and his son Kynon of Powys. That you maintain a strict neutrality in any new campaign that may or may not be about to be waged."

"And if I abide by these wishes?"

"He will consider the maintenance of the protection of our family that was long ago promised to Farinmael at Deorham, and may even allow you to live with Gwen openly and in peace."

I told him nothing of what I knew of Ceawlin's plans, for both of us would have been compromised. My brother looked at me, and asked me, staring directly into my eyes.

"And you, Rhuadrac, what do you say?"

"Brother, do not force my hand in this matter at this time, for truly I do not know my answer. Sitting here in this place, full with the spirits of Farinmael and our kinsmen and our friends on that sad but glorious day, I know for sure that my pledge never to raise my hand in battle against my fellow Briton is a true one. I will not break it. But to join my fellow Britons in a war against Ceawlin is impossible for me too, for what of Ulla? I will not lose her."

There was silence in the space we sat in. Torquato had stood up, and prowled the clearing just next to us, Cormac all the time keeping him just where he could see him. I knew Torquato well, and even though my brother may not have been fully aware of it, I knew that he was ready to pounce if he had to. Although he could not fully follow our conversation, he knew that a moment of crisis had come.

Cormac too, stood up and moved away to look out over that darkening space, no doubt thinking back to the last time we had stood here, and the changes that had been wrought in all of our lives since that day. Perhaps he thought too of that last moment on the battlefield when he noticed me at his side, and we both thought that our last moment had come together. He came back over to me and placed his hand on my shoulder.

"You speak the truth, brother, your position is impossible. There is much else of which we could speak, but now is not the time. Let us eat and drink now, and you can tell me more about your adventures, then we will sleep on the matter tonight, and talk again tomorrow morning."

Then he looked across at his giant shadow, and said:

"And I shall see if I can make some sense out of this great Roman clown."

He addressed Torquato directly in the Roman language:

"You can relax now soldier, this is my brother, and I would outdo any man to protect his back in this world, so you need have no fear for his safety."

Then he nodded at him.

"But your concern is welcome, for I know that he has a good man at his shoulder."

With that, he gave a curt order to the two Hwicca men, and the three of them began to unpack provisions from the horses.

We broke up, and I told Torquato the outline of our talks so far. His face was sombre, which was not usual for him.

"Aye, well, so be it. Your brother has much anger in him, I can sense it. In truth, Rhuadrac, I already know that he is a formidable warrior, but then, so too am I. For tonight I can relax, for he is genuinely pleased to see you, I know that, so there will be no trouble tonight. Let us see what tomorrow brings."

Lighted boughs were brought, and soon enough we had a campfire burning, and the shadows lengthened on the rocks around us. Far away we could hear a pack of dogs barking in the forest. The direction of the breeze must have changed. As on that night that now seemed so long ago, I could hear the Boyde, swollen by recent rains, flow down the narrow channel in the valley below. To my left, some lone bird, perhaps a bittern, cried a long and mournful cry, and to my ears then it sounded like some form of elegy for all of our friends who had left us. On that cry there was as if a covering of moving wings, and echoing cries, as birds of all kinds made wing to the wood behind us.

Throughout our conversation, Aisha had said little, for she regarded it as warrior-talk, and I now asked her how matters fared for her.

We had spent much time together as children, for we had discovered that our sense of humour was exactly the same, and we always laughed at the same things. As we grew from childhood, we had spent less time with each other, for the men in my family became warriors, and the women would be trained by my mother in the ways of women, which is the right and proper way.

She blushed slightly, for I was four winters older than her, and she held me in some esteem, which perhaps had grown on the strength of the tales of my adventures in the Frankish lands, for they had achieved some small repute at that time.

Like my brother, her looks favoured our mother, for she was dark, and slender, and gave out a sense of having a solid strength within her. She was not inclined to speak of herself and her own plans, for she had always been a quiet girl, which was right and appropriate. I do not think I had once seen her lose her temper, and between us Cormac and I had sometimes wondered if she was not destined for a nunnery, for we knew that she was much influenced by our mother.

"My life is well, Rhuadrac, and it has now improved again to see you in such rude health. I am content. So, tell me more of this Princess Ulla, for Cormac tells me that you are much taken with her."

"Aisha, this woman is like no other that I have met. She tended me after Deorham, personally nursed me back to health. But that is not the reason we have a pact. From the first day that we talked, it was as if we had known each other all of our lives – as if she was part of our family – but that I had not set eyes on her before that moment for some reason that I could not understand."

Aisha looked at me carefully. Her smiling dark eyes looked into mine just as they had done so many times when we were children, perhaps when we were planning to run away for the day to the woods or some other childish adventure. I could see the deep affection she held for me was just as it had always been.

"And this woman, this Gevissa princess, does she share these thoughts?"

"Aisha, she does. We cannot live without each other, and we will find a way, somehow, to live our lives together. This we have promised to each other by solemn oath. I have spent seven winters with her image printed on my mind, every minute of every day, and I know now, since returning to Ceawlin's Hall, that it has been the same for her."

Aisha smiled then, a deep and wonderful smile, and asked me no more questions. I could see that she was delighted for me.

"I am pleased for you, brother, and your words fill me with hope for your happiness, for all of our happiness. I will pray that this matter is resolved for you."

Just then she looked away from me and glanced across at Torquato.

"Who is this giant Roman who travels with you? He is the first man I have seen who is nearly the size of our brother. He has a strange face, and from some angles it is almost noble."

I told her about how I had met with Torquato.

"So, a debauched man then! What is his family?"

"I know very little about it. He is not a man for great reflection . . ."

This was to say it small; in those days I thought that I had never met another man who so little rated the value of so-called deep thought.

". . . though he did tell me once, when I pressed him on it, that his parents died when he was no more than a boy. He has hinted to me that at first he was much thrown about by life, but he does not say much about those times. By some strange fate, he was finally taken in as an apprentice fighter by some grizzled rough old mercenary who for some reason took pity on him. This old man, Ranulph, was a harsh and often cruel taskmaster, but he proved to be the best teacher. So Torquato has spent nearly the whole of his life in or around warbands, rough men who taught him about life as they saw it. But they saved his life too, for otherwise he would have had nothing, probably would not have survived. These men were paid mercenaries. By the kindness of the gods . . ."

My sister looked puzzled when I said this –

". . . he eventually grew to his present size and prospered in such circumstances, so the choice of mercenary has been a natural one for him."

Aisha looked at me then, and again glanced across at Torquato with a strange expression on her face.

"That is a remarkable story. I will include your friend in my prayers too, for he seems to me to be in some way distant, as if deep down he walks alone along his path in the world."

These words baffled me, for Torquato out of battle was a sought-after man, and in taverns he was always the centre of attention, much loved by women. But Aisha said no more of it, and instead looked across at our brother.

"Rhuadrac, it is our mother's most fervent wish that you and Cormac should be reconciled, for a split family is a weak family, and in these times it is important that one knows where one stands."

I looked at this sister of mine, suddenly aware that there were many matters at play in this meeting. She stared back at me calmly, but with strength. I knew then that there was far more to my sister's ways than I had allowed for.

"But Aisha, Cormac and I have never been apart. I have chosen a path forced upon me by circumstances. If I wish to win the Gevissa princess, I need status in her family. After Deorham, nobody can deny that the Saxons have all of the power in this place. How else might I hope to be with Ulla if I do not play their games, if I do not win gold and status for myself?"

Again, Aisha regarded me calmly.

"All that you say is true, brother. All that I say to you is that you should not forget who you are and where your true family is. Gold and status is all very well, but there are more important things in this life than gold and status, even if the winning of a Saxon princess might depend upon it!"

She laughed then, a light laugh, and looked away from me, and it was clear to me that she regarded our conversation as concluded. There was a calm poise in her words that would have done justice to a Frankish queen or a Saxon princess. Again I marvelled at the disguised strength in this sister of mine, who had been but a child when I had last seen her.

We moved back to the others, and I helped to unload the small barrel of mead and brought out the casks of wine – for Torquato had insisted with a curse that the wine 'of his people' must be brought – and the food we had brought with us. We sat by the fire and told stories of our time apart, and Cormac listened to my tales of the Frankish lands and nodded with approval. When I talked of Torquato, I talked in the British language, and left my brother in no doubt as to the true nature of the man sat opposite him.

"Then truly this man is a great warrior and a true friend of yours, brother."

We both looked across at this great warrior, who even then was draining yet another beaker of wine whilst sprawled across large white stones on the other side of the clearing. He rolled on to his side slightly, then looked across at Cadolan and lifted his plate towards him:

"Oi, fatso, get off your fat arse and go and get me some more beans."

I saw the shadow I knew so well cross Cormac's face: but before either of us could say or do anything, Cadolan strode across the compound and poured what remained of his plate of beans onto Torquato's head.

"Certainly imbecile. Enjoy those if you might."

"Hells bells, what are you doing, you mad priest?"

Then he looked up, and could see that we all watched, and that even I had no sympathy for him.

"Sorry, my mistake, have I said the wrong thing again? Sorry, I will say my prayers double tonight, only don't hit me, holy father, don't hit me!"

Torquato laughed in a pathetic way and protected his head from the imagined onslaught from Cadolan, who looked down at him as a Roman centurion might have looked at a beggar, waved his arm and walked away from him. Torquato stood up and reached for a cloth, and staggered out of the clearing laughing to himself.

My brother spat on the ground and got up.

"We should turn in, brother, for I need to leave early tomorrow to attend to . . . some business. Let us talk again in the morning, as soon as the sun comes up."

He looked across at Torquato.

"Hopefully by then your friend might have learned how to behave properly in front of a holy man and our sister."

With that, he threw what remained in his mead-cup into the ground, and strode off to the makeshift tents.

The rest went to their tents. I went over and talked to Torquato for a little while, but he grew maudlin, as sometimes happened when he drank too much. I left him there, singing some mournful Latin lay to himself, a giant Roman warrior, my friend from across the sea, drunk, singing himself to sleep there in the place where Farinmael had talked to his warriors.

As I lay down on my travel blanket that night, my mind was full of the role that fortune plays in this life, and the way that it throws all of us about like puppets.

*

At first light I threw back the cloth of the tent entrance. A light-blue mist sat over the valley, and I could hear the sharp cry of a hawk circling overhead, no doubt about to pounce upon its prey. I moved back into the tent and reached for my tunic, breeches and boots. As I dressed, Torquato stirred and groaned in his place over on the far side of the tent, and levered his massive frame up onto his mighty left arm.

He hung his head.

"By the power of Jupiter's crotch, but my head feels as if it might burst!"

He looked at me, and it was a sorry sight. I could see that he had the head-fever, for he had drunk too much wine the previous night. I watched him turn over and bury his head back into his travel blanket, and I laughed. I had often seen him like this when there was no danger about us, and I knew that he would be unbearable for the rest of the day.

I moved out of the tent, and saw that Cormac was already up and dressed.

"Let us walk awhile, brother, for I must leave soon."

We walked a little way along a track leading from the camp. The mist still lay, blue and slow-moving, in the valley below us, and fell like a light wet gauze upon our skins.

Cormac looked at me and said, very directly.

"I have lain awake for some time, Rhuadrac, and I have decided to take you into my trust again, for you are my brother, and although I know that you have lost your heart to the Saxon king's daughter, I know that you will not betray me. Of that I am sure."

"Brother, you had no need even to say it, and it troubles me that this matter should keep you awake."

"It is not that I distrust you. I know the power of the heart in the affairs of men, and I know how it can impact on his head, his way of thinking. But anyway, my mind is made up, you are my brother, and I trust you. That is the way of it, for better or worse."

He looked at me and smiled, and I knew that some great weight had lifted off his mind during the night.

"This is my news. I am chosen to be chief of a fighting force comprised of West Britons from the upper Severn Valley, the few remnants of our war-bands from the lower Severn, and a few new bands of renegade Saxons who have had enough of Ceawlin's ways. The word is that he is now mad, that he is not a good lord, and so they feel that any allegiance that they may have owed to him is no longer binding upon them."

My eyes had widened at the mention of the Saxon renegades, for this was indeed news. The effect of all of my brother's news together confirmed beyond doubt that Cormac was now in open conflict with Ceawlin, and that the protection he had enjoyed was now a thing of the past. I had been sure it was the case, but still it saddened me, for I knew now that I had to make up my mind as to my allegiance for sure, and I could not see my way forward.

We walked for a while in silence.

"So, what do you make of it then?"

"I fear for you, for you are dead set against the Gevissa king, and not even his fellow Aenglish kings will challenge him now, such is his power in the land."

"Well, maybe so, but our own people are not yet all vanquished."

He said no more, and we walked on for several minutes.

Cormac looked at me.

"Even today I am to meet with Brocmael, the Chief of the Britons in Powys, and a great king, and we are to make plans to challenge the power of Ceawlin in our land."

The bulk of Brocmael's land lay away to the west and north; I was surprised that my brother was seeking alliances so far away from his own region.

"I have no choice, for our people are defeated here in the Hwicca country."

I could see that the pieces in the game were already in play, and that events had already begun to unfold. There would be new battles and I would be a part of them.

Standing there, we looked out over the valley through which I had seen the war-bands converge on Farinmael's camp on the eve of Deorham. The blue mist was now almost gone, and I could see the great wooded valleys of the lower Severn unfold before me, and I could hear the gentle rush of the Boyde in the valley below, on its inexorable way down to the mighty Severn.

The old fire began to flow through me; I was sick of the mind-corrupting politics of Ceawlin, of the Franks, sick of all of the machinations of all of the so-called great men and women that I had met. I wanted to walk a simple path in my life again, a path where I could regather my energy, and standing there on that path with my brother I knew where my allegiances lay.

"Cormac, I am a Briton, and you are my one true brother, and I am with you."

I said it quietly, and Cormac looked at me and he knew that it was true.

We said nothing for a few minutes. Cormac looked at me.

"What next for you then? You realise that Ceawlin will treat this as a great act of treachery, for he has been your sponsor?"

"I understand it, but my allegiance to him concerned the land of the long-haired kings only, and he has prospered there as a result of my work. I owe him nothing now."

"We will need to make plans, for as soon as he knows that you are tied in with me then our family and kinsmen will be at the mercy of the Saxon king. I will leave the farm and take our family to Penwyrn, Brocmael's stronghold."

He paused and looked at me.

"What then of Princess Ulla? What is your plan there, and how may I best support you?"

"Ceawlin is away on the Saxon Shore. I will go to her and see if I can bring her back with me."

He looked away from me.

"I know that your bond is strong, but you cannot tell her of the plans that I have just outlined to you. She will be compromised, we will all be compromised, and I do not see how she can be with us."

"No, standing here, nor do I, but I do not see what other path lays open to me."

Even then, though I knew beyond doubt where my allegiances lay, even then I did not tell my brother what I knew of Ceawlin's plans. Such was the confusion of that time, and the delicate balance of power between us. Through no wrong action of my own, I was completely compromised at that moment. Ulla had to be safe, and I knew, standing there, that her safety must be my first priority.

We stood there for a few more minutes in silence, and below us, the Boyde continued to flow on its path, as it must, and as it still would when our little tale had been long-lost in the annals. I looked across at the scarred face of my brother.

"I will meet you at Brocmael's camp at Penwyrn in seven days time."

We clasped hands, and I knew that, even in the face of the difficulties in front of us, my decision was the correct one.

Eventually we turned and made our way back to the camp.

III

Cormac and his small band got packed and made ready to leave. Cadolan and Aisha embraced me warmly, with some sadness, but I assured them that they would be seeing me again soon. Neither Cadolan nor Aisha would acknowledge Torquato, for I fear that they had written him off as a no-good, a debauched reprobate.

I looked at him now; he looked terrible. The head-fever had caused him to wrap a cold wet towel around his head, and he looked up from under this towel at the departing band and I knew that he was suffering.

My brother stood in the middle of the clearing and offered me his hand.

"Good luck brother, let us meet again soon, and we can then more properly plan our next moves."

He swung up onto his horse and looked across at Torquato.

"And as for you, well I suppose I must see your clown's face again at some point. Just watch my brother's back, that's all, if you know what's good for you."

Torquato looked up from under the towel.

"Whoa, now I am really wetting my breeches. What will you do? Give me the evil eye? That will be the right one then, I suppose."

For some reason Aisha looked away, and I thought that I could see her shoulders shake a little. My brother looked at Torquato, then looked back at me. Slowly, he threw back his head slightly and laughed, just a quiet laugh, but there was mirth in it.

"Evil eye? Ha ha. Well, then. Perhaps I do begin to get your measure, you Roman buffoon. Rhuadrac, take care, we will meet again soon!"

With that they were off, but not before I noticed Aisha give Torquato a sly glance, before she too wheeled her horse around and followed my brother out of the clearing.

We watched them go, Torquato scratching his sore head.

"I'll tell you what. If nothing else your family has at least one beautiful woman in it, for I would not have believed that somebody with a mug like yours or your brother's could have a sister with a face as sweet as hers."

I looked at him sharply. I was astonished to see that he was serious, and that he looked almost bashful, but I decided to put it down to the head-fever.

*

I waited for Torquato to ride off the worst effects of the wine, so it was not until we had struck camp late evening the same day that I told him that I had decided that my future lay with my people. I would leave Ceawlin's authority and take up with my family. I said nothing about my brother's plans.

He heard me through. It was his choice; he could either stay with Ceawlin, where in all probability he would become a rich freebooter, with gold and land, or he could come with me, or he could return across the sea.

He crossed his arms over his chest.

"So, let me see if I understand this correctly."

He made as if to be working something through in his mind.

"So. Firstly, I can stay with the king of the Saxons, the most important king in this land, and grow rich doing what I do best, bedding the hundreds of women who would throw themselves at such a powerful, handsome warrior."

He paused, as if imagining these delights in his mind.

". . . Secondly, I could return home to my beautiful country, drink the best wine and eat the best food and bed the most beautiful women in the world, living off the proceeds of our adventures for the rest of my life."

Again he paused, nodding his head contentedly.

". . . Thirdly, I can come with you and face a certain and grisly death against impossible odds in this freezing cold land at the end of nowhere, and end up with my head stuck on a pike and each hand stuck on a pike next to me, like a puppet in a freak show."

He paused and grimaced, a disgusted look upon his face.

"That is a good summary of your options."

He thought a little more.

"Do I have to drink that mead-piss?"

"No, I will get you wine."

He nodded, then hesitated. He looked away from me.

"Is your sister likely to be around?"

I looked at him guardedly.

"Yes, my sister will be with her family."

"And do you think that there is any possibility that your sister might one day talk to a waster like me?"

I looked at my friend closely. There was not a hint of debauched wit in his face and he looked back at me in almost a childlike way.

"Well, I suppose that you could become a great cause for her, and she could devote the rest of her life trying to save your black soul . . ."

I looked at him; I was surprised to see that this lion of a man was hanging on my next words.

". . . mind you, if you behave as you have in the last couple of days, you will have no chance at all, because she is like my mother, and she will not suffer fools. And if you do talk to her, you must obey the proper rules, for she has been brought up in the proper ways, and will drop you like a hot coal if you press on her. You will also have me and my brother to answer to."

I looked at him, and could see that he was soaking up this information.

"On the other hand, she has talked with me about you, but I am sure that it was nothing but pity."

Torquato thought on my words for a few moments.

"What did she say of me?"

"Well, she said that from certain angles you have almost a noble face."

He held his chin with his fingers and moved his head from side to side.

"I must find a polished metal and check. Did she really say that?"

"On my honour."

"Then my mind is made up, and I am with you."

I laughed, for I knew that his mind had been made up all along. I slapped his shoulder.

"Good man, good man, you ruffian, for in truth I would have sorely missed you."

He caught my arm. There was a serious look on his face.

"Have no fear, Rhuadrac. No fooling around, I think that your sister has a sweet face. She seemed to me to have a strength to her, as if she understood this world, knew the right things to say, and the right things to do. She seemed rooted in some way. You have this too – so does your brother. That is how a family should be. A man cannot live like a leaf blowing through some forgotten forest all of his life. I would much appreciate a woman like your sister in my life. I will obey the rules if she would consent to talk with me. I would like the chance to know her better, that is all."

He walked off to unload the horses, and I marvelled at his words; I had never before heard him use words in this way.

Later, we had drunk just a couple of claw-beakers of his Lombard wine. It was almost dusk, though I could still see the rolling downs spread out before me for some distance. A thin cold wind whistled around us. We had travelled well, and were close to the place of the Hanging Stones, called also Stonehenga, near the town of Ambresburh, and with luck we would be back in Ceawlin's Hall by close of day tomorrow.

Torquato sat back on a rock with his feet up in front of him.

"I am surprised by the beauty of this land of yours, Briton. There is much fertile land here, and in some ways it makes me think of my homeland. There is something else though, something underneath the skin of this land that I have not known anywhere else."

I looked at him. Again his way of speaking surprised me.

"There is something . . . ancient and wild about this place. We all know that only barbarians live here. But that is not what I mean. There is something ancient and wild about the hills, and the valleys, these great plains, the lakes. I have not known it anywhere else . . ."

His voice trailed away. After a few minutes he shook his head.

"So! I suppose that the plan is to try to bring the lovely Ulla back with us?"

"That is the only reason we return. That and to try the men, and see if any are with us, for every man, especially battle-hardened warriors, will be of use to us. What is it?"

Torquato had sat up straight.

"Hold a moment, I hear something."

I had long ago learned that my friend had an almost impossibly keen sense of hearing, and it had saved our skins on several occasions in Gaul.

"We have been tracked for at least the last ten furlongs. At least eight horses, war-band, no provisions loaded onto them. Now they have decided to try our mettle."

I could hear nothing, but Torquato had got to his feet and looked over to the west.

A minute or so later I could see the dust thrown up by several horses approaching the camp; they came straight in, bristling with spears and knives, their leader pulling hard on the reins of his black stallion just a few yards from where we sat.

This man had a crazed look to him; his face was deeply lined. His head was covered by sparse grey hair, and long white hair draped over his mouth. I did not expect him to be so old. Torquato laid his hand on my arm and moved ahead of me to meet them, and I could see that his senses were on full alert. Gone now was the clownish face of a buffoon; instead, the lean and calculating face of the warrior I knew him to be looked into the faces of the men who had ridden up. I knew that he was weighing up the odds, looking at the arms they carried. It was a Saxon war-band, probably renegades, and it seemed to me that they looked for trouble.

Their leader addressed Torquato.

"Who are you, and what is your business here?"

"We are emissaries of Ceawlin, King of the Gevissas, returning now to his hall from his business in the land of the Hwicca, with important information for him."

They talked in the language of the Saxons, but I could understand the gist of it. The chief warrior pointed at me.

"This man is a Briton. What is he doing in this part of Wessex?"

"As I say, we are on Ceawlin's business, and this man is a chief of the Gevissa king. He is himself just returned from Ceawlin's business in the land of the Franks."

The lead warrior turned and talked briefly with the man behind him and they both laughed. As they did so, I noticed that Torquato had opened his stance, and that he had removed the retaining clip from the scabbard of his Roman sword.

The Saxon chief turned back to Torquato.

"We have talked and, unfortunately, we do not believe you. So, you can give us your horses, or you can die . . ."

He got no further, for, in a blur of sudden controlled movement and gleaming steel, Torquato's sword bit deep into his neck, and he fell from his horse, dead before he hit the floor.

The horses of his war-band reared up as his fellow warriors realised what had happened, and they leapt from their horses. Before I could unsheathe my sword from its scabbard, Torquato was in amongst them with a lithe grace. In his first cross-step he took out the leader's second-in-command with a short stab in the guts; with his second movement head-butting a man coming at him from the left; with his third kicking his assailant full in the belly, before despatching him with a chop of his sword to the back of his head.

The other warriors watched this and drew back. Torquato crouched, waiting for their next attack, fully alert, the lines in his face etched by concentration. I saw that intent look I had seen so many times on his face, that same look I had also seen many times before on the face of my brother Cormac.

The man he had butted got up and came at him again. Torquato waited for his rush, then, with a sudden movement to his left, he picked the man up by the throat with his left hand and with his right hand ran his sword through the man's heart, throwing his twitching body away on to the rocks.

It was enough for the rest of the Saxon war-band, for they remounted their terrified horses, and sped off, back down the trail they had come.

Torquato wiped off his sword with the towel he had tied around his head in the morning, and then casually threw the towel onto the face of the warrior who had by now stopped twitching behind him. He walked over and kicked the prone body of the old chief.

"This one should have been picking grapes from the vines in his allotment by now. Renegade war-band – no more than robbers and murderers. It is good to know that I still have my skills, for I was starting to get soft with all of your family business. I suggest we leave here, Rhuadrac, for they may well return reinforced."

Once, when we had been on a mission in the land of the Visigoths, on the north rim of the Mediterranean Sea, we had witnessed a travelling circus. The circus had a caged leopard with it, and later we had witnessed this animal baited by warriors in an open theatre. It had occurred to me then that my friend's skills were like those of the leopard, for he was lightning fast, but graceful. He had been honed in the skills of men who fought for a living since he had been a child. His prowess as a warrior was very different to that of my brother, for Cormac relied upon his phenomenal power and strength to sweep away all before him.

We packed up the horses and moved off west into the dull red glow of the sun, before we skirted back to the south-east road after a few miles. There we made camp for the night, the hoar frost thick on our furs when we woke up the next morning.

*

It was late at night when we arrived back at Ceawlin's Hall. One of Ceawlin's young warriors, who knew some of the British language, came looking for us in the stables compound as we fed and watered our horses. He seemed nervous and hesitant.

"Olric has given orders that you are to report to him as soon as you return."

I liked neither the mention of orders, nor the need to report to this man, Olric. I held no allegiance to him. He meant nothing to me; what I had seen of him I had disliked instantly.

"Tell your master I might get around to it tomorrow. Otherwise I will do as I see fit."

The young warrior made as if to say more, but thought better of it, turned and left the long timber barn.

Torquato threw a green woollen blanket over his steaming horse, fixed a feedbag over its head, smacked its haunches, then turned to me.

"Think on now. You have made up your mind to leave the Saxon king. Stirring up trouble now will only make your departure from this place more difficult. I suggest that we pay this so-called chief a visit – make him think that you are still with Ceawlin. Otherwise we may never get out of this place in one piece."

I thought about it. The barn reeked of horseflesh and dung.

"You're right. We'll pay him a visit."

Several torches still burned low in the main hall. We could see Saxon warriors grouped around the top hearth which still threw out a low flame. Others sat at the end of the top table. Olric stood at the hearth, listening to the young warrior who had brought his message to the stables. He looked up as we approached.

"So, you have deigned to grace us with your company after all."

He smiled, but there was neither warmth nor mirth in his smile.

I nodded.

"You had something to discuss with me?"

"Let us two talk in private . . . alone please."

Torquato had made to go with me. I gestured to my friend to stay where he was, and I followed the young Saxon chief to the side chamber.

There were a couple of torches burning in the room, but there was no glow from the hearth, the fire having long since burned out. There was a cold chill in the room, and I could hear rain beat against the window.

"A storm is coming, I think."

I did not reply.

"You wished to discuss some matter with me?"

Olric looked at me calmly, not in the least surprised by my lack of cordiality. This was business, nothing else.

"What news from the meeting with your barbarian brother?"

I remembered that Cormac had violently turned Olric out when they had met.

"He is well. He told me that you two had . . . met."

A cruel sneer passed over the Saxon's face. I could see that this man harboured grudges. There would be a day of reckoning with my brother if he could arrange it.

"Yes. Did you tell him what the king told you to say?"

"Yes."

"And his response?"

"He said that he would think about it."

"Really? How strange. I have heard reports that he is seen often with certain of the more . . . settled amongst the Hwicca people. Even that he has a following of sorts amongst them. Is that not so?"

"I know nothing of such matters."

"Oh, come now, Briton, he must have said something to you?"

"He said nothing of such matters to me. Why should he? He is my brother, but he knows of my allegiance to Ceawlin."

"Yes, of course, of course. Yes, our once mighty chieftain. Tell me, how do you find the king since your return?"

I looked at this schemer closely, saying nothing. His words somehow did not surprise me. He continued, no change in the understated tone of his voice:

"He makes his plans, he would be *Bretwalda*. Perhaps you think that he over-reaches himself?"

He watched me closely as I replied.

"I have every reason to think that Ceawlin is a master in such strategic matters – his plans have obviously had much thought. I wait to see how I might fit into them."

"Yes, of course, the right and proper answer of a thegn."

Olric moved over to the dead hearth, idly kicking over a few cold ashes and splinters of wood.

"You understand that there are many amongst his own people who question his actions . . .?"

He did not look at me as he said these words, and he talked very quietly.

". . . and there are some who think that . . . others . . . may be better placed to take the Saxon cause in Wessex forward."

Still I said nothing.

"You realise that those forces I allude to, in alliance with those elements of your people that could be mustered . . . might have a great influence on the outcome of events?"

I listened carefully to these words. The Saxon had not declared any open opposition to his chief; this might be a test. Either way I would not be drawn on it.

"I know nothing of these matters. Frankly, you surprise me with your words. Better to concentrate on the support of your chief, rather than talk of plots in side rooms!"

The Saxon looked at me carefully; his light-grey eyes betrayed no anger, no hint of agitation.

"Plots? Are there plots then against the king?"

The cold grey eyes regarded me with disdain, then hardened.

"You are a fool, Briton. Have a care, you are out of your depth in this hall, and there are many who despise the presence of a British mercenary in this place."

"I have no argument with you, Olric – not yet anyway. But make no presumption of my regard for you. I met many schemers in the land of the Franks, and I despise such people."

"Your likes and dislikes do not concern me, unless they affect the balance of power in this kingdom."

I gritted my teeth and walked towards the door.

"No doubt you go now to find your . . . close friend, the good and loyal daughter of the king?"

My hand had touched the handle of the door. I turned back to him at these calculated words, making sure that he saw no stirring in my manner. I was sure that he had somehow guessed the truth about Ulla and me. One wrong step now and it was unlikely that my war-band would leave Ceawlin's Hall alive.

"Do you seek to make veiled threats against certain people in this hall? Speak your mind if so."

"I know much more of your plans, Briton, than you might suspect."

It struck me then for the first time that this man must suspect me of some plot against those holding power in the Gevissa lands; in his world, my pact with Ulla could mean only one thing – that I sought power in the Gevissa kingdom.

I laughed into his face.

"Saxon prince, you do not know me, and I laugh at your petty power games. There is nothing in your world of intrigues that interests me. Mark my words though – do not seek to harm those persons who do interest me, for you will one day reckon with me if you do. Think hard on what I say, for I swear it is the truth."

I slowly turned back to the door, not taking my eyes off the face of the Saxon. Olric said nothing, just continued to stand there, the sneer not leaving his face, the pale eyes still guarded.

I left the room, slamming the door as I did so.

I made a sign to Torquato to say nothing; we left the hall immediately.

"I will find Ulla and tell her of my plans. Get the men together, tell them also.

Find out how many wish to come with us. The sooner we leave this place the better."

With that I left my friend, and went to find the Gevissa princess, running through my mind how best I might tell her of my decision.

*

". . . I cannot believe that you have said this. No, it is not possible, not now, I cannot leave him."

Ulla pulled her white robe more closely around her, and the temper I knew so well flared in her face.

"How dare you lie with me, how dare you talk to me of love, and then ask me to desert my father, as if I was some kind of traitor, a stab in the back, to my own father, who is a great man, a great chief amongst my people?"

Her eyes filed with tears and I could see that all would not be well with us.

"Rhuadrac, you place me in an impossible position. Why do you not stay with me? My father brings new ways to your land, and a new language, and he will make this land strong and powerful, with a place in the world, not some provincial island fit only to send mercenaries and . . . and shopkeepers to the Frankish lands. Rhuadrac, why can you not see this? You could be rich beyond your dreams, with much land in this new country, and a powerful chief . . ."

I half-turned from her, for my mind was made up.

"Ulla, my people in this land are the West Britons. You have always known this, and I cannot sit back and watch my land be taken from my people. For I am no longer a freebooter in the land of the Franks. These are my people, and to go against them now would make me a traitor to my own people."

"But I had such hopes for us, Rhuadrac, I thought maybe, in a few years time, children, and in your own hall, and much land to farm, and we would grow old together . . ."

The first rush of temper was now subsiding in her, and I could see that the grim reality of our situation was just beginning to seep into her.

"But it is impossible . . . what is it you intend to do?

Then she thought again.

"No, do not tell me, for we will be compromised, we will all be compromised. Oh, my love, we are lost, there is nothing now for us."

Ulla sank to her knees, and I could see that all of the convoluted thoughts and possibilities were even now beginning to filter through her mind. I knew that, work it through as she may, there was no hope for us at this time, that one or the other of us must make a choice, and I could not oppose my own people.

A sudden gleam came into her eyes.

"Why do we not go away together? Just you and me, away from the madness in this place, just you and me, make a new life for ourselves, in another place somewhere, where none of this can affect us . . ."

"Ulla, my love, you are the daughter of Ceawlin, king in Wessex these twenty-four winters. The man who would be *Bretwalda*, who would create this Aengland of his. There is nowhere to go, for everywhere you would have a value, a price, and you would not be left alone in any place."

"Why must I not have my own life? Who said I could not have my own life? I am Ulla, daughter of Ceawlin, I can do as I please!"

The colour rose again in her face, and she looked at me with a quiet fury:

"Do not test my patience too far, Briton. Not even you might do that."

I waited for the fury to calm away, then I lifted her up and took her in my arms. She buried her head into my chest, and cried then, great sobs breaking out of her. She understood that we were in some danger now, and that our lives together may not take the path that she had dreamed of for all of the seasons I had been in the lands of the Franks.

Presently, she calmed down, and gently pulled away from me.

"Rhuadrac, you must go from this place. You must go now, this very morning, before the return of my father. You cannot see the world in the way you see it and stay here. You must go away, my love."

She walked away from me. I made as if to hold her again but she held up her hand, and stopped me.

"No, my love, it cannot be the same. You must leave me, you must leave me now, this minute, because I will not leave my father, not now. If my mother had been alive, perhaps then . . ."

But her voice trailed away. It was impossible for us.

"Go now. Take care, my love."

"Ulla, be sure to tell your father nothing of our pledge to each other, for he will be angry when he knows that I have gone. Although I know that your father will never cause you harm, still, you must not be compromised in this matter, for in matters of strategy, nothing is straightforward in these times."

She replied quietly, not raising her head.

"I have already decided in my own mind that I will tell my father nothing concerning us."

She was still the king's daughter, and she was already working through how our situation might be perceived.

"Keep a close eye on Olric. I am sure he has guessed about you and me. Is there anybody in the hall who you might rely upon until your father's return?"

Ulla looked at me with surprise in her face.

"What do I have to fear in this hall?

"I do not trust your cousin."

Ulla thought on my words. Her face was full of defiance as she answered me, her words suddenly cold.

"Crida is here. He is one person at least whom I might rely upon."

Her words were not lost on me.

"Then go now. Find Peg and both of you seek his protection until your father returns. It seems to me that there is nothing but scheme and counter-scheme in this place."

I talked from the heart, for I had felt nothing but compromised since I had first set foot in this king's hall.

I looked at her then and she looked at me. We drank each other in.

"We will meet again, Ulla, daughter of Ceawlin, King of the Gevissas. I promise you on my life, I will find a way to make this work, somehow."

She had lowered her head. I walked across to her and kissed her glowing black hair, and the scent of her body filled my senses.

"Take care, my love, I will come to find you again one day."

She said nothing to me.

With that I strode to the door, and with no further backward glance, closed it behind me. It felt as if I had torn out my very heart and left it in that room with her.

*

I had arranged to meet with Torquato at the stables. Now I could see his great shadow in the place that we had appointed. As I got nearer, I could see that the bodies of three Saxon warriors lay strewn around the floor of the wooden barn.

"A welcome committee for you, I think. They made it clear that neither you, nor I, nor anybody else in our band, are meant to leave this place tonight. I begged to differ."

I nodded. It did not surprise me that Olric took steps to stop me leaving Ceawlin's Hall.

"How did it go with the men?"

"They are all with us, already out front, waiting for you to join us. None of them have any great love for the Saxons. Felix tried to argue against it, but changed his mind when he saw that everybody else is with you. We need to keep an eye on him though."

He looked at me then.

"And you?"

I shook my head grimly.

"Impossible."

"In a way it speaks well of her though, for to leave her father is a mighty ask of her."

"Well I know it, but it does not make it any easier for me."

"Where is she now?"

"I do not trust Olric after his words to me. She has gone to seek the protection of Crida until her father returns."

Torquato said nothing, though he frowned slightly. His face quickly became like a mask again.

He put his hand on my shoulder.

"We will find a way, brother, we will find a way."

He had never called me brother before, and I was glad of his words.

"Loosen the reins of the horses, untie them, stir them up. We will need to buy some time."

Even as the Roman did as I asked of him, I ran over to the wall of the barn, lifting a flaming bough from the tightly coiled rope that fastened it there. I flung it into the dry hay that stood furthest away from the horses; immediately a great flame leapt up. The horses, now loose, began to fret, to stamp their hooves and rear up, and their noise rang through the night.

Taking my horse by the leather rein, we ran around to the front of the hall. In the lee of the west flank of the building, I could see my war-band gathered. Scipio sat in the driver's position in the covered wagon; the rest of them calming their restless horses, all ready to go, waiting for my arrival. Saying nothing, I leapt up onto my horse. As I did so, a commotion broke out from behind the hall; the whinnying of horses filled the air, mixed with the shouts of Saxons. Torquato shouted to me:

"They have found their comrades. We go now!"

As one, we dug our heels into the side of our mounts and leapt forward down the track that led away from the hall. Even as we did so, riderless horses began to gallop past us; Saxon warriors ran out into the track, trying to stop us, but they were too late, as we rode hard for the main gates that led away from the hall, the shouts of the Saxons fading behind us as we sped away into the night.

*

And so it came about that two days later, I, Rhuadrac, brother of Cormac, the legendary champion of the dead King Farinmael, with my friend Torquato, the giant warrior, the freebooter from Rome, together with the remaining warriors of our war-band, crossed under cover of darkness once more over the border into Hwicca country in the west of the land that is called Alba. In three days hence we would meet at Penwyrn with my brother and the great chief of the Britons in Powys, Brocmael, the warrior-chief that the verses speak of. We would once more prepare for battle with the Aenglish invader, namely Ceawlin, King of the Gevissas in Wessex, the man who would be *Bretwalda*. But the man who was also father of Ulla, the woman from whom I had hoped never to be divided.

IV

We had followed the Roman Road from Winche over the Ridgeway and crossed onto another of the Roman roads just after, that which led from Calleva and passed over the Fosse Way at Corinium. From there we rode to Gloucester and on to the banks of the Severn itself, which we could follow all the way through the great forests to Penwyrn. The journey as far as Gloucester was hard going. Everywhere we could see the effects of the Saxon settlements; even the old Roman villas had been colonised, and their Romano-British families either put to the sword, chased off, or absorbed into the Saxon way of living. In each one of the old villas that we passed, we could see the timber outbuildings of the Saxon settler, and in several the canvas stalls of the day markets that the Saxons had brought with them.

We moved slowly, no longer under the protection of the Wessex king, for by now I was sure that Ceawlin would know that I had left his allegiance and he would treat it as the worse kind of treachery. Had he not built me up, made me, a young warrior caught up in a calamitous defeat of my people, a man of some substance and status? I felt no remorse on this score, for I had served his purposes well, had been instrumental in the fall of Uthwine, and had therefore done much to consolidate Ceawlin's power amongst his own Wessex tribe.

On the fourth day, we had just cleared the Forest of Wyre, and were by now in the territory of the ancient Carnovii, a region where Ceawlin's power was not strong, for we had left Gloucester and its environs far behind us, and we were less than a morning's ride from the great city of Uriconium and Brocmael's stronghold at Penwyrn.

It was a cold evening. Above us a clear night sky was shot through with blue and silver stars, and the crescent moon cast a strange half-light upon our war-band. To my right rode Torquato, and on my left rode Veostan.

Veos was second only to Torquato in warrior prowess; his face was the battered face of the career warrior, a man who had fought for his living since late childhood, and that experience had left its mark on his character. He trusted nobody until he knew them properly, but once he was sure that he could trust a person, then that person was accepted fully by him.

Like Torquato, he had a love for life, a quick humour. He also had a prodigious appetite for beer. He took much pleasure in baiting the Roman, but rarely succeeded in these baiting contests.

But what intrigued me most about this man was not his warrior prowess, which, as I say, was considerable, but the way that he saw the world. Although he was not in any way an educated man, he was forever asking questions of those who had been taught, for he thought this a great prize. I had discovered by then that many warriors shared this trait; that many men who lived and died by the sword were full of such questions, but they asked their questions quietly, never in groups, and only to those men that they trusted. But of all those warriors who shared this mannerism, none asked more questions than Veos.

Now he was looking up at the shimmering night sky laid out above us.

"Now then, Chief, you are a learned man, are you not?"

I had been asked this question many times by Veos, and I replied in the manner that he knew and trusted.

"I know my alphabet, I can read and write down the written form of this Roman language . . ."

Veos spoke the version of the Roman language used in Gaul, which, though not a polished version, was easily understood by both Torquato and me. ". . . and I know the verses of the Roman poets well."

"Tell me again the names of those poets you mentioned to me."

"Well, like every man who has learned the Roman language I know the author of the *Aeneid*, who was called Virgil . . ."

I had been astonished by the widespread knowledge of this poet's work in Gaul, for every man who could read the Roman language seemed to know of it.

". . . and I know Statius, and the writer Ovid, who wrote his *Metamorphoses* . . ."

"His what?"

"*Metamorphoses*. Where human characters turn into trees, or flowers."

"So?"

He thought a moment.

"This Virgil then. What did he say about the stars, these lights that rise from the sea every night and sink back to the ocean floor before dawn?"

"Why Veos, you are just like young Pallas."

"Who's that then?"

> *"His left young Pallas kept, fixed to his side*
> *And oft of winds enquired, and of the tide;*
> *Oft of the stars, and of their watery way*
> *And what he suffered both by land and sea."*

Veos muttered the last few words quietly to himself.

"Not bad. My people do not write down our songs, we sing or say them. See, we believe that carved out of the Milky Way up there is the path to Asgaard, and us warriors will one day walk that path to the Otherworld."

Torquato snorted.

"By the gods, but you two are going soft. Veos knows enough about the winds, I can tell you, and it was me that suffered, for I slept next to him last night!"

"Torquato, for a Roman, you are an uncivilised ruffian."

"Maybe so. Anyway, think on this – the dewy night is falling fast from the sky, and the setting stars are speaking to us of sleep."

Then that rascal flashed me a grin with that big mouth of his and galloped on.

"What was he talking about?"

"I think that he is telling me that we need to concentrate on a place to camp for the night."

Ahead of us, on a slight slope on our left-hand side, I could see yet another of the old Roman villas that were numerous in this region, set out in well-laid gardens that sloped down gently to the valley floor. The white walls of the villa shone luminous in the moon-light, like some strange ghost of itself. I could see no evidence of timber outbuildings of the Saxon type in its grounds; it seemed to me that it was as yet free from Saxon influence.

I was right in this. The villa was occupied by an old Roman-Briton. Once this man had established with some relief that we were not Saxons but a band of mercenaries led by a Briton, then he was delighted to meet with me, and was happy for us to strike camp in the grounds of the villa. This delight only increased when he learned that I was the brother of the giant, that champion of Farinmael of whom he had heard in the verses

This man's name was Salemnis. He told me that he was a town councillor at Uriconium. When he heard that I could speak the Roman language well, he was happy to talk with me, and at length he invited Torquato, Veos and me to supper with him and his family.

Soon enough we were stood around a huge oak table in a small hall of the villa. All four walls were inlaid with a small blue-brick mosaic set out in a criss-cross pattern. The floors were made up of heavy tiles. Set into these tiles were more examples of the small blue-brick mosaic as on the walls, so that the room had a pleasing aspect under the yellow flames of the torches set into their coiled ropes.

I looked across at Torquato, who had put on his best gold tunic for the occasion, had even washed his face. I could not help smiling at his obvious discomfort, for as soon as he was asked to conform to the correct ways, he was always immediately unsettled, like a poor swimmer who finds that his feet no longer reach to the floor of the rock pool in which he swims. He was now trying to look distinguished and knowledgeable as this man Salemnis told us about the Roman-Briton ways of building, a subject about which my friend knew not one thing, for all such matters bored him beyond patience.

Salemnis stood noble in his light-purple tunic, pinned at the shoulders by two old iron crossbow brooches, which had been a sign of city-office in the Roman times. He was talking about Uriconium, of its wealth and grandeur in past times, and what had been lost by the passage of time. It had obviously been a great Roman city in the old times, before the time of our forefathers.

I complimented Salemnis on the attractive appearance of the mosaic, which caused Veos to question the means by which they were set into the wall and floor. The old man, who appeared to be a great expert on the subject, began a learned commentary on this theme.

At that moment the rest of the family of our host arrived.

Salemnis had two daughters, both of whom were long past childhood, older than me. They were two sturdy women, good looking, and I noticed Torquato's eyes light up on their arrival. The wife of our host also came in with them, an attractive elder woman by the name of Flavia, with her grey hair piled high on her head and held by various kinds of hairpins; she was much covered in gold, with rings on most of her fingers and elegant gold brooches pinned her red cloak at the shoulders.

The meal was then served up, servants bringing the food in many-coloured dishes, but mostly in bowls that gleamed bright red, made by a method that my people had learnt from the Roman potters.

Salemnis looked at me and sighed; it seemed as if he had decided to take me into his confidence:

"I have not slept well in recent days. Rumours are rife that the Saxons in the south, the Gevissas, are gathering for a move through the upper Severn."

He looked at me with a sudden intensity, gauging my response. I showed no reaction.

"If that is so, it may be that this villa and my family face some danger – the Saxons have no love for us Roman-British."

Again he looked at me.

"It is said that you are well known to the Saxons."

I was astonished. By what means did this news circulate?

"Perhaps you can tell me what they are like? As you see, I have daughters. If the tales about these heathens have any truth . . ."

His voice trailed away.

I understood him.

"It is true, I know the Gevissa king and his family."

I could see that all at the table wanted to know what I had discovered.

"There are good and bad amongst them. They seek to establish themselves in this land; they seek to prosper. Their ways are not our ways. They intend that their way will prevail. But in truth, at root they are much like us."

Salemnis and Flavia looked shocked.

Flavia threw down her napkin on the table.

"Like us? But they are heathens! The tales of their rapes and debaucheries swamp the land. Their ways are unnatural, with their warrior-gods and their tree-gods! They are the worse type of heathen, and they seek to destroy all that is good here."

"So I had been brought up to believe. But I have reason to doubt that now. At root they think as we think. Their culture is not our culture. But their instincts, their needs, their fears – all these are just the same as ours."

Salemnis saw the flush pass through his wife's face and sought to talk of other things.

"So, this talk of expansion into the upper Severn. Might there be any truth in it?"

"Who can say what the Gevissa king thinks?"

I had no intention of stating in this villa just how much I knew of Ceawlin's plans. This Salemnis was a local grandee, with many friends in power. I wanted to be at Brocmael's Hall, talk to that king face to face, before I decided to reveal how much I knew.

"On the other hand, it is said that the people are converging on Penwyrn in this time of unrest, so that they may know some protection. For if there is any substance to the rumours, I know from my experience at Deorham that the Gevissa king will strike hard and fast through the land. He will bring together many thousands in his armies, and none would be safe if he chooses to move north."

I looked hard at Salemnis. This man had shown generosity to me and my men, strangers to him. He and his family would be in grave danger if Ceawlin succeeded in his march north.

The old man looked at me, his head tilted slightly to one side.

"Yes, I see your reasoning."

He inclined his head slightly, and looked away from me. I could see that he had understood me.

We then talked of other things. Veos plied many questions at Salemnis, so that even that man's great knowledge was sore tested. Torquato soon lost all interest in the polite conversation, and spent all of his time talking to the two daughters who sat opposite him. They had all drunk much wine; even now he was laughing with them on inappropriate subjects, so that they would giggle in an apparently confused way, and colour up, blushing.

The older daughter leant forward and placed her delicate hand across the Roman's tattooed arm.

"You are a very big man aren't you?"

"Let me tell you, you are not the first beautiful woman to tell me that!"

Much giggling broke out, and Flavia looked across at her husband, her lips pursing.

Salemnis shrugged his shoulders.

Torquato now pressed on with his nonsense.

"To think that I will soon have to go to my cold hut, whilst you two lovely ladies rest warm in your firm beds . . ."

The younger sister looked at him full in the face, and said, in a barely concealed whisper:

"We all know where you would sooner be!"

The two women dissolved into giggles and earthy laughter, and the rascal looked across at me with a knowing smirk on his face, smiling. I just managed to prevent myself laughing at the rogue's outrageous behaviour in this civilised place.

Salemnis and his wife frowned at each other, and I could see that the old man now regretted his decision to allow these uncouth warriors into his home.

It was all I could do to get Torquato away from the table at the end of the meal.

"Well, sir, we thank you for your hospitality and good company."

But the Romano-Briton could barely bring himself to look at me.

"Yes, well, I trust your journey continues well. No need to see us in the morning. Goodbye, Goodbye!"

I turned to thank his wife, Flavia, but she had already left the room.

Torquato had taken full advantage of the wine supplied by Salemnis; it was an ordeal for Veos and I to get our ruffian friend back to the stone and timber round-hut that had been provided for our billet. Halfway there he turned around, staggering a little as he strode back towards the villa.

"By the green fields of the goddess Isis, but my bet is that those two could do a turn or two."

We ran back to him and eventually got him back to the hut.

"Be quiet you dog, and get your head down. We have a full ride before us tomorrow, and we need to sleep. I meet with the great chieftain Brocmael and my brother, and we need all of our strength for the day ahead."

"Yes, Cub-General, right, exactly so."

I had cause to wake up during the night. Turning over in my travel blanket, restless, I could see that my giant friend's own blanket was empty, and that he was nowhere to be seen.

I could not myself sleep then, for my mind was full of many things. Tomorrow I would see my mother again, who I had not seen since before Deorham. I would also see the rest of my family, and my old teacher, Cadolan, once more. I would meet for the first time the Powys king, Brocmael, whose reputation as a wise king was second to none amongst my own people.

But then, my thoughts, as always, came back to the princess, Ulla, daughter of the Gevissa king. Some ancient and sacred knowledge had passed between us just a few short nights previously.

I thought of her open and beautiful face, her wide honest eyes, her dark hair, her wondrous skin, her full womanly body, the very scent of her. I thought of her fiery spirit and her quick temper. I wondered what she might be doing, what she might be thinking, at that moment. She did not leave my mind until I finally slept again, and fell into restless dreams, for even then the absence of the Gevissa princess haunted my mind.

V

At first light we were straight up and on our way. The day was crisp, cold and bright, and an almost blue frost lay on the ground at the early hour of our leaving.

Ahead of us lay more woodland, for it seemed that the whole of this region was covered in forest. By following the bank of the Severn we made good progress, so that before midday we had passed to our right the strange lone hill called the Wrekin. Soon we were on the great Roman Road, and had passed over a ford in the river and found ourselves on the outskirts of the old ruined white city of the Romans, called by my people, Uriconium.

I had long heard tales of this city from my Uncle Gavin and my mother. Gavin had told me that this place was one of the greatest cities in the whole of the

British lands and for many years in the old days had been a major Roman garrison. It stretched for almost two hundred acres within its walled precincts, and at one time some five thousand souls had lived within or around its walls. For a long time now it had been deserted by the Roman garrisons, and its bathhouses and council chambers had long since fallen into disuse.

Some forty winters before the time I speak of, at the time of the Great Darkness of which our forefathers tell in the verses, the days when the sun grew cold, the city had fallen into complete disuse. Very little would grow in those times, and what was grown was kept for each family, and nothing was left over for the barter markets, and so they fell away at that time. So too had the Great Death passed through here soon after, and great suffering came to the people.

In recent years some form of recovery had taken place. Now the Powys king, Brocmael, had decided to make use of it. This king was a Christian king, and he had instructed that a great timber hall be built on its main street, and into this timber hall he had established a bishopric and a congregation of monks.

Such tales had my Uncle Gavin told me.

But my mother told me other, different, tales. She told me what was whispered amongst the old people about this place. On some dark winter nights, as the wind whistled and howled through the empty white-stone halls, and nothing stirred in the deserted streets, those left in this once rich, proud but now time-defaced city would sometimes hear, distant at first but growing nearer, a sound as of an army marching. Then those listening would hear too the jangle and clank of metal, and harsh rough commands barked out. For now the spectres of the long-dead Roman legions once more strode in measure through the city, striding with relentless purpose to cruelly subdue the latest rising of the Britons. At such times, those poor souls left in the abandoned city would bolt their doors, and shutter their windows, and light more candles. So they would sit in their ruined shells, barely daring to breathe, until the tread of the proud ghost army could be heard no more.

I looked about me now. It was early in the afternoon. A bright sun was high. No ghosts walked the land; it was clear that the Roman legions were long gone from this place.

I have never seen such wide streets, for they made Corinium's streets look like those of a village. It was a market day and all sorts of barter trade was being carried on under the makeshift awnings on the trestle tables.

Great high columns still stood on each side of the main street, and though some of the covered walkways had collapsed in places, it was still possible to see how this great city had become spoken of in hushed tones amongst my people. Great part-demolished white-stone buildings were still standing, and these appeared to be used now for trade and marketing.

To our right, dominating the centre of the main street, a hundred or so paces before the crossroads where the Roman Road met another wide street in the very heart of the city, was the timber wall of the bishopric. Strangely, there were no windows set into this great timber wall, for I learned later that this was the rear of the building, and that the front of the building looked out onto the east side of the city.

On our left-hand side I counted some four or five other timber buildings, of some size too, but none of the size of the main building to our right, which dominated this central part of the old city.

Many people thronged the main street, and I could see from their dress that they were Britons like me, or Roman-Britons like Salemnis, and even one or two in German or Frankish garb. Not all Germans were Saxon invaders, and some of their merchants were peaceful men and had even made some small settlements in our land. They were accepted for what they were, and generally left unmolested, provided that they did not venture into the mead-halls.

We must have made a strange sight, my war-band and me, as we rode slowly up the main street of this strange city. Only I was a Briton, and it would be clear to all who saw us that we were a mercenary war-band. Our presence must have been one more clear indication that trouble was brewing, that the relatively peaceful days of their past few seasons were numbered, and that war would soon be let loose upon them once more.

On my right rode Torquato, who had been strangely quiet during the morning. I could but imagine how this rogue had spent his night. He kept falling into a doze on his horse, only to wake up suddenly when I called him, pretending that he had been fully alert all of the time, before dozing off again. Just then he roused up from his doze and caught sight of something to his right.

"Hey, General, the one in the middle looks just like you."

We all looked to where he was pointing. An old Roman stone column stood on the left of the timber wall, and on this stone column was a headpiece. Into this headpiece had been carved three heads, with curled hair swept back from their foreheads.

The one in the middle had a big nose and a pronounced chin.

I did not acknowledge the ruffian. But then I became aware of the quiet laughter of my war-band as they all glanced and nodded at each other. Then I laughed too, for as usual there was some truth in the great clown's mockery.

Felix, who rode on my left, did not laugh.

He spoke to me now in that distant voice of his and looked sideways at me with his sly eyes.

"So, Chief, will I be able to barter in this city?"

"You can attempt to, but do not take any time over it, for I want to reach Brocmael's Hall before dark. What is it you need?"

"My sharpening tools are all blunt, and I will trade two of my least accurate darts to replace them."

"So be it, but say little, for we are not known in this place, and we have business elsewhere."

Felix dismounted and went in search of a blacksmith's forge.

We all then dismounted, and I indicated to the men that we would not spend any time in this place. Any sort of drink was unwise. We wanted none to know of our business and we would leave for Brocmael's Hall as soon as Felix returned.

We broke up, Torquato remaining with me as we strolled down the left side of the main street. There was a busy bustle about the place, as men and women of all descriptions hurried here and there. From time to time livestock was driven down the central thoroughfare. Great carts loaded with feedstuff and hauled by huge yoked oxen trundled past, the farmer no doubt keen to strike a bargain at some granary store buried in the labyrinth of this huge wrecked city. I could see two-horse chariots, old relics of the Roman times, no doubt many times repaired and maintained by their proud Roman-Briton owners, who travelled mostly in pairs upon each carriage.

Again I was struck by the sheer size of the ruined buildings around me. At one point, just beyond the great thronging crossroads where the two main roads met, I could see to my right a great ruined structure. I pushed open the huge oak door that still stood at its entrance. Beyond it, a huge basilica, bigger than anything I had seen on my travels, stretched out for some two hundred paces before me. Many columns still stood on either side of this structure, and some of the old timber beams still stretched across the high roof space.

Torquato was impressed, but somehow sad too. As he talked, his deep voice echoed slightly through the cavernous space.

"This compares with anything I have seen in my own land. I did not know that my people had come so far, had built so much, in this strange island on the edge of the world."

My friend and I walked up through this hall, walking further away from the continuing hubbub of shouts and cries, the whirr of cartwheels and the ringing hooves of horses back at the crossroads as we did so. We could see that dark-blue and white mosaics had been set into the aisles. At the far end, to our right, a huge white-stone wall reared up, and this must have been the entrance to some inner chamber, for two great timber doors still stood at its centre, and we could see how the stone floor under the doors had been worn down by the numbers of people who had used it.

I stood back from the wall with its doors and marvelled at the thought of the Roman soldiers who had stood here, like me, and walked and talked as my friend and I did now. Just at that moment they almost stood before me – not as men who lived hundreds of years ago, but real flesh and blood men who breathed the air as I did now, men with beating hearts. Were they steady men, with a wife, sons and daughters? Did they take lovers? Did they perhaps have a secret meeting planned with some dark lady of the love-arts that evening, before they left for battle tomorrow? How long had they been here? What had happened to them in this place, so far from home?

One of the doors was open, and we could see that great stone walls, partly destroyed, still stood at either side, and at the rear of the building. Several marble pits, lined with mosaics, lay on each side of the great hall.

Torquato scratched his head.

"These are the remains of a bathhouse. They are as good as any such place that I have seen in Rome. To allow such a magnificent building to go to ruin is barbaric."

"Aye, maybe so, but to have bathhouses in this climate in any event is decadent. No wonder they had to leave, they were soft, like women!"

Torquato looked at me sideways, but said nothing.

We retraced our steps to the crossroads, and the hue and cry of the vibrant day markets once more assailed us.

Just then a commotion broke out in one of the buildings in the small square of shops to our left as we moved down the main street. I could see through the window that the building, which was little more than a ruin of a small hall, was some form of mead-shop. There were men sitting on rush mats on the floor, and slave-girls ran up and down with claw-beakers. Men with ribboned hair, dirty faces and wild unkempt moustaches clotted with food and drink shouted at each other, or grabbed at the slave-girls. One of this band had bent a girl over double by the neck, and was turned away from her, and laughed with his fellow tribesmen.

I turned to Torquato who looked at me with raised eyebrows but otherwise his face was stone.

"Leave it alone. It is none of our business, we are passing through, that is all."

I walked away five paces, then stopped, and looked at Torquato.

"But then again."

We turned about, and threw back the cloth that stretched over the shop doorway.

The fellow now had the slave-girl by the hair, and was trotting her around the shop space with a leer on his face, and flicking up her tattered gown, amidst much yelling and cursing and hysterical laughter from his drunken friends.

I looked at this man as a sudden silence descended on the room.

In truth, the presence of Torquato and his giant warrior frame in such a place would always silence such a gathering, for they knew that no good could come to them through his presence.

I felt an almost uncontrollable rage rise up in me. The man in front of me was a West Briton. I could see from his clothing and the strange ribbons in his hair that he was one of the remnants of the Kimbroi people, a bloodthirsty tribe whose terrors had several times been described to me by my Uncle Gavin. The cruelty of this tribe was sung loud in the verses, with their grey-haired priestesses, all clad in white. Their strange and inhuman rites had long ago made me terrified as a child, and had passed into the dark legends of my people.

I looked at the man, who now let go of the slave-girl. She ran over to the side wall and watched with terrified eyes.

"What dignity and honour is there in what you do? What sort of a man are you?"

This drunken fellow looked at his ribboned tribesmen, but they were now silent, all looking closely at Torquato and me. Some slowly moved their right hands closer to the hilts of their swords which they had removed and placed by their sides whilst seated on the floor. Torquato stepped to the middle of the room, placed his right hand on the hilt of the short sword in its scabbard on his right shoulder, and slowly wagged the first finger of his left hand from side to side.

"Not a good idea."

They all knew enough of his Roman tongue to move their hands away from their bodies.

With a spring, the drunken Briton charged at me. I stepped to one side and rammed his head into the timber and stone wall of the shop, and he fell to his knees, whimpering. As he turned towards me, I cracked his jaw with the hilt of *Saesbane,* and he crumpled up in a heap on the floor. I lifted him up by the scruff of his neck and led him bent double around the floor of the shop by his hair. One or two of his tribesmen reared up at me as I did so, but I lashed out with my foot, catching several of them full in the face.

"Not laughing now, lads, heh? Not laughing now then?"

Torquato placed his hand on my shoulder.

"Rhuadrac, that is enough. Let's go, we have business to attend to."

The rage left me and I came back to myself.

"Very well then. You are right."

I let go of the drunk, who slumped to the floor, all of this in complete silence. I gestured to the slave-girl to follow us as we left the shop

The slave-girl ran out after us.

"Take me with you, for they will kill me for this."

I looked at her. She was not yet fully a woman, she had seen perhaps some seventeen winters. She had long red hair, and green eyes, and the curiously white skin of her face seemed somehow stretched thin over the wide cheekbones; there was much beauty in her face and slender figure, though I could sense that she had lived through brutal times.

"What is your name?"

"I am called Megwei. I am alone in this world, for my parents are dead, and I have no reason to stay in this place any more."

"Very well then, you can come with us to Brocmael's Hall, which is our destination – but there you must fend for yourself."

There was such gratitude in her eyes that I knew that I had made the right decision.

Torquato looked at me sideways.

"I think that we both need some battle action, and soon."

I reflected on his words as we left the fabled white-stone city some ten minutes later, the girl Megwei behind me, Felix back in our ranks, and I knew that he was right.

VI

We left the city by the route we had entered, passing back over the ford in the river and following its path now to the north-west.

The territory of the Carnovii contains many hill forts, and Penwyrn had been known by my people since before the time of my forefathers. Brocmael's stronghold lay some twelve Roman miles from Uriconium, in fertile wetlands that were full of wildlife. A thriving community had set up there, and it had become a place of barter and trade on designated market days. It was set in the dense woodland typical of this region; the camp itself lay atop a mound in a clearing, and below this clearing was a lake, and the lake was ringed with trees. In the past, before our father had been lost to us at Bedcanford, Cormac and I had come on expeditions with him on several occasions to fish in this lake, so that the area was well enough known to me.

As we moved closer to Penwyrn, we had begun to ride past a steady procession of people of all kinds: traders, farmers, warriors travelling in ones or twos or in small war-bands, all converging on the warlord's stronghold. This in itself was a sure sign that messages had begun to circulate that the Saxons from the south, the Gevissas, were on the move again, and that this time it was the upper Severn Valley that was their target.

Soon we were in sight of Penwyrn itself. A great wooden fence ran around the perimeter of the camp, and we could see that sentries had been posted.

I explained our business, and when I mentioned that I was the brother of the giant Cormac, Farinmael's champion, the sentries stood aside, so that we came into the camp and my war-band got their first view of it.

We took the main track that cut through a small incline. Ahead of us I could see a band of warriors stood outside one of the huts, and they stopped talking and looked across at our strange mercenary war-band as we approached. I held up my right hand as I came up to them:

"Friends, my name is Rhuadrac, brother to Cormac of the West Britons. Where might I find him?"

At first they were silent. Then the eldest warrior, a heavy man with a deep scar across his forehead, who wore a sword and two daggers in his belt, spoke quietly to the men around him, then stepped forward warily.

"Rhuadrac of the West Britons. We know something of your story. Why would a Saxon-lover come into this camp?"

Torquato's right arm went immediately to his sword, held high on his right shoulder. I raised my arm to calm him.

"Warriors, I have no argument with you. I am here to fight for my people, the West Britons. It is true that I have earned gold in the ranks of the Gevissa king, but my reasons for that are my own, and I have never raised arms against my own people. Where is my brother?"

The elder warrior again talked to the others with him. There was some shrugging of shoulders. Then again he stepped towards us.

"We think that it is better that you are on our side than against us. You will find your brother in the great hall, with Brocmael and his son, Kynon. There is to be a great feast tonight, for it is Martinmas, and tonight we celebrate the end of the harvest."

I nodded, gently kicked the sides of my mount, and moved off towards the great hall. As we walked away, I heard Torquato say quietly:

"Great news. Now we are hated by both sides in this mad country."

I said nothing in response, but asked him to arrange for the billet of our warband, and went alone to the great hall.

The buildings were in the style of my own people, and bore little resemblance to Ceawlin's Hall, for that was a massive timber structure of high walls. The Great Hall of Penwyrn, which was set in the middle of the clearing, looked as if it was all roof. The main struts that held up the ceiling started low to the ground, and the great thatched and tiled structure of the roof overlay the building entirely, so that it looked almost as if a huge version of Rathgere's boat had been turned upside down. Around it stood many round houses, arranged in typical hut circles, so that huts of between ten and thirty paces in diameter were clustered together. All of these structures used timber for their base, for I have said that this region was all woodland, but in many stone was also used.

The main oak door of the hall was open, so I strode in. The room seemed suffused with the smell of cinnamon, and spices, and there was a great bustle about the place. In front of me I could see several women, including my sister, Aisha, who looked around when I entered, and raised a hand to her mouth with delight. I put a finger to my lips; I had recognised the pale green gown on my mother's back as she bent stooped over the side table at which she and my sister worked, preparing the feast in the evening. I walked up behind my mother and placed my hands over her eyes.

"Well then, this is a fine welcome for the long-lost son!"

My mother turned with a great look of shock on her face.

"My God in Heaven! Where have you been, you silly boy?"

I wrapped my arms around her and she buried her head in my chest, and great sobs burst out of her, then she held me away from her and looked me full in the face, as only a mother can.

"Well then, you are a fine man now, and your father would have been proud of you."

I knew that I always reminded my mother of my father, for she always said that I had his features. She was herself hardly changed – the long once black hair still piled high on her head, quite white now in places, the clear blue eyes, her noble face, perhaps with a few more fine lines around those eyes. My mother's small face was intelligent, the face of a deeply thoughtful person; she did not say much, but what she said was always considered. She was capable of great rages if she thought that her children had in some way belittled themselves. She was after all the second daughter of an Irish king, the great Tiernan of Breffni, and she expected her children to never lose sight of that fact.

Now she reached for the cloth that my sister held out to her and dabbed at her eyes.

"Well now, but this is a stupid way for a woman of my years to behave. Tonight you must tell me everything that has happened to you in your winters over the seas, of the people you have met, what you have learned. For tonight we celebrate *Quadragesima Sancti Martini*, and tomorrow our celebrations must end."

Her strong voice still held all of the beautiful lilt that is typical of her people. I remembered our father told Cormac and me often that he sometimes asked our mother questions so that he could simply listen to the sound of her voice, which he had found enchanting, literally so; he could refuse her nothing when she talked to him.

"Mother, when I look at you now I know that I have been too long away. It seems to me that none of us can say where this life will send us, or who it will send us to meet, and that sometimes it blows us around like puppets."

She smiled at me with those knowing eyes of hers. She took note of the chain and cross at my neck, and looked directly into my eyes.

"You not only look like your father, but you speak like your grandfather, for he would always talk about fate too, and how we are all captive to its power. Aisha has told me all about the Gevissa princess, my son – you should not lose hope. Your father had many trials to face himself before we could be together, but we knew we would be together, and it happened, so I know that we can shape our fate in this life."

She looked again at the cross at my neck.

"Sometimes we must just put our trust in a higher power."

Then she hugged me again, wiping her eyes as she released me.

"Now – go to your brother. I know that he is keen to see you. We shall talk later, and we will talk of your time in the land of the Franks. You will tell me all about this lady, Ulla, and we will make our plans!"

I hugged them both, then strode over to the door set into the far side of the hall that my mother indicated, and I could feel my mother's eyes on me all the way over to the door.

I rapped on the door and a firm West Briton voice bid me enter.

The room was a small chamber, set under the eve of the high roof of the main hall, so that the roof slanted sharply into the back wall of the chamber. In one wall was an open hearth, in which a low fire burned, and a many-coloured rug was laid out on the floor. Night had fallen so that no daylight came through the small window set under the eave, but the room was lit by two or three torches, which gave off a dim glow.

Over on the far side of the room I could see three men seated around a small heavy table; the unmistakable frame of my giant brother, an older man with grey hair, who I took to be Brocmael, and another warrior, about my age, who must be Kynon. All three had now stopped speaking on my entrance. It seemed to me that they did not expect a stranger at that moment, and that neither Brocmael nor Kynon were overly pleased to see me.

My brother immediately stood up and came over to me.

"How is life with you, brother?"

We clasped hands. I could see that he was well pleased to see me, but knew also that there was pressing business in this chamber, so we would talk freely later. He turned to the other two men in the room.

"Chief Brocmael, Lord Kynon, this is my brother, Rhuadrac. As I have explained to you, he is with us, and I hope he brings a war-band with him."

King Brocmael was not a young man; he had a large frame, though was slightly stooped, so that he did not seem particularly tall. His hair was black-grey, as was his beard. He had the face of a thinker, not of a man of action; the face of one who would prefer the library to the battlefield.

As I looked at his son I knew that I looked into the face of a true warrior. He was tall and lean, with an etched face, so that great ruts ran down each side of it. His dark eyes were deep-set, and a ridge ran along his forehead, so that he seemed to be permanently frowning in concentration. He wore his black hair long, in the West Briton fashion. He had the frame and face of a man who competes in the short races, and not only runs well, but wins.

Brocmael waved me over to where they sat. Kynon looked at me now with an iron face, and did not offer me his hand. Brocmael offered me his, but even so I thought that I could detect a reservation in his voice as he talked to me.

"Rhuadrac, we welcome you to this hall. Your brother has told us of your decision. We know of your great bravery on the dark day at Deorham, for the poets already speak of it. We know of your work for the Gevissa king in the land of the Franks, we know too that you have now broken with him . . ."

Brocmael stood up and paced a few steps towards the door, then turned back to us.

"Yet even as we speak, this very same Gevissa king, this Ceawlin, whose power no other king has yet found a way to match, has been reinforced with ships from the Saxon lands. We know that he is now marching with his son, Cutha, and even now moves his army east to the land of the Hwiccas in the lower Severn valley, and has already begun to make new conquests."

Brocmael paused and looked at me. He had walked back to where I sat; he now placed his left hand over my right arm which lay on the table between us.

"I must know now, Rhuadrac, what do you know of this Ceawlin's plans, and what are your intentions in this matter?"

It was clear to me then that they had been discussing this very matter when I had appeared at the door.

"I will tell you straight, Chief Brocmael, for I hate the speech of a man who says one thing but thinks another. I once thought that this Ceawlin was a wise and noble warrior. In truth, so too he was, for I am the only Briton still living who witnessed the dignity and honour with which he treated our great King Farinmael on the death of that great warrior at Deorham."

I retold the story of the death of Farinmael.

There was a silence, and I could see that all three men were deeply affected by it, for it was a true warrior's close, and perhaps they wished that they too might have such an end.

"I tell you in all truth that this happened in the way that I describe it. I was greatly shocked by what I saw, for this was not the way I had been thought to think of the Saxons, who I had believed were heathen dogs. Because of the nobility of this Saxon king, and the warmth and respect I received from his . . . family, I was prepared to work for him in the land of the Franks. But only on the condition that I would not fight against my own people, by which I meant not only the West Britons, but all of the British, men who speak our language and live in this land."

"All of this is well and good, Rhuadrac, and it matches with what we know of your story, and what your brother has already told us."

As Brocmael spoke, Kynon had got up from the table and had begun to pace the room. I continued.

"But whilst in the land of the Franks I received letters from Ceawlin's Hall, telling me that a great tragedy had occurred, for his wife the Queen Acha was killed in a riding fall. This event caused him great despair, and it changed him, for something broke in him, and he has not been the same man since –"

Kynon broke in across my words.

"Must we listen to this? I have no interest in knowing the life story of this mad Saxon swine."

But Brocmael seemed to be intrigued by my story.

"Kynon, I would hear the rest of this story, it talks of the true affairs of kings. It interests me, and I want to know more about this Ceawlin. To prepare to defeat an enemy, it is well to first know him, and the way he thinks."

". . . as I say, Ceawlin is not now the same man. I was ordered to return to his hall, which I did, arriving back there just a few nights ago. I then saw for myself the changes wrought in him. He talks of nought but power, and that he would be supreme commander of the Aenglish in this land. He sees great visions of the future, with great ships bearing his crest sailing between great towers down a snakelike river to the open sea."

Brocmael too had now got up and slowly paced the room. He looked somehow suddenly older. The flickering light from the torches cast shadows on his face, so that he looked heavy, and weary of the affairs of men.

Only then did I recall the tale I had been told by Gavin a few winters previously – that Brocmael's own wife, by name Morganna, by all repute a good and holy woman, had also died, in her case during the difficult birth of a child. It occurred to me that it was perhaps the first time he had heard men speak of a Saxon king in this way, and that something in this story fascinated him. It was as if it gave a window into his own life, and the hardships of a king.

"So, Rhuadrac, there is some sadness in this story you tell us of our enemy. For you paint him as a flesh and blood man like us all, and so no doubt he is."

He paced the room again. By now Kynon had stopped moving and stood with his back against the far wall. My brother had been silent throughout. He knew that I must state my case myself, and persuade the chief and his son by my own words, for otherwise no trust would be forged between us.

Brocmael turned back to me.

"But we must deal with this life as we find it, not as we might wish it to be. What do you know of the Gevissa plans?"

He spoke directly.

I knew that this was a moment of truth, and one that I had known that I would have to face once I made my decision to join with my brother. I could only hope that my words did not in some way compromise Ulla, but the game was in play, and powers greater than ours would decide the final outcome.

"Before I speak you should know that I do so with no pride, for there is a sense in me that I betray this Gevissa king. He was good to me after Deorham and in the land of the Franks, and I earned wealth and status because of his sponsorship of me. However, he thought that he could use me against my own people, and I have never given him reason to think that. In this way too he has proved to me that he is much changed and his mind off-balance, for the man I first saw at Deorham would not have made this mistake."

Brocmael looked at me and spoke with some warmth in his voice.

"I believe you, Rhuadrac, son of Advil. I can see that your position is difficult."

He glanced at my brother:

"I know also of your bond with the Gevissa king's daughter, because your brother thought it right that I should know."

I looked at Cormac, who raised his eyes to mine and nodded.

"These are strange times for us all, brother, and there can be no secrets when our very existence is at stake."

"Very well. Then you might understand how much I have been wracked with these issues since my return."

Brocmael placed his hand on my shoulder.

"I believe you, Rhuadrac. Tell us now of the Gevissa king's plans."

"Ceawlin himself told me that his plan is to take Carlegion, or Chester, as his people call it."

At this assertion all three of them looked at me sharply.

"For if he takes Chester, he will finally crush our people and he will separate the north-east of this island from the west, just as surely as Deorham cut off the south-west from us here in the west. Therefore he is coming here, to Penwyrn, to break your power and to take hold of Uriconium, for he has strategic plans for that city. If he succeeds and presses on to and takes Chester, he believes that there will then be nobody to stop him becoming *Bretwalda*."

I stopped speaking. A silence descended on the room. Finally, Brocmael spoke.

"You speak plainly, Rhuadrac, and it does you credit. But the information that you give us is sobering."

He paced the room. Nobody spoke.

"It is certain that we must meet with this Ceawlin in all-out war, and if we fail, this land of ours will be forever in the hands of these Saxons, or Aenglish, or whatever they now call themselves. On the other hand, they will be very far north from their strength, so it surprises me that the Gevissa king should be so ambitious. It tells me that this once-famed strategic thinker is overreaching himself."

He again paced slowly up and down the chamber, his head bent in deep thought. He stared at the timber floor for a moment then looked up and snapped at me.

"And your strength? How many men?"

"Not many, with me, just eight in all. But they are elite warriors who have been trained for all of their useful life in the battle arts. If they are well treated and there is a prospect that they might earn gold and perhaps a little land, they will be a great benefit to you."

Cormac looked at me.

"The Roman freebooter. Is he with you?"

"Torquato is with me, so are others that will impress you with their skills."

Cormac seemed in some way pleased, but then he frowned and said:

"I say nothing about the Roman's skills as a warrior – I have never witnessed them, and I trust you in this matter. But I have never before met a man who can so readily make other men angry."

He turned to Brocmael and Kynon.

"I tell you both, this man, who certainly looks like a warrior, will rile you, he will stir you up, and you will be sore tried to see any use in him."

Brocmael laughed lightly.

"In my life I have learned that warriors, like all men, come in all shapes and forms. There will come a moment when we will learn the truth about this man, for better or worse."

He walked over to the hearth, and raked up the fading coals with the iron stave. Then he turned back to us.

"But that is enough for one day. We have much to think upon. Rhuadrac, you are welcome here, and tonight you will be our guest of honour. I understand that these matters have not been easy for you. You can tell me more about this Gevissa king, for in truth I have never heard a Saxon described in the way that you have painted him, and it much intrigues me."

At that we broke up, and Cormac and I went to find our own people, promising to return to the hall for the Martinmas feast that evening.

*

We met with our mother and Aisha who were still in the great hall. Our mother smiled at me as we approached.

"There was a time after Deorham when I was sure that I would never see you both standing together again."

She took stock of us both. I hugged her again and then gently pulled her down to sit next to me at the table.

"What happened after Deorham? I heard something of it."

My mother wiped her hands on a towel, collecting her thoughts.

"As your brother knows, we have Cadolan to thank for our own survival. He insisted that we travel westward into the old Briton kingdoms without delay. Even then we were sure that we were finished when we were seized by the Saxon war party. We did not know that the Gevissa king had talked with Farinmael. We did not know that even then you were under the protection of the Gevissa king. Cadolan acted with great bravery then, for he refused to let the Saxons pass him until they convinced him by mentioning both your names. They told him that Cormac, King Farinmael's champion, and his brother Rhuadrac, were under the protection of King Ceawlin. Until that moment, we had all made peace with the Lord our God, for we were sure that we were finished."

"Mother, you have the Gevissa princess, Ulla, to thank. She had made provision for your safety even as I was barely conscious, recovering in Ceawlin's Hall from injuries I received in the battle."

My mother nodded, glancing at Aisha.

"Then that is one more reason why I would like to meet with this woman, for she seems already bound up with the affairs of this family."

"I can but hope and pray that you do meet her, for nothing would give me more pleasure. You talk though of Cadolan – is he here?"

My mother, Aisha and Cormac all smiled.

"He is here, and we have never seen him happier. Brocmael has asked him to help supervise the monkish singers come up from Dumnonia who are to entertain us at the feast tonight, and he is taking his duties very seriously."

My mother then looked at my brother, and said to me:

"But others are here too, Rhuadrac. Cormac, tell your brother your news."

I looked across at my brother, and a great beam of a smile crossed his warrior face, which, scarred as it was, lit up with delight.

"I would have told him later. Well, little brother, Gwen is here."

"I will be delighted to see her, Cormac. Is she well?"

Cormac grinned.

"Brother, she is blooming, she is radiant. She has never been better."

I looked at all three of them.

"What is it?"

"She is with child, Rhuadrac – you will be an uncle in three months time, should our mother's god grant it to us."

Cormac's grin became a broad smile, and I punched my fist into his giant mitt with a great roar of delight.

"Brother, this is the best news I have heard in many months!"

I paused.

"So, the limb of the tree shall grow stronger then, we can begin to look forward again."

My mother looked at me with her head slightly raised, as if she was thinking back to another time, to other conversations.

"Truly, Rhuadrac, you have the looks of your father, but you have much of your grandfather's ways about you also. There is a verse-singer in you, of that I am sure."

*

I went off in search of my warriors, promising to bring them to the feast that evening. I arranged for Torquato, Veos and Gregor to join my family beforehand, so that my mother could meet some of these friends of mine, comrades in arms who had all fought and learned together in the land of the Franks.

I found them soon enough, sat on furs around a good fire in one of the round houses that look like beehives. Torquato stood up to meet me as I entered and took me away from the hearth.

"General, we will need to do something with the slave-girl. The rest of the men are already arguing about her, and it can only mean trouble if we do not do something about it."

In truth, I had already mentioned Megwei to my mother and sister. They had agreed to take her in, to find work for her in the compound. I explained this to Torquato, who nodded approvingly at the news.

"Good. Gregor seems to be much taken with the girl, and he would have drawn his sword against Felix if I had not stepped in."

I called Gregor to me now.

Gregor's land was further east even than the German lands of the Saes, but he had no love of them, for they had committed terrible acts in his land, and had forced him to take the path of a mercenary warrior at a young age. His parents had been cut down in a brutal massacre of all the adults in his village by the Saxons. All those children who by some kind fate had survived had been cast out. It was solely by his own wit and invention that he had made his way eventually to the land of the Franks, where he was taken in by a master-swordsman, one Clovis. This Clovis had himself been killed at the siege of

Avignon, a battle where I had fought on the side of Guntrum Boso, and which was the place where I met Gregor.

"So what is this commotion that Torquato mentions to me?"

"I sought only to protect the honour of this slave-girl, for Felix would ridicule her, even though she did nothing to provoke it. I can see from her face that she has suffered enough in recent times – I know what it is to be left an orphan, and things have not gone easily for her."

It was said well enough, and I did not doubt that Felix with his sly tongue might well have said enough to provoke my young friend.

"Very well then. Tell Megwei to come with us, for we go with Torquato and Veos to meet my family. It is my hope that my mother and sister can find a place for her, where she might do work and earn her living in this community."

So it was, that soon enough, my warriors, Megwei and I arrived at the home of my family at Penwyrn.

My mother and sister met us outside the front entrance:

"You are all welcome. Any friend of this son of mine is welcome to my home, and I trust that our hospitality does justice to the homecoming!"

I noted the glance that passed between Torquato and my sister. Torquato had put on his one good gold tunic and looked generally scrubbed up. I could see that he was on his best behaviour. I did not miss the shrewd secret glance that my mother gave Aisha on Torquato's arrival, nor her cool appraisal of my giant friend as he bowed too formally on being introduced to her. I could swear that my friend's face reddened at this moment, though it may have been a trick of the flickering torchlight.

My family's status, always strong because of my father, now made stronger by the marriage of Cormac and Gwen, was obvious to all in the size of the round beehive hut circle that had been made available to us.

It had one large central room, in the middle of which was the hearth under the roof space, so that the smoke could pass out easily. The lower wall was made of turf encased in stone, whereas the higher wall was of timber, and great timber ribs had been set into the timber as the height of the building advanced, with crossbeams. The roof space was made of thatch and wattle. A window was set in above the stone doorway.

In two or three places in the lower stone section of the house were recesses in which furs and rush mats were laid out, and I could see that these were sleeping places. I was told that my mother and Aisha slept here.

A second hut was joined to this one by means of a small vaulted arch, and was used as a sleeping place for Cormac and Gwen. A third hut was available as an eating place, which also served as a sleeping place for Cadolan. A fire was burning now in the central hearth, and torches set into rope coils in the walls cast a gentle light over the hut.

My mother and Aisha talked now to Megwei, deploring the rags in which she was dressed, and led her off into a small side section partitioned off by a timber wall.

At that moment, Cormac and Gwen came into the hut. Cormac, as Torquato had before him, bending almost double to get in through the entrance door.

I had not seen Gwen since a few nights before Deorham; she was much changed. Her graceful tall figure was much fuller, for she was well advanced in her child-bearing, and her face literally glowed with a rude health under the dancing light cast by the torches. Her light-gold hair fell in curls practically to her waist.

It occurred to me then almost with the force of a blow, that I had been the last of my people to see her father alive. I recalled with sudden clarity that moment when he had departed this world, and I was seized with a sense of the curious mysteries of this life. It was Farinmael's enemy, the Gevissa king, Ceawlin, who had clasped Farinmael's arm like a brother at the end. This king, now once more enemy to us all, was the father of the princess Ulla, a woman quite as beautiful as this woman who now held out her arms to me in genuine delight.

"Rhuadrac, you are now as handsome as your brother, and you look wealthy, too, as the brother of a king's champion should look!"

I hugged her, vague memories of her great warrior-father still stirring in my mind.

My brother was introduced to Veostan and Gregor, and I could see that both, even Veos, who was a veteran of many battles, were awestruck by his gigantic frame. For in the hut under the flickering torches he looked even more monstrous; his black hair had grown long and wild, and his scarred face still wore the eye-patch on his left eye. I could tell that they were silently calculating their chances against him in battle, as lifetime warriors are wont to do, and I could see that this calculation was producing only one result, which was not in their favour.

"Torquato, step forward man, come and greet my brother as a friend."

Torquato slowly stepped out of the shadows. Neither man put forward his arm. Cormac looked at him and nodded curtly.

"You are well, I trust?" The words were spoken sharply, with no warmth.

"Yes, I am well. I trust that my friend's brother is also well?"

"Yes."

There was a pause, then Torquato said, in a slightly too-formal voice:

"I congratulate you on the condition of your wife, and I hope that things go well for you both in the future."

Cormac's good eye fixed itself on my friend, who did not flinch.

"Well then, very good, that is well said."

I smiled to myself, for I knew the capacity of these two men. I knew too that they both understood that each had met a match in the other, which was an event that had never before happened to either, so that each was, as it were, circling the other, not dropping his guard for one moment. But I could see too the silent mutual respect between them. I was pleased that my friend had for once got his words right, so that the natural edge between him and my brother was not made worse.

The slight awkwardness in the room was dispelled as the canvas of the partitioned room was swept aside and Megwei stood there with my mother and sister at each side of her. The poor girl flushed red to the roots of her red hair which had been piled on top of her head and held by several green brooches. She now wore a green gown of my sister's, which was a little long for her, and had around her neck a necklace of many-coloured beads, and stones of the type called amethyst. I knew this necklace to be one of my mother's prized possessions, for it was originally from the Egyptian lands. My father had won it in battle, having been presented with it by Farinmael himself. The effect was astonishing; such was the transformation in this girl that all of the men in the room exclaimed with quiet delight. I could see that Gregor, whose eye it was that Megwei had first sought, looked up into the smoke-filled ceiling, closed his eyes and shook his head.

I laughed and clapped my hands, and proposed a drink of wine before we made our way over to the feast in the great hall. A stone jug and beakers had been set aside at a small wooden trestle, and I poured enough for each person in the room, then stood in the centre of the room, facing them all:

"Family and friends, my heart is full at this moment as I look at the people gathered in this room. For me, knowing that I will see my old teacher Cadolan later, only one person is now missing, but I will not speak of this person in these troubled times . . ."

I saw my mother and Cormac exchange glances, and was surprised to see that Aisha and Torquato did likewise.

". . . for this is a happy occasion, Gwen is with child, and with the good grace of the Christ-God of our mother, our family will go forward. We can look forward to a time when the troubles of this time are behind us, and some peace comes to this land, and we can all make true plans with our lives. So now I toast Gwendolyne, daughter of the great warrior-king, Farinmael, and wife to my brother, in the hope that the new life that is within her might help to bring some light to this land in the future."

With that, we all drank, then strode out amidst laughter through the brisk cold of the moonlit compound to the feast at the Great Hall of Penwyrn. My mother linked her arm through mine. Cormac did likewise with Gwen. Gregor and Megwei talked earnestly in a young, excited fashion in some half-learned version of the British tongue that Gregor had learnt on his travels. I saw that my sister Aisha was engaged in some deep conversation in his own language with my Roman friend. Veostan walked amongst us, quite content, asking my brother many questions on the construction of the hut that we had just left, telling us all, after his fashion, how huts were built differently in his native land over the sea.

VII

All was laughter in the great hall. Many torches blazed along the walls, so that light played everywhere, and no shadows yet fell on the floor.

Men, women and children sat at many tables, and there was a loud hubbub of shouts and shrieks and clattering of dishes as women ferried backwards and forwards between the tables, laden with plates of meat from the large hearth set in the centre of the hall. Many beakers of mead and wine had been drunk by the men and women, and children ran about to and fro between the tables. Harps and lyres were being played.

It was good to be back amongst my own people, and to hear my own language spoken on all sides. I reflected on that strange night I had spent in the hall of the Gevissa king, and the violence at the end of it.

Here, everything was different, for there were no weapons to be seen, and the men and women mixed openly, and children played under the tables. There was no sense of the violence of men, only celebration, and thanksgiving that the harvest was finished, that the work in the fields was largely done for another year, and that the early nights of winter lay before us.

I was sat at the main table nearest the hearth, very close to Brocmael and Kynon, who sat at the centre of the table. Brocmael's second queen, Ina, sat next to him on his left. To my left sat Cormac and Gwen, and Aisha had been placed between me and Kynon. The king's son was talking to my sister with great earnestness, and I could see that Aisha was listening very carefully to what he said.

My mother had been seated at her request at the head of a table of young children. I could see her telling them some tale; perhaps one of those I had heard many times myself as a child, of some old Irish lord from across the sea who after a battle met with an angel, and had turned to her God as a result of this meeting, and was therefore saved to everlasting life. I could see that the children sat spellbound listening to her, because as I knew well, my mother was a very fine storyteller.

I could see my band of warriors at a nearby table, some talking to the women serving the food and drink, others talking amongst themselves. Gregor sat next to Megwei, and still they talked. I could see that they were absorbed in each other and I thought of Ulla. I remembered how we had seemed bound to each other from the moment we met, and I smiled now to watch these two. I hoped that they could make something good for themselves.

I saw too that Salemnis and his family were there. He had taken my advice and had brought them up to Penwyrn for their safety. I saw too that Torquato had been met with squeals of delight by the dignitary's two daughters, an event that had not escaped the notice of Aisha.

I was surprised to see that Torquato did not seem his usual self; he kept looking across to my table, and I could see that he was watching Aisha and Kynon, and his face was like stone. I took note; it would be better for Torquato to enjoy himself, for there were many women in the room, and already several had tried to speak with him.

Just then, Brocmael stood up and quiet descended over the hall.

"My people, we are gathered here to celebrate St Martin's Eve, and we have already broken bread together, and ate meat, and drunk a little wine. For tomorrow we begin the great fast, in preparation for the birth of our Lord. Be happy this night, for you should know that we have trying times in front of us. I have received definite information this day . . ."

He looked across to where I sat.

". . . that what we have heard rumoured is true.The Gevissa king is drawing together his forces in the south. He prepares to march on up through the Hwicca territory in an attempt to spread his kingdom further from that territory and to come up into our lands. He means to try us, so once again we must prepare to meet him and to defend our lands from these damned heathens."

The hall was silent as the people there assembled pondered the weight of his words.

"But all of that is for tomorrow. Tonight we shall eat and drink, we will thank God for our blessings and we will have verses and some singing too. Where is the verse-maker? Bring him out, let us hear his verses!"

With that, Brocmael sat down and the harps struck up the tune that marks the arrival of the poets. There appeared from the back of the hall a lean-looking fellow, quite young, with blonde curled hair and a cheerful face. It was clear to all that he was a verseman, for he carried a lyre and leapt onto a table near the harps and cleared his throat. Quietly strumming his lyre, he began to declaim, in the verse form of the Powys people that they call *warrior's triplet*, against the steady melodic beat of the harps:

"Brocmael's Palace is bright tonight
With torches, with fires
The people laugh and shout and poets sing!

Brocmael's Palace is flushed tonight
With the blood of roast meats, with wine
The people eat and drink and make merry!

Brocmael's Palace is alive tonight
The bright torches flame in the roof
The people are happy round the hearth of their prince!

Brocmael's Palace is at peace tonight
The child plays next to his mother
The people thank God for the close of harvest!

Brocmael's Palace is at rest tonight
For the field work is done
The people turn away from the ploughed furrow!"

As the poet continued to sing and speak his quiet verses of thanksgiving, I noticed Torquato get up from the table and leave by one of the side doors set out along the wall beside my table. Excusing myself to Brocmael, I got up and followed him. I found him leant back against the lower stone wall of the hall.

"So, you great ape, how is it with you? I did not see you up to your usual tricks in there!"

"Ah, Cub-General. No, you are right, maybe I sicken with something, for I do not seem part of the feast, somehow."

I looked at my Roman friend and could see that his great spirit was subdued. We said nothing for a few minutes. The night was cold and clear, and the compound was gently lit by the moon, so that already I could see that a light frost was beginning to form over the meadow into which the great hall had been set. Many stars hung in the heaven-tree above us, and our breath came as smoke.

"I see that your sister is close to the king's son."

Torquato spoke quietly.

So. That was the problem.

"You and me are not winning in these matters, Rhuadrac. I think we would be better off in battle, for there at least we can try to control the outcome, and we might go down, but we will go down fighting."

I said nothing, for there was nothing I could think to say that would lighten my friend's mood.

Only rarely did I see him like this. I remember once, in the land of the Franks in the city called Tours, I had found him in similar shape. I found out eventually that, just a few days before I had first met him, a great friend of his had been dragged from a tavern and robbed and murdered by brigands whilst he had been drunk. Torquato, who had promised to meet with his friend that night, had instead been bedding a woman, so that Torquato blamed himself for the death of his friend. It had taken him weeks to recover from it, and from time to time it would return as a memory to haunt him. I had learnt that my friend set high expectations of himself in the matter of friendship, and he believed that he had let himself down.

"Come, Torquato, let us return to the feast. There is still plenty of time to meet some laughing serving wench, who might willingly fill your night with joy, and keep your clodhoppers from freezing! I see that Salemnis is here at this place, and that he has brought his lovely daughters with him."

But Torquato did not laugh. Instead, he turned towards me and placed his large hand on my shoulder.

"I'm tired. I think I will turn in. Give my respects to your mother."

So saying, he lumbered off into the night, making his way to the hut that had been prepared for him.

I returned to the great hall. The poet was still declaiming. I could see that his work was appreciated, for men women and children sat rapt, listening carefully to his every word.

"God's Dove circles the palace tonight
All are warm in His embrace
The cold dark winds blow against the oak door in vain!

God's Dove is with the people tonight
The child lies calm in her mother's arms
The warrior sips wine, and his wife's bed bids him welcome!

God's Dove watches over all in the palace tonight
His spirit flows gently o'er the lake below
Let tomorrow's storms come – they have no place in the palace now!"

The poet played two more quiet notes on his lyre, and stopped speaking. He stood up, bowed, and stepped down from the table amidst a quiet clamour of mugs and beakers being pounded on tables. His gentle verses had been well received, for they matched well the happy mood in the hall.

I returned to my place at the top table. Aisha caught my arm as I went past and whispered into my ear as I bent down to her.

"Where is your Roman friend?"

"He was . . . tired, and thought that he might turn in for the night."

"Well, that saddens me, for I had hoped to speak with him again tonight. There is more to your friend than one might guess in a first meeting with him."

I sat down at the table, wondering what it was that Aisha wanted to speak to Torquato about.

Brocmael waved his arm to the back of the hall, and out of the side chamber poured a phalanx of monks, all dressed in grey robes, their heads shaven. They lined up in front of the great hearth, in four ranks of five. I could see with delight that my teacher, Cadolan, fussed around them, standing one monk here and another there, generally trying to organise what seemed to me to be an already well-organised group of monks. The choirmaster, an elderly man with no hair and a kindly face, pointed out a place for Cadolan on the front row, then stood in front of the choir with his arms upraised.

Brocmael stood up again. The choirmaster lowered his arms.

"Monks of Lanwethinoc! You are welcome here in this palace tonight. For we know that you have taken risks to come by boat from your Bishop's hall in Dumnonia to come here at this time. You are doubly welcome, and be sure to give my thanks and greetings to your good Bishop Wethinoc upon your safe return!"

With that, the king sat down.

The choirmaster looked back to the choir, hesitated, then looked back to Brocmael. Finally satisfied that he would not be further interrupted, he looked back to the choir, raised his arms once more, then threw both rigidly in front of him. Immediately a glorious sound filled the hall, its Latinate murmur filling all corners of the hall with its wondrous otherworldly texture:

TE DEUM laudamus: te Dominum confitemur

I took stock of the people around me. Brocmael and my mother were enthralled by the sound, for they had closed their eyes and were lost in its majestic cadence; my sister, Aisha, too, was impressed, for I could see that she lowered her head and smiled. Cormac and Gwen looked at each other and then they too smiled; Kynon looked bemused, as if this was a vaguely pleasant interlude before he could get down to the serious business of the night.

Sanctus, Sanctus, Sanctus, Dominus Deus Sabaoth

My warrior-band seemed mostly bored. Veos, though, seemed entranced, as if it might have been the first time he had heard such singing, and he was curious as to how it had been created, for he looked with a question in his face at the choirmaster. Gregor and Megwei, meanwhile, continued to talk between themselves, and I smiled as I watched them, for I was quite sure that they were but barely aware of this glorious singing:

Te gloriosus Apostolorum chorus

Aye, and this glorious monkish chorus continued to sing in their wonderful harmonies, as if we had been visited from heavenly singers, for it was a beautiful sound, and as good as anything I had heard in the lands of the Franks. The flames from the torches and the hearth had by now begun to cast great shadows over the walls of this hall in the middle of Britain, and still this harmony from the Otherworld rang out amongst us

Miserere nostri, Domine, miserere nostri.

The last grace notes reverberated around the hall then fell away, and there was a silence in the hall. Then loud applause burst out from the benches, and the people gathered there banged their mugs on the table. My teacher, Cadolan, stood there with a great beaming smile on his face. I could see that tears rolled down his cheeks as he was momentarily reunited once more with those whose way of life he had once tried to maintain.

Cormac had stood up at the table and indicated that I should follow him. Kynon had also stood up, and was making his way to a side chamber behind the place where he and his father had sat.

I followed them, and found myself in a small room with no hearth, but with pegs lined up along the walls, and from these pegs hung leather cases, and in the leather cases were manuscripts. I took it to be a reading room, and it was warm enough from the heat generated by the fires in the great hall.

Kynon stood over against the far wall.

"The king will be listening to the choir for the rest of the night, and will ask for several repeat versions. I thought that we could make good use of the time to talk."

The words were neutral, neither mocking nor warm.

Cormac stood in front of Kynon.

"Yes, of course. What do you wish to discuss?"

"The king and I have been talking through the information you brought to us, and we have been making plans. We would like your views on those plans . . ."

Cormac and I nodded, and waited for him to continue.

"There are advantages and disadvantages to consider if we allow the Gevissa king to make his way through the upper Severn to meet us here. The advantages are that his lines of communication and supply will be stretched, he will be far from his home base, and there is no love between him and his German countrymen in Mercia so they will not be persuaded to come to his aid."

We both agreed.

"The disadvantages are that a defeat for us Britons here, in our own stronghold, will be decisive for him, and there will be no second chance for us. It is likely that the scenario you painted will come to pass, and the Gevissa king will be in a position of great power not only over the Britons, but over his countrymen also, so that none in the land will be able to withstand him. Our communications with the Britons in Gwent and the Irish in Dyfed may be cut off, so that our chances of gathering again to throw him over will be much reduced."

All of this made sense to us. We waited for him to tell us what conclusion had been reached.

Kynon looked at Cormac.

"You have hinted that there are Saxons amongst the Hwiccas that are disillusioned with the Gevissa king?"

"That is true, for I have heard them speak myself. They are settled men, their lands give them what they require, they have no need to make further war, which they now begin to see is the plan of a power-crazed man, a man who is no longer fit to lead them."

"Do you believe that they can be stirred up, told that to fight against Ceawlin is to fight in defence of the lands that they themselves have now planted, and tilled, and ploughed? Stirred up so much that they might be persuaded to march with us east of your own land to meet the Gevissas before they reach the upper Severn Valley? In other words, if we act quickly now, before the Saxons begin their march, and we march down the upper Severn and, together with the Hwiccas, we meet in battle with Ceawlin on the borders of his own land?"

Cormac and I looked at each other. I said:

"It is a bold plan. I know the way that Ceawlin thinks, for I have planned many strategies with him in Gaul. He thinks that the Britons are nearly finished. He will not expect his own people to rise against him. He will not expect a march against him, only stubborn defence in a place of his own choosing. As a plan, what you say has many good parts to it."

Cormac frowned.

"The Hwiccas are Saxons. It is one thing not to fight for a king, it is another thing altogether to fight against him. We might at least try them to see if they will stay neutral, for if they will, that is knowledge worth knowing."

Kynon bowed his head slightly, acknowledging that such a position was itself desirable to the Hwiccas joining with Ceawlin on his march east of the lower Severn.

Cormac continued:

"And if I can persuade the Hwiccas either way, who can you bring to the field?"

"Gwent, Gwynedd and perhaps the Irish in Dyfed, even. If we use boats, parts of Dumnonia and the far south-west Britons. Already this evening our men go with my father's letters to these kings. Later tonight the choirmaster will be told of our plans. The Gevissa king might be in for a nasty surprise."

We talked with Kynon a little while longer. We agreed that Cormac would leave with me and my war-band in the morning to return to the lower Severn, to see if the Hwiccas would join us, and, if so, to prepare for battle with Ceawlin on the northern borders of his own land.

Cormac and I left the great hall and stepped outside into the cool night air. My brother looked up into the night sky, now dense with stars.

"So it starts again, brother. Maybe after this I will have something to talk to my son about, something more than being the failed champion of a dead king."

His words surprised me. I had not known that these matters still rankled with him.

"Your son, if your child is a son, will be proud of you in any event, Cormac. It is what you are as a man, not what you have done in this world that they will consider – and anyway, you have already done much in your life."

"We shall see, Rhuadrac, we shall see. But what of you and this dilemma with the Gevissa princess? What will happen there?"

I too stared up into the vast night sky. I felt suddenly alone, even though I stood next to my brother and great friend. I felt alone standing there under the stars, and I did not really understand why.

"I do not know, brother. I really do not know. Perhaps I will pray to our mother's God, the Dove that the poet spoke of."

With that, we both turned and went back into the hall.

By now the choir had finished singing, and though the torches were starting to burn low and the shadows had begun to stretch over the walls, I could see Cadolan standing with my mother and Aisha, and they were all laughing. Cadolan was beaming, and it was plain to see that singing with his fellow monks had made this a special night for him. He was flushed, and sweated a little, and even as we spoke he reached for what was plainly not his first beaker of wine.

"May the Lord God be praised, but I have never heard better singing. Could you hear me Ethna, did my voice carry?"

Cadolan and my mother had known each other many winters – she had known him since she had first met my father and they had been through many a crisis together.

"Cadolan, your voice boomed from the front of the choir, where no doubt you had been placed so that the people could clearly hear your voice even amidst such beautiful singers."

"Boomed? Yes, that's it, boomed! By God, but I myself could feel the strength in my voice tonight. Rhuadrac, did you hear me? Could you see me there, singing with my fellow monks, providing a beautiful *Te Deum* for the people of this place? I had to correct them a few times in rehearsal you know, just one or two points, the descant, the upper harmony – specialised matters of course, so I cannot possibly go into detail."

"Cadolan, I heard you and I saw you, you were magnificent."

"Magnificent? Yes, I think so too! Magnificent!"

We all laughed. It was rare to see our friend and teacher so animated. It was clear that this experience had meant much to him.

Then the king himself came across to join us, and he talked long to my mother about the singing of the choir, for he was obviously much moved by it, and turned then to Cadolan.

"I hear that you have wonderful organising skills, Cadolan – the choirmaster himself singled you out for special praise, telling me that you have a remarkable voice."

Cadolan positively pulsed with pleasure.

"It's the weight you know. That's what does it. A man needs a bit of ballast behind him for the high notes, or he will not make them. Mark my words, he will not make those high notes!"

Cormac and I had a few words with Brocmael, confirmed that we had spoken with his son, had agreed on the next steps, and would leave tomorrow for the land of the Hwiccas.

"Then Godspeed to you both and to your men. Your mission is crucial if we are to have any slight prospect of success."

With that, he wished good night to my mother, sister, and Gwen, congratulated Cadolan on his work once more, then moved back to his son and his family, and soon after left the hall.

On the way back to the huts that night, Aisha caught up with me and drew me aside slightly.

"Tell me truthfully, why did your friend leave the feast tonight?"

I hesitated, and looked down at my sister, we who had been friends since all of those long years ago. My heart felt glad to see her again, and I no longer felt alone, for we were kin, and whatever was to come in life, would come, and I would meet it squarely.

"Aisha, you should know that my friend . . . hoped to talk with you also tonight. When he saw you deep in conversation with Kynon during the feast, I think that he was sad, for he felt he had no chance of talking further with you."

"I think that your friend is a very silly man, Rhuadrac."

But she smiled as she said it.

"You might tell him that the Lord Kynon was talking at me all night about the duties of a wife, about what he knew to be the duties of a wife, and that wives must know their place before their men, and treat their men with respect at all times. You might tell him that I did not care much for such conversation, for I was bored, and did not get to say one thing in all of the time he was lecturing me."

Then she paused.

"No, do not tell him any of that, let him work it out for himself."

Then she laughed an artful laugh. I looked at her, with her fearless eyes and spirited temper, and it struck me again that there was far more to my quiet sister than I once had allowed for.

"Aisha, you should know that Torquato, who I love like a brother, has lived the life of a rogue, is a great sinner, and has broken the hearts of many women in the land of the Franks. He is the way he is, and though I believe he has a great kind heart at root, he knows nothing of the ways to treat a woman properly. He has been a freebooter all of his life, and he knows only the ways of the freebooter. You must have a care in your dealings with him, for he may cause you distress even when he does not mean to."

Aisha fixed me with a smile.

"You leave that for me to work out, and let us see if your friend is the man that I think he is."

With that, she ran across to where my mother stood waiting for her, and I made my way back to the hut of my war-band, thinking of puppets, of leaves blowing in the wind, of the vast open spaces of the star-lit night sky, of the beautiful harmonies of the monkish choir led by my teacher, Cadolan, and then, once more, of Ulla, the Gevissa princess who seemed now more than ever divided from me.

*

PART IV

In the Land of the Hwiccas, Fethan Leag, Aftermath

I

The next morning we rose with the first light, for we had much ground to cover and time was of the essence if Brocmael's plan of forcing the battle early was to have any chance of success.

Torquato and I met with my brother on the way to the horse paddock. He was dressed much as he had been on the eve of the Battle of Deorham, for gleaming *Gaeallon* was strapped across his back, and his mail shirt hung at his shoulder. I confess, it was good to see him dressed in this garb, for I knew that the farmer's life had not really fulfilled him, had made him brittle, and now he looked what he truly was, a warrior from head to toe. The change in him was marked, for he was full of high spirits, and I could see that the start of the battle-spirit was even now starting to flow through him.

"So, then, no more nonsense, we go to proper work!"

He smiled, and even clasped Torquato by the arm and shook it vigorously.

"Now then, soldier, you and I can go about our work properly, heh? No more hanging about, discussions, plans, waiting for the real work to begin!"

Torquato, still subdued from the night before, smiled and nodded.

"Aye, big man, this is about all you and I are good for, and it is about time that we had the chance to prove it."

We got the horses ready and met with the rest of my war-band, already mounted at the main gate of the compound.

We left the fortress and turned south-east, towards the ford at Uriconium, for that was the quickest route back down to the lower Severn and the land of the Hwiccas.

At each side of me rode Rama Bec and Little Sigfeldt.

Since we had arrived in my homeland, a jest had started up between me and the Syrian. He would tell me that he thought of this place as a land inhabited by barbarians, a belief made certain by his brief visit to the city of Uriconium, because he refused to believe that such a city had simply been allowed to crumble away.

"In my land, we had cities like this many hundreds of years ago, and they still flourish today, great centres of commerce, and the world's trade passes through the gates of such a city. Yet here? You have a few barter markets hiding under some threadbare canvas, and sometimes you sell good products, but it is a village compared to my land. All is still forming in this place, all is becoming something else, nothing is settled, whereas in my lands we know our culture, and we have known it for many centuries!"

Then I would defend my land, and I would tell him that Britons also journeyed to the lands east of Gaul, and even traded with Scipio's land, for I had seen goods from the great country over the southern seas bartered in British markets. Then Rama Bec would laugh quietly, for he thought the matter was beyond dispute. Britain was a barbaric place compared to the land of his forefathers. From the descriptions this master-storyteller gave me of his land, I could not disagree with him.

As we rode, I talked from time to time with these two men, and I could tell that both were happy to be on an expedition, for that is what these warriors lived for; no matter what they appeared to be, they were true fighting men, trained in the battle arts, and like all such men they only felt fully alive when the battle or the promise of battle was once more underway.

After a few furlongs I pulled up next to Torquato.

"You are very quiet today, you big lump. What is it?"

"Oh, nothing, nothing that the next battle will not put right. Nothing at all."

"My sister talked to me last night."

"Oh?"

"Yes. She wanted to know where you had got to."

The sullen look disappeared from Torquato's face.

"What did she say then?"

"Oh, nothing much. She did say though that she missed the opportunity to talk to you."

"Well, there was no chance. She spent all night talking to that walking statue."

"Apparently not. He spent all night talking to her. And she did not like it. But you have got to work out why she did not like it."

"Oh? Did she say that?"

"She did, and one or two other things also, but I cannot tell you those things."

Then I laughed into the bemused face of my friend, whipped my horse and rode on.

*

A day and a half's ride later we had crossed back into the land of the Hwiccas. By now we travelled with extra caution, for already we had seen several advance parties of the Saes, but we had matters to attend to, so we had agreed from the outset that we would only engage with the Saes war-bands as a last resort.

Cormac headed for a farm to the east of Corinium. There he knew a Saxon, one Edelwine, who had some repute amongst his fellow Hwiccas as a leader, for he took the lead at the tun meetings and was prepared to speak his mind.

Cormac told us that this man had said, at the right time, when the right people were in the room, that he could not see the purpose in further war – had not the Hwiccas good land to till and to plough? Did not their wives and children grow fat in this fertile land and their farms prosper, and were there not markets for their produce? Even the Britons were bearable, up to a point. Why then would they join with Ceawlin to make further wars? What was in it for them? More wars could only increase the land and the gold of the king, it could not improve the lot of the Hwiccas, for they had fought in the past, and had fought well; now they wished to enjoy their land, and observe their own ways in the temples, and watch their children grow.

So had this Edelwine talked with Cormac in the room, and then they had broken bread together and found that they could talk, so were friends after a fashion. Edelwine had made his meaning clear to my brother. He was for settlement, and not war. He was for putting down roots in this green and fertile land, and he saw no reason in threatening his own prosperity to further the power urge of the old Gevissa king.

But it was one thing to settle in this place; it was another to take arms against your own people to defend it, and that was the burden of our visit, to try these Hwiccas, to see if they would join us against the Saxons of Wessex.

We arrived at the site of Edelwine's farm in the early evening, to be met by a strange sight.

It was unusually warm, as often happens at Martinmas, and there had been light rain earlier in the day, so that the soil gave off a moist earthy smell, as of ploughed fields.

We had come by way of the high ground, from the north-east, to take advantage of the view offered down the gently sloping valley to the farm. It was as well that we did, for on reaching the crest of the hillside we could immediately see that a large Saes war-band, as many as perhaps forty warriors, was encamped in the grounds of the farm.

I looked across to my brother and Torquato.

"What do you make of it?"

My brother replied first.

"Not good. Either the Saxon has joined with his countrymen or the Gevissa king has heard of his speeches and has sent a war-band to try him and his loyalties. My guess is the second option – Ceawlin will want to root out anybody capable of stirring up the people before he takes his men through to the upper Severn, otherwise his line of supply and retreat will be exposed."

Torquato nodded.

"That sounds right. Do we pay them a visit or do we move on, try another route?"

I thought for a moment.

"I suggest that we pay them a visit, but quietly. If we find that this Edelwine has joined with them, then we move on. If he has not, and they mistreat him, then his rescue will bring us favour in this region, if the feeling against the Gevissa king is as strong as we believe it to be."

So decided, we explained to the men our thoughts, and I told them that the three of us would attempt to reach the farm immediately, for by now dusk was falling, to see how matters stood. Veostan was given clear instructions to leave one man with the horses and then move the rest to the flat floor of the valley, so that the farm could be reached in minutes if the need arose. If we had not returned in two hours, then he was ordered to take the men back to Penwyrn; again, if he saw five sweeps of a lit bough in the small copse to the right of the farm huts, he was to bring the men in and to expect hand-fighting. With that, Cormac, Torquato and I moved off the crest of the hill and headed down into the gentle valley below.

Torquato led the way. I had long ago learned to appreciate his tracking skills, beaten into him from childhood by the mercenary lifestyle; he had been taught by skilled men that a wrong step, a false move, could easily result in disaster and death. We kept low and followed the bed of a small stream down into the valley, walking through the stream itself as we got down to the valley floor. We could see and hear soon enough that Cormac had been right.

The farm was a cluster of round houses, mostly of wood and wattle, no doubt built up from the ring post structure so typical of the design used by my people. This farm had once belonged to a Briton, Sagolan, but he had been lost at Deorham, and since then Edelwine, who had fought and won praise in that battle, had taken the farm.

Cormac had told us his story. A season later, Edelwine had called for his wife and children to come over in new boats from the land east of the Franks, and he had built up the land and the stock. Now, more of his relations had joined him, and several more huts had been constructed in the compound.

On one side of the compound, away from the huts, we could see several campfires, and fur-clad figures moved around in the glare of the flames. The smell of woodsmoke and roasting meat filled our nostrils, and we could hear loud guttural laughter drift over from the camp. Between this open space and the huts we could see several prone bodies of all sizes, still laying where they had fallen in various twisted shapes in the mud.

Torquato grunted:

"Definitely a raiding war-band. Those are men, women and children on the floor, hacked down where they stood, no chance to defend themselves. Perhaps this man Edelwine is amongst them. There is something going on in the main hut. We need to take a closer look."

By now, Cormac and I too could hear shouting and growls coming from the round-hut in the centre of the compound.

"Around the back first, listen, then in through the front door."

Cormac and I nodded in agreement.

Torquato led the way in zig-zag fashion across the now dark boundary of the farm compound, then cut directly to the back of the main hut.

As we got closer, the howls and screams grew louder, and we could still smell burnt meat, which puzzled us. Cormac and I reached Torquato who was crouched against the mud and wattle wall of the hut, listening intently, and peering through a small gap between the wattle and one of the internal fence posts of the hut.

Torquato pointed away from the wall and we moved back twenty paces. He whispered:

"I think your man Edelwine is still with us, but only just. Hot irons, to the flesh, now they are moving to the eyes. Five men by my guess, but there is a woman and three children also in the room. Speed is everything. We need to move now."

I held up my hand.

"You two in the hut. The noise is likely to bring over the rest of them. After the first rush I go to the copse to bring our people in. None of the Saes can go free, for Ceawlin will learn of our presence here, which will be fatal to our plans."

Cormac and Torquato nodded, and I drew *Saesbane* from its scabbard. Cormac drew his short sword and moved to the front. He looked at the two of us and smiled, and I knew that cruel smile, for I had seen it after Deorham, and it unsettled me still.

"Go!"

In one movement the two giants were around the side of the hut and in through the front door. I heard a muffled exclamation and one silenced half-shout, then the sound of thuds and half-screams.

I crouched at the side of the hut and watched the campfires some thirty or forty paces or so away from me. Two huge makeshift torches of wood and straw had been set up on poles on either side of the clearing between the fire and the huts; two or three warriors had turned towards the hut on the sound of the half-shout and now stood up, looking at each other. Hesitantly, they reached for their spears on the ground beside them. Just then, a loud male scream pierced the compound space, to be immediately stifled in mid-scream. As one man the war-band warriors began to leap to their feet, reaching for their weapons, and already the first two or three began to hesitantly walk towards the hut, still not sure if the cause of the scream was the continuing sound of torture or something else.

Just then, Cormac and Torquato stepped out of the hut. Cormac held something in his left hand. Both warriors strode towards the campfires, for the sight of these two giants had stopped the Saes in their tracks. Cormac raised the object in his left hand.

"Your leader appears to have lost his head."

So saying, he dismissively tossed the object by its hair into the space between where he and Torquato stood opposite the war-band. As it landed, the Saes warriors stared at it, then took several steps backwards.

Cormac turned to me as I ran up to them.

"Leave the first rush to me and the Roman, brother. As they come, take the bough from the fire and bring the rest of your people in."

I moved around to their far side and moved away perhaps ten paces.

Cormac swung *Gaeallon* down from his broad shoulders, and my brother and my friend took up their battle stance, standing shoulder to shoulder.

Even as they did so, a great howl rose up from the Saes and they came at them. The first three or four men to reach my brother were immediately scythed down by *Gaeallon*. Even before my brother's first movement had completed the sweep of its arc the Roman was in amongst them, his oddly graceful strokes taking out three of the Saxons in a blur of sword and knee and head, each move measured, fatal, precise.

I had already reached the nearest fire. I snatched a bough from the flames and ran the ten paces to the copse and swept the bough over my head, swept it five times towards the hillcrest, and, dropping it, turned back to the fight.

The Saxons had withdrawn back again some fifteen paces, in awe of the power and skill of the men in front of them, realising for the first time that these two giants that faced them were in some way exceptional, and that they had never seen their like before.

I ran back to my brother and my friend. Both barely registered my arrival; each had on that stone face that I knew so well, each deeply concentrated on what was in front of them. I took up my place at the left side of my brother. Again the Saes came at us, and again *Gaeallon* swept through them. Then they were in amongst us, and I fought for my life.

But I had learnt from the best teacher, who was Torquato, and so I too knew better how to feint, and to parry and to use my opponent's rush against him. I brought *Saesbane* down across the neck of a Saxon, even as I parried a thrust from a second with my shield and kicked another full in the guts with a third movement, driving *Saesbane* through his ribs as his body fell forward.

As I leant to retrieve my sword, I felt a great rush of iron just above my head as *Gaeallon* cleaved through the air into the head of the second Saxon even as his dagger plunged towards my exposed neck. But I had no time to think or to thank as another Saes came at me with his spear and I parried and cut deep into his right hand at the wrist before finishing him off with a short stab through the ribs.

Beside me Torquato moved with that measured flow, all of his movements learned and perfected over many years, never leaving his back exposed, his eyes almost trance-like as his limbs moved expertly, all of his blows killing blows, for so he had been taught, and I knew that he would not waste energy in the execution of his dark arts.

Alarm and fatigue swept through them, and again the Saxons fell back, and I could see that already they had lost almost half of their number.

I breathed heavily, for the fighting had been full on, and I had not fought in many weeks, so that my heart and lungs were not yet battle honed. Torquato, I knew, trained every day, so that his state of preparation was always high, for this was his work and he treated his work with the utmost respect. My brother was some freak of nature, for I never saw him prepare for battle, but in battle he was a champion, and I only saw him tired once, and that was in Ceawlin's Hall after Deorham.

I took in great lungfuls of air and looked at Torquato and my brother, both of whom seemed barely troubled. Cormac, his scarred face intent and fully alive, looked at the Saes war-band and then back at me and said:

"Your man Veostan must bring his warriors in through the horse paddock and cut them off, otherwise these farmers will turn and run after the next charge at best."

"Veostan is time-served Cormac, he knows what will be required, you can have faith in him, as I have."

We could see that there was already confusion in the Saxon ranks opposite us. Four or five of their bravest men were exhorting the rest to charge again, but some others held back, unsure, real fear in their eyes, some backing away towards the fires.

Just then, Veos arrived running with the others, and sure enough he came through the copse in which the Saxon horses were held, so that the line of retreat of the Saes was now cut off. We could see that real fear then descended on the Saxon war-band, for even though they still outnumbered us by more than two to one, they had seen the full force and power of the warriors in front of them. Now they could see that more expert soldiers reinforced them, and cut off their line of escape, so that the outcome was certain and they were finished.

Cormac wiped a huge forearm across his brow and spat, lifting *Gaeallon* as he spoke.

"Now let us see this business through to its close."

So the matter was concluded; the Saes war-band was destroyed, and their end was pitiful. They could not have thought that such destruction could have come to visit them out of the dark, even as they had sat down to their meal at the fire, their grim work of destroying the farmer's family completed.

On our side, there were no more than flesh wounds and bruises, and we stood in the clearing between the huts and the fires amidst the fallen Saxon war-band, their ranks laid out vanquished before us. There was no exultation or celebration, for unlike battle, this was work, mercenary business, and no false pride would be taken in the destruction of so many lives.

I shouted to my men.

"Do not waste their food – eat what can be salvaged, but no mead or wine, keep your heads clear tonight. Then dig a pit; destroy all evidence of what has occurred here tonight; this way we might at least buy some more time for our mission against Ceawlin."

Cormac and Torquato had returned to the central hut, and I followed them there. It was a grisly sight; the bodies of the Saxons had been removed. I could see that two cartwheels had been set up; a man had been tied to each, and the body of one of the men was still tied to one. A brief glance at him was enough to tell me that he was finished and that terrible torture had been inflicted upon him, for his body was a red mass of wheals and burns, and his eyes had been put out with the hot irons.

Another man had been cut down from the second wheel; he was still alive and was being treated with water and cloths by a heavily built woman of middle years, who I took to be his wife. Cormac confirmed it and told me that this man was Edelwine, and that it was his brother who had been put to death next to him.

"He is in bad shape now, but he will survive and recover quickly enough, for we arrived just in time; your friend was right, for his eyes would have been put out also. In front of his woman and children . . ."

Cormac's voice trailed off, and I followed his eye to the corner of the room, where two girls cried in each others arms, and a boy of about sixteen winters stood away from them, clenching and unclenching his fists and grinding his teeth. I could see that his young face was deathly pale, and I knew that what he had witnessed in that hut that evening would not leave him, but would colour his thoughts for the rest of his life.

I moved over to him and placed my hand on his shoulder, talking to him in the language of my people, which I could but only hope that he might understand.

"Have courage, lad. Your father lives and will soon recover; your mother and sisters need you to be strong now. This is one part of life only; do not let it fill your head forever, there is also beauty in this life if you keep your eyes open and alive to it."

But the boy turned his terror-stricken eyes from me and wrenched his shoulder from under my arm and cowered back against the wall of the hut. Torquato and Cormac stood at my side and I saw them glance at each other at my words. Cormac stepped forward.

"Leave it to me, brother, I will tell him your poet's words."

Cormac said something in the Saes language to the lad, who looked at me doubtfully and said something to Cormac in his own language, which Cormac heard through, then turned back to me:

"The lad's name is Edel. He is saying that he cannot believe that his own people have done this. He cannot believe that it is the Saxons themselves who have killed his uncle and the rest of his family."

The boy had stopped speaking and his eyes filled full of tears, and he looked away to the far corner of the room, his body pressed close to the wall of the hut. His mother came over to us; her heavy face was drawn and pale, but I could see too that she was grateful, though bewildered by the events of the day. She talked in the Saxon language, sobbing from time to time, but collected herself and finished what she had to say. Cormac spoke her words:

"She says that the Saxon war-band arrived at the farm huts at sun-up. At first they had appeared friendly, but the talks with her husband and his brother had turned ugly when the talk turned to war against the Britons in the north. Edelwine had refused to fight, and it was then that the Saxon leader had accused him of treachery, as the Gevissa king had long suspected. The Saxons had then turned on the family and killed them, torturing Edelwine and his brother to find out who he was in league with."

The Hwicca woman said something else, looking at both me and Cormac as she did so. Cormac then looked at me and smiled grimly.

"It would seem that we are now notorious in these parts, for the Saxon leader wanted to know if Edelwine is in league with the giant and his brother, who are themselves traitors and have spurned the protection so generously granted them by the Gevissa king."

All three of us thought on these words for a moment. I looked at the woman's exhausted face and said to my brother:

"Then we must move quickly. Ask her if her husband is fit to talk."

We could ourselves by now see that her husband was struggling to raise his heavy body, and had managed to lean his weight on one arm and look across at the body of his dead brother, and then his large head dropped, his long hair fell down to his chest, and a great moan went out from him.

The woman moved back to her husband and wiped his brow with the wet cloth, talking to him and gesturing over to us. Edelwine lay back on the skins on the floor and groaned, but nodded and the Saxon woman indicated that we should try and talk to him.

We knelt next to him and he started to talk in a version of our language that we could understand. He spoke haltingly and feebly, and sometimes coughed and caught his breath, but for all that, he spoke clearly enough and we knew that we were listening to a strong-minded man whose thoughts were now set.

"I am . . . pleased to see you, Britons. Another few minutes and these bastards would have killed us all."

He paused and coughed up some blood. His wife wiped his mouth with the cloth.

"This madman, this great king of ours . . . I am sure this was his intention, to finish us off, all of my family. All of us Saxons from his own land."

He winced and coughed again. We waited for a few minutes as he wrestled with the pain wracking his body. He looked at me then.

"What is your name?"

"I am Rhuadrac, brother of Cormac, who you know."

"Ah yes, Rhuadrac of the verses. There is word amongst our people that you and the Gevissa princess are strong with each other. Is it true?"

I was shocked to hear of this, here in the Hwicca country. I looked into the face of this man, this Saxon farmer, who seemed to know so much about my affairs.

"It is true. But I ask you and your family to say nothing of it, for much trouble will come to her if her father is made aware of it."

"I understand, I understand."

He paused again, the air in his lungs coming in long wheezing gasps. He looked across for a few moments at the body of his dead brother, then looked back to us.

"My mind is made up. I will do all in my power to stir my people up against this mad Gevissa king."

Edelwine said this in a quiet voice, and we knew that such words did not come easily to him.

"There will be a meeting of the hundred in four days' time. All of those who wish to speak on this matter will be allowed to do so, should they wish to. If I am strong enough, I will attend, and I will make my voice known.They will hear what has happened here today, at the hands of their own king. My people will hear from my lips that the giant Briton and his brother with his war-band have saved what is left of my family. Then we will decide what we will do with the plans of this king of Wessex."

"If you think that this is right, then so be it."

He looked at me, Cormac and Torquato.

"You three should come with me. If the meeting goes well enough, come and state your case."

He looked across to Cormac.

"You should know that my people sing of your strength in our verses. You will be allowed to speak, for you have earned the respect of those that fought against you at Deorham and survived to tell of it."

Cormac looked down at the stricken Saxon and nodded once.

"So be it. We will come with you and state our case, should the moment prove right."

Edelwine lay his head back onto the floor.

"My brother was a simple farmer who came here across the seas with his family at my invitation to settle in this fertile land. And now he is butchered by his own people."

We could all see that he needed to rest, that the events of the day had begun to pour back into his mind. We turned to go.

"These were not the actions of a wise lord. There can be no more allegiance to such a madman."

At these words he ceased speaking and asked his wife if he might drink some water, for his body was wracked with pain and he could barely breathe.

We left him then, and walked over to the campfire. We could hear the sound of digging in the copse, with heavy weights being lugged about, and I knew that Veos and the others were carrying out my instructions.

II

During the next three days, whilst Edelwine recovered, we made our plans. Little Sigfeldt was sent back to Brocmael with a wax-wood that would tell the Powys chief that we had met with Edelwine, that he was for our cause, and that Brocmael should continue to prepare with his allies for an early strike in the battle.

By the end of the second day, Edelwine was much recovered. He could now stand again, and move around slowly. He asked us to help prepare what for him was a sacred ritual. He wanted us to prepare a high pyre of wood and sticks, and to place on this pyre the family of his dead brother, wife and children. We did this with heavy heart and limbs, for it was grim enough when warriors had to be cleared away after conflict, but this was far worse, and it went against all of the harsh rules by which these battle-scarred men had learnt to live; in this way, my men were exceptional.

Veostan in particular was unsettled by it, but insisted that he himself would carry each child to the pyre, which he did, weeping quietly throughout, and nobody could answer his questions as to why the children had had to suffer in this way. Later, I saw that Scipio sat with him, neither man saying much, though Scipio would occasionally say quiet words, and place his hand on the shoulder of his friend.

It was with great sadness that we watched from a respectful distance the firing of this pyre in the early evening of the second day, for though it was not our custom, I could not but think that there was some quiet nobility in it, as the pyre burned down even as the thickening shades of night fell around it.

I knew for certain as I watched the grieving faces of Edelwine and his remaining family that they suffered as my own people suffered at such times.

Later that night, Edelwine walked slowly over to the fire where I sat with Torquato and Cormac. He was a heavy man, quite tall, with long grey hair and a full beard and the strong features of one who led others, who spoke his mind readily, and expected others to do likewise.

He took his place by the fire and said nothing for a while, perhaps reflecting on the grim ritual he had overseen earlier in the evening. No doubt too he thought about the strange truth that he now sat at the fire of the men who had been his enemies when he had first come to this land, and that it was these same enemies who had now saved his life from his own people.

I silently sympathised with him, for these mixed and confused loyalties were a thing of the times, as I well knew, and none of the old certainties could be taken for granted anymore. What would be created out of this time of change, no man could say.

It was a clear night and a light frost covered the land. The cleansing fire burned bright, and beyond the smoke and the sparks shone innumerable bright lights.

Eventually, Edelwine threw a couple of boughs onto the fire; a shower of sparks flew up, and the rest of the boughs flared up momentarily too, so that the light lit up our faces. We sat there wrapped in skins and furs, the scarred and thoughtful face of my brother contrasting sharply with the aquiline features of my Roman friend, both of whom stared into the flames, thinking their own thoughts. Edelwine then began to speak in a quiet voice:

"Tomorrow we will go to a Roman house to the west of Corinium, for a folkmoot has been called, and there we will meet to decide our next step. There we will talk with the elders and chief speakers of the Hwiccas. There has already been much talk in quiet rooms about how we might plan for our future, for many, though not all, believe that the Gevissa king now makes too many demands upon us. We have fought for him in the past, and won him much power and status, but he will not be satisfied and will make himself more powerful. By doing so he threatens the very gains that we have made in the past by fighting by his side. Now some of us grow tired of battles, not because we are not prepared to fight when we have too, for that is the measure of a man, but because we do not see the reason for fighting, for here we have what we need and do not need more."

All that he said was as Cormac had told us. I noticed that he called Ceawlin the Gevissa king and never Ceawlin. This seemed to me to point to the division in the Saxon ranks, for already they drew distinctions between themselves.

"But you should know that what I have just said is not shared by all of the Hwiccas. Some believe that to rise up against the Gevissa king, or even to refuse his call, would be a great treachery. In the old land our way of living is based on loyalty to the chief. Our idea of a free man is a man who bears arms and who fights for his lord when called upon, and not to do so is to abandon our ways, to become worse than you Britons. Such a thing is a disgrace in the eyes of our gods, who are battle gods, and Thor himself, the thunder god, son of Woden the Almighty, will exact a terrible revenge upon all of those who bring such disgrace upon our people."

He said nothing for a while, but continued to stare into the flames.

"In truth, it is difficult to know what to think in these times, for there are portents in the sky most nights, and strange groupings of the stars around the moon, and it all points to some form of calamity."

The Saxon drew a hand down his lined and noble face, probably thinking of his brother and his wife, and the children who had been given such little chance to understand the ways of this life. A shadow crossed over his face, and again he said nothing for some time, just stared into the flames.

"You men seem to me to be good men, who say the right words, and show the right respect for proper things, so how then are we to judge these matters? What is important in this world? Gold and glory, status from the battle? Or to try to understand the thoughts of our fellow men, no matter who they are or from where they come, to try to understand how they too see this strange world? For we too all must surely leave it one day."

We said nothing, just let this man think his thoughts aloud, as was the natural thing to do on a day of grief, and we understood that.

After a few minutes Cormac looked up from the fire.

"Edelwine, what you say is true. My wife, if the god of my mother will allow it, will deliver us a child before the seasons grow warm again. But what am I to tell this child? What is he to believe? Does he fight against the Saes, your people, who have come to this land for many years now and keep on coming, and take our land? Or does he seek out those amongst the invaders who, like you, speak wise words, who work the land, who do not look to fight anymore but seek to work the land, to grow it, and to build the land and make it stronger? I tell you, there have been times when to meet and kill your people was everything to me; no other thought occupied me, and the better the job I did of it, the better I felt . . ."

I looked across at the scarred face of my brother, which itself told a thousand stories, and I was surprised to hear him talk in this way, for usually he kept his thoughts to himself.

". . . but now that I know that my child will soon be born, it makes me take pause and consider further the future. A father who looks always to fight an enemy is perhaps a foolish father, when the enemy proves to be a man who talks sense, when that man has no wish to fight for the sake of fighting, but who wishes to cultivate the land, and grow his family strong."

Edelwine looked across at my brother, and nodded, but said nothing. Eventually he got up slowly from the fire, blinking hard at the pain in his body as he stood up. He bade us good night in his strange language, and slowly made his way back to the main hut, looking across to the blackened earth in the space near the copse where the funeral pyre had stood, and drew a hand down his face as he did so.

Torquato stood up from the fire and stretched out his long frame.

"By Jupiter's furrowed brow, but everybody in this strange land is a philosopher! Life is what it is, the day ahead will be what it will be; that's my philosophy, and my head is clear, it does not ache with the weight of my thinking! Enough for me for one day – good night to you both!"

With that, he strode off to the hut that had been put aside for the men, looking neither at the stars nor at anything else.

My brother and I stayed awhile staring into the embers of the fire, letting the fire burn away, just quietly content to share each others company.

"You know that Aisha is keen to talk with him?"

"I have seen the signs."

Cormac hesitated and kicked up the few remaining embers into flames, watching the sparks glow black red on the scorched wood, before they too drew back, and settled grey on the smouldering limb.

"She could do worse. I know well enough now why you treasure his friendship, for I sense that there is much good in him . . ."

He paused for a moment, thinking.

". . . if there is any good in any of us who fight in this life. In a fight he is what he is – a colossal warrior. For the rest – he is a lost soul."

He paused again.

"Maybe I understand something of that, may our mother's god help us all!"

With that, he stood up, hauled me to my feet, and together we made our way back to the hut provided to us by the grieving Saxon.

*

"I tell you, the Gevissas, under the clear instructions of the Gevissa king, came to my farm, slew many kinsmen of mine, including the defenceless wife and children of my brother, then killed my brother Edelbert too, after terrible torture. They would have killed me, too, had it not been for a war-band of Britons, who by Woden's power had chosen that day, unbidden by me, to come to my farm."

A quiet murmur swept through the Hwiccamen stood in the large hall. Cormac, Torquato and I were stood in a side chamber behind a door, until the mood of the audience could be properly understood. I watched what I could through a ventilation grate set into the wall, and Cormac translated the Hwicca's words as he talked. We were gathered in the large hall of a Roman palace, built of the honey-coloured stone which is typical of the rock in the land of my people. Many torches burned in the hall, for it was the cold months, and night had already fallen.

Edelwine stood at the front of the hall, and was speaking at the invitation of the chief speaker, a man older than Edelwine, called Alfhere, the leader of the folkmoot. We had met him upon our arrival at the old Roman palace, now in Hwicca hands, which was set in the low hills and gentle valleys to the west of Corinium.

Edelwine continued:

"I have talked with the Britons, and they talk sense to me. With reluctance they have accepted us into their land. We work their farms, but, because we have settled here, because we work the farms well and bring work to the land, and produce, they have no argument with us now. It is the Gevissa king who stirs things up, who would go north to new conquests."

Some of the Hwiccamen nodded amongst themselves, but some did not, and seemed outraged at Edelwine's words, and shook their heads.

"What purpose do we have to share in this mad king's lust for power? It is said in the verses:

often, when one man follows his own will, many are hurt

. . . this is true, and it is what we are faced with now. The Gevissa king thinks only of his own status, and some say even that he is mad, that he thinks only of conquest. He will be *Bretwalda* – overlord of all in this land. Yet there is nothing for us in these new conquests; nothing but danger. Here the land is fertile, even more so than the best land in the country of our birth; why then would we jeopardise what we now have?"

Loud shouts broke out amongst the crowd of men in the hall; some did not like Edelwine's words, and tried to shout him down.

Alfhere stood up and raised his arms, and eventually the audience became quiet again.

"Let Edelwine put his full case before us, then we will discuss it and we will decide."

Edelwine stood forward again.

"I well know the rules of the old ways. We owe our allegiance to our lord, for he has given us mail shirts, and helmets, and some of us even battle rings . . ."

Edelwine himself had such a ring, on the middle finger of his right hand.

". . . to go against the allegiance to our lord is a terrible thing, and we risk the rage of almighty Woden himself, and the hammer of his son, the thunder god. All of these things I know. But I also know that to continue allegiance to a lord who has made forfeit his right to that allegiance through his actions is no crime amongst our people."

Angry shouts broke through his speech.

". . . They say this Gevissa, once a mighty and noble warrior, indeed the noblest of men, is now gone mad. I have seen the evidence with my own eyes. I have seen my own family cut down in front of me. Is this the action of a good lord? Are these the actions of a sane man? I tell you, my son saw sights when the Gevissas arrived at my farm that have struck him dumb, for he cannot now speak, and I fear for him. But I am obliged to seek compensation for my brother, for those are the rules we live by – that this man's kin, whether he be king or no king, should pay me what is rightfully mine."

A great hubbub flew around the hall. Alfhere stood up and indicated that Edelwine should sit down. Eventually his voice could be heard.

"Edelwine has had his first say, and for myself I will say that I am made sore in spirit by his words, for if it is the case that the Gevissas have set upon our own people, then that is indeed sobering news. Is there anybody else in the hall who wishes to speak now?"

A short heavy man with a barrel chest moved forward to the front of the room.

"I will have my say!"

"Come forward, Wulfhere, we will hear you."

The man climbed up onto the small dais at the front of the hall. He had an intense face, and strode right up to the front of the dais and began to speak.

"This man speaks treachery!"

A great outcry went up from the hall, and men shouted and raised their arms in the air.

Alfhere moved forward again, his arms held up.

"Let us hear what Wulfhere has to say. But he might choose quieter words, for we will be inflamed otherwise, and none will be heard."

Wulfhere brushed aside the older man.

"Quieter words, he says! This man . . ."

He pointed at Edelwine

". . . has stood here and accused the greatest king on these shores of madness, of behaviours unfitting of a lord. Well then, where is his proof? Who were these Britons? How is it that they by chance show up at the farm of this fool even as a so-called bloodthirsty Gevissa raiding party is there? Is it not more likely that the Gevissas went there to apprehend this traitor, even as he made plans with his British plotters, and caught him red-handed?"

Even as Cormac relayed the gist of all of this to Torquato and me, uproar broke out in the hall.

Cormac looked at us.

"Time to make our entrance, I think."

So saying, he threw back the door of the side chamber and strode out amongst them. *Gaeallon* lay slung across his shoulders, his wild black hair fell long, with the skins draped over his massive shoulders, the eye-patch over his battle-scarred face. He strode out, every inch the giant barbarian Briton that even the verses of these Hwicca people had already made legendary.

At his right shoulder walked Torquato, the giant mercenary, his right hand touching the hilt of his sword in the scabbard set high on his right shoulder.

The crowd of Hwiccamen literally moved back away from them as they strode up the hall.

Cormac planted his feet in front of the dais on which still stood Wulfhere, who now said nothing. I heard later from Cormac what his precise words had been. He talked in their Aenglish language.

"I will have my say, for this is my land too, even though you Hwiccas looked to make it your own after Deorham. I know this Gevissa king, as does my brother."

Cormac pointed to me stood beside Torquato.

"This man, this Ceawlin, was once a great and noble king, and my brother saw much evidence of this with his own eyes. But then a tragedy befell him, as it can all men, even the strongest amongst us. This man's queen, the lady Acha, was killed in a fall from a horse. All men know this, for it is said in the verses, and all right-thinking men understand the nature of his loss."

A quiet hum rolled through the room, and many men nodded their heads.

"The Gevissa king was devastated by this loss; his mind became off-balance, and his vaunted strategy skills became less. He now makes mistakes, and over-reaches himself, so that all of your current prosperity becomes threatened."

Again men nodded, and muttered amongst themselves.

"My brother saw all of this change in him with his own eyes, for my brother was once his thegn, a position earned by his own conduct in the land of the Franks."

The hall fell quiet. Most of the men in the hall knew of these events through the verses or by word of mouth; they knew of the tragedy of Acha, and rumour had long since suggested that the Gevissa king's behaviour had become strange after her death. Even my name was known in their verses, because my fate was a strange fate, and I now knew from Edelwine's words that even my pact with Ulla was rumoured amongst them.

"Let me now tell you what happened at Edelwine's farm three days ago, because I saw it with my own eyes. You can believe me or not, at this moment it is of no consequence to me. Edelwine knew nothing of our mission. I have been sent by Brocmael, King of Powys in the north, to see how the Hwiccas stand in the tumult today. Are the Hwiccas for this land, or are they for the Gevissa king?"

Much muttering went up again from the floor of the hall. Cormac then described what had occurred at the farm, sparing no detail.

A quiet had settled upon the hall at the description of Edelbert's fate, for he was a simple farmer like them, and the mood became even more sober when Cormac described the family pyre, for this was a powerful image in their minds, and it conjured up many things to them.

For some reason as Cormac talked I was struck by a magnificent mosaic of reds, greens and deep-blues, set into the floor just in front of the dais. It displayed several circles, and in the first circle was some Roman deity playing a harp; in the next circle were birds of various kinds; in the outer circle, separated from the last by a beautiful interlaced pattern of green leaves, were great feline creatures, and then a final circle of the green interlaced leaves, all of the circles set into a square, where the interlaced leaves again formed the inner core of the design.

Even as I mused on the beauty of this design, Cormac stopped speaking. Alfhere again moved to the front of the dais.

"Well, the mighty Briton has spoken his mind, and we thank him for that. You have elected me chief speaker in this town of Corinium, so let me now tell you my thoughts."

The room became quiet, all intent on his words.

"I have heard enough over the last two seasons and now today to believe that this Ceawlin, the Gevissa king, is no longer the mighty and noble king that he once was. So let us all take note, even powerful kings are merely the puppets of the gods, as we all are."

All in the hall remained silent, reflecting on this sobering thought.

"Therefore, for myself, I feel no need to pledge allegiance to this lord, and the events at Edelwine's farm have determined my mind on this matter. I will not lift my hand to assist the Gevissas in their march north."

A few angry shouts resounded around the hall at these words. Alfhere held up his arms for quiet.

"We know already that the Gevissas have amassed a great army on the Saxon Shore, reinforced by new boats from the old land. Even now they are moving north, and have already made new conquests to the east of this land of ours. They will be on our eastern border in no more than three days."

He paused, so that the full importance of what he had just said and what he was about to say could have its full effect.

"To fight against one's own people is a matter of great consequence, and I will instruct no man in this hall today that this is the right course of action. I will neither support not resist the Gevissas in this matter. I have a great fondness for this fertile land in which we now live, and I would live out my days here, and I wish only to plough the land that was earned by my warrior's arm at Deorham. But let each man decide for himself, for he must wrestle with the gods himself if his decision should be the wrong decision."

A great outcry again broke out in the hall, and a couple of scuffles broke out over on the far side, quickly stopped.

Then several men from the floor came up to the front and supported these words, and said that they were for neutrality, and would neither support the Gevissas nor would they fight them.

So the matter was decided for them in this way.

We watched as Wulfhere and a small band of men left the hall. We knew that our time was now limited, for the Gevissa king's outriders would know all about this meeting before sunset tomorrow, and Ceawlin himself would know of it by the morning of the following day.

As we left the villa, several men came up to Edelwine and pledged their support, saying that they would fight with us against the Gevissas. To them too, the land they tilled and ploughed was now of more importance than the diminished Gevissa king.

Cormac told them to make plans to protect their families, and to meet with us in two days time in the valley of Edelwine's farm, for we would prepare to battle with the Saxons once more at a location east of that place, because it was now not in the interests of either side to make war in the land of the Hwiccas.

III

The general place of battle was now settled.

The armies would meet to the east of the confluence of the rivers Thames and Evenlode, to the east even of the Wychwood Forest. My war-band had marched there by means of the Roman road known as Akeman Street, which ran north-east from Corinium. Ceawlin's army we knew was marching north from Gwenta through the Vale of the White Horse to meet us, so that we would meet somewhere between the old Roman city of Alcester and the monkish town of Aylesbury.

Brocmael and Kynon had been as good as their word. We arrived in the place called Fethan Leag in early afternoon, and already the gently sloping woodland was thick with the tents of the British forces. To the west we could see the red standards of the Cunedda kings of Gwent; to the north the green standards of the Irish now settled in the land west of the Picts, and to our right and south the green-reds of the South-West Britons, who must have crossed from Dumnonia by boat to reach this place. It was clear to Cormac and I that we were reinforced and greater in number than at Deorham; this would be a battle that included the Irishmen led by Chief Aidan from north of the Roman Wall, Britons from as far west as Dyfed, from Powys under Brocmael and from as far south as the West Welsh from Cornwalia.

We crossed over to the east of the plain, for there we could see Brocmael's red and gold standards, and soon enough we arrived at his camp. This was much bigger than Farinmael's camp at Deorham; several large tents were set out in full rig, and again the horse paddock was set up behind the tents, so that in front of the tents was a large open space. I could see that a great hearth had already been staked out, and that roast meats were being prepared, and barrels of mead and casks of wine were being set up in one corner of the hearth space. The eve of battle would once again be the scene for a modest feast.

It was wise for kings to prepare for battle in this way, so that their people knew that the king thought of their welfare at these times. It was as good a way as any for a man to prepare for what might be his last night in this life.

I was surprised to see that a company of monks was also present on the camp ground; I had never seen this before. I felt somehow unsettled, because to me then battle was one part of a man's life, and the care of his soul was another, and I did not much appreciate this confusion of the two. Cormac agreed with me when I mentioned it to him.

"Aye, I generally respect the work of these men, brother, as we have been taught by our mother, but I do not see how any good can come from their presence here in this place."

We struck our own camp to the side of Brocmael's tents, and soon enough the men were hard at work looking to their weapons, sharpening swords and spears, testing shields, practising in the meadow next to the tents.

Felix in particular was edgy; he had seen no action since coming to this land, for he had watched the horses during the affray at Edelwine's farm, and his manner was becoming more withdrawn by the day.

I stopped by him now as he sharpened one of his deadly darts, every now and then lifting the point to his eyeline and checking its weight for balance.

"So, Felix, you will see some action soon enough?"

"It is about time as well. I joined your band to make gold, not to wander around this barbaric land from north to south, always camping, always talking, all practise and no action. I want gold on this mission, and I mean to get it. I will be looking for this Ceawlin's chief warriors, and they should look to their defences, for I will take no prisoners tomorrow."

So saying, he turned suddenly and with a controlled yet convulsive movement fired the heavy razor-sharp dart at the tree that stood twenty paces behind him. It thudded heavily into the centre of the rough circle that he had burnt into the bark of the tree.

All of this was said and done in the usual cold manner; the man's eyes were cold, his tone was cold, I could never find any human warmth in him. But then, perhaps that is what his work had made him, and which of us was any different?

"Well then, fair enough, that is what you are here for. I understand that if you do not earn gold with me then you will leave me, and seek your fortune elsewhere. Those are the rules we live by."

"Yes, they are, and believe me, if I have nothing more in my sack from this mission by tomorrow evening, I will drop you like a stone and I will find another man amongst these kings to follow. One who better understands the needs of a mercenary like me."

I left him then, still weighing the balance of the dart he held in his hand, and I walked on to others in my war-band.

Scipio worked the trident and net expertly, the accuracy of his throw of the net at a wooden stake exactly precise, the follow through with the trident cold and efficient.

It would be soon too that he returned home to his family and his own land.

"So, young chief, explain to me again what brings us to this field in your land."

I talked to him about Ceawlin's latest plans, about his successes in the southern lands of this *Britannica Sancta*, and of how he now wished to extend his conquests to the north-west and make himself the most powerful man in the land.

Scipio heard me out, then he looked at the floor, and some fleeting sadness seemed to pass through his face:

"So, the once noble man you described to me is no more."

He thought on his words for a few moments, then looked at me searchingly, some profound sadness in his eyes:

"Always this is the way. Does nothing good last?"

I said nothing, but for a moment I glimpsed the great heart of this man from the southern lands.

We were silent for a few minutes, Scipio working the trident and net with a simple deadly method.

Then Scipio looked at me again. Now he smiled.

"You tell me that this man has many palaces, and his family is strong, yet still he wishes to make war, and let many men be killed in this field?"

Then his shoulders began to shake, and the great wide smile lit up his face, and he threw his head back and laughed at the stupidity of kings, who would come to this field and sacrifice the lives of many men in pursuit of their ambition.

After a few minutes he calmed down again.

"But I should not laugh, for the men who seek power are the same in my own land across the great sea. This stupidity has made me rich. Soon I will return to my family in my own land, and try to forget the stupidity of such men. I will cultivate my land, myself and my family made strong by the stupidity of these so-called great men."

I left him there, still laughing quietly to himself, and went to find my brother.

I found Cormac sat upon a stool outside of our tent. He had the war-helmet of our father on his knee, and the great belt buckle was slung over his shoulder; both objects gleamed in the pale sunlight, and I could see that he had spent time with the cleaning oils. These family treasures had been restored to him by Ceawlin after Deorham, and now I noticed that the hollow bronze crest of the war-helmet had been fashioned with a golden eagle, and I asked my brother what this might mean.

Cormac looked at me, his eyes bright:

"Well, brother, that is the eagle of the king of Powys."

He grinned at me then.

"Tomorrow I am back in service, for Brocmael asked me before we left for Edelwine's farm to be his champion in the battle. I take back my old role, and we shall see who or what the Saxons have to show us this time."

I clapped my hand on his shoulder, and was pleased for him. I could see that the old spirit was beginning to rise in him and that by the battle's start tomorrow he would be distant from me again. I worried less for him now than at Deorham, for I had seen many battles, and by now I was sure of his extraordinary prowess. I left him to his preparations and went off to find the Roman rogue, to see what he made of these British preparations for battle, a matter he treated with serious consideration, because it was part of his work.

I found him between the tents and the horse paddock, practising his 'steps' as he called them. These were a set of coordinated foot and sword arm movements designed never to leave his back exposed in battle, so that he could about-face in one movement of the hip and knee and instantly be facing the opponent behind him. Veos sat watching the Roman.

I watched him for a while, not wishing to disturb his practise, which was a serious matter for him. He had lost none of the grace in his movement, and I congratulated him on his skills, a rare thing between us, for usually we bantered with each other. But this was the day before battle, and we would talk proper words at these times and ridicule each other again the day after the battle, if we survived it.

Veos now stood up.

"Come on then, Roman; ten minutes hand to hand with swords – if you're up for it!

Torquato laughed.

They circled each other; an occasional sweep, or thrust, a block and turn. Then Veos stepped in, thrusting with the sword, but Torquato easily turned him away, causing him to expose his back to the Roman.

"Veos, for the hundredth time, you must not thrust with your full weight like that; it becomes a simple matter to turn you around."

Torquato was for a moment deadly serious. I had heard him mention this several times in the last few months of their training. It was a flaw that had crept in to the sword style of the Scandic warrior, and Torquato worried for his friend.

"Oh, it is nothing! You underestimate your own abilities – for once!"

Both men laughed.

They completed their training and towelled themselves off.

Torquato threw down the towel and looked at me then, some scheme in his mind.

"Rhuadrac, I have been thinking whilst I practise. What say we go and have a look at the enemy camp? Just you and me, like the old times, for I am sure that your brother is occupied with other matters this evening."

I thought about it. I led a war-band; they would need their leader tomorrow. Torquato anticipated my thoughts.

"No risks, just a look at the perimeter, for this is thick woodland, the night begins to draw in, and the exercise will do us good. I will wager my skills will allow us to have a quick look-see and be back here in good time to make final plans for tomorrow."

I agreed with him and we made our plans.

We had been told that the Saxon forces had arrived and encamped to the east, for this place Fethan Leag was largely woodland, carved out of which was a great central plain. It was known by all that the opposing armies would meet on the central plain tomorrow.

I told Veos that that we would return within two hours.

We decided to go by foot, which best suited Torquato's tracking skills.

The woodland was dark, for by now the sun had set and its last rays threw a red-orange glow onto the high branches of the trees. A heavy damp moistness seemed to pervade the air, even though it had not rained for two days or more. There was the occasional cry of a bird, perhaps a nightingale, or chaffinch, and when these cries came they seemed too loud, so that the sound echoed through the glades that we moved through. But then after a while even those cries faded and the birds slept, so that we were left with only the muted two-tone call of the night-bird.

Once into the centre of the forest, the light seemed to fade completely.

I was dependent on Torquato, who seemed to know the path, for he moved forward steadily, not once pausing to pick up the trail again.

After a walk of perhaps four or five furlongs or more, Torquato raised his hand and we stopped. Ahead of us we could see a camp, and I knew that we had reached the Gevissa ranks.

Fifty or sixty paces in front of us, in a place with the tree cover starting to thin out, stood a group of Saes warriors, with heavy furs over their shoulders, each holding a spear.

I guessed that these were sentries, posted at one of the perimeters of the camp. I remembered back to the first time that I had encountered the Saxon – in the forest before Deorham, when the very sight of them had sent fear down my spine. Now, I was older and wiser, and I knew that these were men just like me, and their battle dress and guttural language no longer struck fear into me.

Torquato gestured to his left, and we padded through the woodland, going no nearer to the sentries, but working our way nearer to the tents that we could now see in some detail. We were at one end of the camp, which we could see stretched out for some distance away to our right. We knew already that the Saxon numbers were considerable, but the Britons would not be outnumbered in the manner of Deorham. Tomorrow would at least see some sort of parity between the two armies.

Before us was a tent of some size, and it seemed that we had stumbled upon a senior warrior in the Saes ranks, for the wolf's head standard that I knew so well flew from the top of the canvas enclosure. Many sentries stood at the front entrance, so that it was clear that here was a man of some importance and rank.

Even as Torquato was indicating that we should work our way around to the right, so as to better see the size of the Saes numbers, the full moon glided out from behind some thick dark cloud, and the space behind the tent was suddenly lit up. Seconds later the canvas at the back of the tent was thrown aside and a tall man stepped into the half-light.

I could clearly see Ceawlin, the Gevissa king. I was shocked by his appearance. He wore a long white gown, and sandals, even though the night was cold. On his head he wore a laurel garland, with what seemed to be feathers strewn around its rim.

I looked at Torquato, and he looked at me. Neither of us said anything.

Ceawlin moved to the centre of the space, and looked up at the clear night sky. He seemed to be shouting at the stars, and raised his hand and shook his fist at the moon. But then his tone became calmer, as if he was talking to somebody else. There was nobody else in the clearing. Then he looked directly at us. He held out his hand, as if beckoning to us.

Both of us immediately lowered ourselves to the floor, peering through the bushes in front of us. A chill breeze passed through the space we lay in, and rustled the foliage around us.

Ceawlin continued to talk gently, and listen too, as if he debated lightly with somebody whom we could not see. Suddenly he smiled, and held both arms out wide as if somebody walked towards him. Then he closed his arms as if he held somebody there, and began to make steps around the clearing, seemingly dancing. Three steps forward, two steps back. He held his arm aloft, as if somebody pirouetted in front of him, and he smiled. Then he moved again, circling, three steps backwards, two to the side, all of the time moving slowly, and talking, as if he conversed with some spirit there.

As he moved, two figures stepped out of the tent and watched silently from the corner of the clearing. I could see that it was Cutha and Crida.

Suddenly, Ceawlin stopped moving and closed his arms abruptly to his chest; there was a great anguish in his face; he sank to one knee, and sobbed into his hands.

"Father!"

It was Cutha who had barked out the word, and I knew he had called to his father so that he might snap him out of this strange trance.

Slowly Ceawlin stood up, drew his hand down his face, looked sorrowfully into the woods where we were crouched, then turned to face his son.

They talked in an excited fashion, or, more properly, Ceawlin talked in an excited fashion. His son spoke carefully, in measured tones, and I had the impression that he was trying to calm his father by the firm words that he used, but I could not understand enough of their conversation to make out what was being said. I distinctly heard the word "Ulla."

Just then, Cutha stepped back into the tent and reappeared moments later, and there was somebody with him. I heard a sharp intake of breath and a muttered curse from my friend beside me, then Cutha stepped forward and I could see her. For it was Ulla, my woman, who stood there in the half-light.

She was more beautiful, more graceful, even than she had been when I had last seen her, for her dark hair was lifted from her gentle shoulders by brooches, and it shone like black glass in the half-light.

But her father stood at a distance from her and seemed barely able to look at her. There was a great rage in his face. His daughter seemed to be pleading with him, almost begging him on some matter, but he would not even look at her.

Then the king turned and shouted at her and raised his arm as if to strike her. Crida sprang forward and held the king's arm. The king turned on him in fury too, but Cutha stepped in and used soothing words, his hands making calming gestures. Slowly Ceawlin's rage subsided. He lowered his arm, staring at the young thegn, and then at his son. He turned away from his daughter, barked harsh words, sweeping his arm behind him, as if dismissing her.

I looked at Ulla's face. I could see the soft glow of anger there that I had seen so many times before. She wore a light-purple gown, and over her shoulders she had placed a deep-red woollen shawl. She suddenly seemed alone and vulnerable, standing there in the clearing, looking at her father as if her world had just crashed around her. Just then I had an overwhelming urge to stand up and call to her, and might even have done so, but then I felt the massive hand of my friend around my mouth, and he silently lifted me backwards several paces, away from the tent, and I lay there on my back, my mind reeling.

I had not thought it possible that she could be here, on a camp next to a battlefield. The thought had never entered my head, so that I was shocked by the sight of her. What had brought her here? Why here, where I would face her family in pitched battle in the morning? What was she, a woman, doing here in this place for warriors? Why had Ceawlin raged at her, dismissed her in so final a manner?

After a couple of minutes I held up my hand to my friend, indicating that I had recovered myself sufficiently to be trusted. We made our way back to the tent, but now the moon had disappeared once more, and Ulla, Ceawlin and Cutha had gone back into the tent. I indicated to my friend that I wanted to watch at the front of the tent for a few moments at least, in the hope that I might catch a brief glimpse of her again.

After about ten minutes, a group of six warriors on horses drew up in front of the tent, and between them they held two spare horses, both fine-muscled greys. Ceawlin, Cutha, Crida and Ulla then stepped out of the front entrance. Peg was with her, which for some reason reassured me, but even that doughty lady looked frightened, as well she might, as a Briton in the Gevissa camp at this moment.

I could see that Ulla was dressed to travel, for she had over her shoulders skins and furs, and some form of short bonnet on her head. She looked first to Crida, and touched his arm with a tenderness that set my teeth on edge. She then turned to her father and brother, and held each of them by both of their hands and looked deep into their faces, and said something slowly in her language to each of them.

Ceawlin barely looked at her.

With a graceful light movement, assisted by one of the Saxon warriors, she leapt up onto one of the greys. Peg, with more effort, got up onto the second grey. The group of warriors wheeled about, and Ulla was gone, riding south out of the Saxon camp.

The two Saxon chiefs and the thegn waited until the sound of horses disappeared into the woodland, then quietly turned and went back into the tent, Ceawlin's face like stone.

Torquato and I slowly backed away further into the thick woods. I was still shaken by the shock of seeing her here, for I had not thought it possible.

Torquato whispered to me to follow him. Soon enough I could see that his warrior training was still in full flow, for he was making his way around to the right, so that we might at least have some idea of the Saes strength. We walked the full perimeter of the camp, and we could see that the Saxon numbers were at least equal to those assembled for Deorham, if not greater.

We worked our way back around to the place where we had seen the two

Saxon chiefs, but now nobody was to be seen or heard. We backtracked the way we had come, and soon enough we were back in the British sector of the field.

I sat down on a rock in a clearing on the edge of the forest. The moon had again broken through the night cloud, and its silver glow lit up the small clearing in which I sat with my head in my hands. A thin covering of frost sparkled grey-green on the grass at my feet. To my right and slightly below me, I could hear a brook gurgling on its way through the forest. My head was still reeling, for I had been so close to her.

Torquato remained standing. Eventually he spoke.

"Sorry, brother, I would not have suggested our little mission if I had thought for one moment that she might have been here. I have never known it before."

I said nothing. My friend continued:

"I know enough of their language to have heard that she is banished from her father's kingdom, banished from his sight forever, and that you are the cause of it. She had come here to plead her case with her father, but as you could see, his mind is like iron. She is exiled from Wessex, Rhuadrac. He has washed his hands of her."

I looked down at my feet. The frost sparkled grey-green on the grass.

Torquato continued.

"The young chief was insisting that she be taken from the place of battle and returned to a safe town before she is sent to the Saxon lands. I think that he thought only of the safety of his sister; they have now taken our strength, and they know that tomorrow will not be the easy victory obtained at the last battle."

I let his words drift away.

I had guessed as much. Now, Ulla was to pay a dear price for her pact with me. She knew only the life of a princess; I could not see how she might survive back in the land of the Saxons, for she had been born here, in Britain, and there was nothing in her forefathers' homeland for her. I groaned at the thought, for my first instinct was for her safety. I saw no way that our dilemma might be resolved.

Torquato looked down at me.

"I had the impression that the Gevissa king is looking to make an example of you after the battle tomorrow, and perhaps his daughter too."

Torquato let those words sink in.

"But the young chief insisted that a battlefield is no place for such matters, and he persuaded the Gevissa king that she must go from this place, and so she did, as we witnessed."

He paused. A further thought suddenly stuck him.

"What in Jupiter's name was the Saxon king doing, dressed like an emperor of my own people, prancing around the clearing like that?"

"Could you not understand?"

Torquato looked at me and shrugged his shoulders.

"He danced with his spirit-queen, with Acha. Her spirit is alive in his fragmented mind."

I looked up at the Roman mercenary, who stood with a look of wonder etched on his soldier's face.

"Friend, in truth I am shocked to see Ulla in this place. Let me be still awhile whilst I return to my senses, then we will go to my brother and Brocmael, and explain what we have seen, but Brocmael must not know that we have seen the Gevissa king's daughter leave the camp."

I did not tell Torquato my thoughts, but no doubt he guessed them. It was probable that Brocmael, or perhaps more likely Kynon, might have considered sending a section of his horse-warriors to attempt to capture Ulla. Ceawlin's daughter would be a great prize capture and hostage on the eve of battle.

My friend nodded and said nothing.

As always, he accepted my words, for he had decided some time ago that he was my friend, and to him this was a bond as strong as brotherhood; he simply accepted that this was how I had reacted to seeing Ulla. He moved over to another rock in the clearing and sat down, his booted feet up on a rock in front of him, his chin settled onto his chest.

We stayed in the clearing for some time, neither of us saying anything.

I wrestled with my thoughts. I had not thought that I would see this woman I loved before combat with her family and her people tomorrow. At first, such a thought seemed suddenly grotesque to me. A leader of warriors cannot go into battle with doubts. On the field of battle his mind must be clear, because others rely on him. It was clear that Ceawlin now knew everything about his daughter and me, and that had resulted in much trouble for Ulla, for she was exiled, and there was nothing I could now do before the battle. What if I should not survive it? What would happen to her then?

I thought of Deorham, and Farinmael, Gavin, Oisin and Fintan, and I remembered the bravery of all the men who had died there. I thought of the easy manner with which Ceawlin had dismissed my people when he outlined his plans to me in his hall. In this way I remembered why I would be fighting the Saxons the following day.

I thought it through till the moon was finally lost behind a bank of clouds. After the battle, I would seek out Ulla.

I had settled my thinking, and was strong again in my mind when we got up to push on back to the British camp.

*

Torquato and I arrived back at Brocmael's tent to find that some sort of ceremony was in progress. Various delegations from all of the British sectors had already paraded around the area in front of the central hearth, and the princes and kings of those regions had come to Brocmael's tent, for it was Brocmael who had called together the tribes, and they met now for the first time together.

The sentries, knowing me from Brocmael's table at Penwyrn, took us straight through to the king. He was holding court in his tent, and several men bustled around him. All heads turned when Torquato and I were immediately brought up to him, for this action spoke of some sort of privilege to these kings and princes, to whom status and position was everything.

"Rhuadrac, you are welcome! I have talked to your brother already, and I know of the general success of your mission to the Hwiccas, so that at least we can expect little interference from them on this occasion. Let me introduce you to my other guests: here we have Aidan of Argyll; here, Rhin-Hir of Gwynedd, and Meurig of Gwent, and here the great Constantine himself, most saintly man, from Dumnonia, and Aircol, son of Vortiporus from Dyfed."

In truth, I have never had sight on first impression of a greater bunch of schemers and thieves then this group of men introduced to me that night. Only Aidan of the Irish-Scots struck me as a true warrior; he stood away from the group of chiefs, watchful, and by his side stood two men who may have been his sons, so closely did they resemble him. These three men watched on, and I could see that they were measuring the fighting-worth of both myself and Torquato, the true sign of a battle-served warrior. Constantine, by now an old man, also seemed above the fray, and he greeted me warmly, with friendship in his eyes. The others would barely look me in the face, or dismissed me outright with a sneer of indifference, and I took an instant dislike to at least two of them there on the spot. There was not one amongst them fit to have put the fur-skin on Farinmael's shoulders.

"Brocmael, this warrior and I have thought it fit to establish the strength of the Gevissas in camp. We have visited their tents, and our estimate is that they have at least eight thousand men, with perhaps five hundred on horse, so that we can expect horse charges either at the outset of the battle or during the day."

My news created a stir in the group of chiefs around Brocmael. Such a number of horsemen was unusual, and the size of the army facing us caused some alarm. Few of these men in Brocmael's tent had led more than skirmishes in the past, and their presence at Deorham had been notable by its absence, as the wise men say. An army of the size that I described was a new idea to them. Of these kings and chiefs, only Aidan was known to me. He had won renown on the battlefield; many tales were told of his wisdom and bravery – a man born to the role of king, and confirmed in it by the great Columba himself. This Columba's name was always whispered quietly by my mother when she told me the mysterious tale of the crystal book and the angel, which was often.

The chief called Meurig, a fat man with a sunken chest, few teeth and wandering eyes, who had been one of those who refused to look me in the face when introduced, now looked me up and down, then said:

"Rhuadrac? Rhuadrac? I remember now. Are you not Farinmael's man, who became some sort of servile messenger boy, a freebooter in the pay of the Gevissa king himself? What are you doing here in this place, and why should we believe you?"

I touched the hilt of *Saesbane* and Torquato's arm went straight to the scabbard on his right shoulder, and a space opened up between Meurig and I, whose shoulder-men too reached for the handle of their swords.

A sudden silence descended over the tent. Aidan and his sons had stepped further away, and now watched the scene even more intently. I knew that Torquato would have already ran his experienced eye over the strength of this king's guard, assessed the number of sentries in the tent, would have worked out the best points of exit if required. I was quite prepared to run my sword through this fat slobbering clown who had somehow gained power over his people.

"Have a care, prince. I am not inclined this night to listen to your sly insinuations, for I have no allegiance to you, and I will kill you here on the spot if you accuse me of lying."

Meurig turned pale; he well knew that I would carry out my threat. I looked into the face of a scheming bully who had spent a lifetime issuing orders for his own pleasure; the face of one who did not know how to react when faced with such straight-talking.

All in the tent became quiet.

Just then my brother walked in. He could see that some altercation had occurred. He walked straight through the silent audience and up to my side.

"What goes on here?"

I stood with Cormac and Torquato at each side of me. The thought occurred to me at that moment that we could have laid waste the combined chiefs of most of the west of Britain in no more than five minutes, and none there would have had the power to prevent us. Again I could see that Aidan looked on with great interest, measuring the worth of this group of Britons, and it seemed to me that there was some amusement in his face, for he looked at me through narrowed eyes with a particular fascination.

Brocmael stepped forward. I suspect that he too recognised the havoc we could wreak amongst his carefully laid plans, for he was quick to break the tension.

"Nothing at all, Cormac, nothing at all, just a little dispute between friends. It is nothing. Come kings, princes and warriors, let us eat and make plans for tomorrow, for that is when we face the real enemy!"

Slowly I removed my hand from the hilt of my sword, but refused to take my eyes off Meurig, who looked away and smiled the smile of a weak man.

"Of course, Brocmael, you are right, and of course if you trust this freebooter, then of course, we must all trust him, is that not right, Aircol of Dyfed?"

This Aircol, whose father had gained infamy as a man who ruled as a tyrant over his people, a man with thick lips and watery eyes – without doubt another robber – spoke in a high piping voice:

"Of course we must, for tonight we enjoy Brocmael's hospitality. Tomorrow is of course another day."

The sly insult and threat behind his words was not lost on me.

Then this group of princes broke up, and Brocmael led the way out to the central hearth.

Aidan and his sons came across to where we stood. All three men were powerfully built; they wore thick tunics of red and green, woven around their bodies from shoulder to hip. Around their legs they had black leather strappings, and from their ornate leather belts hung the longswords of the Irish in the north, with much gilt in the pommel. They wore their hair long and swept back from their faces with oils. The face of Aidan was much lined, and long ruts ran down each side of it; his dark eyes were hooded. It was the face of a leader of men who had survived many battles in his life. But his eyes shone with a keen spirit as he spoke to me in heavily accented British, the lilt in his voice instantly making me think of my mother.

"You are the son of Advil, I think?"

There was a question in his voice.

I glanced at Cormac, who was now regarding the Irish king with some wariness.

"Yes I am. How do you know that and what is it to you?"

I had not yet thrown off my irritation with the Dyfed king.

Aidan's eyes smiled, and he nodded at his two sons.

"This is the son of a brave man, a wise man, a hero at the Battle of Culdrain, where even holy Columba himself was involved."

He turned to me then.

"As Brocmael told you, I am Aidan, King of the Dal Riada, north-west of the Roman Wall, and this is my son Arthur, and this my nephew, Bran."

"And this is my brother Cormac . . ."

All three of the Irishmen looked up at my brother, and there was no disguising the muted awe in their eyes; at that time Cormac had come into his full maturity, his giant frame bearlike.

". . . and this my friend from the Roman homelands, a mercenary."

Torquato did not move forward, and barely nodded his proud head in their direction, not relaxing his gaze for one moment.

I looked back at Aidan.

"How did you know me?"

"Because I knew your father well. We fought side by side at Culdrain, and he saved my life twice in that battle. You could be him, so much do you look like him."

Both Cormac and I were surprised by the knowledge that the Dal Riada king knew our father.

"And I knew your mother too. Ethna, is it not? Your brother follows her colouring. The love of your father and mother for each other is legendary in the annals of my country across the sea! Are they both well?"

"My father is dead, killed by the Saxons at the Battle of Bedcanford, some thirteen winters ago now. My mother fares well, but would fare better with my father by her side."

Aidan nodded his head and said quietly:

"I am sorry to hear of the loss of your father. He was a good man."

Then he smiled at me again, and grasped my shoulder.

"Unless my senses have begun to deceive me, from what I have just seen he has every reason to be proud of his sons! Feast well tonight, and may God walk with you in the battle tomorrow. Afterwards perhaps we can talk, if God in high heaven smiles upon us. If not, then the sons of Advil of the Britons will always be made welcome in the Dal Riada territory, should you some day decide to visit us."

With that he turned on his heels, and together with his shoulder-men walked out of the tent, nodding briskly at Brocmael and Kynon as he did so.

Cormac looked at me.

"What was all that about then? With the Dyfed king?"

"A gross insult from the fat man, which I neither invited nor looked for. Brother, who are these robbers that we are now in league with?"

Cormac looked at me. The scarred face was full of thought, and I could see that his thoughts were the same as mine.

"Aye, I understand you. Dignity is laid low in this place. Brocmael, Kynon, maybe this old man, Constantine. Aidan and his men. Those are true kings and princes. As for the rest of them – from what I see, not one of them deserved to stand shoulder to shoulder with Farinmael, or with our father."

I told my brother then of the mission we had undertaken, and that we had seen Ceawlin, Cutha and Ulla.

"What, his daughter here? He is mad then."

"It was all I could do not to shout out to her when I saw her, and Torquato had to take steps to prevent me from doing so. She is exiled from the Gevissa king's land, Cormac. She is to be sent to the north German lands. But have no fear, my thinking is straight again now, for she has left the Saxon camp, and it becomes again a battle between warriors. How it will go between me and her, I know not, but it is a matter I will address after the battle."

"We will find a way, brother, we will find a way. But for now, we have more pressing matters to attend to. This battle tomorrow, even if half of our allies are brigands and thieves, will settle all of our immediate futures, so we must look to our survival first."

Brocmael came over to us.

"It is unfortunate that you had to hear such words, Rhuadrac. Have no doubts that my son and I are of one mind as to your loyalty to the cause of the Britons."

He shook his head, and his face again looked older.

"I have learnt in my years as the chief amongst my people that sometimes you must sup with the devil when faced with an even greater evil; many of these so-called princes and kings are little more than robbers, but the threat we face tomorrow forces our hand in these matters. The Saxons would rid the land of all things British, and our very way of life is threatened. We have no choice but to make allies amongst brutes so that the greater good of our people is protected."

I might have argued with him, for Brocmael's words were similar to my thoughts before Deorham, and my experience since that day had taught me that such matters were perhaps not so clean-cut. But the night before battle was no place for it, so I let his words pass. He looked at me now with some warmth in his eyes.

"I have a request to make of you. As perhaps your brother as mentioned, I have asked him to be my champion on the field of battle tomorrow . . .?"

I inclined my head in acknowledgement.

". . . I have hopes that you and your war-band of warriors . . ."

He looked at Torquato at my right-hand side.

". . . will act as the personal bodyguard of my son tomorrow. There will be much gold in it for your men, though I know of course that such matters will not sway your own thinking."

The last words were said quickly, Brocmael no doubt remembering my reaction to Meurig's insult.

I thought it over. Kynon would be in the thick of the battle and I had no argument with the prince. My men would at last have the promise of gold, which was the least they deserved after following me across the sea to my own land. No doubt too that my powerful war-band would likely be reduced in numbers after the battle, and I did not doubt that this thinking also formed part of Brocmael's design.

"Of course, Chief, it will be an honour for me and my men to perform such a duty, and we will do so with pride and all of our strength."

I could see that the Powys king was pleased with my response. Even in battle, a good man will make what provision he can to protect his family; my small war-band was a formidable fighting unit, so he had chosen well.

The rest of the night was spent drawing up the battle plans. Brocmael's army would take up the central part of the field, with Kynon representing his father in the eye of the centre, so that my thinking was right, and my men would see much action.

The left section of the field was allocated to Rhin-Hir of Gwynedd, who was a quiet man, thoughtful, who listened rather than spoke, but he accepted his duties willingly. I thought then that I had perhaps misjudged him with my first impressions, for he spoke quietly but firmly when accepting his part in the battle. The right flank would be taken by Constantine's lieutenants, for Constantine was too old to wage battle himself. The men of Argyll, Dyfed and Gwent would be held in reserve, a strategy which suited Meurig and Aircol, and a plan which did not surprise me in the least, and they would only come into the fray if matters went badly with the early exchanges. But I could see that Aidan's son, Arthur, was angry to be in reserve, and may have said something aloud had not his father laid his hand on his arm and shook his head curtly. The Irish-Scots had good cause to fear the Saxons in the north of Britain; if the British could halt their progress here in the mid-lands all well and good, but the Irish would only lose their own men in this British battle if it could not be avoided. I could see the wisdom in his thinking.

The planning over, the rest of the evening was spent in such entertainment as was available.

I was surprised when Brocmael clapped his hands and the monks were summoned, and when they arrived they formed up into a choir, and they sang their godly hymns for us.

In Penwyrn, such singing had been much to my taste, for it was in keeping with the events of that night, but here it seemed to me to be out of place, and I could not reconcile the religion of my mother with battle. The two things seemed to me to be opposite sides of the same question. In peacetime, have a care for the soul. In battle, have a care for the arts of war, and survival, and if survival, expect gold. So I thought at that time, but Brocmael thought differently; to him, everything was a matter for the soul, but I could not see it. I knew that my brother thought as I did, and we retired early, so as to be ready for the fray in the morning.

Torquato had left the hearth at the first sight of the monkish choir.

*

We awoke to a crisp cold day with high blue sky. The air was curiously still, and clear of clouds.

Cormac had retreated to that place that was his alone on the day of battle, and I indicated to Torquato that we should leave him to prepare his mind for the task ahead.

We went out to the wagon, and I selected those elements of the booty that I had won on the battlefield in the land of the Franks that would serve me in the day ahead, all of which had been prepared by Gregor the day before. I chose first a gleaming mail shirt, with tight steel mesh, but which was also light, so that I could move freely in it. Next I took up the bronze helmet with the boar's head crest, which had side panelling, so that the side of my head would gain some protection. I also pulled out the gold belt buckle, and the shoulder-clasps that matched it, which were my real treasure, for although they had little value for the protection of my body, they conferred much status on me as a warrior. Only a man who had taken such items in hand-to-hand combat with a prince might rightly wear such treasures on the field.

I chose a shield made in the old Roman fashion, with a central iron boss overworked with hardwood, which was about six-hands-widths long and three across, and was made concave, so as to fit my body more closely. Finally I drew *Saesbane* from its scabbard; Gregor had done a fine job, for the steel at both edges shone razor-sharp, and its iron central shaft was strong, with no sign of fatigue.

Torquato chose items similar to my own, but he would take no shield. His training told him that it was a false defence, and that a man had better rely on his own reflexes, his own speed and skill, than trust to such protection. But he put on the gold helmet won in Lombardy, and the gold shoulder-clasps that matched it, and chose his favourite mail shirt, light with tight mesh like my own, but in his case made to the old Roman design. He placed three daggers in his belt, and took out his own short Roman sword, which he wore in a scabbard on his right shoulder, which had long been the fashion of his people.

Thus attired, we moved out of our quarters with the rest of the men and made our way to Brocmael's tent. All was hurry and bustle, for the battle-spirit was in the camp, and nothing and nobody would now rest until the battle was done. Brocmael himself was clad in warrior gear, but we knew that he would play a watching role, in at least the early stages of the battle, for his son was of age to fight for him, and that was what had been agreed at the battle talk last night.

Kynon made a fine sight, for his armour was all of black, and the eagle crest of his family was on his chain mail shirt and on his shield. At least this man looked every inch the warrior amongst the Britons that day, even if other kings did not.

His face was set, and he gave brief instructions to me as to the conduct of the battle.

The British forces would form shieldwalls for the first assault, if as expected, cavalry were to be set upon us. If those charges were withstood, we were to advance upon the Saes ranks at once, so as to benefit from the confusion in their ranks. I passed these orders on, and talked to Felix carefully, for if we met with cavalry, his darts would play an important role in the battle, at least in the early stages.

Soon enough we were in place on the central plain carved out of the woodland at Fethan Leag. A light breeze blew in the clear air, and for the last hour I had heard the steady beat of the devil drums of the Saxons, but they held less fear for me now. I had known many battles, and I understood that these devices were there to strike fear into the heart of an enemy, but once their purpose was known, their power to instil fear was much less. Now I listened carefully for a different reason, for I knew that once that rhythm changed, the battle would commence.

Horse-warriors ranged up and down the front ranks of both sides, and standards of all colours shook out on the light breeze. I looked around me at my war-band, and my heart swelled with pride, for I had fought with these men before, and I knew their value.

The devil-drum beat slowed. Three riders came forward from the Saes ranks, and I could see that Cutha was amongst them. I was reminded of his father's garb at Deorham, for he too wore the gold and niello of a king, and the wolf's head crest was emblazoned on his shield and mail shirt. A red cloak was draped over his shoulders, and a king he looked, too, as he rode out to the middle of the field.

Brocmael, Kynon and my brother rode to meet them. I wondered then if the Saes had a champion to test my brother, for Ceawlin well knew his strength. He would not risk losing face at the start of this battle unless he thought Cormac could be beaten.

A parley took place in the centre ground. I saw Cormac dismount, and the armies at the centre of the field were bidden to close up. A challenge had been thrown down. I knew then that Ceawlin had found his champion.

A flicker of apprehension shot through me. Ceawlin knew the strength of my brother, yet he had accepted the challenge. The first advantage was his.

The central ranks of both sides had closed to within fifty paces of each other. Cormac stood alone in front of us, now stripped to the waist, with *Gaeallon* held calmly in his right hand, one of the blades resting easily on the ground.

Slowly, a ripple went through the Saxon ranks, and a space opened up in the centre.

A man strode out from their ranks then, but such a creature I have never seen before or since, for he was neither Saxon, nor Briton, nor any other race of man that I have ever seen before. I had heard of such men though, this race of giants who fought as champions since battles had first been fought. They came from central Asia, from the region of the High Mountains. Amongst mercenaries they were called by one name only: a Chinaman.

I looked at Rama Bec over to my left. There was real awe in his face, for one of his stories was happening for real, now, in front of him. I looked at Torquato on my right, who looked back at me, and there was real concern on his face too, which must have mirrored my own, for this was a myth made flesh. The Chinaman of legend stood before my brother.

Wherever this creature came from, he was gigantic, bigger even than Cormac. His hair was shaved, but for a tiny line that covered the centre of his head and ran down his neck into a thick plait, and a thin beard covered his upper mouth and fell to his jaw. Great leather bands covered his upper and lower arms, which were massive. Otherwise he wore nought but three-quarter breeches and boots, and carried only a short dagger. He was the heaviest man I have ever seen, for, though his waist was firm as a wrestler's, slabs of flesh hung from his chest and thighs, and he moved ponderously, as one who never takes orders, but only threatens all who have dealings with him.

The two giants looked at each other then. Cormac, taking note of the arms borne by his opponent, threw aside *Gaeallon*, and even then his own sword. Seeing this, the Chinaman did likewise, for they would meet hand to hand and try each other's strength.

They circled each other, each man assessing the strength of his opponent. Then, in a sudden and huge expense of energy, each man stepped right up and threw several blows straight into the face of the other; a sound as of mighty axes hitting oak many times rent the air, but neither man gave ground.

Suddenly, the Chinaman, moving with the speed of a viper, took one step back and then sprang forward, catching Cormac behind the neck with both hands, and in the same beautifully balanced movement, all of his weight transferred to his upper torso, butted my brother full in the face, between the eyes.

The blow staggered Cormac, which I had never before seen, and he fell back two or three paces, fell down at his left knee and the Saxon ranks bellowed their approval. The creature followed through and his great swinging fist swung up from near the floor and caught my brother flush under the jaw, sending him sprawling onto his back.

Then the Chinaman leapt at Cormac, making as if to strangle my brother, and his huge hands tried to grip my brother's neck, but Cormac held the giant's arms, and with a roar kicked out at the brute's midriff, lifting the creature off his feet and throwing him onto his back, and the British side roared its appreciation. As Cormac leapt at him, the Chinaman kicked out with both feet and again sent Cormac sprawling.

The two champions picked themselves up and again circled each other.

The Chinaman came at Cormac, again moving with astonishing speed for one so colossal, and Cormac too stepped forward, and went to lock his opponent's arms, but tripped. Instantly the creature was upon him, taking him by the head in a lock. For a moment the assembled crowd was silent. I feared for my brother's neck, for this monster was tightening his grip over that neck, and I thought that I would see the life drain out of my brother. I saw that my brother sought some purchase for his legs, which slipped from under him.

My right arm moved to touch *Saesbane*, for if this brute finished my brother then I would finish it, or die in the attempt, and to hell with the right protocol when champions fought.

But Torquato moved his left arm over mine, without looking at me.

"No. He is not finished yet."

I saw then that something else had happened, for Cormac had found his foot purchase. He had broken the headlock and had now slipped round to the front of his opponent's belly. It was then that I saw that cruel smile pass over my brother's face. His clasp was around the small of the Chinaman's back, then his wrists locked, and every sinew in his massive arms and back and bull neck strained as he lifted that monster clear of the floor. He leveraged his full strength on that man's spine and he shook his opponent like a mannequin, smiling as he did so, even as the watching ranks on both sides fell silent; he applied even more pressure to that spine. I saw then the back of that Chinaman from the High Mountains begin to arch and his face twist into a grimace. I ground my teeth, for I knew the sound that I would hear next, but no scream, no sound at all, went out of the dying man as the vertebrae in his back cracked with a sickening sound as of a young branch snapping cleanly, and his body fell limp, broken, gone.

Cormac swung his opponent's lifeless body onto the floor next to him and staggered a few steps and again fell to one knee and hung his head. Then he stood up, and reaching for his sword, went over to his opponent and put his hand to the giant's neck. He stepped back; with a clean efficient stroke to the back of the neck he finished the Chinaman off. The monster's body twitched once, then moved no more.

Cormac turned around, wiped his brow with the back of his massive forearm, and picked up *Gaeallon*. With the gesture I knew so well, he raised his right arm bearing *Gaeallon* and shook it at the Saxon hordes, and roared at them again, did they have one who might face him?

I looked at Torquato, who nodded his head once and said only:

"Magnificent."

The cheers and roars went out from the assembled British ranks, and the Saxon army backed away just as I had seen at Deorham.But now I knew what would soon come at us, so I told my men to prepare, told Felix to stand ready, and then watched as my brother rejoined our ranks. I saluted him once, full of pride, and pleased that I would have my brother at my side again as the Saxons came at us.

Then the drums began to beat more quickly, and my heart began to thump in rhythm with it, but all of this I knew from before. So even as Kynon ordered his men to form the shieldwall, I walked up and down before my men, now slightly retreated behind the shieldwall which was six ranks of men deep. I calmly issued orders, reminding them that if we met with cavalry, the priority in the first charge was that Felix must be given the position to wreak most damage with his darts. Our job was to achieve that position, even whilst we provided Kynon, who had retreated with us on my suggestion, with as much protection as we could offer him.

Still the beat of the drums increased. Then, on the blast of horns, the Saxon ranks parted and their cavalry suddenly hurtled towards us. Now there was no time to talk, or even to breathe, for the Saxon horses ate up the ground. We barely had time to see the face masks of their riders before they hit the shieldwall. All became a tumble of flying hooves, and the acrid smell of sweating horseflesh, as the shieldwall absorbed the first collision. Men cried and shouted and screamed. Some were pinned to the floor with the spears of the horsemen, and others dragged riders from their terrified mounts and stabbed them, whilst still others wrestled on the floor, their bodies clasped together and barely moving, for this was a death grip, and one wrong move meant certain death to one or the other. All was a mass of seething unthinking horse and human flesh, merged, seeking one thing only, which was to survive.

All of this time my band circled for position, still together as a tight war-band, for we had not been part of the first collision, as our job was to see how the shieldwall fared against the first wave of cavalry. We could see that although the first three ranks were splintered, the rest of the shieldwall held; now we could concentrate on the first of our tasks. I looked to the horsemen coming through, and just behind the lead horses I could see a fine warrior, who had the wolf's crest on his shield, so that this must be one of Ceawlin's high-status men. I could see that it was neither Cutha nor Crida, which for reasons I knew not was a relief to me.

I pointed the chief warrior of the cavalry out to my men, and we moved as a group, clearing fighting men and bodies from out of our way. Felix moved in our centre, his weighted dart in his hand. The second wave of cavalry came at the shieldwall, and at that moment Veos, Gregor and Torquato, who formed the first rank of our war-band, fell to one knee. In one movement Felix sprang up and threw his dart. His aim was true, for it hit the warrior-chief full in the chest with a thud, and he fell backwards from his horse, finished before he hit the ground.

I nodded at Felix, even as the Saxon cavalry fell back, for we had killed their chief, and seeing this, they had retreated to regroup. Kynon clapped me on the shoulder.

"Good, good, that was fine skill."

But in moments the Saxons came at us again, even before the shieldwall could fully reform, and the horses waded through us again. This time the depleted shieldwall splintered, so that the Saxon cavalry came through our ranks and pressed on to the second wall behind us. Again, we moved together as a band, and again I saw that the chief who had led their second charge was isolated. He had barely time to turn around his horse from the initial charge before Felix had again done his deadly work, and he fell to the ground, the dart protruding from his back. Now too the Powys men took up their spears and attacked the cavalrymen who had come through the shieldwall, which by now had reformed in front of us. A terrible slaughter took place, for only fifty or so horses had come through the gap, and the Powys men set about finishing off these Saxon horse-warriors, who fought bravely but were no match for the overwhelming numbers that now swarmed upon them.

I looked ahead of me. The Saxon cavalry in this sector had now fallen back, their leaders dead. I looked away across the open plain. The horse-warriors had also charged the Dumnonia and Gwynedd positions to our right and left, and it seemed to me as if they had achieved more success, for it looked as though both those armies had fallen back slightly. I looked to Kynon.

"We have resisted the first charge, the chief warriors of their cavalry here are dead, do we move forward or not?"

Kynon looked across to the left and right. He did not much like what he saw.

"Our allies have fallen back, a forward thrust through the centre here might isolate us further up the plain."

He thought for a few moments.

"Yes, we will go forward and take the risk."

So saying, he strode to the front of his men, raising his sword, and pointing it towards the Saxon ranks.

"Men of Powys, we go forward, we go forward!"

Our battle ranks slowly began to move forward, gathering pace with every stride, until their jog became a stride, then a gallop, charging on towards the Saxon ranks, who I could see by now had formed their own shieldwalls even as their cavalry had fallen back. My men and I ran at a steady pace, for we were battle trained, and already I could see that those who were not, who had sprinted forward at Kynon's command, even now were slowing down. It was then that I heard a familiar bellow at my side, and I looked up to see Cormac, his scarred face set, his eyes alive with the battle-spirit. I said nothing. We would talk later.

A great cry went up from the men of Powys as we closed on the Saxon ranks. I had caught Kynon's arm as I caught up to him, and gestured that he should fall back, for a brave prince giving orders was better than a brave prince dead on the first collision with the shieldwall. This he did.

On my quick nod in reply to his pointed finger and raised eyebrows Torquato raced on with my brother, and I watched as they hit the Saxon shieldwall together, Cormac hitting it with his full weight and clearing men away from in front of him, Torquato hanging back slightly, watching with his expert eye for the gap into which he could glide and cause most damage. Together they fought there, and I was reminded once more of Deorham, but this time there was more science in Torquato's support of my brother. Many ranks of the Saxons fell then in front of *Gaeallon*, as Cormac waded amongst them hefting the battle-axe with the deft double-handed movement I knew so well. Torquato wrought havoc next to my brother, in and out of the Saxon ranks, in, out, step, in, out, step, all measured, each blow a killing blow. The Saxons could not get near either of them to inflict damage, for no sooner had *Gaeallon's* arc swept through them than Torquato was there, picking off the Saes warriors expertly, as he had been taught to do over a lifetime. Such was the success of these two that the Saxons immediately fell back, for they could find no way to get at them.

But then a horn rent the air; all looked up, and we saw that another band of horse-warriors rode at us from the top of the clearing. At their head rode a warrior on a magnificent white stallion, and I thought for a moment of Brindowen, before Deorham.

As the cavalry approached I could see that Crida rode at their head. We were unprepared; I had no time to form up my men so that Felix could wield his deadly art.

The cavalry came straight at us, and it occurred to me then that Ceawlin had seen our position, and understood that he needed to take steps to eliminate us from the battle.

Then the horse-soldiers hit us, and every man fought for his life.

Crida aimed straight for me; in a sideways movement I sprang away from the lunge of his spear and grabbed hold of the shaft as I did so. With a wrench I pulled him from the horse. As he sprawled onto the hard ground in front of me, I saw Cormac charge at the horse of the second-in-command; the horse reared as Cormac drove into it, and its rider fell backwards, hitting the soil with a sickening crunch.

Before me Torquato cleared several men from in front of us. At my back Veos and Scipio fought expertly, the net like a deadly web for the warriors who then felt the full force of the trident's bite. Veos fought with his Scandic sword, striking with clean blows, and Sigfeldt darted amongst them. I saw with sickening clarity Rama Bec's mace and chain strike full into the face of a Saxon even as he got within six steps of me.

All of my men fought then for the life of their chief, because it was clear to all that Ceawlin had decided to make an end of me on that battlefield. But he had reckoned without the skills of my war-band. Even as Kynon's men ran up to engage with Crida's cavalry troop, it was clear that they would not succeed in their mission, for they could not get to me. Cormac and Gregor fought side by side then, and together they began to force back Crida's horse-warriors, most of whom were by now unhorsed. On each side of them my men fought expertly, Veos and Scipio together, Rama Bec and Sigfeldt together, all of them expert in their art.

But now Crida had regained his feet, and although only a few yards in front of me, had immediately been engaged by Kynon's men. These he had fought off with ease. All around him his men had begun to fall back, but still he sought me out and came up to me, even though he now stood isolated before me and Torquato. I knew then the courage of this man.

Into his path stepped Torquato.

They fought then, those two fine warriors. Both were big men. We saw then that Crida too was expert in the sword arts. They clashed, and I saw a sight I have never seen before, for my great friend was toppled; but even as he fell, he rolled backwards and sprung up to his feet, instantly regaining his stance. Crida leapt forward, slashing his sword in great arcs at the Roman, or thrust it at his chest. But at each move Torquato was ahead of him, parrying, blocking, each movement precise, just so. The great clang of metal rang out then on the field before me.

Though Crida fought with great strength, it became clear soon enough that he could not match the Roman. He lifted his sword in a great two-handed movement and as he did so we could see that his strength was beginning to fail him. As it came down at Torquato's head the most-skilled mercenary of all met it there halfway; he held the downward stroke of Crida's blade in one movement; in the next he threw it away from him, threw the Saxon warrior backwards, so that he went sprawling onto his back.

Even as the mercenary stepped forward to deliver the final blow, I shouted to him:

"No, Torquato!"

The Roman stopped in his movement, even as the blade fell towards Crida.

All movement seemed to stop in that place momentarily. Crida's men had fallen back before the combined force of Kynon's men and my war-band; to my left stood Cormac, the reins of the great white stallion in his hands. I walked over to him, took the reins, and led the horse to Crida.

Slowly he got to his feet.

I gave him the reins of the stallion and placed my hand upon his right shoulder.

"You are the friend and guardian of one who is precious to me. I will not cause her pain. You are free to go."

The Saxon looked at me then, some astonishment written in his features. With an angry look on his wild face, he shook his head, in one movement remounted his horse, turned it away from me, and galloped off into the woods that ringed the clearing.

Both Cormac and Torquato looked at me, a look of some confusion in their faces. But then they shrugged, and looked about them, for the battle still raged on.

The men of Powys fought like tigers. It was soon enough clear that we had achieved major success in our sector. The Saxons fell back generally from the charge of these brave men, so that we continued our charge on over the open plain, until we found ourselves to one side of the field, close to the wooded area into which Crida had driven his horse after his reprieve. The Saxons in the central part of the field had fallen back into this wood and the decision now was whether or not we should follow them.

I again looked across the open plain behind us. Both Constantine and Rhin-Hir's men had fought back, so that they too made progress into the Saxon positions to left and right. I was puzzled though, for I had not yet seen Ceawlin or Cutha, though I knew of Ceawlin's habit of watching the battle from a vantage point, and perhaps this he did even now.

The first phase of the battle was over, and many dead warriors of both sides lay over the open plain, but it was clear that the advantage lay with us at this stage at least, for the Saxons had broken away from in front of us and had retreated.

I again parlayed with Kynon. I had been impressed with his fighting skills, for he had not shirked for one moment to join in the rout of the Saxon shieldwall, once the first collision had been seen through. He and I had fought side by side all morning and we had seen off many of the Saxon warriors between us.

"We might explore this woodland before we engage again, because I am puzzled as to why we have not yet seen the Gevissa king and his son. The Saxon chief I spared made straight for this sector. I suspect some sort of trap, and my suggestion is that my war-band go ahead to see what is in front of us."

Kynon readily agreed, but insisted that he go with us, and he cleverly pointed out that I could hardly refuse this request, for otherwise he would have no bodyguard, and I had given my word to his father that I would protect him with my life. I laughed, warming to this proud warrior's sense of humour, even if his words had bored my sister senseless at the feast at Penwyrn. Kynon gave orders to such of his chief warriors who remained standing to hold the present position, whilst we checked for traps ahead of us and I explained what was happening to my men before we moved off into the woods.

Torquato led the way, and Cormac protected our rear with *Gaeallon*. At first we could see very little, for although the sun was high and bright on the open plain behind us, in amongst the trees all was shadow, and it was cold, and again I was aware of the moist damp smell in my nostrils, as if it was exuded from the very floor of the forest itself. I could hear no cries of birds, and it occurred to me that others must have passed this way before us and disturbed them. Ahead of us we could see a clearing, and Torquato held up his right arm as a signal for us to stop. In the clearing we could see many figures. On my friend's signal we dropped to our haunches, and watched as he edged forward to the very rim of the clearing itself. In a couple of minutes he was back, and Kynon, Cormac and I crowded around him.

"Almost the top prize. The Gevissa prince is there, reading maps on a table, and with his personal bodyguard, unless I am mistaken."

"How many men?"

"I counted twenty-five, and these will be seasoned warriors, not farmers."

His eyes shone, and I knew that his instincts were fully engaged, for this was what he had been trained for.

I gave the word to my men, and we carefully crept forward. We would have the element of surprise, but the clearing was a large one, so that this would not count for much.

Cutha was there, in full battle rig, and around him were men who all wore the wolf's crest on their mail and shields, so that these must have been some of Ceawlin's best men.

Just then the white stallion galloped into the clearing – Crida. He dismounted and went up to Cutha and they talked. Cutha then put his right arm to his great friend's right shoulder, they clasped hands, and then Crida remounted and rode out of the clearing.

I turned to Kynon.

"Looks to me as if there is some greater plan going on around us. We should move quickly here."

I looked at Cormac to my right. He nodded. I looked to Torquato to my left, who also nodded.

I looked at Kynon.

"This is your battle, Chief. What do you say?"

The Powys prince drew his sword.

"I say that we pay them a visit."

With a yell he raised his sword and leapt from the cover of the woods, straight at the Saxons, and my war-band and my brother were right behind him.

The Saxons looked up, deep surprise on their faces, but even as they did so their survival skills in many battles sustained them, for already they reached for their swords, already three of them stepped in front of Cutha, and they stood ready to repel our charge even before we were within five paces of them. So battle was joined, and I knew at once that these men knew their work, for Kynon reached them first and already their lead warrior engaged with him. I could tell from his first stroke that took Kynon's blow away from his chest and straight away put Kynon onto his defence that these men were real warriors, trained in the battle arts.

Then we were engaged on all fronts, for we were outnumbered more than two to one. I crossed swords with a man with black-grey hair first, and he parried my stroke and stepped gracefully to one side, an advanced manoeuvre, one that Torquato himself had taught me. I turned and he came at me then, but I too parried his thrust, and myself stepped to one side, but as I did so I thrust my blade into his side, and he fell to the floor, and he would play no further part in this battle.

To my left I saw Scipio sink slowly to the ground, caught full in the neck by the blade of a young long-haired Saes warrior even as his trident struck another lunging Saxon in front of him. I cried out, but I had no time to think, for immediately another Saxon came at me, and I ducked, and I stepped, and I parried, and now the Saxon was on his defence, for I had him just where I wanted him, and I thrust a killing blow hard through the ribs of the mail shirt that he wore. Even as I removed *Saesbane*, I cried out in despair as I saw Veos fall in front of me, a sword in his back. These Gevissa warriors were highly trained in the battle arts, and we had met the best men, and this was true fighting, for we were all hard pressed, and had little time to think, only to fight and to try and survive.

On the far side of the clearing I could see that my brother and Torquato engaged several warriors of the elite guard, but I had little fear for them, for both of those warriors were exceptional. I could see Gregor in front of me, and the young warrior defended the Powys prince expertly, for Kynon had fallen to the floor under the onslaught of three of the Gevissas. Now Gregor parried, and moved, then fixed a Saes warrior with his blade, and with an expert thrust despatched him. Still the men of the wolf's crest came at him, and still he expertly defended the Powys prince. Then I was at his side, and together we drove off five of the bodyguard, for they had decided that Kynon was their prey, so that Gregor and I fought for our lives then, moving, cutting, throwing them off from our shields, and still they came at us, and still we fought. I could sense that Gregor was growing tired at my side, but still they came at us. Then I heard a great roar and I saw the blade of *Gaeallon* cleave the air, and two of the Gevissas fell under its arc, for my brother had seen our need, and he was there next to us.

The Saxons fell back, for I did not know it then but Cormac and Torquato had already wreaked havoc amongst their numbers, and these men were the last of the guard to fall, so that in moments it was all over. Now only Cutha stood before us, standing proud, surrounded by his enemy, but not one trace of fear showing on his face.

The skirmish was over. Cutha's guard had been destroyed, but we had taken heavy casualties ourselves, for I could see that not only were Scipio and Veos down, but Rama Bec and Little Sigfeldt were also down, dead or wounded, I could not say. I saw that Kynon was wounded, but thanks to Gregor he would live.

Now the crucial moment was at hand. I came forward, and as I did so Cormac and Torquato moved back to the centre of the clearing, so as to act as a guard, for we did not know if other Saxons were near and might come upon us at any moment.

I came up to the Gevissa prince; he stood there tall, proud, and composed, but kept his shield well up against his chest to afford him at least some protection. His face was pale, but no fear showed in it. He it was who had first downed Kynon with a sword-thrust to the thigh, and if not for Gregor he would have finished off the Powys prince at that moment. I was moved by his quiet pride, for he held his head high, and I could see his father and his sister in his actions. The thought occurred to me that in other circumstances, in a different life, this man and I might have been brothers, and I suspected that we might have made good brothers too.

I put my sword in front of me and leant on the blade. I spoke in the language of the Romans, for I wanted him to know that I sought the middle ground in our words.

"I will not fight with you, Gevissa prince. As all now seem to know, your sister and I have a pact, and out of respect for it, I will not fight with you now."

I said no more, for I had no intention to sully my relationship with this man's sister in some open display of bravado.

"You know, Rhuadrac, my father once had great hope in you, for he valued your way of thinking highly, and hoped to make a shoulder-man of you one day."

"Gevissa, your father placed too much reliance on my ability to fight and deceive my own people, for some matters are beyond gold and status, and that is one of those matters."

I could see that these words struck home with him.

"I fear that my father is much changed since the . . . tragedy in our family. Much changed . . ."

His voice trailed away.

". . . Briton, we are strangely met here, but you have the advantage of me and I would appear to be your prisoner. I doubt that I will be shown any leniency if I am taken down into the British ranks. I would therefore ask that we talk here for a few moments, for there are matters of great consequence to me, and to my sister, that I would discuss with you now, whilst we have the chance to do so."

I looked around this clearing in the woods; no doubt the battle still raged on the open plain behind us, but my people were here with me, and I had Kynon safe, if wounded. I knew that Cutha was right; the cut-throats I had met last night would not spare a Gevissa prince.

"Cutha, I will speak with you, but we do not have much time."

Cutha stepped towards me, and smiled, and put his shield to one side so that he could take off his helmet. Just at that moment, even as he raised his arms to remove his helmet, something heavy flew past my right ear. As I looked up, the weighted dart hit Cutha full in the chest with a thud, piercing his mail shirt. He stopped dead in his tracks. He blinked hard and looked down at the red stain spurting under and through his mail shirt, and then he smiled a distant smile, and fell forward, staggering into my arms.

As I lowered him to the ground I looked around me in shock, and I could see that the Gaul, Felix, stood there with a mocking leer on his face, slowly weighing a second dart in his right hand. In a moment, Cormac had him by the throat, knocked the second dart from his hand, and lifted him from the floor. My brother looked at me.

"We all heard you say that you would talk; the Saxon prince was defenceless. This snivelling gold-seeker thought that he might take some more plunder. What would you have done with him?"

"Hold him there."

I looked back to the face of the fallen warrior in front of me. There was much of his father in him, but his eyes reminded me of another, much closer to my heart, and I could barely bring myself to look at him brought so low. I bent forward and lifted his head in my arms, and I spoke into his ear:

"Cutha, I would have spared your life, even though we are enemies on this field, for your sister is everything to me, and she always spoke of you in the highest terms, with great pride . . ."

The Saxon looked at me, and his mouth filled up with blood, and I could hardly bear to look at him, for his eyes reminded me of another. He tried to lift his head.

"Rhuadrac . . . you are everything to my sister too . . . she cannot live peaceably without you . . . She talked of nothing but you during your time in the land of the Franks. So I feel as if I know you very well . . ."

He tried to smile, but then he gripped my shoulder and grimaced, and the blood ran out between his teeth.

"You must go to her, Briton, and find her, and protect her. Olric has poisoned my father against her . . . he tells my father that she is in league with you to take his kingdom from him . . . she has been exiled from my father's sight . . ."

A spasm of pain convulsed his body.

". . . and even now there are plans to take her from this land. She may not be safe when my father learns of what has happened here . . ."

His tongue moved in his mouth as he tried to say something else to me. I moved my head closer to his:

"Try to . . . find . . . the good man . . . in my father again . . ."

Then he smiled at me, and seemed almost to rally, for he lifted his head, and said clearly:

"Ulla tells me that we will make good brothers, Briton . . ."

His head fell back, and the soul of this proud warrior left this life forever.

I knelt with my head bent over him for several moments. Then I looked up, and Cormac still held the Gaul, and he writhed in my brother's grip.

I looked around the clearing, now littered with the sprawled and probably lifeless bodies of warriors; Veos, Scipio, Rama Bec, Little Sigfeldt, the Gevissa elite warriors, and now this prince, Cutha. All good men.

I looked at the Gaul then.

"This evening, after the battle, we will have a final reckoning of your share. You will be allowed a minimum amount of gold. Then you are on your own. I will have no more dealings with you."

Felix said nothing, but I saw hatred flash through his eyes.

My brother left him then and went over to tend to Kynon.

I stood up and walked over to the fallen warriors of my war-band; I saw at once that Scipio, Rama Bec and Sigfeldt were finished – Sigfeldt laying across the body of the Syrian, as if in some way shielding him. I saw that a calm and peaceful look, though full of wonder, played across the early dead features of Rama Bec, and his eyes were open, as if he witnessed new and wondrous stories in the lands in which he now walked.

These men from many lands, this war-band, had walked and slept and broken bread with me through many seasons in the land of the Gauls; we had seen many battles, had stood together at times of greatest need. Now, in moments, they had been taken from me. A terrifying dizziness momentarily assailed all of my senses. I lowered my head and closed my eyes, my right hand coming up to my face as I fell onto one knee. I reached for the bronze cross I kept always on my person, and I held it clenched firmly in my right hand.

Eventually I looked across at Torquato who stood near to me; his face had taken on the blank mask I had come to know at these times. This was the consequence of battle. You live or you die. If a warrior is skilled, and has good fortune, then he might survive to give quiet praise to his dead comrades. So he had been taught, and so he conducted himself. But in truth I knew that his real thoughts at these moments were wrapped up deep down inside him. No flicker of emotion crossed over his features. His eyes met mine, as if daring me to speak; after a few moments he nodded towards the prone body of Veostan.

"Our wounded comrade lives still."

Veos lay on his side, his eyes still open. Slowly I stood up and walked to him, then knelt by his side, the Roman with me. The Scandic warrior's battered, good-natured face was deathly pale; the sword that had felled him still bedded deep in his back:

"How many wounds, Chief?"

"Just one, Veos, but I fear it is too many, friend."

"Ah, so be it. The Roman told me always to watch my back in these skirmishes. It looks like he was finally right."

He winced, and the light in his eyes grew dimmer.

"Chief, after the battle, you will return here and see us out in the right way? I have that journey to make, remember?"

"Aye, Veos, I remember. I promise to return."

Torquato looked into the face of his fallen comrade, then briefly looked away into the trees, the muscles in his jaw clenching.

Veos too followed his gaze into the trees, and said, in an awed whisper:

"Why then, what sort of bird is that?"

I looked up into the branches but could see nothing.

"Can you not see it? Look, there now! So white, so beautiful; I would not have thought it possible. Perhaps it is returning home from these winter lands?"

I again looked into the branches but could see nothing.

I looked back to Veostan; I saw then that he had died.

I bowed my head, then looked across at Torquato.

As I did so, I saw Torquato's eyes widen at some sight beyond my shoulder. In a sudden blur of movement he pushed my right shoulder slightly with his left arm, causing me to sway away to my left. In a flash of heavy black metal, a dart hit the bole of the tree in front of me, juddering there.

"You British bastard, I will have my full share of that gold . . ."

But Felix saw that Torquato was already moving, leopard-like, unfolding his massive frame with great speed. Felix ran then, but Torquato was after him. They clattered off into the foliage that surrounded the clearing.

We all moved towards the centre of the clearing, my brother supporting Kynon.

In a short time Torquato returned, wiping the blade of his sword.

"The Gaul will kill no more defenceless princes; the gold-greed has left him for good."

*

We had no time to dwell on these matters, for the battle still raged on the plain behind us. As we left the clearing, Torquato caught up with me and fell into step. I said to him:

"Our friends are lost. We need a cold heart and cold reasoning, friend, now is not the time to lose sight of the purpose of the day – but thank you, once again."

He placed his large hand on my shoulder. As he did so, long blasts of several horns rent the air from the far side of the plain, and a great cry went up, and we could see whole squadrons of Saxons pour down the far side of the plain. Torquato looked at me.

"It looks like the Gevissa king has decided to join the fray."

We watched as the Saxons thundered into the men of Gwynedd, who had been making great strides forward on the far left flank of the plain, and could see a wide rift open up in their ranks as the Saxons hit them. Even as we watched, a second wave swarmed down the right flank, and immediately Constantine's men fell back, for they too had already been fighting for most of the morning.

"Where are the reserves, where are Meurig and Aircol?" I said, through clenched teeth.

Still the Saxons advanced down the plain, and still there was no sight of the reserves.

"Where are those robbers? The day will be lost!"

Even as I spoke, I heard a low roar come from behind the British sector, and then we saw that the Irish army under their king Aidan had come onto the field.

Another great clamour went up from the British ranks, and still more warriors flooded over the plains before us. I found out later that Meurig and Aircol were for fleeing the field at the sight of the Saxon counter-surge, but the lead warriors of both Dyfed and Gwent ignored them, and, seeing the Irish surge forward, brought their warriors onto the field anyway, for they could see that all was still in the balance. They would fight proudly for their land, even if those in power over them would not.

From where we stood we could but watch as both sides fought furiously in the centre of the plain; it was clear that Ceawlin's intervention had prevented a rout, but still the battle raged, and if anything it was the Irish and British forces that were making ground.

By now Gregor had reached Torquato and I, and Kynon too, though limping, arrived, half-carried by my brother. I spoke to the Powys prince:

"We will head for Brocmael, and find out what strength is left in the Powys forces, for perhaps our forces too can remuster, for it seems to me that Ceawlin's warriors are losing ground, and one more surge may be decisive."

Kynon nodded in agreement, and we moved down the small slope from the wood and onto the plain, making our way around the side of the field, heading for the place where we had left Brocmael watching the fray that morning, for it had been agreed that he would come onto the field only if it was required.

The Powys king was still where we had left him. I was surprised to see that he was watching the battle with several monks; they did not leave us when I arrived with Cormac, Torquato, Gregor and the limping Kynon, who greeted his father with the words:

"It is nothing, Father, little more than a flesh wound in the thigh, given to me by the Gevissa prince himself, who is now dead. These warriors have already done more than we could have asked of them – my life has been saved several times because of their intervention."

Brocmael looked at his son, satisfied himself that he was in no danger, and turned to me and Cormac.

"Your names will ring out in the verses after the work you have done today. But the day is not yet finished. I think we get the upper hand, now that the Irishman Aidan has come in to the field with Dyfed and Gwent. I believe now is the time for the decisive move. What do you say to me?"

We all agreed that a move now with sufficient men may well prove decisive.

Brocmael turned to his shoulder-men and gave precise, measured instructions. His personal bodyguard was to lead the last charge, with as many men as were still fit to fight.

In front of us, many men still stood or sat, or lay on the ground, tired, but not yet exhausted, for they sensed, as we all sensed, that the day was turning our way, and that one last drive could make it ours.

So it was that the Powys king came onto the field, flanked by his bodyguard carrying the eagle standards. He charged straight at the Gevissa forces, and the Powys men charged with him, and Cormac, *Gaeallon* in his right arm, Torquato and I were in the vanguard this time, for there were no more shieldwalls to negotiate, now it would be hand to hand, each man for himself.

We charged straight into the most concentrated area of the battle. In front of us we could now see Aidan himself, flanked by Arthur and Bran, even as they were pressed backwards by more warriors wearing the wolf's head silhouette on their shields. Even as we strove to get to them, we saw Bran, nephew of Aidan, fall as three men set about him – he struck out at the man to his left, just as a short spear was thrust into his right side. He fell in a wide sprawl of shield, sword and war-helmet, dislocated. Now Torquato and Cormac had reached him, and with three short blows cleared away the Saxons around him. But we could see that we were too late. Already the Irishman Bran was finished.

Barely pausing, Aidan ran onto into the fray, his son Arthur by his side. We joined them, and the Irish and British forces swelled all around us, and we knew that the momentum was with us. Together we plunged straight into the heart of the Saxon forces.

The effect of the charge was immediate. The Saxons saw the eagle standards, they saw the Powys king, and they saw too the legendary giant champion who had vanquished the Chinaman from the High Mountains. Then it was that the spirit of those brave men was broken, for some who had survived the first engagement had now fought for many hours. There was no wholesale flight from the field, but the tide of the battle was decisively turned, for ground was given immediately, and the momentum of the fighting was on the side of the British, for we moved forward in every sector, and the Saxons were being driven back towards the woods that ringed the open plain, and the British followed them.

About sixty paces ahead of me I could now see the Gevissa king himself, seated on a black stallion, the wolf's head crest prominent on his shield and mail shirt. He was dressed exactly as I remembered from Deorham. Now he sought to lift his troops, but he could see that the battle was going against him.

Then I saw that he said something to his shoulder-men, for as always the old man Willem and the young thegn Crida were next to him. All three of them then galloped off the plain into that part of the woods in which we had met with Cutha and his elite warriors. The battle went on in front of me, moving away from me now as the Britons continued to press home the advantage gained by Brocmael coming on to the field, and I could see Torquato and Cormac right up at the front, still causing havoc in the Gevissa ranks.

Now I stood back and watched the woods. I could but imagine the scene when Ceawlin came upon the clearing and found the body of his dead son.

Just then it was that the battle seemed suddenly stupid to me. This should have been a moment of triumph, but I felt none of it, could only feel keenly the stupidity of kings, and the chaos wrought by the ambitions of those who seek power in this world.

Still I watched the woods.

Finally the Gevissa king reappeared, but I could see that the battle-helmet had gone from his head, and the shield had been thrown from his grasp. Even from the distance at which I stood away from him I could see the white hair and the fine lean features of his face as he raged, and mouthed oaths at the sky, and shook his sword at the sun. I watched as the black stallion reared and bucked and ran in circles, as its master cleaved at the trees and the branches and the fresh air with his sword, and I thought then that the madness of the man had finally claimed him forever.

Next to this madman sat Crida. I saw that his head was bowed, and his horse stood stock still. I remembered then that Cutha had been his great friend.

But then there were three loud blasts of the Saxon horns; then again, repeated, three loud blasts of the horns. On the second series of blasts the Saxon army turned and ran, and fled for the sanctuary of the woods. They were chased as far as the wooded perimeter, but there their pursuers stopped, themselves exhausted.

Great cheers went up from the British side, for victory was ours. The Saxons, though not completely routed, had fled, and we were in possession of the field.

In this way the combined Irish and British armies had put a stop on the Gevissa king Ceawlin's march to the upper Severn Valley.

I looked back to the woods, but Ceawlin was no longer to be seen.

I looked around me. Dusk was just beginning to fall at the end of a short winter's day, which had been clear and lit by the gentle warmth of a winter sun.

Around me I could hear everywhere the baleful cries of the mortally wounded. A low dull moan, sobbing, an occasional agonised cry.

From somewhere near me I could hear what seemed to be a boy's voice saying simply:

"Mama, mama, are you there? Why have you left me here, mama?"

Then I heard the plaintive voice no more.

Elsewhere, the living celebrated the victory. The cheers continued to ring around the plain at Fethan Leag, whilst bodies of dead men and the wounded lay all around the open plain. A great stench had begun to fill the air, and already black scavenger birds were landing on the edge of the field, some already in amongst the dead men.

I thought of Veos, his questions now forever silenced. I thought of Rama Bec; no more would his tales be heard at the hearth. No more would Little Sigfeldt sit quietly in his company. I thought of Scipio, and his laughter just yesterday at the folly of kings. Scipio was dead. I would find some way to get his share of the spoils back to his family, somehow, for he would not himself be taking to them the gold that he had earned.

I hung my head low then, on that field, and there was suddenly no sense of glory in what we had done that day.

But I had other matters still to attend to, for I knew that the fury and madness of the Gevissa king would not now be easily assuaged.

*

Later that night I sat around our own hearth back at Brocmael's camp. With me sat my brother, Torquato and Gregor.

Earlier we had gone back to the clearing in the woods to find the bodies of the men in my war-band. We all took flaming torches. Brocmael had insisted that some of his men come with us, for there would be work to be done there, and they too carried lit boughs. As we walked, long shadows fell away from in front of us; strange formless creatures seemed to scurry back into the undergrowth. High above us some strange night-bird sent out a shrill four-note *Ha-Ha-Ha-Ha* nearby; then again, more distant, *Ha-Ha-Ha-Ha* – its inhuman cry echoed around the dense hanging branches.

So it was that we found ourselves back in the place where we had met Cutha's elite guard. There was no sight of the Saxon dead; no doubt Ceawlin would honour his warriors and his son in the Saxon way. The bodies of my fallen comrades had been strung up in the trees, and there was clear evidence that their bodies had been despoiled; the Saxons had performed some terrible rite there. But I did not dwell on those matters. I preferred to think of my warriors as they had been.

We made up pyres, for none of my men were of my mother's faith. We lifted them onto biers, placing swords, shields, mace and daggers on their chests, with Scipio's net and trident by his side. Then, with that strange night-bird still crying out in the echoing dark – *Ha-Ha-Ha-Ha* – a chill breeze plucking at our backs, we burned them there, the sparks spiralling away up into the black night.

It was a sombre moment, but it was the right way, and it was as they would have wished it. I hoped that even now Veos took the warrior-path, striding out through the stars to find the warrior-heaven of his people, there just as he believed it would be.

As we stood there, I found that I held the silver and bronze cross, given to me by Cormac after Deorham, held tight in my right hand. Still I carried it with me always.

So now we had put that grim business behind us and returned to our own hearth. None of us had the stomach to visit Brocmael's tent, for we feared that Meurig and Aircol and others like them would be there, no doubt telling all that would listen how they had saved the day. Aidan and his men would in all probability seek their own company too. The first few claw-beakers of wine had been supped, and a mild euphoria had gripped my brother and friend, for they were born warriors, born to fight, and I shared none of my misgivings about the battle with them, for I was beginning to understand that I perhaps saw this life in a different way to them. They had fought, and fought like the elite warriors they were. They were happy, and so too did they deserve to be.

"By the power of Hercules, but I thought that I heard the very ground shake when that Chinaman rumbled into view! So they do exist then."

Cormac looked at my Roman friend and laughed quietly.

"Aye, he was a big bastard for sure, and he was real enough when he caught me with that head-butt. I could see that I needed to be on my mettle. His big mistake was to think that he had the headlock on me. He did not; that was exactly where I wanted him, for I was confident that I could break him if I got the armlock on him. More fat on his belly and less on his chest would have helped him."

"That Crida knew some good stuff; lucky for him that your brother has principles!"

So they talked, and it was good to be in their company, for these warriors were my family and friends, and they were good men too.

Cormac looked across at Gregor.

"Now then lad, what's that you're drinking?"

Young Gregor looked across at my giant brother, even now still a little in awe of him.

"I drink mead, for it is quite like the beer in my own country."

"Well, let me pour you another cup, for you proved you are a man today, and you are a fine warrior. Your defence of Kynon in front of Cutha's elite guard was the work of a master, and I was proud to stand by your side in your war-band."

I could see that Gregor's chest swelled, and he lifted his chin, for my brother's words thrilled him, as they had been meant to do.

"And as for you . . ."

Cormac looked at Torquato, who looked back at him warily.

". . . I have never set foot on a battlefield with a finer warrior, and from this day on you are my friend."

He held out his arm.

Torquato stood up, and smiled quietly.

"Yea, big man, your brother told me all about you when we were in the land of the Franks, but in truth, you are an even mightier warrior than he described, for sure."

The two giant warriors clasped their hands together and threw their arms around each other, and rocked from side to side.

I smiled for these two men, so different in character, yet who shared so much. I was pleased that they had broken bread in this way, for although alone they were formidable, together they had proved unstoppable on the field of battle. I knew them both well, and I knew that the edge in their relationship would be back again as soon as the after-battle euphoria fell away.

And so they talked of the battle, of Kynon, who all agreed had proven himself as a fine prince, and of the delay in the Dyfed and Gwent ranks coming onto the field. So too Aidan and his people. The reports were true. Then they talked of Cutha in respectful terms, and both Cormac and Torquato looked at me. My brother spoke first.

"You are quiet, Rhuadrac."

"Yes, brother, matters weigh on my mind, but I have no intention of spoiling the after-battle talk. Carry on, it gives me great pleasure to hear you two rogues and wasters talk of these matters."

Cormac looked at Torquato, then back to me.

"We would know what it is that troubles you."

With some reluctance I outlined my thoughts.

"I know Ceawlin well. He will be devastated by today's events. Not only has he had his progress north up the Severn Valley halted, but, and for him this will be much worse, he has lost his son, so that he now has no natural successor to his kingdom."

We all thought on that for a few moments.

"What then do you think he will now do?"

"I think he will mourn tonight, then somebody will feel his wrath."

"Who then?"

"Maybe the Hwiccas, because he will regard their actions as treason. If they had fought on his side today, their presence on the field may well have turned the battle in his favour."

What I said made sense to them. We did not know if Edelwine had survived the battle or not, but we knew that a small force of Hwiccas had fought on the British side that day, though most had stayed away. Cormac thought on it.

"We should find out if Edelwine survived, for perhaps he should warn his people to expect trouble. What else concerns you?"

I looked into the fire in the hearth.

"I fear for Ulla. She has been sent into exile. Even now she is being taken to the Saxon Shore, from there to be sent to the land of the Saxons. But now I fear that her fate may be even worse than that. In his madness, I am no longer sure that Ceawlin would not harm her, for he will blame me now for the death of his son. I will become the focus of his rage, for I know from Cutha that Olric has convinced the Gevissa king that I seek to use Ulla to make claim upon his kingdom. To this king, disloyalty is the greatest crime a man can commit. Now he will see even his daughter as having betrayed him. If not the king himself, then others might be a danger to her, for Ceawlin's Hall is a viper's nest of intrigue at the best of times, and now her pact with me is known by all."

We all thought on these words.

"Cutha himself, with almost his last words, told me that I should try to find her, for she will need as much protection as she can get in these mad times. Crida alone cannot provide it."

Cormac stood up.

"Brother, we see your concern. What do we know of the whereabouts of the Gevissa princess?"

Torquato looked up from the fire.

"When we listened in on their conversation last night, I think that Cutha may have mentioned that she was to be taken back to the great hall in some place called . . . Silthcaster . . . Silchester, something like that."

This was news to me. I looked at my friend, a question in my face. He shrugged his shoulders.

"I cannot be sure; my knowledge of their language is not perfect, but I think that a place of that name was mentioned."

Silchester, or Calleva, was known to my brother and me, though we had not been there. It had fallen to the Saxons in the time before Bedcanford and had been a strategic loss for the British. It was an old ruined Roman fortified city, not unlike Uriconium, though not quite on the same scale as that city. Since being deserted by the Romans it had been used by the British as a marketplace for trade. It had high-walled ramparts, and it was now deep in Gevissa territory.

Cormac looked at me, then looked at Torquato.

"Why Silchester?"

I thought on this.

"It is safe enough, away from the battle, but not so far as Winche. It may be that, having thrashed us Britons at Fethan Leag, Ceawlin planned to go to

Silchester himself, and take her back to Wessex to make some sort of example of her in his own territory, as proof that not even his daughter would escape his wrath if she schemed against him. Perhaps she would be paraded before her own people in disgrace before being sent away. Who can say what this man's thinking is any longer?"

Cormac thought on my reply.

"If Torquato is right, and Silchester is the place, I vote that we go and see. I am in no rush to go back to farming just yet."

His scarred face smiled.

I too thought on it. My friend's information was not sure. Calleva was quite deep into Saxon territory. On the other hand, three or four men could cover the ground quickly, and with Torquato's skills might just avoid capture.

"I vote too that we make the attempt."

I looked at Torquato.

"Yes. But what do we do if she is not there?"

I thought on this.

"If she is not there, then I will press on to the Saxon Shore, for I will not allow her to be taken by boat from this land whilst I still breathe."

Torquato and Cormac looked at each other. Cormac talked for them both.

"Then we will do likewise."

I looked at Gregor.

"And you Gregor; how do you see it?"

"I go with you."

"You have no need to take the risk, Gregor. You have proved yourself today, and the Powys chiefs are in your debt. You can expect much gold."

"That's good. But you forget two things. First, you are my chief, and I follow you until we decide you are my chief no longer. These are the rules we live by. Second, I have now met this Megwei who you brought to me. I am young, but I understand something of these matters."

There was a pause, then we all laughed. Gregor flushed to the roots of his hair, and his temper flared up, but we calmed him, for what he had said was well said, and Cormac ruffled the lad's hair warmly.

"Well then, but we will have a beard on your face in no time!"

We made our plans then, and decided that time was of the essence. We would try to get a good night's sleep that night, give our excuses to the Powys king in the morning, and strike out for the Saxon lands straight after.

*

The next morning we woke early. The sun shone in a high blue sky. I washed in the ice-cold, clear-running waters of a nearby stream, trying to restore some life into my aching limbs, sore and bruised from the previous day's battle. Cormac and I then went off to see the Powys chief.

Brocmael told us that he would be sad to see us leave so soon after the great victory, but on hearing that we had 'family matters' to attend to, he wished us godspeed. He insisted that we took four of his best horses as a token of the esteem in which he held us, for he thought that Cormac and my war-band had been the difference in the balance between the two armies. Kynon too was full of praise for our conduct on the field of battle, and together they promised us a feast in our honour 'and much gold' when we returned to Penwyrn. We thanked them both, and I went so far as to ask for a fifth horse, for if our family business was successful, we would have need of it.

We asked around the camp and discovered that Edelwine had survived the battle. He had fought in the last phase only, for his wounds from the skirmish at his farm had not yet fully healed, and we found him in good spirits, but it soon became clear that he too shared my concerns as to what the Gevissa king might do now that his ambition further north in the Severn Valley had been crushed.

"A Saxon mind like his thinks only of power, and ambition, and the strength of his family. He will regard the refusal of my people to support him as unforgiveable, and we can expect some retribution. As for me and my family, what is left of us . . ."

There was still a great sadness in his eyes. I was not sure that he would ever fully recover from the events at his farm.

". . . I have already given orders that they leave the farm and move into Corinium, to a safe house, until at least some sense can be made of all of these recent events. As for the rest of it – well then, the Hwiccas are hardy people, and if the Gevissa thinks that we will stand around and be butchered by his army he will be taught to think again. He will store up hatreds that will surely come to plague him in the seasons to come."

We left him then, and I was again struck by how nothing was certain anymore. Now Saxon had begun to fight Saxon, so that it was no longer the case of the British against the Saxon invaders. The battle lines were becoming confused, so that it was no longer clear who fought whom, or what, in truth, it was that was being fought for.

We came across Aidan's tents. The mood seemed sombre as we approached it, and we remembered that their kinsman had lost his life in the thick of the fighting yesterday. Even as we arrived, a solemn ceremony was taking place, and we could see priests dressed in the cassocks of the Irish Christians intoning their rhythmic celtic chants. We paid our respects and stood quietly at the edge of the group of mourners. Then Aidan looked across and saw us.

He moved over to us and said a few brief words:

"The day after a battle never changes."

His face was set; he looked older, profoundly saddened.

We said nothing, for it seemed to us both that words would have no meaning for him at that moment.

Aidan held up his arm, and each of us in turn clasped it.

"I was right. Your father would have every reason to be proud of his sons. Remember, you are welcome at any time in the Dal Riada territories – may peace be with you."

We thanked him, and he moved away to say a few words over the body of his fallen kinsman.

*

We left Brocmael's camp and headed south-west, for we had decided that we would cut back to the edge of the land of the Hwiccas, which had been our homeland, and pick up the tracks we knew well. We would then go down to Calleva by the Corinium to Cunetio road, the very same road taken by Ceawlin all of those long years ago before Deorham. In this way we hoped to avoid contact with the main retreating Saxon forces, who we thought would be likely to take the most direct passage south through the Vale of the White Horse to return to their strongholds.

We made good progress in the early stages. It was near noon when Torquato, who was leading our small band, held up his hand, so that we slowed to a trot. Ahead of us we could see smoke; it was clear that something was in flames. We left the main path and climbed into the hills, so that we might have a better view of what had occurred. Looking down into the valley, we could see that the village below us was on fire, and that several bodies lay about in the central street. Whoever had caused the problem had moved on, because we could clearly see village folk milling around in the central area. We decided to go in and establish what had happened.

Men, women and children walked or ran through the main enclosure, and some were recovering bodies that were strewn here and there, and there seemed to have been a great robbery too, for boxes and chests lay all over the enclosure, with stoved-in lids, their contents ransacked.

We saw a man dressed in British clothes, so we hailed him, and asked him what had occurred here.

He was an old man, who dressed simply, with breeches and an old green tunic, with an old green cap on his head, and we guessed that he was a farm worker, now working for the Saxons.

"It was complete madness. I never thought that I would see the day when Saxon fought Saxon, but that is what happened here. A Saxon war-band came, and they were looking for their own people, and they killed them and robbed them. We received reports that this had happened also in other villages before ours, so that it seems that the Saxons seek to leave waste the farms of the Hwiccas, who are their own people."

We could see that these were new ideas for him, for he seemed to be completely bewildered.

"Have a care for your safety Granddad, for the Saxons have suffered a defeat to our British forces just yesterday at the place called Fethan Leag, and they blame their own people amongst the Hwiccas who would not fight for them."

The old fellow pulled the cap off his head and danced a jig where he stood.

"Good boys, well done. Give these Saxon heathens a good hiding did we? Good work, boys, good work."

We left him there, on that village street on the edge of the Hwicca lands, an old man dancing a jig because his people had secured a victory over the Saxon invaders, even as the village huts burnt all around him. The Saxon settlers were now feeling the wrath of the Saxon king who would be *Bretwalda*.

With this evidence that the Gevissas had turned in anger upon the Hwiccas already, we decided to press on without delay, and to cut across country to reach the Calleva road, to head south.

This we did, and soon enough we picked up the road to Cunetio, which we knew would take us through Calleva. With luck, we could even be there before nightfall if we drove the horses hard.

At one point we left the road and climbed the high hills to our right, or to the west on a map, and from there we had a commanding view of the plains set out all around us. We were surprised to see that fires burned in all sectors – behind, to the side, in front of us.

Cormac looked across at me:

"Looks like the old king has finally taken complete leave of his senses. His war-bands are firing every town or village they come across, whether it be their own people or not."

I could say nothing at first, for the evidence was in front of us; the Gevissas seemed to have decided to torch their own lands, because we now rode through Gevissa settlements, and still we could see the fires burning.

"Perhaps he has decided to teach a lesson to all who might think about rebelling against his rule, whether they have done so or not?"

This seemed to strike the right note concerning his madness, which was some sort of power madness, and Cormac nodded his head in agreement.

"Maybe so, maybe so."

We rode on, avoiding the towns and villages, but still making good progress. The sun had dropped below the land some time ago; we had passed over the river Kennet, and we could see several huts set out along the Corinium Road, which suggested that we were getting close to a settlement. We skirted behind the huts, for we presumed that Saxons occupied them. Rejoining the road soon after, we could see the lights of Calleva set out on the higher ground in front of us. It stood on a low hill, really a vast plateau slightly raised above the surrounding flatlands, and was surrounded by woodland on three sides. We could see no evidence of fire there; either Ceawlin's men were now behind us or Calleva would be spared the looting and robbery that seemed to have fallen upon other townships that we had skirted.

We dismounted in a copse, and shared out the strips of dry salt beef, bread and water that we had brought with us.

"So, we have reached Calleva, or Silchester, or whatever this town is now called. What next?"

Cormac looked at me, as he increasingly did since I had come back from the land of the Franks, for he was happy to leave the planning to me.

I had been thinking about this for most of the journey down from Fethan Leag.

"Torquato thought that he heard mention of a great hall. My father used to talk of a palace in the centre of this town, called the Forum, from Roman times. My guess is that she will be there, or if she is not there, then somebody there will know where she might be, if they can be persuaded to tell us."

We decided to press on to the western boundary of the city walls, and there to secure the horses in a hidden place, for we were sure that they would be needed if we were to make an escape from this city.

We found a thicket deep in a wood not far from the city walls, and tied the horses up there. I asked Gregor to stay with them, for they would be vital to the success of our mission, and without a guard over them we could not be sure that their presence would go undetected.

Gregor reluctantly agreed. So it was that the three of us – Cormac, Torquato and me – headed for the west gate of the ruined city of Calleva, to see if we could find the Gevissa princess there, and take her back with us to Penwyrn

*

Ahead of us we could see the high turret-like walls, at least five arm-widths in height, and although they were crumbling since the departure long ago of the Roman legions, still they provided a formidable obstacle. The walls were made of rough stones set in cement, and every arms-width or so a row of stone slabs had been set lengthways over the stones, so as to bond them. Then the stones and cement were piled on top again, and a further bonding ridge of stone slabs laid lengthways, and so on, and in this way the colossal walls of this city had been constructed.

At the west gate, a plain wooden bridge was laid across a wide ditch, about four long paces wide. The west gate itself had two arched entrances, presumably for the flow of traffic when it had once flourished under the Romans. Those days had long since gone; although the city was still occupied, now it served as a trade centre. Most of the whitewalled buildings were no longer used, though some were, for we could see lights through the open gate, so some sort of Gevissa community had been set up here.

From where we stood we could see no evidence of sentries on the gate, which made sense, for now we were in Gevissa territory, and no Gevissa would expect a Briton in this place.

We dropped back into the dense foliage of the woods.

"We all three go in, keeping low, Torquato leading. If we are found, after the events at Fethan Leag, we are dead men. So we keep together. If one is discovered, the other two will leave him and press on to the Saxon Shore. We make for the Forum. If we see no sign of her there, we make our way back here and decide if we push on for the Saxon Shore or spend more time searching here."

Both men looked as if they might say something, but then both looked at each other, and smiled. This was their business. They would decide if anybody was to be left behind. They said nothing, just nodded at me.

We agreed that Torquato would approach the gate first. He drew his sword and set off, keeping low, zig-zagging, then we saw him stop and suddenly drop to the floor just before he reached the bridge. He ducked under it, into the wide ditch.

It was then that we heard what he had already heard – several horsemen, coming down the road that we ourselves had just left, heading for the west gate also.

They swept across the bridge, and I could see Crida, Ceawlin's shoulder-man, on the first horse. In all, we counted twenty men – a Gevissa war-band, covered in dust, some holding torches, who all looked as if they had been riding all day. Perhaps these were the warriors responsible for the attacks we had seen in the Hwicca country. We could see from the light of their torches that there were no sentries at the gate, which was undefended. They carried on across the bridge and into the city through the open gate, turning to their right, making for the southern quarter.

Cormac and I saw Torquato re-emerge from the ditch and swing himself onto the bridge itself. Then he hurried forward, bent double, and ran up to the gate, lying flat against the rampart of the wall on its left-hand side. It was obvious that he could see nothing in front of him. He waved to us, and Cormac and I sprinted forward, keeping low, and reached the Roman mercenary.

I told them both that I had seen Crida at the head of the Gevissa war-band.

"Perhaps here to tell Ulla, if she is here, about Fethan Leag and the fate of her brother, and take her to the Saxon Shore, or do whatever else it is that Ceawlin has ordered him to do."

All three of us looked at each other in the dusk.

Cormac spoke first.

"Then there is no time to waste."

Torquato turned away from us and ran through the gate and looked up the street to his left. He came back to us:

"All clear – through the gate, turn left. Keep running to the first building on the left, no lights. Keep going north until we can see the main square."

We nodded. Torquato went first. We heard nothing. Cormac followed, then I ran too, ducking low, turning left, ran further, and turned into a doorway. In this way we made our way up the street. We could see both timber and stone buildings. Some were deserted, but in others we could see lights and hear voices. I could see both Cormac and Torquato ahead of me, moving between the doorways of unlit houses, and I followed. After a few minutes I saw them turn right under an arched gate. Again I followed them. I found myself in a small courtyard garden. Torquato and Cormac were already running lightly down the path, towards what seemed to be a deserted white-stone building. I watched and saw Cormac hoist the Roman onto a ledge, from which Torquato swung up onto a small roof and disappeared over a second ledge. In moments he was back and waved to us to follow him. Cormac lifted me high onto the small roof. I hoisted my brother behind me, and together we climbed over the ledge and up a few steps to the proper roof of the building, where we could see Torquato lying flat on his stomach. He was looking out over the old Roman town.

A full moon glowed in the clear sky, throwing a febrile light over the white walls, and there were a few lit torches in the street below, so that now we were ideally placed to see the layout of the city.

Immediately in front of us we could now see a building that could only be the old Forum, for it dominated the centre of the city; it effectively formed a walled village within the city itself, for its walls ran left and right in front of us. Even from where we lay, we could see torchlights burning in the first floor of the building, so that it was clear that people were residing there.

We moved away from the lip of the roof. I spoke first.

"If she is here, she will be in that building, I am sure of it."

Cormac looked out across the imposing rear wall of the Forum that now dominated the street in front of us.

"Then we need to get into the central courtyard to get a better look of the layout."

Torquato spoke:

"There is an archway set into the building on our left-hand side. I think that we can gain entry there."

We agreed, and soon enough found ourselves in the open square of the Forum itself. To our right rose up a magnificent basilica. On the three other sides of the square we could see shop entrances and porticoes. Some were still in use, for we could see canvas awnings over a few of them. In other places, rough timber structures had been erected, not unlike at Uriconium, no doubt used by the Gevissa traders on market days. But it was the basilica that held our attention. To one side stood a row of giant columns in the Roman style, and here we guessed was the main hall of the city.

Then we saw that eight horses had been tethered in a makeshift paddock in the centre of the Forum, two of which were grey.

Torquato glanced at me.

"One of those greys is the horse that the Gevissa princess rode when she left Ceawlin's camp."

I had noticed it too. My mouth was dry. Suddenly I was certain that she was here, in this place.

We fell back into the shadows of the ruined buildings. Deep inside the basilica we could see that there were rooms, and lights flickered in those rooms. Just then we heard hooves, and the war-band we had seen before swept through the main entrance of the Forum, on the opposite side from where we stood, and galloped up to the makeshift paddock.

Crida and three men dismounted; all except Crida held torches in their hands. Crida stopped and looked at the ground for a moment, and it seemed to me that something heavy weighed on his mind. Then he straightened up, barked orders to the rest, and he and the other three warriors holding the lit boughs ran over to the basilica and turned left. Crida pounded a wooden door with the hilt of his sword. The door opened, and the bright torchlight lit up the area under the arch, and I could see old Peg standing there. The Saxon warriors roughly pushed past her to get into the room behind her.

The warriors left behind now dismounted. They too drew boughs from a pouch in each saddle and poured some clear liquid over the rags tied to the end of the bough. A flint was eventually struck and then each man took his lit torch and began to scorch the rough canvas tied back over the market stalls. Fires began to burn in the courtyard in front of us. I looked at Torquato and Cormac.

"They mean to torch this place. If we are to succeed in this mad mission, then we must move now."

So saying, I stepped out of the shadow of the basilica and stood in the moonlit courtyard. Even as I did so Cormac swung *Gaeallon* down from his shoulders, and Torquato too drew his short sword.

The Gevissa war-band stared at me, at first not certain what they were looking at. They could not have expected a Briton in that place, but then one or two in the war-band recognised me, then saw Cormac, and they drew their swords, and their fellow warriors did likewise. Before they could move at us, the three of us were in amongst them. Then they came at us from all sides, but they fought exceptional warriors. Cormac and Torquato scored first, the Roman taking two Saxons out of the conflict instantly with that step, parry, step, in, out manoeuvre that I seen so many times. Cormac swung *Gaeallon*, and two more of the Saxons fell.

But then they were behind us, and these were elite warriors too, and even as I pinned one against the wall with *Saesbane* another's sword cut deep into my left shoulder, near the arm. I cursed twice over, once with the pain that immediately seared down the whole of my left arm and twice for the fact that I had not put on the shoulder-clasp which had protected me yesterday. I wheeled about and caught the next thrust of the same warrior with *Saesbane,* knocking his sword from his grasp and sweeping my sword across his neck. A third came at me and we blundered into each other at the chest, each with the force of our momentum. I saw his blue eyes close up, then I threw him away from me and with a single thrust under the ribs, finished him.

Now the Saxons stood off from us, for we had almost halved their number already. I could see that Cormac bled slightly from the side of his head, although Torquato remained unscathed. With a roar we went at them again, and the fighting spilled out from under the eaves of the building into the open Forum. I could see the wooden shutters in the room that Crida had entered get thrown back, even as three more of the Saxons fell in front of my brother and friend.

Cormac lifted a fourth off the floor with a mighty heft of his battle-axe and threw the man at the two Saxons rushing in at him. I ducked and sidestepped in one movement as a heavy sword almost took the head off my shoulders and I thrust *Saesbane* into the side of my attacker. Suddenly, the remaining warriors in front of us broke off the engagement and ran towards the room under the arches of the basilica which we had seen Crida enter.

As they did so I heard the sound of shattering glass, and noticed that smoke poured out of the unshuttered window. The other two heard it too, and we watched as the flames burst with a great roar of noise up the outside wall of the Forum.

Even as this was happening we saw Crida and the remaining warriors of his war-band cross over through the arched passageway from the burning room into the hall across on the other side of the basilica. Between them they shielded two women whose heads were covered with wet blankets. I knew that Ulla was there, and my mind was blank for a few moments, because she was still safe, and she was so close to me now. My shoulder began to throb and burn with pain, but the battle-spirit was on me, and the pain could be dealt with tomorrow. We watched as the flames leapt out of the open door of the room and licked at the makeshift timber awning set into the stone archway that led to the great hall. From the inside of the abandoned room came the sound of falling stone and masonry, as the fire wreaked havoc with the ruins of the building, now made like tinder with all of the makeshift wooden shop enclosures that ran through the porticoes of the building.

The Saxons ran through into the hall, but we could see that the great stone doorway had lost its oak door many years ago, so we followed. Through the black smoke that even now began to pour out of the hall, we could see the Saxons over on the far side of the hall, and we saw them turn over tables so as to make some form of barricade there. Even as we came into the hall, I saw one of the women take the towel from her head. It was Ulla standing there, in this mad place, with flames running around the timber frame of the ceiling even as we stood there, with the shadows of the three of us making great shapes over on the far wall.

I saw then that Ulla was aware for the first time who it was that pursued her. Her arms dropped to her side and she stood in disbelief, looking at me no more than thirty paces from her, with my giant brother and my friend at my shoulder.

I saw her hand come up to her mouth, and suddenly all things seemed to stop for whole minutes in that place, but in truth it could only have been a matter of moments.

Beside her stood Crida, and I saw him drop his sword to his side. Peg too stared in disbelief, and her hands came up to her mouth.

Ulla made as if to walk to me. Crida called to her. She stopped and turned to him. She reached out for his hands, held them for a few moments, then touched his cheek gently whilst saying something to him, then she turned away from him. I saw his head drop to his chest. Ulla then held Peg's hands to her cheek, and whispered some words to her.

Then, looking almost as if she was in a trance, Ulla clambered over the make-shift barricade. Crida and his men did nought to prevent her, and she walked, than ran to me, there, in that hall. She ran straight up to me and she smiled, and I smiled too, and we held each other.

Everything had stopped around us. The Saxons dropped their sword arms and shields. Cormac and Torquato dropped their weapon arms and waited, watchfully, eyes focused on the Saxons in front of them.

Cormac looked at me.

"Go, brother. Take the Saxon princess. You are wounded. Leave this to me and the Roman. We will give you time. We will meet in the copse with the horses before the night-shadows grow long. If we are not there then, go without us."

I looked at my brother. With the guard who had been with Ulla in the room, there were still perhaps twelve or more of the Saxons facing us, all warriors of Ceawlin's elite corps.

"Go. Go now!"

I looked at Ulla. She looked at me; there was some fear in her grey-blue eyes, but no doubt, no doubt at all. I nearly laughed at the madness of it all, for even as we looked at each other, another wall fell in the outer archway.

"Brother, one hour, make sure that you are there!"

With that I put my right arm around Ulla's shoulders, and I led her out of the hall, through the archway.

Even as I did so, the stone doorway, now shorn of its supporting timbers which lay in blackened ash below it, fell asunder behind us in a shower of bricks and debris and dust, and as I looked back I could see that the doorway was completely blocked and that no man could get out of that hall by that door.

Ulla and I ran to the tethered horses and she took the grey and I took a black stallion, and we turned them about and raced for the main gate of the Forum. The flames roared out of the basilica behind us, and it seemed to me as if the whole Forum might finally be destroyed, for the timber outbuildings and the temporary shop awnings would be more fuel to its advance.

We reached the main gate and turned right, in front of it, away from the long corridor that ran down to the south gate and made our way around to the west gate. There were by now other people on the street – market traders, farmers, and all were looking back at the Forum, for the flames by now leapt into the sky. I could see no warriors, which was just as well, for I guided my horse with my right arm, and my left arm hung uselessly against my side.

We reached the west gate and clattered over the bridge. In five minutes we were clear of the city, and ahead of me I could see the copse. We slowed to a walk. I asked Ulla to wait for me as I went forward, but I need not have worried, for Gregor was still there, with the horses, and he had jumped up at the first sound of my horse.

"We have the Gevissa princess. She is just behind me. Cormac and Torquato bought us time. We left them fighting Saxon warriors in the great hall of the Forum. We will give them until the moon swings over the south gate. If they are not back by then, we will leave."

Gregor nodded, and then turned to see Ulla, and he blinked hard, for the woman was a beauty, and he was still a young man.

I lifted her down from her mount with my one good arm, and we walked over to the side of the clearing, Gregor sensibly leaving us in peace. We held onto each other then, but said nothing, and that silence was right, for there was nothing that we could say that might capture the turmoil inside us.

I lifted her chin and kissed her then, and held her again, and still words would not come for either of us.

Finally I lifted her chin again.

"I told you that I would come to find you."

"Yes."

Then suddenly she pushed away from me, and I saw the colour flood into her face as I had seen it do so many times in the past. But now there was a deep sadness in her eyes, and fear too. She spoke quietly

"Crida told me that you killed my brother yesterday."

"I did not, Ulla. He died in my arms, bravely, as a warrior. He was killed by a rogue warrior in my band, a man who paid the price of his actions with his life, at the hands of my shoulder-man. Your brother and I had agreed to parlay, for we would have talked of many things, but the despicable fool who killed him thought only of gold. Even as your brother was dying, he asked me to come to find you, for he was worried for your safety, and he asked me to come and protect you. His dying words were to tell me that we would have made good brothers."

Ulla spoke quietly, as if to herself.

"Ah, Cutha! You would truly have been the king of kings."

She sobbed then, great cries pouring out of her, and I held her silently.

"He asked of me one more thing also, something which puzzled me, and puzzles me still."

She looked up at me, still distraught.

"What was it?"

"He asked me to try to find the good man again in your father."

She pushed away from me again, but this time more gently.

"Cutha was a great man, and would have made a great king. He was trained by my father, when he too was still a great man. I am proud that Cutha was my brother."

I said nothing, but the little that I had seen of her brother confirmed her words.

"As for my father – well there my brother's last wishes will be disappointed, for he is completely mad now, and no more the man he once was."

I went across to her and held her again, and the sobs wracked her body.

"Crida told me that he had been given instructions to fire every third town and village between the Hwicca lands and Silchester, including the Forum of Silchester itself, and to loot those places too, as a lesson for all those who might think of defying my father."

She looked at me, and I could see that these orders of her father struck her as the actions of a madman.

"Crida himself would at first not look at me. I had the impression that I was not meant to leave the room that he was torching."

She looked at me to allow the weight of her words to sink in.

"But my father chose the wrong man for the task. Crida is my friend. He has sworn to protect me. He would not carry out the king's instructions.

But he told me that my father now believes that you killed my brother because you have designs upon his kingdom, and that you will use me to achieve that purpose."

I looked at her now. Her black hair lay in fronds over the wide-set eyes, and the colour burned in the high cheekbones. Again I lifted her delicate chin, and said to her, very quietly:

"Ulla, I have no interest in your father's kingdom, but I do make claim upon your soul, and hope that you still make claim upon mine."

Her eyes were black, and I knew then that nothing had changed between us. Again I kissed her, and held her in silence. She spoke quietly.

"How can my father so misunderstand me?"

"He has power madness, and believes that everybody sees the world in the way that he sees it. To him his kingdom has become everything, and therefore he believes it must be everything to all others too."

I spoke firmly then.

"We will wait for the return of my brother and friend, then I will get you away from here, and take you to the fortress of Penwyrn, close to the City of the White Stones. My family and I will protect you in that place. We will make our plans for the future, as we did once before, for your father will never again threaten the upper Severn after his defeat yesterday."

I could see her sadness, but I could see also that something was strong within her, for by some miracle we were together, and somehow we would make sense of the madness of our lives.

So we talked for a little while, and even there we started to make our plans.

But now I was beginning to get concerned for my brother. The night-shadows began to grow long; still there was no sign of him. Together the three of us led our horses and the spare mounts to the end of the copse. Now we could see that the fire had taken hold beyond the Forum, for a great red and yellow light lit up the night sky above the ruined city, so that it glowed within its walls, like some gigantic lantern.

Still I could not see my brother or my friend. Smoke belched out from the west gate, and other people fled out through it, but none that I recognised. My left shoulder pulsed with pain.

Then from that gate I saw a great form emerge, with another smaller form at its side, and both figures ran across the bridge and made their way towards us. The giant figure carried something across its shoulders. I saw that it was my brother, and that he had Torquato on his back, and with them was Peg. They ran towards the copse, and we rode out towards them. My brother lifted his bloodied head when he saw us, and gave thanks. Peg ran up to Ulla, and both women hugged each other for a few moments. We got the prone body of my friend onto the ground, and splashed a little water into his face from our hip flasks, and slowly he revived. We got him onto a horse, and we rode then, and drove our heels into our horses till we were well clear of the ruined city.

*

We found a quiet grove in a forest that was at least ten Roman miles or more from Calleva. We all dismounted, and Gregor went to find wood for a fire.

Cormac ran his hand roughly over the back of Torquato's head.

"Thick as a rock, as I suspected. You will have a lump the size of a goose-egg tomorrow, but you will live."

Torquato shook his head, his face still very pale.

"What happened then?"

"Later, let's get this fire burning."

We shared such of the provisions we had between us, which was not much, and soon enough the fire had flared up. Agonising jolts shot through me from the pain in my shoulder. I said nothing, for I had more than adequate recompense for my pains. The gods alone knew what was going through Ulla's mind, but I could see that she was content within herself, and knew that she had made the right decision. I could see that having Peg with her now was a great comfort to her also.

She looked at me.

"What has happened to your shoulder? Let me see."

She peeled back the torn shoulder from my tunic.

"That needs to be treated, or poison will set in."

Torquato half-stumbled over to his horse, and then came back to us, a silver flask in his hand.

"Pour this on it."

Ulla took the flask and poured the clear spirit into the wound.

A great spasm of pain again shot through my arm. I said nothing.

Torquato grinned at me, even as he took the flask and took a long pull from it, wincing as he swallowed the clear liquid.

"What a waste! This stuff is so good it makes my teeth go soft."

I managed a weak smile.

"Thank you. At least my needs will save you a bad head tomorrow."

Ulla tore strips from the hem of her gown, and did what she could to bandage the wound, which even now had begun to bleed afresh.

"The bleeding is good – it will clear any poison."

Cormac had barely met Ulla before, and had never talked to her. Now he looked at her thoughtfully.

"Lady, I have always known that this brother of mine would walk through fire for you, and now he has proven it."

He smiled gently at his own joke, then looked at me.

"I grow more and more confused by these times, for now me and the Roman have a Saxon chief to thank for our lives."

He explained what had happened when we had left him. He looked across the fire at Torquato.

"You were not felled by a Saxon sword, which will be a relief to you."

He then looked at me.

"Just after you left, the stone doorway of the hall fell in. That collapse caused part of the roof to come through. A whole beam swung down and caught this big lump on the back of the head. So I stepped in front of him and shouted at those Saxons to come and do their worst, if they dared. It was then that the Saxons charged me. I had some success."

I could see that Cormac was telling just as much of the story as he needed to.

"But even as I had got through most of their ranks, I felt the point of a blade between my shoulders. It was the Gevissa king's shoulder-man, and he had me dead to rights."

I looked at my brother.

"So what happened?"

"I do not know. Nothing happened. He stepped in front of me, threw *Gaeallon* across the hall, then held his sword across his chest and bowed to me, muttering some gibberish. Then he smiled, told me to pick up the Roman, talked to this lady, who nodded, and she took me out of a back way, and then we came to meet you."

"Crida was saluting you."

We all looked at Ulla.

"He was saluting you by making the sign of Thor, the thunder god. My people grant this salute only to the greatest warriors. He spared your life because you are a champion warrior."

Ulla said no more. Nor did my brother, but eventually he wandered over to the side of the grove, deep in thought. I could see that the confusion that had first gripped me all of those years ago was starting to affect him too. There were good men on both sides, bad men too.

We slept for a few short hours afterwards, Gregor and I taking turns to act as sentry. Otherwise I lay with my good arm around Ulla, and this time I knew that she would never be divided from me, and the pain that burned in my shoulder was a small price to pay for the peace that entered my soul that night.

*

We made our way back to Penwyrn unscathed, even though we had many small skirmishes on that journey, and avoided real dangers only by the skin of our teeth.

On the final day of travel, when we had safely crossed back into the reaches of the upper Severn and the protection of the king of Powys, Cormac and Gregor pressed on ahead, so that all could be made ready for our return with the Gevissa princess. I did not anticipate difficulties; both Brocmael and Kynon were obliged to my war-band and me, and they already knew of my pact with Ulla. But I wanted to take no chances; a great battle had taken place, and this lady's father had been the king of the enemy forces, so precautions needed to be taken.

As we hove into view of the fortress, we could see a crowd had formed outside of its main gates, and the lines of people stretched all the way down to the rim of the lake. As we approached, a great shout went up, and cheers rent the air, for we returned as victors of a battle that had decided the future of these people, at least for the time being. Ulla was treated as a great curiosity by the people, for many had never seen a Saxon princess before, and she held her beautiful head high as she rode amongst them, her chin raised, the colour high in her face, looking every inch the daughter of a king. Beside her rode Peg, her eyes wide in her flushed face, and the thought crossed my mind that this must too be a strange journey for her, returning to the lands of her people after so many winters spent with the Saxon invaders.

Ahead of us, just in front of the gates of the stockade, we could see Brocmael and Kynon. To their right, I could see Cormac and Cadolan, who both smiled at me, and Gregor, and with them were the womenfolk.

I could see my mother, Aisha and Gwen, all of whom wore their finest robes of all colours – deep-purple for my mother, green and red respectively for Aisha and Gwen – all of whom had gone to great lengths with the make-up palette and wore fine brooches in their shining hair, and all of whom regarded Ulla with the greatest interest. I could see Megwei too, also dressed in fine clothes borrowed from my sister for the occasion, holding on to the arm of Gregor.

Brocmael stepped towards us as we approached. We dismounted, and he, Kynon and my family walked forward to greet us. I saw Kynon's eyes narrow with great curiosity, and not a little interest, when he saw the Gevissa princess

"We welcome you back, Rhuadrac, son of Advil!"

He turned to Ulla. His face was grave, but there was affection there too – the affection of a man who was a father and understood the life of a king, and that of a king's family.

"Your father and I have been enemies, princess, and many have recently perished as a result of the ambitions of your father in this land. But I believe in Almighty Jesus Christ, and I do not visit the sins of a father upon his children, therefore you are welcome in this place, and you will be given my full protection whilst you remain in the land of the king of Powys."

Ulla bowed slightly in response. She was calm and dignified and she was the daughter of a king, and she would have her say. She talked in the language of her mother, which was the British language.

"I appreciate your words, British king. I am here because of my pact with this chief . . ."

She looked at me.

". . . but I do not accuse my father when I stand in this place, for he bears the weight of kingship on his shoulders. His decisions are made always in the interests of his own people as he understands them. It is not for me to criticise his actions. However, you should know that my mother is British, and so I too am part-British, and that I grieve when I hear of the many dead on both sides, for part of me dies with them all."

Brocmael acknowledged her words with tact, for he understood that he spoke with the daughter of a king, and it was said well. All who heard it were impressed with her words, so that she was received quietly, and with not a little awe, into that community from her first arrival. Peg's face too shone with pride, pleased that Ulla had retained all of her proud dignity.

Now Brocmael turned to me.

"If Rhuadrac would indulge the wishes of an old king, perhaps he would allow my son to lead Ceawlin's daughter into my hall?"

I said nothing, merely nodded. But the words of the cunning old king did not escape me. Kynon was a prince, and he had no woman. Ulla was the daughter of the Gevissa king and much might come from an alliance between them. It suddenly struck me that it was not only in Ceawlin's Hall that I would need to have a care.

As Kynon walked up to her, I saw Ulla's eyes open wide for a split second before she recovered her composure. Kynon had the face and frame of an athlete.

He took Ulla's hand and held it high. Then, in a curiously formal fashion, he walked with her through the gates into the fortress, amidst some gentle applause from all who stood there.

They made a handsome couple.

Brocmael followed his son with me at his side, and the crowd followed us in.

Brocmael turned at the top of the small incline and held up his arms:

"Good people of Powys! There will be a great feast of rejoicing tonight. The giant Cormac, my champion, who has surpassed even his previous deeds on the field of battle, with his brother and his war-band who also have brought much glory upon themselves – these will be the honoured guests. But the most honoured guest will be this beautiful Gevissa princess who has shown great courage to come amongst us, and who has already spoken to us in the words of a princess."

Again some quiet cheers went up in the compound. Brocmael held up his arms again.

"There will be singing and verses, and all who are not bound by the forty-night fast shall eat and drink through the whole night, for the land is for now safe from the Saxon threat, and the people shall give thanks for it.

More cheers rang out, then the crowd broke up, no doubt making ready for the feast, and it occurred to me that many fasts would be broken before the night was done. I noticed that Kynon kissed Ulla's hand before he let go of it, and she looked full into his warrior face and thanked him, before coming over to where my family stood. It seemed to me too that Aisha frowned when she saw Kynon do this.

I said nothing to Ulla as she joined us.

My family, with Ulla, Peg, Torquato, Gregor and Megwei walked over to the hut enclosure that had been provided to us. My mother talked with Ulla in a lively open fashion and it struck me then that these women, so different in character, culture and age, were yet well met, for both were the daughters of kings, and both had left the comfort of the privileged life they had known, for they knew not what, to start a new life. But my mother was no fool; she understood the ways of kings. Already she was bringing Ulla into my family, for she knew that my peace of mind depended upon it.

Even as we reached the main hut, my mother turned to us and made clear to the men that we should go over to the hall, or in some other way make ourselves busy, for the women had much to discuss.

I looked at Cormac, Gregor and Torquato, and smiling, shrugged:

"No sooner is the battle over than the real chief makes her orders known! Men, I think that we are banished to the hall, to drink and to relive the battle, to mourn for our lost friends, and to speak again of the events of Calleva."

*

That night I lay with Ulla for the first time in a hut that belonged to the Britons. It had been Cadolan's; with good grace he had moved out to another hut group, smiling the smile of an old man, and looking at me in a fatherly way.

Now Ulla and I lay naked beneath fur-skins. We had been curiously distant since our arrival at Penwyrn. My left shoulder burned with a dull ache, though the signs were that it would heal well.

Ulla lay with her head on my chest. She looked up at me now. The flames from the still-hot coals lit up her face, and I could see that she looked concerned.

"What is it?"

I was silent for a while.

"You seemed much impressed by the Powys prince."

"Why would I not be? He is a powerful man, a great king's son; a most handsome man too."

I hesitated, then glanced down at her. Then I saw that mischievous look in her face. She smiled up at me then, that wonderful open smile, her white teeth perfect in the light of the fire.

"You are a very silly man, Briton!"

So saying, she threw back the furs and rolled her lithe full hips across me, sitting astride, straddling my body. She looked down at me, her hands pressing down at each side of my head, the black hair falling about her shoulders, her black eyes glowing out of that gorgeous face, her trembling hips rolling expertly over my body.

"Now, let me see if I can make you forget all about your silly thoughts, if only for a while."

*

So a new life started for us all then.

Ulla became a part of my family. Both my mother and my sister in different ways were devoted to her, and she to them, for the British way as lived by my family was much to her liking. She was reminded of her own mother, and not of the mad ways of her father, whose memory continued to torture her quietly, but about whom she refused to say much. Peg too flourished in the British community at Penwyrn. She had been a long time away, tied by loyalty to Ceawlin's queen, Acha, but we could see that her true home lay here, with the British people and the British ways. She became as much a part of the family as Cadolan, and became indispensable to the smooth running of the family homes.

Between Ulla and Gwen there was always some tension. She was, after all, the daughter of the king who had destroyed the proud army of Farinmael. Gwen, strong heart that she was, wrestled with this knowledge, and tried all she knew to throw it off, but sometimes, especially in the early days, a deep anger would flash out between these two proud women.

One day, not long after Ulla first came to Penwyrn, Cormac and I sat in the great hall with Ulla, Aisha, Gwen and our mother. There was to be another feast that evening – the feast of the birth of the Christ-God. Bright sunlight shone through the glass set into the roof of the hall, and a light humour prevailed amongst us.

Ulla, caught up in this mood, then mentioned some small fond memory of her father, the way he would listen to Queen Acha sing a song, then clap his hands and say:

'"Bravo! The Britons have a nightingale!"'

We had smiled at this quiet tale, for we knew that it was a sign that Ulla was beginning to relax in the family, learning to drop the guard she still adopted when she and I were not alone.

Gwen, now towards the end of her child carrying, fell silent. A deep flush passed over her face, and she would occasionally glance at Ulla.

Finally, she could contain no longer the anger that wracked her.

"I would be happier not to hear glad mention of certain persons when I am in the room."

We all fell silent. Gwen was Farinmael's daughter, yet she rarely reminded us that she was the daughter of a king.

The colour came up into Ulla's face, and I knew what that meant.

"Do you, perhaps, speak of my father?"

Gwen looked coolly at the Gevissa princess.

"I mean no other."

"If I choose to speak of my father, a great man, then I will do so."

There was a brief pause. My mother stood up and started to walk over to the two younger women. Before she could say anything to them, Gwen exploded with rage:

"A great man, you say! This man is a power-mad fool. His ambition alone killed my father, a man worth ten times the value of that Saxon heathen! Thousands of good men have died due to his land lust, his power-craze! How dare you say this man is a great man?"

Ulla flushed deeply, turned away from Gwen, and looked at me:

"I should never have come to this place."

Both Cormac and I stood up now, at a loss as to what to say.

My mother spoke, using quiet words:

"These emotions are still too raw for all of us. Ladies, you must give yourselves time for these wounds to heal. Gwen – you cannot allow yourself to become so angry, you have another to think of, you must be calm."

Gwen looked at my mother, then at Cormac. Without saying another word, she turned and walked out of the hall, holding her proud head erect. Cormac shot me a glance, then followed her.

Ulla again repeated; "I should never have come to this place."

So, we went forward, slowly at first, because these matters that caused us such grief were real and not easily forgotten.

My brother and I learned at these moments to keep space between the two women, taking our mother's advice, to allow time for these wounds to heal.

My initial fears concerning the intrigues of Brocmael and his family proved unfounded. Soon, the bond between Ulla and me was obvious to all, for we were inseparable now, and it was clear that we would make our life together.

A couple of months after Fethan Leag the whole family made ready to move down to farm enclosures in the borderlands between the lower and upper Severn.

My brother and I were given a sizeable parcel of land each, next to each other. The borders of our properties would run along the dividing line between the kingdom of Powys and the land of the Hwiccas. These farms had become available because the previous farmer, a widower, and his son, had perished at the Battle of Fethan Leag. These were good lands, well-tended, suitable both for grazing and for planting wheat and oats and barley, and would provide us with more land than we had had in my father's time.

Cormac and I made plans for a modest hall of our own, in a plot of land we agreed would be shared between us, so that we would not entirely cut ourselves off from the way of the warrior, which had played such a great part in our lives.

A few nights before our departure south from Penwyrn, the time had come to face facts – Torquato and Gregor were not farmers, and though they too had been offered land by the Powys king, neither were of a mind to take it.

Gregor had already come to his decision. He would return to his own lands with the gold he had acquired as a freebooter, much added to by his actions at Fethan Leag. He would take the slave-girl Megwei with him.

It was a sad day when we waved them off from the gates of Penwyrn – a loaded cart with them, and a small band of warriors for their protection until they reached the land of the Kentish king, through which Brocmael had arranged for a safe passage for them to the coast. After that, they would be on their own, with Gregor's warrior-skills only to rely upon.

Gregor turned to me finally as he picked up the reins, and he spoke to me quietly, so that only myself and Ulla, who held my arm, might hear his words.

"Chief, you have been a fine leader. I speak for all in the war-band, living and dead, when I say that we came to these lands only because of our respect for you, for we all thought you the best chief that we had known. Even the Gaul. It is sad that it ended for him the way it did."

Neither of us could think of anything more to say about it.

"Perhaps me and this lady will return to your land one day, in many years time, with our family too if the gods should grant it. We will come to see you, and discover how the great young chief chose to live out his days."

With that, they were gone, Megwei holding onto his arm as if she would never let go of it. I was much moved by his words, for none of my war-band ever spoke openly of such matters.

Now of all my war-band, only the great Roman rogue was left at my side.

Away from battle, he had started to resort to his old ways, for he was listless, and drank too much, and his foolish ways soon came upon him again. None of this was a surprise to me, for I knew him too well, but it caused problems in my family.

His return from battle had been greeted warmly by my sister, but soon enough it became clear to us all that matters did not run calmly between them.

Almost a half-season had gone past since our return from Calleva. By now I had often seen my sister talk to Torquato in a quiet rage, for the change in him out of battle was astonishing to those who did not know him. Though he made a great attempt to pick up the way of life at Penwyrn, his wild heart was not in it.

One day, soon after Gregor and Megwei had left the fort, I went to see him in the hut that had been set aside for my war-band when they had first arrived at Penwyrn – now only he remained in it.

I was therefore surprised to hear earthy laughter coming from the inner room as I pressed open the door. I shouted the rogue's name. Suddenly he appeared at the door, as naked as the day he was born, slowly arranging his tunic about his shoulders.

A female voice came drifting through into the room.

"Who is it? What do they want?"

Then another, sleep-filled, satiated, careless of the world:

"Come back to bed, you wild man . . . ignore them, whoever they are . . . or perhaps they want to join us . . .?"

I remembered those voices. The two daughters of Salemnis, no less.

Torquato looked at me now, a surly look on his face. He still talked to my sister, and I could not but be disappointed with him, though his actions did not surprise me.

I looked at him coolly.

"If you have a moment when you have finished your . . . labours, I will be over in the hall."

Torquato said nothing.

Even we could find nothing light to say to each other at that moment.

Several times after this I found him drunk, talking to the serving wenches in the hall, fooling around with them. He began to earn a reputation, and men would move away their women if they sought to talk to him.

Here at Penwyrn even I was embarrassed, for this was not the land of the Franks, this was the temporary home of my family. I feared that some conflict between my brother and Torquato was inevitable, for my mother had had cause to mention his behaviour several times.

Now my brother began to grow angry with the Roman.

At this time, Cormac met with me at the lake one morning. We had come to fish, a rare pleasure these days. There was much wrangling going on around us – this was the time of Gwen's argument with Ulla. Now too was Torquato becoming a problem.

It was a very cold day, not long after the Christ feast. The lake was not frozen over, which was a relief, so we could at least attempt to catch fish. A high sun shone over us, and occasional bird cries would ring around the light woodland surrounding the lake.

We said nothing to each other for a while. It was good to be in each other's company, with none of the family troubles to distract us. We had already talked over the estrangement of Ulla and Gwen, and had decided that we would keep them apart for as long as was necessary for the wounds to begin to heal.

Cormac now cast out his line again, the tightly-wound wool snaking out expertly from the stout oak rod. He watched the bait sink into the pool, the ripples of water slowly dispersing out and fading away.

"We need to do something about the Roman."

He did not look away from his line.

"Our mother has had to speak to me. She fears that he begins to bring disgrace upon our family."

I said nothing. I knew that it was true.

We did not speak for some time. Then Cormac turned to me again.

"We both know that the man was never made to be a farmer. He is a fine fellow, after his ways – a great warrior. But we see now that our life will not be all battles and war. Much as some of us might wish it to be so."

These last words were said quietly, almost to himself. I looked at him, and I knew again that his warrior self was the man he preferred to be.

"I know it brother, I know it. But this man has been my great friend these last few years. I cannot bring myself yet to tell him that our paths must now go different ways."

Again we said nothing for a while.

"I know the man. He will come to his decision himself. One day he will be gone, like those ripples around your bait, no trace of him remaining."

"Aye, well let us hope that the day comes sooner rather than later, because I will not allow the name of our family to be disgraced in any way further, not even by this man, great fellow that he is amongst men."

We said no more on the matter, but it concerned me. I did not want these two men to come to blows, for one or the other would likely be lost in any such contest.

That night I met with Torquato in the hall. I could see that he had already been drinking, but not too heavily, so that he was in high spirits. I knew him well enough to know that this mood masked his real emotions.

"Now then, Cub-General, farmer, consort of princesses, how goes your life today?"

I looked at him. The old ways were passing away everywhere, not least between my great friend and me, for a different way of life now offered itself to me, and I would take that path. Both of us knew it.

"Now then, you rogue, you know well enough how my life goes. I will make my life with Ulla, and my warrior days are behind me for now at least. I think of family, and land and property, and I have a mind to make a success of these things."

The great Roman rascal looked at me with a gleam in his eye, but there was some sadness too.

"Well then, brother . . ."

That word had a resonance as he said it.

". . . I wish you well, but we both know that I was never cut out for it."

"What next for you then?"

"I think that I might take a look over at your Kentish lands. There is always much work there for a freebooter like me. I hear that they are always fighting somebody, either invaders or neighbours or each other. You remember the good Princess Bertha from our time in Gaul? She took a great liking to you once. Well then, we know that she is taken as wife by the Kentish king. I might go over there and offer my services."

What he said made sense. One part of our mission on Ceawlin's work had involved the protection of Ingobert, the widow of Charibert, the old king of Gaul, and her daughter, Bertha, when they had become entangled in one of the many in-family fights of that strange land. We had done our work well, so that the queen had promised us both work in any future time should the occasion arise. Bertha would remember Torquato well, for she had taken a great liking to me, though I had gently guided her to look elsewhere.

It was a good plan, and I was sure that he would find work in Kent. I told him so.

"Aye, well maybe that's what I will do, and make more gold."

He was suddenly serious.

"Your sister is a fine and beautiful woman, Rhuadrac. I would bring her nothing but disappointment and pain. She will be better off with this prince, Kynon."

In his typical fashion, Torquato had blurted out what was really on his mind. We had all seen that Kynon had continued to walk with my sister. It seemed to us all that he had begun to make some progress, not least because Aisha became suddenly attentive to him again, when Ulla had arrived and Torquato reverted to his old ways. We knew that progress was being made, if only because we sometimes saw that Aisha talked to Kynon, and that proud prince was, for once, listening.

I looked at my friend. Then we both laughed – a sad laugh, but one which acknowledged that he spoke the truth.

"I had hopes that you two might make a life together just a few short weeks ago, you know."

"So too did I. But that was when the battle-spirit was upon me, and my brain worked properly and life made perfect sense. I step out of battle and the warrior-way and nothing seems to make sense to me anymore. My words and actions often no longer make any sense even to me."

I knew that he spoke the truth. He took a long pull on the claw-beaker that he held in his hand.

"Let us drink, little General, let us tell each other tales from the land of the Franks, and our battles here, and the rescue of the beautiful princess."

I raised my glass:

"To your future adventures in the Kentish lands!"

I paused.

"May your rampant blade be forever engaged in action."

He looked at me then. The aquiline face creased into the huge grin I knew so well and the gold teeth flashed. Then he nodded ruefully.

"Aye, well, I'm good for one thing out of battle, at least."

Then we both laughed, and we drank and we talked nonsense. By the end of that night we agreed that the battle just gone and the mission to Calleva was equal to the best of our adventures.

The next day my friend was gone.

I found that he had left me his Roman sword, and with it a message in Latin on a wax-wood.

'To a good chief: from Torquato, Roman.'

*

PART V

A New Life

I

A new phase of my life had now started up, taken up by family matters and the mastery of my farmlands.

Ulla and I were then married, in the Christian style, and Cormac, Aisha and Peg stood witness for us. Cormac and Gwen, soon after, became the parents of a son, whom they called Finn, after the Irish king of legend.

It had become clear that Ulla and I too would soon become parents. The time of Ulla's confinement drew near, and at this time Peg once more proved her worth to the family, flourishing in the role of midwife.

Soon enough it was obvious that the child's arrival was close at hand and Peg drew me aside. Over the years her size had increased; she was a buxom woman, her hair was now largely grey, though wrapped up in coils upon her head, and still the gap-toothed smile shone out of her flushed face as she gave me my instructions for the day.

"I don't want you anywhere near here today. Go away. Go and walk around the hills. Go fishing. Just don't bother us today – we've got real work to do here!"

I took her advice and spent the day walking in the grove by the stream that Ulla and I would visit whenever we needed to be alone, just to talk about our lives and how matters had turned out for us. I threw an occasional line out into the waters, listlessly. After a restless day, I returned to the farm compound. It was early evening. I remember that a fierce sunset threw out its fiery glow over our homelands as I walked down the hill towards home. I could see that white smoke billowed out from the roof-vent – that was promising.

As I entered the yard, I noticed that Peg was sitting on the stone doorstep laid out in front of the main entrance. She looked tired, but happy, and her long grey hair had fallen down over her shoulders. She had her arms clasped around her knees, and her head was thrown to one side as she looked wistfully into the ground in front of her, looking just like a young girl. At the sight of me she leapt up and came running towards me.

"A boy, Rhuadrac, a boy, and as fine a boy as you ever did set eyes upon!"

I smiled and hugged her, and pulled her hair gently, then pushed my way in through the main door of the hut. My mother sat peaceably on a chair just next to the door, and her eyes met me as I entered, full of a mother's love. Then she nodded and smiled too, as if some dim memory was stirring in her own heart.

Ulla lay on the furs that had been strewn about most of the floor space in the hut. Her long dark hair was loosened, and she had never looked more beautiful, more desirable to me. As I came into the room she gave me a look that I will never forget. In her arms nestled what looked to me to be a bunch of rags.

With great pride in her voice she gently held up the bundle to me.

"Here, take him. It has been a long journey for us both."

I took our son from her tentatively, and with fear and mingled pride took him out into the light. My heart leapt when I saw him. So tiny, so defenceless, so dependent upon his family to survive! I knew for sure in that moment, whatever life had in store for me and the Gevissa princess, it could never be the same again.

We agreed to call him Cadwalla, a name that spoke to us of both our fathers.

Between the second and third winters of this time, both Gwen and Ulla produced healthy daughters, whom we called Eilea and Acha respectively. In the following year Ulla produced a second son, whom we called Cuthan.

I knew great contentment then. Now I was more suited to the farming life, and my properties thrived and the land prospered. My life moved in harmony with the seasons. I learned to love the spring with its new shoots, the summer with its work and harvests, the heavy fruits of autumn and the dying of the land in winter, only to bring forth the new shoots of spring once more.

The rhythm of this new life fulfilled me. It was almost as if we lived in a great cavern, but this cavern, with Ulla by my side and the cries and sounds of the growing children within it, was a wondrously lit cavern, so that I had no reason to leave it, or even to think of leaving it.

Cormac too made a success of this life. It seemed to me that his actions at Fethan Leag had in some way repaired his belief in himself as a warrior, for he would no more be remembered as the failed champion of a dead king.

This period we would later call the quiet time, the time of new life, when no invader came to trouble us, and we talked only occasionally of the battle times, and that was at the feasts.

We built our hall, and we threw feasts, and this hall became known throughout our region as Brothers' Hall, and many from Powys and from the lands of the Hwiccas came to our feasts there.

We had achieved some modest fame through Deorham and Fethan Leag and our names were read out in the verses. As I had first learned in Scapthar's tavern, Cormac's prowess as a warrior had became the stuff of legend. My tale too was sung by the Saxons and the Britons alike, for it was strange to them, and my family became known as the-family-of-the-new-hope in the Hwicca language, which joined words together in this way.

Ulla was content and thrived with her new family. She watched our family grow, and it was only occasionally that I would find her in tears, because she thought then of her father, or of her brother, and the calamity that had come upon her family, for something had broken in her father when her mother died.

Then all I could do was listen to her quiet lament, for she had known the glory of her father in his noble years, and she found the changes in him impossible to accept. So too would she lament for her dead mother and her dead brother, and would sometimes wonder if her family were cursed, for only she amongst them all would have the chance of any sort of lasting happiness in this world.

Slowly too, the breach between herself and Gwen was cured. Eventually they saw that they had more in common than not: both women were proud and strong; each was the daughter of a strong man – though each would say, when pressed, that she was the daughter of an even stronger woman. Both women had now married into my family. Both too now had children of the same age. In their own way they grew close, and even became great friends, though neither would probably have confessed to it.

My mother took great delight in her growing family, for she had a new audience for her tales, and old Cadolan too took down his books – he had new students to teach, and now these children would speak British, and the newly forming Aenglish. Cadolan insisted that spoken and written Roman should be taught them too, for that was the language of scholars and was well known in the foreign lands.

The bond between Aisha and Kynon continued to grow, so that finally they were married in the Christian manner. Cormac, Gwen, Ulla and I stood witness for them. Aisha went back to live at Penwyrn. They too had children, for their son Selyf Sargaddau was born in the second year after Fethan Leag, and their daughter Ina in the third year after that battle. Cadolan took great pleasure in the Latin and Aenglish names of Selyf.

"Ah, Solomon. He will be wise, mark my words, and a great warrior!"

We heard occasional news from the Gevissa lands, none of it good for Ulla. Olric had started to grow in status at the expense of her father. Ceawlin's power was much reduced, for his proposed march on the upper Severn had not been understood by his people. He had then suffered a reverse at Fethan Leag, and turned upon his own people in a rage. Although he was not yet destroyed, his grip on power had long begun to weaken.

In all of this time I saw and heard nothing of Torquato.

II

In late summer of the second year following the Battle of Fethan Leag, as soon as the harvest had been brought in, in the period before the new planting had to start, Cormac and I took our families back to Penwyrn.

Together we loaded a cart with a treasure chest, and we set off for the great continent in the southern lands to fulfil my silent promise to Scipio.

Perhaps I will one day set down the full story of that journey; we saw many things, and for my brother it was his first journey out of our own land. But here I speak only of what happened when we reached the city of Constantine.

Our journey took us many nights, and the winter months were almost finished by the time of our return. We had heard of a trade route by sail boat from the southern tip of Dumnonia to the north of the land of the Visigoths, to the region of Cantabria. From there we travelled by road for many days through the great central plains of that land – itself a land wracked by battle, for their king Liuvigild made many conquests at that time. We travelled on to Recopolis, a magnificent new city built by that king in the Byzantine manner, and finally, after many days, we reached the Spanish province on the south-east coast of that land, and then to the boat-place at Cathago Novo.

We travelled from that place by boat to the north-east coast of the great southern continent itself. Scipio had told me many times that his family lived there, in a city in a ravine. This city was called Constantine, in the Exarchate kingdom. He had told me that he was married to the most beautiful woman in the whole of that place, that her name was Mounira, and that they had four children.

We reached the city on a warm cloud-filled day almost two months after we had begun our journey.

It was a magnificent sight. I could see why Scipio had named it in the manner he had, for the whole of the city was set into a great ravine carved out of the rocks that surrounded it, and even I had never seen anything like it.

We had found in the Spanish province a fellow by the name of Alanus, who could speak the African language. He let it be known in the places where mercenaries gathered that there were foreign mercenaries in the city who wished to speak to Mounira, the woman of Scipio, he of the trident and net, who had gone to seek his fortune in the land of the Franks.

For ten nights we heard nothing. Early on the next night, we were summoned to the sentry gate of the hut compound in which we slept. A woman and four children stood there, and Alanus told us that this woman claimed to be Mounira, the woman of Scipio, mercenary soldier.

This woman was very well-made, tall and long-limbed, her short black-grey hair curled back from the forehead of her delicate face. Her face was of indescribable beauty, for its bone structure was fine and regal, and the high cheekbones sat under long, wide dark eyes that shone like jewels, and her face was full of a dignified calm. Those dark knowledgeable eyes looked at me now with pride, but also some fear, as if she knew the purpose of my visit.

This woman had no need to prove to me that she was Scipio's woman; she had brought her children with her, and the oldest boy was about fourteen winters, and he could have been the young Scipio himself standing in front of me. As I looked at this young lad, who must surely be Scipion, a sadness must have crossed over my face, for the woman looked at me steadily and then spoke to Alanus, a question in her voice.

Alanus turned to me.

"This woman wishes to know what news you have of her husband."

I looked then at Cormac, then back at Mounira.

"Tell her that I bring the worse news, for her husband is dead. He died as a brave warrior should, at my shoulder in battle, and he brought much glory and honour to his family."

Alanus hesitated slightly, then talked quietly to the woman in her own language.

I saw a great shadow pass over her face, and she shook her head slightly. The children had fallen silent at the words of Alanus, and dropped their heads. The woman walked away a few paces, then rested her arm on a wooden fence that ran around the compound perimeter. We saw her hand come up to her face several times. Scipion went quietly to stand next to his mother.

We said nothing.

After a while, the woman came back to us, then lifted her head with pride and said something to Alanus.

"The woman thanks you for bringing this news, though she would sooner not have received it. She would like to know why the blonde-hair and the giant have made the journey over the seas to tell her this?"

"Tell her that I was the chief of the war-band that her husband served with much valour. Tell her that Scipio talked of her always. Tell her that he amassed much treasure in the foreign lands because of his great skill in the battle arts. Tell her that he told me always that this treasure was to make his family strong, that he would have returned to her after this final battle, and his family would be strong always through the treasure that he had earned. As his chief, I have brought his treasure to his family."

Alanus raised his eyebrows at this information, then he repeated all of this to Mounira.

This dignified woman then looked at me steadily for a long time. Then she turned to Alanus again and spoke quietly to him.

"She says that she understands why Scipio would choose you for his chief. But she asks, of what use is treasure to her now, when her man is not here to share it?"

I looked into the wide-set eyes of this dignified woman then, and I knew that she and Scipio had been well met, and my sorrow for them both deepened.

"Tell her that when her sorrow passes, she will need it. The children need to be protected in this world, for she now has no man, and the treasure will help in that."

Alanus talked again to Mounira, who listened to what he said with her fine head angled to one side, her eyes opening and closing slowly, as if she now wished the conversation over. Mounira then stepped lightly across the room in a simple graceful movement and put each of her hands upon my shoulders and looked directly into my face and said something in her own language, then left the room with her children.

Alanus looked at me:

"She thanked you. She said that your journey and your words will help to keep her strong in the coming months. She will think on your words, and return tomorrow morning."

The next morning she came alone to the compound. We carried the large chest that held Scipio's gold with us at all times, and now we took it with us to the covered wagon, and opened its lid.

Scipio's battle gear was there: helmet, mail shirt, shoulder-clasps, belt buckle. In two leather pouches were jewels of all kinds, and a necklace of spun gold, with red and blue amethysts set into its links.

Mounira held the mail shirt to her cheek for some time, sobbing quietly.

Then she opened each pouch and poured the contents on to the floor of the wagon. She told Alanus that she would select three jewels for each child, and then three for herself, which she did. She lifted the necklace to her neck – the red and blue amethyst stones gashed bright in the early morning sun. She felt its stones as if distracted in some other place, and then placed the necklace into the pocket of the red robe that she wore. She picked up the mail shirt that had covered Scipio's heart, and the belt buckle that had girt his loins, and then she stepped back from the wagon and said something to Alanus.

"She says that this is all that she needs. The rest is the fruit of battle, and she wants none of it. It is for you to do with as you please. It has cost Scipio his life, and that life was to her more precious than anything that these treasures can buy."

She said one more thing to Alanus, walked across to me and touched my face gently. Then she lifted the sack that she carried and walked away from the wagon and out of the compound.

"She said that she hopes that you and your family thrive in this life."

I never saw her again.

*

Alanus was well rewarded for his work with us.

As for the rest, we took a few jewels to cover the cost of our expedition, and the remainder we gave to a wary bishop in the city of Toledo who seemed honest enough, explaining that he was to use it for the care of the wild children we had seen roaming the streets of that city, because we thought that would please our mother and Cadolan. We had no further need of another man's gold, won through the strength of his own arm.

After many adventures, we eventually returned to our farm compounds safely.

Many months after this journey, I was ploughing the high field at my farm.

It was the end of the summer months, and I had started to get the the harvest in. The day had been long and warm, only now had the the sun's heat begun to cool. The work had been hard, and my limbs ached with the effort. As I ran the plough through the final furrow of the day, I saw a sliver of coloured glass thrown up by the well-kept blade catch the soft rays of the sun and glint like red-blue fire, like jewels, like amethysts.

I thought then of my friend Scipio. I imagined his laughing black face before me. Then I thought of Veos, all of them, Farinmael, Gavin and my father. Gone, all gone, and gone irretrievably, never to return. For a few moments a deep sadness bewildered all of my senses. Then I heard a voice calling me.

"Rhu-ad-rac."

I saw that Ulla slowly climbed the high field towards me, and she smiled as she walked with Cadwalla strapped to her back in a sling. She was big with our second child. I looked at the climbing form of this magnificent woman, and then I smiled, too, and shouted her name in response, waving to her.

"Ulla!"

This life is long for some of us – for others, brutal and short. One man might choose to step out into the world to find his fate, another will stay at home fearing it; each man dreading to lose that which he loves the most.

Whichever path a man chooses, one day his fate will find him.

III

The Hwicca Saxons had stayed and tilled the land. For the first time in British memory the remaining Britons had not been driven out, but had been forced to pay tribute to the Saxon conquerors, and to work on their lands.

Eventually though, a great mingling had come to take place, so that the tribute paid by the Britons was no different to the tax paid by the old Hwiccas themselves to the local tun, or ham. Now new families were beginning to grow, comprised of neither one nor the other side, but of a new type, and these Hwiccas had already shown that they had no inclination to forsake their lands for new conquests.

The reprisals carried out by Ceawlin on his retreat from Fethan Leag had caused much resentment, so that the local tribe had become stronger, and looked to its own defences. Many were inclined to regard any encroachment upon their territory as an invasion of their own land, so that the tribal loyalty was to the land, the tun, and the folkmoot – the last a meeting place where opinion was freely given and then decisions made, as I had witnessed before Fethan Leag.

This settlement of the Saxon Hwiccas brought some good news for Peg. The Hwiccas were good farmers, and their knowledge soon became known to my brother and I, who both had much to learn about the farming ways. We took in a man called Edwin, not a young man, who was quiet and a good worker, very practical with his hands, and both my brother and I learnt much from him. He would look at a field and turn to me and say, with the few British words he had mustered in his time in Britain:

"Not here. No good for barley. Too much water."

To me it looked like any other field, but over the seasons we came to see that he was right, and we came to trust him.

It was soon clear that he had taken a great liking to Peg. Several times I saw her take a stick to him, and shoo him out of a farm hut, but she smiled as she did so, and it seemed to me that there was a good trusting bond between them.

One day Peg came to see me and Ulla. She looked as if her world had fallen in upon her, for she seemed in some distress, great sobs welled up out of her.

Ulla asked what it was that caused her such distress.

Peg turned her large blue eyes to Ulla.

"Only that fool Edwin has asked me to be his woman . . ."

Another great burst of sobs came out of her.

I asked her to be calm. I never did like such naked emotions.

"What is the problem with you, Peg? I'm sure this is good news?"

"And I'm sure you understand nothing, as always . . ."

Here Ulla turned away and smiled. For some reason she always loved the manner in which Peg spoke to me.

"But he is a good man, a good worker . . ."

"It has nothing to do with him. He is all of those things . . . but, but . . ."

Here her lips trembled, so that I feared that another burst of sobbing might be unleashed upon us.

"If I go with him, I will have to leave you both, and the children . . ."

Now all was revealed. I looked at Ulla, who raised her arched brows, as if to say – so, what do you propose?

I thought on it.

"Well then, that is not a problem. There is plenty of room in the compound. We will build a new hut, and it will be for you and Edwin. We cannot do without you, Peg, nor Edwin, so the matter is settled."

Now another great burst of sobs came out of Peg, and I turned to Ulla.

"Try to calm her down. I will go and check that repaired wheel on the wagon. Calm yourself, Peg, for mercy's sake, all is fine now, is it not?"

With that, I left the hut, and left the women to make the necessary arrangements.

IV

It was the anniversary of Deorham, now some fourteen summers in the past.

We had sent out word that there was to be a feast at Brothers' Hall. Over the years the battle had come to be celebrated by both those Britons who survived it, and those Saxons who had fought in it, because it had changed the shape of the land in which it had taken place.

Brothers' Hall had been constructed in a meadow that bordered both my farm and that of my brother. It lay at the foot of a valley set amongst hills, with a stream running through narrow banks in the grounds.

When building the hall, my brother and I looked to merge the best of the British and the Saxon building, but included some Roman techniques also. Craftsmen who knew the Roman techniques flourished in this region, because so many of the old Roman buildings still required to be maintained.

Our hall had a low roof, but not so low as the hall at Penwyrn. The main facing wall, behind the top table, had been constructed in stone. Every two arm-widths we had caused a double line of red tiles to be inserted, so as to bond the stone, in the old Roman way. This facing wall had then been cemented and plastered, so as to present a smooth face to the hall itself, again in the old Roman style.

The other three walls of the hall were all in timber, and we made full use of mortised joints in the eaves, and fine timber architraves had been designed into each corner, for this reminded me of the room to which I had been brought after Deorham, and Ulla recognised the design.

A complex mosaic had been set into the floor underfoot. It was tiled in dark-blues, reds and whites. The pattern was British, so that it was of loops and swirls, rather than the zig-zag and geometric patterns of the Romans. At the head of the room, beyond the top table and before the smooth wall, a large hearth had been set out. Another was set up in the centre of the room, for the rest of the benches in the hall had been laid out in a great circle fanning out from the top table.

The roof was of thatch and wattle, and came low down the sides of the timber walls when viewed from the outside, but the roof space on the inside of the hall had been left as a great open space, but for the main beams and rafters, all jointed together by expert carpenters. We thought that this magnified the songs and the verse-readings, and on a few occasions we invited monkish choirs also, so that my mother and Cadolan too might have the enjoyment of the space.

Around the walls we hung skins and hides – wild boar, wolf and stag. We mounted shields, and swords, including *Saesbane*, and even a battle-axe very like *Gaeallon* – which had been lost at Calleva – so too our mail shirts, shoulder-clasps and belt buckles. In pride of place in a glass cabinet at the side of the top table was the war-helmet of our father, Advil.

On the wall opposite this helmet, we had set up another glass cabinet, and in this we placed Torquato's sword and message, and we put over this cabinet another inscription, punched out by the smiths onto bronze:

'This sword belonged to the Roman, Torquato,
First-equal amongst warriors with Cormac, kings' champion'

Cormac himself insisted on this inscription, and I did not try to dissuade him. It sounded right to me.

Although both Cormac and I had great respect for the religion of our mother, there could be no doubt that this was a warrior's hall.

We set up a small chapel in a side chamber so that our mother and Cadolan might each enjoy some quiet moments there. Further up the hall, on the same side as the chapel, we had built onto the side of the timber wall a small chamber, also of wood, where we could hold meetings as and when the need arose.

As Cormac and I looked over the hall now, there were signs everywhere that preparation for the evening's feast progressed well. The mead and wine tables were set out, and barrels and casks had already been set up. Both hearths had been lit, so that smoke rose up to the roof, in which the smoke flaps had been left open, and it made a clean exit there. We had arranged for the slaughter of cattle, and sheep, and goats. There would be chicken too, and already the great iron spits over the central hearth were beginning to turn. Great loaves were set out on tables, with whole cheeses, so there seemed little danger of the local population starving when at the feast.

Already the guests had started to arrive. It was towards the end of the summer months and the days were still long. This day had been a fine day, full of the sun's warmth and high blue skies with a few white clouds.

As my brother and I stood at the wide-open double-door entrance of the hall, the smells of roasting meat from the hearth and freshly baked bread was in our noses, and a dull red glow lit up the surrounding hills as the sun began to slip below the horizon. All seemed well with the world that evening.

One of the first guests to arrive was Edelwine and his son, Edel. This man and his family had remained close to us after Fethan Leag, for we felt bound in some strange way. The shared experience at his farm when his brother and his family had been butchered had in some way bonded us.

What was certain was that Edelwine himself had never really recovered from it, The thought that he had invited his brother and his family over to their doom at the hands of his own people in this strange land had continued to haunt him, and he could not dismiss it from his mind.

Edel himself had grown into a fine warrior, tall and strong, but he was generally reserved in his manner, and brooding, like one who swims in the river race, but is always in the second or third rank, and does not push on to win the race even though all know that he is capable of it.

He too had never fully recovered from the ordeal at the farm. Edel had lately earned himself a reputation as a stirrer of men – at the tun-moots and the hundred-moots he was known as a powerful, if not particularly wise, speaker, for he was happy to ferment anger against the Gevissas at every opportunity.

For all of that, Cormac and I greeted them now with some warmth, for they had become good friends in the intervening years since the Battle of Fethan Leag, not least because Edelwine was a very knowledgeable farmer, and several times his advice to Cormac and I had proved invaluable. He it was who had brought Edwin to us.

"Soon enough for the harvest, then?"

"Three more weeks, we think, then if the weather holds we will bring it in."

"Sounds about right. A good crop of wheat?"

"Excellent, at least as good as last year and probably better."

I turned to the farmer's son.

"How are you, Edel, and what news from the hundred-moot?"

I knew that a folkmoot had taken place at Corinium earlier that day.

"There is ferment again in the land of the Gevissas. I will not talk of it here, but perhaps we can speak later this evening in your chamber, for it concerns your family."

"So be it, we will make a start after the feast. We will have verses, and choirs. Later we will find some time to talk of these matters."

Then the guests began to arrive. Kynon and Aisha were amongst the first, having travelled down from Penwyrn during the day. There were already flecks of grey in Kynon's hair, but for all that he still looked very much the warrior-athlete. Aisha was resplendent in a green gown, with matching green brooches in her dark hair.

"Are the children with you?"

They were not. Selyf had been ill, so that he was being cared for back at the fortress, and Ina had been left there with him, as a precaution, to her fury.

"A pity, for Cadwalla was greatly looking forward to seeing his cousin."

Even as I talked, I could see Ulla and Gwen come into the path that led down to the entrance. They had all of our children with them.

Ulla wore a light-purple gown, a royal colour that always suited her, and around her neck she wore the necklace I loved most, for it was the very same one she had worn when I had first seen her after Deorham. The pendant still held the dark-blue stone at its centre, set in gold.

My son Cadwalla favoured his mother – he had dark hair, and lean features, and was tall for his age. Already I noticed a marked resemblance to Cutha, Ulla's brother, which she herself had commented on several times.

At the moment, he was looking up at his uncle, Cormac. He held out his arms towards him.

With a sweep of his arms, Cormac lifted the boy up onto his shoulders.

"Grandpapa's helmet."

The child pointed to the glass cabinet up by the top table.

Cormac stumped off towards it, with the lad slapping his shoulders, as if he might be a horse.

Ulla, Gwen and I laughed, and I reflected for a moment on the changing patterns of this world. For both Cormac and Cadwalla, uncle and nephew, even now were stood in front of a war-helmet once worn by a man who was the sworn enemy of this child's other grandfather. Then Finn held out his arms to me, and I threw him up onto my shoulders, and I too dutifully trotted off to see the fine sword of my Roman friend.

Soon enough all of the guests had arrived, the entrance doors were closed over, the locking beam was put in its place, and the feast in memory of the Battle of Deorham proceeded on its way.

Much later – the verses had been spoken, the choir had sung, and all had eaten their fill.

I had offered a conciliatory toast in memory of all of the men who had fought and died at the battle, and said words that pointed to a future in which all might be united, for the greater good of the land and the welfare of all of our children. All in the hall had drunk heartily to that wish, and the men had banged their mugs and claw-beakers on the tables.

The torches and lanterns had begun to burn low, and the shadows lengthened on the timber walls of the hall. Slowly people had started to drift away from the hearth, heading back to the carts and horses that would take them back to their homes.

I sought out Edelwine and his son. During the evening I had noticed Edel in vigorous conversation with Cormac. I saw Cormac jab Edel in the chest with his finger, a sure sign that my brother was making his views known forcefully to the young warrior. I saw Edel and his father standing with the eorl of Corinium and Alfhere, all deep in conversation. They stopped talking as I approached them. Edelwine greeted me warmly.

"A fine evening, Chief."

I was called by this name by most Hwiccas, because that was how they remembered me – as a warrior-chief of a mercenary war-band, a warrior who had married into a Saxon king's family.

"Yes, I think my mother and my old teacher enjoyed it more than most though."

Even as I spoke, I saw my mother raise her arm to me as she left the hall on the arm of Cadolan. I had arranged for Brocmael's monks to sing for us, and they had both much appreciated the singing. As they approached their old age, both now were even more inclined to such matters.

Edel spoke.

"Is it possible to discuss the matters I mentioned earlier?"

"Yes, of course."

I looked around the hall. I went to Ulla, who had gathered the children to her for the journey home.

"There are matters that need to be discussed with the Hwiccamen and Kynon. Take the children, I will be home later."

Ulla was immediately on her defence.

"What matters? Does it concern my father? Is that snake Olric plotting against him?"

The quiet rage I knew so well rose up in her.

"Ulla, I know not. There has been a folkmoot and certain matters were discussed. They wish to take my counsel. More than that I cannot say."

She frowned, then, shaking her head, she marched the children in front of her, and left with Gwen, muttering to her friend as they went out into the courtyard.

Kynon stood in conversation with Cormac. I gestured to them both, and pointed to the side chamber.

Once we had all assembled there, Edel closed the heavy oak door.

"I am sure that all can be trusted in this hall, but it is sensible to take no chances."

Cormac and I looked at each other. Edel's actions bore a stamp that was long familiar with us – men were plotting, the pieces of the game were in play again.

Edel explained that it had become clear at the moot that afternoon that forces were coming together against the old Gevissa king. Apparently his nephew, Olric, was much stronger now, and had to a large extent gained control over Ceawlin's lands, for the old king had been losing his control of the people since Fethan Leag and there had been countless plots to oust him, all of them ruthlessly crushed. Now Ceawlin was raising an army of those Wessex men still loyal to him, so that matters would soon be settled one way or the other.

Edel looked at the men around him.

"Matters have now taken a decisive turn. Olric himself came up to the moot. He is gathering his army and plans to force the issue with Ceawlin. Even now he is calling on all of those that have a grievance against the old king, for he is all for change, and would declare himself king in name, as he now regards himself king in practise. But there were many at the hundred-moot who are still undecided. To openly stand against the old king is not easy for us Saxons, our tribal roots are strong. It is the greatest treachery to stand against one to whom you have previously sworn loyalty. For families like ours . . ."

Here he gestured towards his father

". . . it is a simple matter. Ceawlin broke the pledge of loyalty by his direct actions against us and it is our duty to seek revenge or compensation from him, or die in the attempt. There are many other families who see it the same way. But for others it is not so clear-cut, even though they know the old king is no longer the man that he was."

Edel spoke boldly, which could only mean that Olric's plans were already well advanced.

All eyes in the room now turned to me, for Edel had spoken against the father of my wife, and the grandfather of my own children. I had learned over the seasons that my word carried weight in these matters amongst the Saxon settlers. As the husband of Ulla and father of their old king's grandchildren, they looked to me for guidance. The Hwiccas had long known my position – I wanted no dealings with the kingdom of Wessex. I wanted my family to be free from the intrigues that seemed to wrack that kingdom at all times. Now that I had Ulla by my side, I had no reason to go against the old king. He was kin, and I had no wish to stir up storms that for many winters now had lain calm in my household.

I looked at them all, then stood up and walked over to the far side of the room. A quiet fire burned in the hearth there. I stood for a couple of minutes with my back to it, weighing up the news I had just received. My family now had strong influence in these matters – my son Cadwalla was in direct line to the Wessex kingdom, I was kin through marriage to Brocmael and my brother had taken Farinmael's daughter as his wife.

If I was so minded, I could cause Olric some trouble. I had no doubt that Edel was here this evening under the express orders of Olric, to try me and to see where my allegiances lay.

"My thinking is this – I will neither assist you nor hinder you in this matter. As you all know, Ceawlin is now kin by marriage to me, he is the grandfather of my children. On a matter of principle I will not take up arms against him. Nor, for that matter, am I much impressed with your choice of king, if you were to replace the old man with this Olric. I have met him, so too has my brother. I did not care for his manner then, and I doubt that it has changed much with the years . . ."

This was dangerous enough talk, against the man who would be king. But I was in my own hall, and I too held power in this place if I chose to call upon it.

Edel's face flushed slightly. He stood up and said, too quickly for my liking:

"Well then, if he was from the very darklands he would be an improvement on the murdering old madman who has now ruled Wessex for far too long."

I looked at this young man calmly. He had suffered at the hands of Ceawlin, as I well knew, but I did not care much for his manner, which was hot. I knew that such warriors did not survive long either in battle or in the discussion chamber.

Edelwine stood up quickly.

"Be quiet Edel. All in this room have much knowledge of the story of the old king."

He watched his son slowly sit down.

"We understand you Chief – what of you, Cormac? How do you stand in these matters?"

Cormac stood leaning back against the timber wall of the room. His gigantic frame dominated that end of the room and his massive arms were folded over in front of his chest. I saw the old flame pass over his face, and I could not be sure how my brother might decide – he had no personal love for Ceawlin. He had made a success of his land, for we had both prospered, but still there was a part of him that fretted and chafed as a farmer, still the battle-spirit lay dormant in his soul. So too was he the husband of Gwendolyne, and dead Farinmael's champion. Those Britons who had started to regain their strength and pride in West Britain looked to him always for leadership.

"I have respect for my brother in all matters, as all here know, and I too understand his position."

He looked at me then.

"Also, though my kinship to the Gevissa king is far less than my brother's, I have learned to have much respect for the Princess Ulla, and even now I think of my own nephews and nieces, direct kin of the Gevissa king himself. I do not think that their uncle should take up arms against their grandfather, therefore I stand with my brother, and my first thoughts are that I too will neither assist nor hinder you in your coming war with Wessex."

I was grateful to my brother. If he decided to take part in the coming battle, what man could say when the scars in my own family would heal?

Through all of this conversation, Kynon had watched patiently from the side of the room. He was the son of a king, moreover of a king that had inflicted the first defeat on the old Gevissa warlord. His opinion had not been sought. I suspected that Brocmael and he must already have been sounded out by those factions close to Olric.

"So be it, you have both made your position clear. Your prowess will be missed on the field of battle, but there is not one who can say that you two have not earned the right to so decide after Deorham and Fethan Leag . . ."

We both nodded at him in gratitude.

". . . for my father and myself, we are of a mind to join with these forces of Olric. It is not in our interests to have a madman in control of Wessex. We have already seen that his ambitions include at least parts of the land of my father, so it is in our interests to stay close to those who would unseat him."

At this point, the Powys prince paused, then turned and looked into the glowing hearth, even as a burning log fell into the grey ash, causing sparks to momentarily flick up into the darkened room.

"It is said that the old king has called on many of his old retainers, and seeks allies in the strangest places. Even the Kentish king, who grows in strength by the season, is said to be outraged at this treason by an Aenglishman against another Aenglishman of his own family. He calls it *civile bellum* in the Roman language – civil war between them, and he is threatening to send forces to support the old king, even though as a young man he once felt Ceawlin's wrath. The tribal customs weigh heavily on these Aenglish."

So the Jutes might be involved too. I wondered in passing if my Roman friend had made his journey to Aethelbert's lands. We waited to see what Kynon would say next.

"So, with such alliances the outcome is by no means clear; it may not result in success for Olric and the British forces."

Again we waited for his words.

"Have you considered what the consequences might be for your family if Ceawlin should prevail?"

Cormac and I looked at each other. Defeat of Olric's army, including that of

Brocmael, would lose us the protection of the Powys chieftain. Our families would be at the mercy of the old Saxon king.

Eventually I spoke for both of us.

"As always, Kynon, you speak wise words. My brother and I will talk upon those words, and let you know our reply."

"That is welcome news, Rhuadrac. The decision of you and your brother may well be decisive for all of those in these Hwicca lands who still are undecided too. Your word, as husband to the Gevissa princess, carries much weight amongst the settled Saxons. Cormac's word, being that of the old king's champion and husband to his daughter, will decide many of those Britons in the next generation who were too young to fight at Deorham and Fethan Leag."

I knew this to be true. I had been invited to many a folkmoot to give my thoughts on various matters. Somehow, the Hwicca people still looked to Ulla and her husband for guidance. As Kynon had said, the old loyalties died hard amongst these Saxons.

Cormac and I walked out into the now much colder evening air. Although heavy black night-clouds were rolling up from the southern horizon, a full moon for now cast its faint silver glow over the cleared space in front of the hall, even as it had at Deorham all of those seasons ago. We could just make out the rolling slopes of our dark farmlands. Nearby the stream gushed peacefully through its shallow bed, though a stiff breeze stirred the leaves of the rooted oaks. By now our children would be asleep in the farm huts.

For a while neither of us talked. Then Cormac broke the silence:

"Kynon talks sense. A defeat for Olric and the British forces throws us open to the vengeance of Ceawlin."

"Vengeance? But we do not know if he seeks vengeance against us. Ulla is his daughter, the children his grandchildren. That bond must count for something."

"He believed his daughter betrayed him. That much was clear from his actions at Fethan Leag."

I said nothing. I could not deny the truth of my brother's words.

"Olric's forces are strong. Brocmael and Kynon stand with him. Perhaps Aidan will again come down from the north . . .?"

"From what we hear, Aidan has trouble enough in his own lands."

I understood Cormac's words. From the few reports we received from the folkmoot, the Northumbrian Engles grew stronger with each season, heading inland and north from the east coast.

"Kynon is right. The strongest reason for us to fight is your influence amongst the Hwiccas because of your bond with Ulla. Your children are Ceawlin's grand-children. It will say much to those undecided Saxon men if the daughter and grandchildren of the old king now stand against him. It will tell them that their allegiance to the old king no longer binds them. They will be free to stand against the man who has once already vented his anger amongst his own people."

I knew that these words again spoke the truth. I had no free choice in this matter. Much as I wanted to keep my family away from the snares of the Wessex kingdom, it had finally come to my door, as I knew that one day it must.

"And you, Cormac? As the husband of Farinmael's daughter, you too will be asked the question – will Farinmael's champion bear arms once more to finally avenge the wrongs done to the dead British king? The Britons here in our land look for a resurgence of the old champion. Those who were but children at Deorham and Fethan Leag are now old enough – they too fret under the Saxon rulers."

Cormac smiled thinly, looking out over our shadowed farmlands. He turned back to the looming silhouette of the hall behind him, the still flaming hearth and torches casting a faint warm glow against the strengthening wind, which even now scattered a few early dead leaves up to the timber walls as the trees began to shed their annual burden.

"Rhuadrac, I have learned to love this life we have created here. The steadiness of Gwen and the children, you and Ulla as hearth-companions whenever we choose to share it. The changing seasons, the crops growing, watching those beech trees there grow copper-red and lose their leaves. Even the winters, with the hearth roaring in the dark nights . . . the tales we share, the laughter."

I looked at my brother. Coming to terms with this way of life had not been easy for a man of his character. But he had won through, he had found some peace for himself in these farmlands on the Hwicca borders.

Now he leaned his massive frame onto the fence that ran around the courtyard of Brother's Hall, dropped his head, then turned and looked at me full in the face:

"In truth, brother, it seems that we have no choice. We have built a good home for our families here, but the world has come knocking at our door once more, as we both knew it must. I will fight against the old king one last time. Perhaps then we will be left alone to live our lives in this valley in the way that we choose."

But then his smile broadened, and I could see that his own words had kindled some excitement in his soul.

"If nothing else, we will taste battle once more."

We walked back to the chamber. Some urgent talk in the room stopped immediately as we walked in. Cormac looked at me and swept his arm towards those in the room:

"Tell them our decision, brother."

"It is decided. We will walk to battle with you once more, and see this matter with the old king finally settled."

Kynon spoke out for them all.

"It is a brave decision that you have come to. I think it is the right decision, and I hope that we all live to thank you for it."

"And Olric? What will his thoughts on the matter be?"

It was known by all that we despised the Saxon Olric, and that he despised us too.

"Leave Olric to me and my father. We will not join in his alliance if half of the Hwiccamen and the lower Severn British do not join us, and you two are key to achieving that."

The matter was decided. We agreed that we would meet with Olric at the first opportunity, at a place to be decided by Brocmael, who would preside at the meeting.

Soon after, all went their separate ways.

Cormac and I made one last tour of the silent hall, from which place all had departed. Outside, a now stormy wind rattled the solid timbers of the hall, and a low moan echoed around the roof joists. There was barely enough light from the torches to make our way, and the flickering light threw our shadows onto the timber walls, so that they made gigantic shapes ahead of us. We walked up to my sword *Saesbane* and the new *Gaeallon,* hung there on the wall.

"So, into battle one more time."

I looked across at the battle-scarred face of my brother.

"Aye. I think that this coming battle will be ferocious, and I suspect that Olric will gain most from it. Even if we settle the matter with Ceawlin, in the seasons still to pass factions will come looking for my family. They will seek the growth of their own personal power in alliance with my son, and they will want to get rid of Olric. That is in the very nature of kingship and those who would have power. I do not care for it. As I get older it strikes me more as a great stupidity with each passing winter."

My brother looked at me then, and smiled. I did not talk often about such thoughts, not even to him.

"Aye, but then, you always were a dreamer, brother. It is a dream for men to think that they can stand apart from the snares and nets of this world."

I looked at him, puzzled by his words. He smiled, and clapped my shoulder.

"I'll tell you something. You remember the day you left Ceawlin's Hall, soon after Deorham, to go to Gaul for the first time? Well, that day I was sure that I would never see you again. I thought that this world would grind you up, like flour in the mill."

These thoughts were all new to me. He looked away to *Gaeallon,* then spoke quietly:

"I learned before you the fragility of dreams in this life. There are many in this world who would snuff out the dreams of others, just like the metal hood of the long-armed pole used by the priests to snuff out a candle in the church. Such people have no time for dreamers."

He stood looking at the new *Gaeallon*, shaking his head gently.

"I have never met anybody more keen than you to seek the best motives in a man's actions, nor one who is more disappointed when those actions reveal that the man has feet of clay."

Again I looked at my brother. For a moment I was reminded of his quiet nature before Deorham, of the gangly youth oppressed by the village bully. But then he collected himself, and turned to me, speaking in a strong voice:

"So I know how you think about such people, and I have known it ever since your return from the land of the Franks. I am your brother, we grew up together, your thoughts are sometimes written on your face."

Then he paused and looked up once more at the giant battle-axe set into its beckets on the dark wall.

"But I have never had any interest in any of this greed for power. It is the thrill of the battle itself, Rhuadrac, the thrill of the battle itself. What champion might they bring out against me this time? What adventures might we have? That is what I seek, and even now my mind begins to think of battle for the first time in many seasons!"

I looked at my brother and laughed at the passion writ large on his face, and slapped him on the back.

"Cormac, you were created in this life for battle, even though your hair begins to grow white. I do not doubt that there is glory ahead for you. But we shall see."

So saying, we strode out of the hall. I saw that Ulla had come back for me, wondering what it was that had kept me there. She stood waiting for me, the now-savage wind streaming back the raven-black hair of the Gevissa princess, the reins of my horse in her hands, her fine wide-set eyes looking at me intently, a question forming.

I would tell her of the decision made this night, and I already knew the distress it would cause her.

So it proved.

*

PART VI

Preparations for Battle: Wodensberg.

I

It was as if an early winter had come to us that autumn season. The tempest that came in on the night of the Deorham feast seemed to herald the start of a storm season unlike anything known before, even by the eldest amongst us. On most days the wind howled over our border lands like some displeased god, bringing with it rains that caused the streams on our land to burst their banks, so that we had to get in the harvest early in order that it might not be ruined. As it was, only two-thirds of it survived, but in the circumstances we regarded ourselves as fortunate – others fared far worse.

On the fifteenth night after the Deorham feast, we received word that a meeting place had been arranged by Brocmael. In three days time we were to travel to the villa of Alfhere at Corinium, the same place that had been used for the folkmoot before Fethan Leag. Olric would be present, and there, plans would be made to join battle against Ceawlin in the Gevissa lands, but not so far from our own territories that we might be isolated. The combined British, Hwicca and rebel Saxon forces would move down to the wide plains south-east of Bath, and there meet with Ceawlin and his Aenglish alliance forces, and no man could know the outcome.

Cormac and I spent the next two days completing the harvest work. On the evening before we journeyed down to Corinium, we stood unharnessing the yokes from the plough horses in the stables. It had been a rare good day, and much work had been done.

"Have the spirits of the princess revived yet?"

I looked at Cormac. Ulla had flown into a rage when I had told her of the decision to make war against her father. To her, Olric was the worse type of traitor. To have her husband join with the traitor in such a despicable act was beyond her worse fears, and she had barely spoken to me since the Deorham feast.

I lugged a heavy blanket over the rail that ran along the centre of the livery stable.

"Slowly, brother, slowly. But it is very hard for her. She cannot gain in any way from this conflict. Either her father is driven out of his kingdom, or he prevails and we are placed in danger here, in our homelands."

Cormac walked over to the stable entrance. He reached up and spread his long arms along the main crossbeam of the entrance to the stables and craned his neck to look out upon the ploughed fields spread out before him. A soft fresh breeze had replaced the wind-lashed fury of recent days, and he gazed across at the full crop bins in the yard. Today had been a good day, more produce had been recovered than we had thought possible.

"All things change, Rhuadrac. By the time the seasons change once more, and we come to replant the crops, these difficult times will already be just another story for the versemen. Ulla will see that our decision is the right one, for our family will be free of the Saxon threat, at least for the near future, and perhaps us British can walk once more with the dignity of the Hwiccamen."

Cormac talked always of the broken respect of the British, though the combined British and Irish forces had stopped Ceawlin's further expansion to the upper Severn Valley at Fethan Leag, still there could be no dispute as to who held sway in the lower Severn. We had established a way of working with the Hwiccamen. We enjoyed the protection of Brocmael here in the Powys–Hwicca borders, but it was still a Saxon tribute in crops that we made in the markets after each harvest, and it was the laws of the tun and the folkmoot that decided all local disputes.

Such facts hung heavily on Cormac. He was a Briton, and the Britons were a defeated people here in the lower Severn. Edwin, who even now forked the hay-grasses into the barn beside us, was Saxon. A good Saxon perhaps, a man we could work with, but still Saxon. To Cormac, never would the two tribes become one. He viewed Ulla and me, and our children, as something exceptional, as a meeting between a man and a woman that was beyond tribal hostility, a union that had been written in the stars as an event that must happen, and he supported our pact with all the strength of his wild warrior heart.

I saw matters differently. To me, all I could see was a great mingling of the two races, invader and British, and my own family was living proof of it, at least here in the west of Britain. Peg and Edwin too. Something new was starting to be forged, which was neither British nor Saxon, but something new and separate, which shared some of the traits of each side, but which was also something different in itself.

I said none of this to Cormac. I looked at him now – grey streaks layered his long dark hair, and his frame had grown thicker. This morning I had called on him just after first light, as was our custom during the harvest-gathering. I had found him on his knees in a field behind his hut compound. Here he had created an allotment, and in this soil-bed he nurtured plants of different shapes and sizes. He had been concentrating keenly on a task – with great care he was planting new seeds in a trench, carefully covering them over with soil, using his massive hands. He had got quickly to his feet when he heard my call, brushing the mud from his knees. So too, during the last few days, as he had worked with the heavy plough on the opposite side of the field to me, I had noticed that he had to rest often, something I had not noticed in him before. The seasons had begun to catch up with him, there could be no denying it.

I replied to him now, even as I thought back on these matters:

"Maybe so, brother, maybe so, but we have to get from here to there, and the crossing will not be easy."

He turned away from the fields and looked at me, his head tilted back, his chin raised.

"In this battle, which is under Olric's banner, I will not stand forward as champion."

He had made a simple statement, but I knew that the admission was not easy for him.

"It is the right decision; we take part because we must, not because we support this Saxon's cause."

We said no more.

II

"Let the war-band chief speak!"

Alfhere stood on the raised platform of the hall and I stood next to him. In front of us, all was agitation.

Before us stood a room crowded to bursting with men of all ages and sizes. So many men had tried to get into the room that the double doors had been left open, and many other warriors spilt out into the antechamber and even into the courtyard of the villa. Most men were Hwicca, and for them this was a gathering of the war-host, for all bore arms of short sword and shield. A few Britons were there, and for the first time I saw that they too bore arms. All were making their voices heard, so that the rhythms of a strange mixed language flowed around the four corners of the hall. Now this general hum of mixed tongues had developed an increased intensity, so that shouts rang out, and some arms were raised, and men argued, and every now and then some guttural laughter would burst out, perhaps at the expense of one tribe or the other. On the dais next to me sat Cormac, and seated on the far side of the platform sat Brocmael, Kynon, and the Saxon warlord, Olric. In the middle were chairs for Edelwine and Alfhere and two other older men – they represented the Counsel of the Wise Elders here in Corinium.

The Saxon, Olric, had changed since I had last seen him. He was now completely bald, and if anything had grown thinner. He wore a royal-purple tunic of the finest silk. His grey eyes showed no spark of warmth, or even interest, and he had greeted Cormac and me with little emotion, barely a flicker of an eyelid. As he watched the folkmoot develop, I had seen a pulse start to beat in a vein at the side of his naked head, and this tic grew more noticeable whenever a British voice was raised to ask a question, and then too his left foot would start drumming on the floor under the bench at which he sat. This meeting was a necessary evil for him. It was clear to me that he would as soon have massacred the Britons present as listen to them, if he was free to act.

Alfhere held up his arms and gradually the hall became quiet, and all there listened to my words. Edelwine had spoken to me beforehand; my word held more sway in that hall than did the word of Olric. The Hwiccamen wanted to hear the thoughts of the husband of the Gevissa princess, a woman whom they always linked with Ceawlin in the good times, when he had ruled them well, and not with the strange times that had fallen upon the old king. I spoke in the British language, and Alfhere translated my words into his own language:

"There are many in this hall who know me. Many times now I have been asked to address this assembly. You know my wife, who is the daughter of the old Saxon king. You know we have children, and some of you Hwiccas call us the family-of-the new-hope, because we mingle together the blood of the two tribes, and we move forward together through life."

One or two of the younger Hwicca warriors growled at this, because I had used the Hwicca phrase to describe my family, but they were told to shut up by the older men in the hall.

"I have taken the counsel of my brother on this matter. I have talked to Prince Kynon of Powys, and also Edelwine and Alfhere of you Hwiccas. We have talked. I have decided. I will join this battle against Ceawlin . . ."

A great outcry broke out in the hall as Alfhere translated my words, and it was clear that some of the Hwiccamen were surprised.

I raised my right arm.

"Hear me out."

Again the hall became quiet. I had gained some status amongst them by this time, as one who spoke his mind in straight words, and one who did not try to win the talk with double words.

"My woman, the Gevissa princess, is sorely challenged by my decision. It goes hard with her. I have decided to once more wage war against her father. I have done this twice before, as all here know. I have also worked in the service of Ceawlin, when he was a good and fair king, and one who then thought only of the welfare of his people. So my life has been marked by the strange progress of this man in the last few seasons, perhaps more so than any other man in this hall."

There was a low murmuring as my words were relayed to them. Nobody in the hall could deny the truth of what I said.

"But I am now a father to my own children. Our children, the children of me and Ulla, the daughter of Ceawlin. And I have seen enough of Ceawlin's actions before and after Fethan Leag to know that my children may not be safe if this man . . ."

Here I indicated Olric, who did not acknowledge my words in any way.

". . . should prove to be unsuccessful in his war with Ceawlin."

Here there was much nodding amongst the older men in the room. All there understood that there had been no human logic in many of the actions of the old king for many seasons-cycles. These men shook their heads and looked older still. They had known Ceawlin as a great king, a noble man who had lost his way on the death of his wife. This thought troubled them, and it troubled me too, always.

"It may be that I do the old king a great disservice. If so, I will acknowledge it before all. Only the course of events can say if my decision is the right one or not. Therefore, for better or for worse, I have decided that I cannot take the chance of placing my children in harm's way, and I will join this campaign against the Gevissa king."

I sat down.

A few shouts rang out around the room. A couple of older men even shouted: "Where is Cadwalla? Let us see the grandson of the old king."

I winced inwardly at these words. I would keep my son out of Wessex affairs, or die in the attempt, but those in this room did not need to know that. I said nothing in reply. Most men there nodded their heads as they talked. They accepted my words, even if some did not agree with them. A great debate sprang up between them, and Alfhere let the talk flow for several minutes, before he once again stood up and raised his arms.

"Now let us hear from the British champion."

Cormac stood up. Still he looked every inch the wild barbarian. The furs were piled on his shoulders, thick studded bands encircled his wrists and he wore the eye-patch, though by then I had rarely seen it for several seasons. The new *Gaeallon* was slung across his shoulders. He missed no opportunity to show these Saxons that the West Britons were still a force to be reckoned with, if only through the force of his own person, and though he was no longer a young man, none there chose to argue with him.

As he stood up, so too did a band of warriors press through to the front of the hall. I could see that these were young Britons, men who had been but young boys at the time of Fethan Leag. They too carried sword and shield. They hung on every word uttered by my brother. He too chose to speak in the British language, though he knew the Hwicca language well by this time.

"You have heard out the words of my brother. Now hear mine. All threats to my brother's family are a threat to me and my own. This is the natural law, and it is a law that both Britons and Hwiccamen understand everywhere . . ."

All in the room murmured their consent.

"Ceawlin has lost his way. Eight winters ago I stood here in this room and told all that he was no longer fit to lead the Hwicca people. It is true, I had my own motives then. I am a proud Briton, and if the Britons grow strong, then that suits my purpose. I make no secret of that before you. But Ceawlin's actions proved the truth of my words. So I say to the young Britons in this hall – show your worth. Show these Saxons that a man might still defend his own territory, even if, for now, he pays tribute to the Saxon lawmakers!"

A few of the young warriors in the front ranks began to bang together their swords and shields. Cormac held up both arms to quieten them.

"Be sure of this too. If this plan fails against Ceawlin, it will spur him on to look again at his designs on the upper Severn. He will roll through here with his allied Aenglish and the Britons of the upper Severn will be at his mercy. Either this joined army of Britons and Saxons will stop him south of Bath, or he will march on all the way to Carlegion . . ."

Here, I saw that the vein in Olric's head pulsed faster, and a sneer moved across his face. It occurred to me that perhaps Brocmael would do well to track the plans of his present ally too in the seasons to come.

"There has been enough land given up to the invaders! Let them be satisfied with what they have, leave what is left of Britain to the British!"

Now he sat down, even as Olric indicated to Alfhere that Cormac had said enough. Again there was much talk in the hall. The younger warriors in both tribes were stirred up, and shouted, and taunted those on the other side, while the older men nodded or shook their heads.

Now Brocmael stood up, and an immediate hush came over the room.

The Powys king had barely changed in appearance since Fethan Leag. He still had a world-weary air, still measured his words carefully and talked in a distant way, as if he was in some other place in his mind. Alfhere said his words in the Hwicca language for him.

"We thank Rhuadrac and Cormac. Let me say that I am pleased with their decision. These two men have proved their worth many times before now, and their presence in our ranks can only serve to further our cause."

Now he turned to Olric.

"Is there anything that Prince Olric would like to say?"

But Olric waved his arm in a disinterested fashion, and shook his head. There was a momentary lull in the murmur in the hall. The Hwiccamen had expected to be addressed by this man who sought to lead them.

But Brocmael moved on swiftly.

"Very well then. Let us find out now how it stands. Who will join us in this action against Ceawlin?"

Gradually, then growing in rapidity, a low din started to throb through the hall – sword hit shield, then louder – sword hit shield. The rhythmic drumming grew louder still. Now the drumming enveloped the room, and I found myself almost mesmerised by this rhythmic drumming in time, and my heart too began to beat in time with it, and a chant of "Aye" and "Aye" started up amongst the Hwiccas, and the Britons in the room took up the chant, "Aye" and "Aye" and "Aye" and "Aye" and the mingled accents sounded wondrous to my ears as the very foundations of the building rocked to the sound of this "Aye".

The host of the war-moot poured outside into the courtyard of the villa. A steady rain fell, and a cold wind blew, but we had achieved our aim; it would be a combined force of Hwiccamen and Britons who would join with Brocmael and Olric in three days time on the march south of Bath to do battle with the old Gevissa king.

III

Once more the two opposing armies faced each other on the treeless plain.

Crashing peals of thunder rolled through the heavens, and jagged spears of light crackled through the thick morning gloom, as rain-laden black clouds whorled lowly above our heads. The rains lashed into our faces. These rains had fallen all night, and water ran everywhere through the lowlands of the open plain upon which we stood. Great rivulets ran through the gorse at our feet and the furs of the assembled warriors were sodden, and hung heavily from our shoulders. But no man would turn his face from it, because the drum beats pulsed with a regular rhythm, and those of us who had fought before knew that at the first sign that the howling storm grew calmer, all hell would be let loose on the plain before us.

Cormac sat mounted on his horse next to me. He wore the full battle rig: the war-helmet and belt buckle of our father, the chain mesh presented to him by Farinmael before Deorham, now tighter on his thickened body; the hollow ash shield was strapped to his back, and he held mighty *Gaeallon* in his right arm. For the first time since Fethan Leag I saw that he wore the amulet, with its flame-breathing dragon, that Gwen had given him so many winters ago.

Our leaving of the women and children before coming south had been fraught; Ulla could barely speak to me, and wrung her hands and pulled at her hair. I had never seen her in such a state before. Before we left, she came out to me, and took up my hand, and kissed it, then whispered to me:

"By all that is holy in this life, take care, husband, for I fear this coming conflict. There is something terrible in it, and I know nothing will be the same after it somehow."

She had said no more, but turned and left me then, going back to our children, even as the howling wind moaned around our farm compound, and the bare branches of the high trees sighed and swayed in the copse, their leaves long gone.

My mother and old Cadolan now said goodbye, my mother with tears on her face. She had seen her family go off to battle too many times. Cadolan too had real anxiety in his face:

"You two scoundrels must take care of yourselves. We have a good life here, and it must be allowed to continue."

Then they had taken their leave of us.

Now Gwen had lingered with Cormac. She seemed reluctant to let him go, and held onto him. He smiled down at her, and he stroked her once-golden hair gently, great love and kindness in his eyes.

"Be calm, Gwen. We will be back before the moon grows thick again. We will have put this business behind us finally, and we can close our door at night, safe in our beds. Then the winter will come, the hearth will roar through the short days, and the new season will be upon us soon enough."

But still she held onto him, and would not let him go.

Eventually he had slowly taken her arms from around his waist, and lifted her chin to him, looking into the eyes of this woman who had shared his life so far, and smiled at her, and she smiled too.

Then had he turned to me, and we climbed onto the covered wagon and made our way onto the track away from the farm compound. As we both turned at the last bend in the track, we saw that Gwen still stood by the fence, as if transfixed, her arm raised in salute, though the moaning wind lashed all about her. Neither of us had said anything to the other.

Now we sat on our horses on the treeless plain, and still the rain lashed into our faces.

Ceawlin had arrived here at Wodensberg first, and his forces occupied the high ground up by the ancient long barrow. Behind Ceawlin and to his right, beyond the rim of the hill, I knew that a great open plain opened up all the way down to Stonehenga, but here, as we approached from the north, all of the paths converged upon the long barrow, and it was here that he had set his banners. Through the never-ending rain we could see his own wolf's head silhouette standards all about the top ground, but other standards were there too, and we knew that, although the Cantawwa king had not sent a force as he had threatened, he had been persuaded by Ceawlin to send a force of paid mercenaries, the best fighting men in his army, who had earned a terrible reputation in the south of Britain in the recent seasons.

It seemed to me that the wind had dropped – the steady rhythm of the sound of the drums on both sides seemed suddenly to be louder. So too did the rain begin to ease, though the black clouds still hung heavy over our heads. Just then the drums from Ceawlin's side stopped beating. So too did ours.

A strange and pregnant silence enveloped the treeless, weather-blasted slopes, and a shiver ran down the length of my back, even as a drop of sweat or rain-water did likewise.

A trio of warriors on horseback galloped out from Ceawlin's side. We looked to our right. For some reason Olric was not on horseback. That strange man sat in the back of an open wagon drawn by two magnificent grey stallions, and he was seated on some makeshift throne. Nor did he wear armour of any kind, but had on the royal-purple robe that we had seen at Corinium, with just one white fleece thrown across his shoulders, and his bald head stood naked. He raised his arm, and so too did a trio of horses ride out from our side, and I could see that Kynon was at their head.

Next to me Cormac grunted.

"So, what sport might we see now?"

He had maintained his word, and had declined the champion's role when Brocmael had suggested it at the last parlay of chiefs in Olric's tent the previous night. Instead, Olric had brought into the tent his own champion, a towering man by the name of Maccus. This fellow was almost as big as Cormac, but much younger. His blonde hair was short, and his beard clipped, which I had never seen before. He had a fine physique, and there was pride and intelligence in his eyes, but I saw no arrogance in the man. He had acknowledged Cormac with reserved respect, and Cormac had nodded a curt response. Now Maccus rode out next to Kynon.

We watched as the horses converged upon the other side. A standard was thrown down by Ceawlin's men, amongst whom I could see Crida. Kynon did likewise. The champions would meet.

Maccus dismounted and stood ready.

From the opposing ranks rode out a lone warrior dressed in black armour, his sword held in a scabbard high upon his right shoulder, in the Roman style, his unhelmeted long white hair thrown back by the easing wind. He carried no shield with him.

I looked at Cormac, and Cormac looked back at me.

"It is Torquato."

Cormac nodded, some great knowing sadness already forming behind his eyes.

"Yes, it is the Roman mercenary. The fates are playing their games with us."

I had not seen, nor heard any news of, my friend since the day he had left unannounced from the fortress at Penwyrn. So he had joined up with the Cantawwa king. Clearly he had flourished, as I might have expected, because I, better than all others, knew of his fighting skills, and now we would see him fight as Ceawlin's champion.

I wondered momentarily if Ceawlin had expected Cormac to face him once more on the open plain. Somehow I could see the crazed thinking of the old king, because he had found none other in his lifetime who could match the prowess of my brother.

Neither had I.

Now Torquato reached his opponent, and with an easy gait swung down from his horse.

Maccus crouched and made ready, but Torquato stood there calmly, taking the measure of his opponent, and with a deliberate movement, flicked the clip of his scabbard and drew the sword from it.

Now Olric's giant champion made to lunge at the Roman. With the practised movement I knew so well, Torquato stood to one side, and simply hit the lunging giant with the broad side of his sword, helping him on his way. Maccus collapsed in a heap on the floor in front of the mercenary. A swell of laughter pealed out from Ceawlin's ranks. Next to me, Cormac lowered his head onto his chest, closed his eyes and frowned.

Now Maccus stood up, and turned, slightly dazed, to face his opponent.

He launched himself at Torquato again, and swept his sword at the Roman with great swinging strokes. Torquato parried them all with ease, and again with a simple movement, turned the giant around and tapped him on the head with his sword, before kicking his backside.

Again laughter pealed around the battlefield.

Next to me, Cormac spat.

"He is toying with a brave man, and I do not care for it."

I did not like what I could see either. These were not the actions of the man that I had known. It struck me then how different Torquato's actions now seemed when viewed from the opposing side. Even now he had turned his back on Maccus, and had raised his arms to his own side. I had never before seen his clownish side exhibited on a battlefield, and I knew that something had changed in him.

Now Maccus came at the Roman again, but the game was all up for him. In a simple movement, Torquato knocked the sword from his hands, and with two quick, clean strokes pierced the side and chest of the young giant, who fell forward onto his knees, then onto his face, dead.

Now Torquato turned his back again upon his vanquished opponent, and raised both arms in acknowledgement to his own side, from which great cheers rang out. Then he turned back to us.

Some shout went out from him, and I knew that he was calling out any other champion who might wish to challenge him from our ranks. Next to me, Cormac stirred. I laid my right hand on his arm.

"You will not do it. No matter what we have just seen, he is still our friend. This is Olric's war. We will not be destroyed by the battles of these power-mad Saxons.

I looked into the face of my brother. A cruel and vicious look, which I had not seen for many seasons, had come into his eyes.

"He should not have made a fool of a brave man. I did not care for it."

"You will stay where you are. We will survive the coming madness of this day, somehow."

Cormac said nothing, just stared ahead of him. This was a battlefield, and my brother's soul lived for the battlefield. I knew that he had pictured himself in Maccus's place, and imagined such ignominy being heaped upon his own shoulders. I saw the rage come into his spirit. Soon all havoc would break out in this place, and I knew then that he would be prepared for it. I knew too that there was no thought of farms, or seasons, or crops in his mind at that moment. But he heard my words, for now the tension in his body relaxed slightly, and I knew that he would not take up Torquato's challenge.

The devil rhythm of the drums began their deadly beat again. Slowly, slowly. Then a faster pulse, and faster still, pulsing ever faster, the sound amplified because both sides beat upon the battle drum. I was reminded that this was a fight between men of the same family, and I was a part of it. It struck me as a great madness, for I knew what was about to be unleashed in this place. I thought for an instant of my Uncle Gavin, and remembered his battle-weary face turning to me just before the mayhem of Deorham, and in my mind I nodded quietly, and straightened my shoulders, and I knew then that I was ready for whatever would unfold before us.

Now the drums rang out an incessant beat, with barely a pause between each stroke, and about me I could feel the tension build, as if some great dam was about to crack, and around me horses reared and bucked and whinnied, as they too sensed the moment of release was upon us.

Now Kynon led his horse up and down our lines.

"No shieldwall. We will fight man to man, let the devil take the loser. Good fortune to every man here today!"

So saying, he turned to face the opposing army, just as the seething mass of men began to move forward on both sides. Even then a great crash of thunder rent the air, and a savage gust of wind blew into our faces, as the first drops of rain began to fall again, but all thoughts of the storm were forgotten.

Cormac and I rode in the first rank, and behind us we too sensed the second and third ranks of men begin to move, that first movement almost unwilled, as a drop of water in a mountain stream first starts its long journey to the ocean, for now the movement forward was unstoppable. We broke our mounts into a trot, and then a gallop, and our yells and shouts and screams filled the silent air as in front of us we could see Ceawlin's horse-warriors approaching. They too galloped over the soaked surface, and now it seemed that they were suddenly rushing up to us as if borne upon the howling wind and we met them there.

The bodies of many men were broken then, in that first clash of the two armies.

As the horses met I swung *Saesbane* with all of my strength at the lead Gevissa horseman to my right. The blade caught him high up on the temple, and he clattered backwards to the floor. I hit out to my left, and a second horse-warrior fell into the mud. Now a warrior from the first rank of Ceawlin's foot soldiers thrust his spear at my side, but I splintered it with my second blow, and brought back the blade and it hit him under the jaw, finishing his battle just there.

Horses and men flashed past me on each side, and my horse reared up, his momentum all stopped.

I turned him back into the fray. We had driven right through to the front of Olric's most advanced position, well into the Gevissa ranks. Ahead of me was a small mound. I could see Cormac now, already on foot, as he wielded *Gaeallon* with the mighty two-handed motion that I had seen many times before, and many of Ceawlin's men felt its bite there, and already strong warriors lay all about him. Now, I too dismounted, and let my horse find his own way in the chaos around us. I fought my way through to my brother, and I could see that a body of men stood with him at his side, and that Kynon was amongst them and so too the young British warriors from the lower Severn, and all had sought him out in the middle of this madness. Now we moved to the mound, and sank our British standard into the softened ground there. The battle was joined in full, as the Gevissas looked to throw us back from our vantage point. We fought like men possessed, and together the Britons fought the Saxons once more.

Then I saw young proud Edel, son of Edelwine, making his way over to us. He felled two men with clean strong strokes, but even as he reached for the war-helmet of one of the Gevissas, a third warrior struck him from behind, and the spear point went through the soft flesh at the top of his shoulder and out of the other side, and I saw him sink to the boggy ground. I made my way to him, slashing, cutting, bringing *Saesbane* down on anything Gevissa that I could see, and reached his side. He still lived. I dared not pull the spear-shaft out of his back, for I knew that it would cause more damage on the way through.

I stood over him and shouted to Cormac, even as he rammed the top blade of *Gaeallon* up under the jaw of a Gevissa man. A thrown spear came at him from somewhere to his left, but it failed to bite through the chain mail shirt that he wore, and fell useless at his side. He heard my call, and he moved to where I stood, and together we dragged the young warrior through the mud and grass back to the mound that had become our rallying point, so that we formed a phalanx around the young Hwiccaman, whose family had been so cruelly treated by his own people.

We fought all who dared approach us, and never before had I seen Cormac fight with such raw energy and power. The tired man I had witnessed just days ago ploughing our fields was gone. As the enemy came up to him, so would he force them back, two or three men at a time, and many Gevissas fell all about him, never to return to their families.

So the battle raged on all around us, but we held our place on the battleground, and threw back all who came at us. Many waves of the *Gevissa* came at us, and time upon time we drove them back from our vantage point. All through the early morning the battle-sides clashed, one side gaining ground, then the other, yet all through those gains and losses we pushed back all those who sought to shift us from our British ground.

Now there was a brief lull in the fighting in our sector.

We looked around us. It seemed to me that already, with barely half a morning gone, the battle belonged to the British and Olric. A desperate massacre of both sides spilled all around us, and there was a cruelty in it that I had never before witnessed. It struck me as strange that men of the same blood could wreak such destruction upon each other, but they did so, and with a ferocity I had never before witnessed.

But there could be no doubt, the momentum was with us, and all around us we could see that it was our side that was winning the day. Only in one part of the field could we see Olric's men fall back. To our right it was clear that some part of Ceawlin's army had success, for Olric's men withdrew from there, and we could see that this Gevissa force was working its way over to our place on the small mound in the battlefield.

Cormac looked at this whirling mass of men making towards us and it seemed to me as if there was an old and distant glint in his eyes. He looked at me and for some reason smiled. Then he turned to the young Britons around him and shouted out above the rising winds:

"Make ready, men. The Cantawwa freebooters are upon us. They are skilled fighters – give them no quarter. This battle will be won or lost, here, in this sector. We fight for our own land, here and now!"

I looked back to the fighting to our right, and saw that Cormac spoke the truth. In the middle of it all I saw my friend, the giant mercenary Torquato, and still he moved with his old leopard movements, and Olric's men fell all about him.

Even there, in the midst of that battle, I knew that some moment of great terror was upon me, but I knew not what it was, only that I could do nothing about it. The forces operating around me at that moment were beyond the control of any human hand – we were being whirled about as if we were but puppets. Wild winds tore at our clothes, deep cracks of heavy thunder pealed across the sky, and splits of wall lightning lit up the land around this devildark morning, and still men toiled under it, intent only on the battle before them, and their own survival.

Now the dread moment was upon us.

Torquato cleared two of Olric's warriors who stood in his way, even as Cormac sent a Gevissa man sprawling in front of him. Now the two champions stood before each other, no other man between them, and there was no more than thirty paces man to man.

For the second time in my life, a strange thing happened on a battleground – the fighting that continued in pockets around the field ceased when the battling hordes saw who it was that faced each other that day. Word spread, and now warriors on both sides came running, and two semicircles formed around the two men – the survivors of the British and Olric's forces behind my brother, and what remained of Ceawlin's Gevissas behind Torquato. I saw that Ceawlin, with Crida and Willem at his side, stood watching from a slope not fifty paces from where I stood, and that terrifying man, Olric, in his strange cart, watched too from just behind his own lines. These Saxons lived for such contests. It captured something deep in their souls.

Now even the winds dropped down, and the rains almost abated, though a low rumble of thunder rolled through the heavens in the near distance.

I stood but five paces from my brother. I saw the wide smile pass over his face, as he then calmly and deliberately removed the war-helmet from his head, and tossed it as if lazily to me. His long grey-black hair streamed back from his proud brow. He shouted across to Torquato.

"Well, Roman, we both knew that it would come to this, one day."

Torquato smiled too, as he slowly unwrapped a blood and mud-stained bandage from his tattooed right arm. I looked into his face. I saw that it was much scarred.

A long white welt passed down the right side of his face from eye to mouth. He looked much older, and the thought struck me that he had seen great trials since we had last spoken, but what those were I could not say. Now he spoke up in reply to my brother. There was a weariness in his voice that I had never heard before.

"Aye, Briton. I was half expecting you at the beginning of the fight. You would have made a better fist of it than the clown they sent out to me. I fear that in my relief that he was not you, I may have made an example of him."

"Yes, Roman, you did wrong there. I was disappointed in you."

Now Torquato wiped clean the blade of his short sword and looked across at me. I saw that another ugly red scar ran at an angle across the top of his left eye-bone.

"Well General, I get to see you at least once more in this life! I thank the gods for it. I have seen many things since we last met. I have spent time in the north of this land. Heed my words, have no dealings with the Saxons there, those men Edelric and Edelfrid of Bernicia are cruel and evil men, monsters – stay out of their clutches!"

He said no more, but looked back to my brother, a mirthless smile crossing over his scarred features.

"It is madness, Briton. These people mean nothing to us, yet one of us will not leave this field alive. The fates are playing with us."

"I know it, Roman, but we have given our battle pledge to the people we support. We have no choice in the matter."

"As you say, Briton, we have no choice. We have given our battle pledge. Perhaps, when we are through, these warriors may go home, and forget the battle."

Both men laughed at this.

"Know this, though, Roman. I respect you as a great warrior, whatever should now occur between us."

"Aye, and you, Briton. The best I have ever met, bar none."

Now I made to step into the space between them, and say something to them, but both stopped me.

"No need, brother. We both always knew it would come to this."

"No, General, this is the way we knew it must be."

Then Torquato smiled, and said again:

"I'm glad I set eyes on your ugly mug at least one more time in this life."

I stepped back, and I looked up at the black banked clouds above me, and I cursed this day, because I knew then that there was nothing I could now do to prevent what must happen.

They both calmly made their final preparations. Cormac removed his shoulder-clasps, the Roman too. Torquato would keep his armour and sword, for he knew that without it he had no chance against the raw power of my brother. Now, for the first time, I saw that he called for a shield from a man in his war-band. Cormac too kept hold of *Gaeallon*, though he removed the mail shirt from his chest. They would meet on those terms in the centre of the ring.

Each man circled the other. Now there would be no more talk. I saw the face of each man become a mask, and I lowered my head, for I knew that one of them would not leave this field alive.

Cormac ran at Torquato, and even as he stood to one side, caught him a glancing blow with the battle-axe, sending him spinning.There was real venom in the blow, and any lesser man would have been felled by it. But the Roman quickly recovered his balance, and in the same movement caught Cormac with a blow on the upper arm, drawing blood. No pain, no emotion at all, showed on the face of my brother.

Now he moved in again, and came after Torquato with the full-blooded two-armed action that I knew so well. The Roman parried, and feinted, and his skill then was admired by all who saw it and survived that day. With some sinuous movement, he managed to turn my brother around, and forced him off-balance in the waterlogged grass, and would have dug his sword into Cormac's back if Cormac had not brought the blade down with the battle-axe and hooked it away from his body, almost throwing it from the Roman's hand as he did so.

Cormac recovered his balance and charged at the mercenary again, and drove him back across the field, at one point hitting him with his shoulder, a blow that lifted Torquato off the floor, and shifted him several paces backwards, so that his feet landed with a splash on the sodden turf, perfectly balanced, and now he came at Cormac, and my brother stepped back. So they fought, at one time the Briton getting the upper hand, at the next the Roman. The circle of men opened and closed with the movement of these warriors, reshaping itself instantly. It was clear that my brother was the stronger man, but the Roman was more skilled, trained in the fighting arts.

Cormac drove the Roman back once more, and the blade of *Gaeallon* drew blood from Torquato's face, but it was a skin wound, and neither man gave quarter. Still Cormac drove him backwards, and still the Roman stopped each sweep of the blade with expert strokes. Cormac was growing in strength, and for a moment it seemed to me that my friend was weakening. *Gaeallon* nearly struck the final blow. In the same movement, Torquato raised his sword in both arms, and in one clean strike cleaved the shaft of *Gaeallon* in two.

My brother stepped backwards, throwing each part of the useless axe from him, even as Torquato came after him in a flash. Now Cormac swept the Roman's feet from under him on the slippery turf, and in the next moment kicked the sword from his grasp. He hit the Roman once, twice, three times, his fists a flashing blur. All could see that the British giant's blows had scattered the senses of the great mercenary, and now men on both sides began to shout out wildly, for this was a true fight between champions, and they knew that it drew to its close.

Now Cormac had the Roman in his rock-like grip, and I knew what would follow next. Cormac tightened his hold, and the sinews of his arms bulged, and the cruel look in his face gave way to a vicious smile, as he began to crush the life out of the Roman. I saw Torquato look down at my brother, his long white matted hair falling forward, deep ruts chiselled into his face, and his teeth ground together as he felt the full power of the Briton. No emotion showed on his dazed, strained features, no emotion at all. He moved his right arm in a sudden move, drew a small blade from a pouch sewn into the side chest of his tunic. In one clean precise movement he stabbed Cormac once, up through the neck and under the left ear.

Cormac dropped the Roman who sprawled onto the floor in front of him – a surprised look on his face. My brother staggered two paces and then fell on to one knee. His head came up and he looked at me then, and made to hold out his arm to me, but crashed onto his side, then rolled over onto his massive back in the cloying earth.

The life went out of him then.

Not a sound could be heard on that battlefield. Somewhere far away, I heard a deep roll of thunder, and I noticed that the rain had started falling again over the treeless plain.

I walked to my brother and looked into his face.

Dead.

No other man moved in that clearing. Ceawlin and Olric had both raised their arms to indicate that nobody was to move – all looked for my response.

Torquato had now staggered to his feet. I looked at him, a distant and puzzled look in my face.

"What is it that you have done here this day, Roman?"

Torquato stood upright. His face was ashen pale, bruised and bloodied. Still no emotion showed on his warrior features.

"He was the better warrior, Rhuadrac. I could not contain his power."

But I looked at the fallen body of my brother again. He was dead, killed by the Roman. The man who was my friend still lived. Cormac was my family. I was bound by the blood bond.

I said again:

"What is it that you have done here this day, Roman?"

"It was me or him. Those are the rules. I knew how he would finish it, so I prepared a final defence."

I said nothing, but with a measured movement drew *Saesbane* from its scabbard.

Torquato understood for the first time what it was I meant to do, and a flicker of apprehension crossed his face.

"I will not fight you, friend."

"Torquato, defend yourself."

He said again:

"I will not fight you, friend."

A great rage surged up in me, and I felt sick in the pit of my stomach.

"You will defend yourself, Roman, or you will die here."

I rushed at him, and although Torquato at the final moment made to lift up his sword arm, he was not quick enough, and I drove the blade of my sword deep into his chest, into a gap where his mail shirt had been stretched and torn in his contest with my brother.

I drew back the blade, and Torquato fell onto his knees in front of me, a look of almost childlike surprise in his eyes.

"Why, you have killed me, brother."

His head fell forward, and the long white muddied hair fell over his face, then he looked at both of his bloodstained hands and said strange words:

"Braxus, you are on your own now . . . I did what I could . . ."

Again his head fell forward, and I saw that he struggled to hide his agony. Once more he raised his scarred face, quiet resignation in his eyes, the trace of some Otherworld smile already around his mouth as he shook his head gently:

"This world is nought but madness, yet I would not finish it here, so far from home."

With that he fell forward, his armour clattered all about him, and the light in his eyes grew dark.

I stood alone on the treeless plain, my dead brother and friend before me.

*

I finally looked across at Olric, and that abominable man threw back his head and laughed lightly, both arms still raised. I took a spear from a man standing next to me, and with a sudden lunge I hurled it at this man who would be king. It struck point-first into the sodden turf a man's stride from where he stood in the strange cart.

"Perhaps you have your victory now, imbecile. I will have no more of this day."

I looked across to where Ceawlin stood, still he too had his arms raised, and no man sought to continue the battle.

I walked up to the Saxon king, and all watched my movements. It seemed to me that a great anguish showed in his face, and he was staring at me. He lowered his head, then shook it. If I had hit out at him at that moment, he would not have tried to stop the blow.

I put my hand onto his shoulder, and I said to him:

"Old man, father of my wife, grandfather of my children, it is time to leave this place of massacre. Too many good men have died already. No more men should die this day."

He would not meet my eyes then. He turned to his old shoulder-man, Willem, and said something to him.

All on both sides now watched the actions of the old king.

Nobody moved.

His horse was brought up to him, and he gave the order that the horns be sounded. Then his horse reared up, and he turned away from the battlefield, and what was left of his forces slowly started to move away from me, away from that place, and there would be no more battle, because Ceawlin had departed from the field and from his kingdom.

*

Kynon came across to me and offered me some words of solace, but I could not talk. Words failed me then.

Now I was alone.

Some ten paces or so from where the bodies of my comrades lay stood a pile of ancient rocks, glistening black under the rain-soaked skies. I sat there, leaning forward onto the hilt of *Saesbane*, trying to make some sense of the events that had unfolded in that place. I stayed next to my brother and my friend for all the rest of that long day. The rains came again, and far away the thunder still rumbled. All around me I could hear after-battle noises – wounded men groaning, or crying out as they were carried from the field. Everywhere around me was the sound of running water, as rills ran thinly over the slanting turf. A sweet and sickly smell started to assail my nostrils. The coal-black ravens and hunting eagles circled the field, wheeling about, giving out their inhuman caws and cries, diving down into the field. But I would not allow them to come near to me or my people.

The storm died away and a watery sun cast a baleful light over a scene of mayhem and massacre. Eventually the shadows lengthened and the land grew dark. Still I stayed there on that field with my fallen comrades, made numb by the events of that day. Somewhere close by the demons and trolls of the Otherworld pressed hard against the veil that separates them from us, but they did not trouble me. Tight-closed in my right hand I held the bronze and silver cross given to me by Cormac before Deorham.

Now only one name reverberated through my brain, as I sat there alone with my loss, the long shadows gathering all about me:

Ulla. Ulla. Ulla. Ulla.

*

At first light it seemed to me that a new world had somehow come to pass. All was strange, and I knew that my life could no longer be as it had been before this battle. A febrile daylight revealed once more the vague outline of the hills above me, and a grey dawn, full of mist and the smell of the sodden earth and fallen men lay all about me. Here and there the shadowed shapes of the living searched amongst the fallen bodies, now and then stooping to carry a prostrate figure from the field. A cold dampness filled the air, and my isolated breath came as smoke. In my freezing right hand I still held tight the bronze cross of the peaceful god of my mother, given to me by Cormac before Deorham. Below my right hand, my left hand rested upon the hilt of *Saesbane.* I looked at the tiny cross. I looked at the expert handcrafted carving in the hilt of the sword made so long ago by old Dermot. I looked at the fallen bodies of my brother and of my friend. Slowly I got to my feet. I sheathed the sword. Taking the delicate silver necklace that held the cross, I placed it around my neck.

A voice. Two voices. The voices seemed to echo around the place I sat in, on the slopes of the ancient barrow, as if made louder by the oppressive mist and the cold damp air. Looking to my left I saw Brocmael and Kynon come striding towards me, and with them they brought several warriors, and it was clear that they had come to assist me.

The old king laid his arm on my shoulder. His wise eyes looked into mine, and I saw that he noted the cross around my neck.

"You must go from this place, my son. There is nothing more to be done here. These men will assist you in whatever you choose to do. Will you take him back with you or will you leave him here, on the battlefield?"

He talked of my brother.

I had barely allowed myself to even consider the question. Once more I thought of Gwen and his children. I remembered how she had refused to let him go, had stood watching us leave the farm. Somehow, she had understood, with her woman's understanding of these things, that she would not see him again.

"We will bury him here, Chief, on the battlefield, at the highest point of the hill, where the ancients buried their warriors."

Brocmael nodded.

"It is right and fitting. And the Roman mercenary?"

This time I barely had to think.

"He too shall be taken to the top of the hill of the ancients, and his body burned there, and his ashes scattered to the wild winds."

And so it was done.

*

A cold and terrible homecoming I had of it.

As I drove the wagon up the track that led into the family compound, I saw that Gwen stood at the gates, as if she had never left that spot. Seeing me, she came running towards me. Already her hand was to her mouth. She ran straight past me and in a frenzy threw back the skins that lay scattered on the floor of the wagon. Now she looked at me, and I could but stare at her.

Slowly the rest of my family came out of the huts, and stood in a curved line around me. I stepped down from the wagon, and for a moment stared at the ground in front of me. Lifting my head, I looked into Gwen's paralysed face and fixed her eyes with my own.

"We have lost him, Gwen. He is gone, killed by the hand of the Roman Torquato, himself killed by my own hand."

Gwen made no sound, but slowly slumped to her knees where she stood. To her right I saw my mother cross herself several times, her eyes closed, shaking her head.

Then a great wailing went out of Gwen, and Peg stepped forward and led her into the main hut.

For a time nobody spoke. I had my eyes fixed upon Ulla, who stood with her arms at her sides, her dark hair falling forward over her lowered head. I understood at that moment how difficult her life had been since she had met me. My brother was dead, lost in a battle against the Gevissa king. She knew nothing about the outcome of the battle, nor of the fate of her father. I spoke out now to all there, keeping my eyes upon Ulla as I spoke.

"There was much slaughter on both sides, but by the the end of the day it is the Briton and Saxon forces under Olric that have triumphed. Olric is now in power in Wessex. Your father is defeated but he is not dead. He has been driven out of his Gevissa lands, but none know where he and his elite guard have now gone."

Ulla received this news in silence, then slowly walked out of the farm compound. I let her go.

Finn now looked at me hopefully, as if this may be one of my stories. He had to learn that it was not, and I saw then a great despair in his young eyes. Cadolan had wandered away, his head lowered, crossing himself. We later found him deep in his papers and parchments, reading his sermons, so did he always deal with crises. For several days later he could barely register another person coming into the room in which he sat. My mother, who by now had collected her wits and strove to bear the news with the grim sad stoicism she had learned to master in a life much touched by battle, put her hand on my arm and talked quietly to me.

"Go to your woman, Rhuadrac. We have to bear a terrible loss, but she too has received sorry news, for this signals the end of her father's power in this land, and none of us can know how it might affect us. I will watch over the children."

I found Ulla sat by the side of the stream. This was a place where just the two of us would go occasionally, to talk about this life, and our plans, and what we might do in the future. She was not tearful when I found her, and she looked at me with those light grey-blue eyes, ringed with green, as I came up to her, a question in her face.

"What now then, Rhuadrac of the Britons? What now then? Your brother is dead. At least my father is not dead, even though that might have been the better path for all of us. It seems to me that many people have suffered as a result of our union."

I sat down next to her, but said nothing for a while. She would know how the loss of my brother burdened me. Eventually I shared my thoughts with her.

"My first thought is for our son. He is now in some danger, for to Olric he will represent a threat, and we must have a mind to that. You and I too will be seen as a threat to him. Others will seek to use us to unsettle the new Gevissa king. We must decide now what our strategy is to be as we go forward."

The deep colour which I knew so well by now flushed through her high cheekbones.

"Strategy! Always strategy! You sound just like my father. I did not mean for you to talk about strategy! We have lost a good man, your brother. I want to talk about real things, matters of the heart and soul, those emotions that count in this life!"

I lowered my head. It seemed to me that some matters were best left unsaid. Sometimes, words can not capture the grief that we feel. Ulla saw life differently – she would say what she thought.

"I want to know about us – you and me and the children. How we might live now that my father no longer rules over the Gevissas, those ungrateful pigs who have thrown him over, and forced him out of his own hall. He made them the most powerful people in the land, and look what they have done to him."

I could tell that the shock of the news we had received would take some time to pass away. I held her then and we said nothing for a while. Eventually she looked up at me.

"What you said about the children is true. They will be in some danger in the future."

"We need not fear. We are in our own land here, and you forget that we enjoy the protection of the king of Powys. Olric will not try anything here – he saw what happened to your father at Fethan Leag. If we stay in this land, our children will be safe from your cousin."

We said nothing for a while. I decided to raise a matter that I had considered for a long time.

"We need to decide what we tell Cadwalla, and when. He has a right to know that others will look to him in the future, for he represents your father's line, and that is of value in these strange times. For myself, I care nothing for these affairs of kings, I would have him free of them. He might seek gold in battle, which as a warrior is the right way, and it will keep him a free man, yet I would not have him involved in the affairs of kings, for I see no worthwhile profit in it."

Ulla did not immediately reply to my words. Then she said something that seemed to place her at a great distance from me, which I did not much like.

"My husband, perhaps you are forgetting that I am the daughter of a great king. My son is therefore the grandson of a great king. We shall have to see how matters unfold, for he will make up his own mind when he is old enough to know the true story of his grandfather, and then he can decide."

We said nothing for a while. Eventually I turned to her and held her again, still in silence.

I watched the woodsmoke rise from my brother's hearth over in the next valley. No doubt Cadolan was taking it upon himself to do what he could to keep the hearth burning in these sad times.

No more would I sit at that hearth with my brother.

A flight of starlings took wing for the woodland over to our right, dipping and rising, dipping and rising, at great speed. Other flocks also joined them, and the raucous cries of rooks filled the air as they too sought a resting place for the night ahead. The day was beginning to fade out, and a slight chill had come over the space that we sat in.

Eventually I stood up, and I raised her up by her arms, and we made our way back to the farm enclosure, even as the dusk fell over our land, and the birds fell silent in the woods.

*

PART VII

Death of a King

A full season-cycle passed; gradually our mourning grew less, but not a day would go past when I did not expect my brother's voice to boom out in the farmyard, as he called me to the fields, or to his hearth at the end of a long day's work.

We heard nothing from the Gevissa lands, which was good by my reckoning, for there was nothing in that place that we did not have here, in the borderlands between the kingdom of Powys and the land of the Hwiccas.

Our fortunes prospered that season; we returned much produce that harvest – wheat, oats, barley, beans and peas – and all sold well at the Hwicca markets, for they were trading men, and farmers themselves, and they knew if a crop was sound or not.

One morning in early spring, I awoke to hear a great commotion in the farmyard; the dogs barked, the geese ran amok, hens and chickens cackled. I could hear oaths from the yard outside, and they were uttered in the Saxon tongue.

"By Thor's hammer, but these dogs are mad! Get away from me, you hounds of hell, or you will have my sword to reckon with!"

Immediately I was on my guard. I swung out of the skins in which I lay; Ulla still slept quietly beside me, and although the children stirred, they did not wake up.

I pulled up my breeches, threw a red tunic over my head, and stumbled into the same worn leather boots that I had worn for years. I took up *Saesbane* from its brackets, and tried to see who it was in the yard, but could see nothing.

I threw back the door, blinking in the bright early morning sun.

I was shocked to see that Ceawlin's old shoulder-man, Willem, stood there, fully armed, as the dogs leapt up at him, and the geese and the chickens and the hens ran around the yard. Over by the fence was a war-band, also bearing weapons, watching us, even whilst they scanned the land around them.

I swung *Saesbane* back over my shoulder, prepared to defend my family.

But the old warrior raised his free arm, and said to me, in my own language, of which he had perfect command:

"We are not here to harm you and your family. There is no need to protect yourself."

Slowly I lowered the sword.

"What is it that brings you to this place? You place yourself in some danger by doing so."

Willem gripped his tunic at his chest, and nodded his head deeply; he had greeted me in the way the Gevissas greet a *gesithas* of the king, a senior comrade, which he was himself.

"The king has asked me to bring you a message, and a proposal."

Ulla's sleepy voice came to me from the hut.

"What is it? What goes on out there?"

"It is your father's shoulder-man, Willem, who calls upon us, in full arms, and he brings other armed men onto our lands, but he tells me that there is no danger to us."

There was a silence from inside the hut.

I understood that Ulla would want time to be able to present herself to such a visitor. Ulla was the daughter of a king, and had been raised as a princess, and she would want to greet her father's comrade as such.

After a few moments, Ulla asked in a wary voice.

"What has brought him here? Is there to be another battle?"

Willem raised his finger to his lips and gestured out of the yard.

"I do not know. I will take him down to the hall and I will find out."

So saying, I stepped back into the hut. Ulla stood in the midst of the sleeping furs, a blanket drawn up over her naked body.

"Dress yourself. I will find out what brings him here."

I lifted the heavy two-handed key from its nail, then led the old Saxon shoulder-man out of the yard. He gave orders to his men to dismount and wait for him there. We turned right down the hill, and headed for Brothers' Hall.

We spoke little as we walked. Willem looked out over the lands of the Severn Valley nodding his head, but said nothing.

By now we had reached the hall, and I unlocked the main entrance.

I could see that the old Saxon warrior had been impressed at his first sight of the hall as we came down the hill and forded the small stream in its grounds.

It was no small structure; Cormac and I had paced out the floor, which was forty-two paces in length.

Willem walked over to the wall-mounted cabinet; he looked at Torquato's sword, and then looked back to me, and said, again in my own language:

"Your brother and the Roman mercenary were the two finest warriors my eyes saw in battle."

I nodded, but said nothing.

I noticed that he was trying to decipher the inscription on the metal plate, and I could see that he did not understand the British language in its written form. I read out the words to him.

"Yes, those are true words."

Now he turned back to me.

"I am here on behalf of Ceawlin."

"Yes, what is it that the old king wants to say to me and Ulla?

"At the end of the last battle you said to him that he is grandfather to your children."

It was true.

"He wants to see his daughter and any children she may have before he dies, and he wants you to take them to him."

I was disturbed by this news. My greatest wish was to keep my children free from the affairs of Wessex, even if Ulla did not approve of it. I could see only trouble ahead for them in the future if they were to become embroiled in the intrigues that swirled around Ceawlin.

"Before he dies? Is he sick?"

"He is not, though he is always harassed by the forces of the traitor . . ."

By this word he meant Olric.

". . . and, though we have found a safe place for now, there are no guarantees that it will remain so."

I looked at the old Saxon warrior. He had the face of a time-served soldier. The hair on his head and jaw was grey, and his once fine physique had taken on the weight of years. His wise eyes had seen much.

"Did the old king say anything else?"

Willem looked at me then and nodded. His reply was measured:

"He wants me to tell you that he has wronged you and his daughter."

I was surprised at these words. That did not sound like the words of the madman that had ruled Wessex for so many seasons. But then, nor had he seemed like that man at the end of the conflict at Wodensberg.

"In what way has he wronged us?"

"He wishes to tell you himself. But I was there when the king talked with the Roman mercenary before Wodensberg. Your friend . . ."

Here the Saxon looked at me closely, moving his head to one side.

". . . talked much about you. He told him how his son had died, told him of his son's dignity at the final moment – he had died as a warrior should. He told him of the treachery of the Gaul in your war-band and of your fury."

I walked over to the cabinet which held Torquato's sword as the old Saxon shoulder-man continued to talk.

"He told the king that the strength of the bond between you and the Saxon princess is stronger than any other he had known between a man and a woman. It reminded the king that this is what the queen, Acha, had always told him – she had understood the true nature of the bond between you and his daughter. He had been much deceived by Olric, who poisoned his mind with tales of your schemes and ambitions."

"Did the Roman say more?"

"He did. The old chief asked him about your character – did you seek power at the king's expense?"

I looked at the Gevissa warrior from under hooded eyes:

"And so?"

"The Roman laughed at the thought. He told Ceawlin that his daughter's husband, though a true and proud warrior, is a man who takes a thousand times more delight in watching the movement of the stars through the night sky then he does in counting the gold in his chest in the morning."

I turned my back on Willem and closed my eyes as the Saxon talked.

But then I collected myself and walked back to Willem.

"Gevissa, you have given me much to think about now. I have little interest in my children getting caught up in the viper's nest of Wessex affairs."

Willem nodded quietly at these words; it was clear to me that I did not have to explain my meaning to him.

"What are the thoughts of Ulla in these matters?"

"She is undecided, but is sure that our eldest son should be told of her father's history at the right time, for it is his birthright."

Again Willem nodded, and I could see that he agreed with her thoughts.

"So what then is Ceawlin's plan?"

"For me and my men to escort you and your family back to the secret camp we have made near the Saxon Shore. No force must be used. The decision is for you and his daughter. If you want no part of it, and do not wish to see him, then so be it. He will respect your wishes."

I paced slowly up and down the space in front of the cabinet and thought about Willem's words.

"Come home with me now. We will eat, and we will tell Ulla what you have told me. I will take my family's counsel, and then decide how we might best proceed."

*

The matter was quickly decided.

Ulla was as astonished as I had been to learn of Ceawlin's proposal, but once she had thought it through she was delighted by it. Ulla had no doubt that the man making such a proposal was the father she had known, and not the power-mad king who had come to throw away his kingdom. She would go to see him; if she could be sure of a safe passage for her children, then they would go with her too. Her father would see his grandchildren, so that he knew that his line continued. Her mind was made up, and I could see that I would not be able to dissuade her.

We took counsel with my mother and Cadolan. Both of them expressed some anxiety, but it was finally agreed that we should make the journey and that they and Gwen and Cormac's children would move up to the fortress at Penwyrn until our return.

*

We set out on the second day after Willem's arrival at the farm.

We took a small covered wagon, which carried Ulla and the children, and Peg too, for she had insisted that she would make the journey and would not be parted from the children at such a time. We had enough provisions for ten days. We did not wish to draw attention to ourselves by bartering for provisions along the road. I drove the wagon, and Willem and his war-band rode at each side.

We took the Corinium Road, and from there took the same road that we had taken to Calleva all of those years ago. In the Calleva environs we saw little sign of habitation, other than a small day market of makeshift stalls. It seemed that the firing of the city by Ceawlin's men had dealt that city something of a death blow. We had heard that a small tun called, in the Aenglish tongue, Dorchester had been set up in the near north-west, and that the people of Calleva had moved there.

From there we turned south, down into the Vale of the White Horse, where we struck camp for the night.

Soon enough we had a fire burning. Now we all sat around the hearth: my family and Peg, and the Gevissa war-band.

To my children, this was the greatest of adventures.

My son, Cadwalla, looked at me with his wide innocent eyes, and I thought again of Cutha, Ulla's brother, whom he so closely resembled.

"Talk to me of your friend Torquato, father, the great warrior whose sword is in the cabinet in the hall."

Across the fire, Ulla's eyes burned into my face; she knew that the burden of his loss, and the manner of it, haunted me still.

"What is it you want to know?"

"Where did he live?"

"Well, he lived here, there and everywhere."

"Where was his family?"

I paused:

"Why lad, this is Torquato's family. We were it."

I saw Ulla lower her head. Across the flames, Willem too lowered his chin to his chest.

Now Cadwalla's eyes opened wide. Such a thought had never occurred to him.

"How can that be? He was not your brother like Uncle Cormac was he?"

"No, son, not like Uncle Cormac – but he was my brother all the same."

Across the flickering flames, Willem nodded his head silently, his face suddenly older.

Cadwalla wrestled with these thoughts for a moment, then moved on to the next thing, as children do.

"Where is my uncle now, father?"

Again I looked into the flames; sparks flew out now and then, and whirled away into the night sky.

"He is guarding the far fields, to keep us all safe."

I could see that Cadwalla was impressed with this news about his uncle.

Now Willem took up the theme.

"Aye lad, what your father says is true. The giant warrior now patrols the shadowlands, where the monsters lurk. He seeks them out, so that you can sleep easy at night!"

I nodded at the Saxon, content with his intervention.

Cadwalla thought awhile. Then he looked at me, his mind immediately on some new subject:

"Father, I know who it is we are going to see."

"So tell me, who is it?"

My son spoke in the Aenglish language.

"Well then, it is Ceawlin, who is the father of my mother, who himself is the son of Cynric, and Cynric is himself the son of Cerdic, and Cerdic was the great-great-grandson of Woden, the father of the gods. Cerdic was a great king, who came to this land with others on three boats and became the king of the Gevissas in the land called Wessex. It is to this land that we now travel, to meet King Ceawlin who is my grandfather, but not the same grandfather whose battle-helmet sits in the hall back home."

All of the Gevissa war-band stirred at my son's words, and then banged their mugs on the stone and applauded him, and he beamed at his unexpected success.

I looked at my son, and then I looked at his mother, who shrugged and carried on arranging the roast meat over the blazing wood.

"My son seems suddenly to be very well-informed as to his forebears on his mother's side."

"Yes, of course. And why would he not be?"

I thought about it. Ulla was right. This was part of the family history of my son. Do what I might to erase it, there was nothing I could do about it.

I looked again at Ulla; there had always been great passion in my relations with this woman, whether it be in physical love, or love in the spirit, whether it be in words or in deeds; all was passionate intensity.

So would it be till the first of us drew our last breath, as we both well knew.

*

By the end of the natural light on the second day we were deep into the land of the Gevissas. Willem had described to me where we would meet with Ceawlin. This place was south of Winche, close by the Saxon Shore, in a place that was covered by woodland, near to a small lake. Now we were within but a short ride of that place, and we expected to meet with Ceawlin the next day.

Our journey down through the Gevissa lands had been uneventful. We had talked to nobody, had not bartered, had passed few people on the road. At one point a cavalry war-band had passed us just south of the Vale of the White Horse, but their business was elsewhere. I had taken the precaution of insisting that Willem and his men leave the road before their horses reached us, because a Gevissa war-band would arouse interest in these lands now, where Olric held sway. The lead horseman in the cavalry had looked at me closely as he rode past, but they did not stop, and soon the dust they kicked up was lost in the next valley.

Now Ulla was coaxing the children to sleep in the covered wagon, and I sat with Willem and his men at the rough fire we had set up in the middle of a ring of white stones under the lee of a high rock. The full moon was high over a mild night, and we had set burning boughs into clefts in the rock that loomed above us, so that the space was well lit. As we made our plans for the following day, Willem quietly stood up and went out of the circle of light around the fire. A few minutes later he was back.

"We will have visitors shortly. At least four men, on horses."

I immediately stood up, and went over to the wagon to get *Saesbane*. Willem and his men stepped behind the wagon, and I sat alone at the fire. Soon enough I could hear what Willem had heard before me – horsemen, coming down from the north, on the road that we ourselves had just travelled. The horses now slowed to a trot, and I knew that they would come right into the camp.

I stood up as they arrived, and to my great surprise Ceawlin himself was at their head, and riding at the side of him was Crida, his shoulder-man.

Ceawlin seemed changed beyond recognition. Gone was the rutted forehead, gone the great strain behind the eyes. He looked somehow younger, yet I knew that he had by now seen some sixty-nine winters. He wore no warrior armour, only a couple of skins over a simple white tunic, buttoned at the neck, and black leggings. Nor did he carry a weapon, which astounded me.

"Rhuadrac, I see. We have been a long time apart, my son."

Even as he spoke, Willem and his men stepped out from behind the wagon.

I looked at the old king, even more astounded. I would not have believed that Ceawlin could have used such language towards me. At his side Crida was dressed all in black, as were the two other warriors who made up their number, but these had held back and now watched and waited just outside of the circle of light set up by the fire and the lit boughs.

"I welcome you, Ceawlin. This is a happier meeting place than the last."

As I spoke, Ceawlin looked over to the covered wagon.

"Is my daughter here?"

Even as he spoke, the rough muslin cloth curtain over the entrance to the wagon was thrown aside, and Ulla stepped down from the wagon and moved over to stand by my side. There was a high colour in her face, and much pride too, for she stood with her head high, looking at her father, herself every inch the daughter of a king.

The old king's face stared stonily at his daughter, and I could see that a thousand emotions raced through his mind. Beside him Crida's face was deadly pale, and he lowered his eyes as Ulla stepped down from the wagon. Her beauty had not altered in the years since he had last seen her.

Slowly, the old Gevissa king got down from the white stallion that he rode.

He did not walk over to his daughter, but they looked at each other then, Ulla by my side, her head held high. Finally, Ceawlin, in a quiet voice, said:

"Daughter, I have been a very foolish old man, and I fear that I have not been in my right mind since I lost your mother. I have caused great suffering to many, even made threats against you, my daughter."

Ulla looked at her father and I could see that there was a quiet joy in her eyes, for she now saw again the man who had once been a great king, and who had ruled his people with care.

"Father, there have been dark seasons behind us, let us think only of the good seasons before them and the future we may yet have. I forgive you for the dark times."

She walked over to him then, and they held each other gently, in the centre of the circle of light created by the moon, by the fire, and by the gentle glow from the flaming boughs. Ceawlin kissed his daughter lightly on the forehead, as I had seen him do all of those years ago, and I saw that there was a deep peace in his face.

Ulla then pulled away from him, her eyes shining

"Let me now show you the future, if you are prepared for it!"

So saying, she ran to the wagon and pulled back the cloth entrance. A child's head appeared, then another, then a third, each head causing Ceawlin to exclaim quietly. They stepped down from the wagon and sleepily walked across to this man who they had never seen before.

Ceawlin looked at my eldest son, and I was sure that he must have thought of his own son, for he looked at him with a great mixed sorrow and joy, but said nothing, his old lean face just looking down at my son. Our son stared proudly back at him, then said:

"I know who you are."

Ceawlin raised an eyebrow.

"Who then?"

My son talked in the Aenglish language:

"You are that Ceawlin, who is the father of my mother, who himself is the son of Cynric, and Cynric is himself the son of Cerdic, and Cerdic was the great-great-grandson of Woden, the father of the gods. Cerdic was a great king, who came to this land with others on three boats and became the king of the Gevissas in the land called Wessex, and it is to this land that we have now travelled, to meet with you."

I saw Willem and Crida glance at each other and nod with approval. But Ceawlin himself passed a hand over his eyes, and knelt down on one knee in front of the boy, and placed a hand on the boy's head, saying quietly:

"In truth, lad, I am but your grandfather, and nothing else now matters to me."

Then Ulla brought across Acha and Cuthan to their grandfather, and announced their names to him with pride. There was great joy in the old man's eyes, but all of it for sure tempered by his own knowledge that his power madness had caused great suffering in the land he had once ruled and that now there could to be no recovery of it.

We talked then, around that fire.

Ceawlin now looked about him; the children still sat with us, but now their heads lolled, and they struggled to keep awake. He looked into the hearth, and I could see how moved he was to see these grandchildren that he thought he might never see. He lifted his head and spoke to us then.

"I ask this of you. Will you come with me now to the camp that we have set up in the Forest of Baer, down towards the Saxon Shore? There is much to discuss, and I have words that I want to share with you both . . ."

He looked at Ulla and me

". . . matters which are of the greatest importance to me. We will be safer in that place."

I could see that something had gone out of the old king. He now seemed lucid and once more fully in command of himself, but yet not like the man I had once seen stride onto the field at Deorham. This was no longer a warrior-king that we had met, or a man deranged by power, but a man who had gone on alone into lost seas, in some way, a man who had found himself again, who seemed somehow at peace within himself.

So it was agreed, and we travelled on that night into the Forest of Baer. Eventually we were led away from the barely noticeable path that ran alongside a small lake, and we moved in to the dense foliage of the forest, emerging after a long walk into a clearing which held many hut enclosures. Such was the hidden nature of this place that six wooden platforms had been set up around the camp, and these platforms held huge cauldrons, and these cauldrons blazed with fierce flames that lit up the entire compound. A central hearth still burned, and many men and women moved around this clearing, so that it was a small community, made up of those warriors and their families loyal to Ceawlin who had survived the battle at Wodensberg.

We were shown to a cluster of huts set up in the centre of the compound, and Ceawlin suggested that we attend to the sleeping children and then go over to his hearth, for he had many matters to discuss with us that night.

So it was that Ulla and I now sat at the old king's hearth, Peg asking that she be allowed to stay with the children after the long journey. Ceawlin offered us food and drink, which we took gladly, all the while his daughter watching her father quietly; I could see that this return of the old king was a matter of profound delight for her, because she had thought that he had been lost forever.

Crida sat at the back of the hut, brooding. From time to time he would raise his wild head and stare at Ulla, then again silently lower his jaw to his chest, listening to everything, saying nothing.

Ceawlin looked at us now and talked in a quiet voice. He used mostly the British tongue, full though of his Saxon accent and some German words, but clear enough for us all to understand his meaning.

"I thank you for taking the risk to come to this place. Daughter, I am pleased beyond words to see you again . . ."

His face made it clear to all in the room that these were no idle words; his eyes shone with tears and there was a father's love in the simple way he placed his hand upon her shoulder.

We waited for Ceawlin to tell us why he had called us to this place.

"To see my grandchildren after all that has gone before is the greatest gift that an undeserving old man can receive . . ."

The old king was silent for a few moments. We could see that he battled with some emotion that threatened to tear asunder his hard won peace of mind, and that there were words that he was determined to share with us.

"As I have said, I have been a very foolish old man in my last years. Many men have died as a result of my actions. Just a few days ago I listened to one of our scops sing a lament for these times, and when he proclaimed the old words . . .

often, when one man follows his own will, many are hurt

. . . I understood that the verse spoke of my actions, and that I will be remembered as the man who caused such destruction in this land."

His words were apt and true. I understood then that Ceawlin was now beyond the power madness that had afflicted him. He bore no false picture of himself in his mind.

"As you know, at Wodensberg there was a great slaughter of men on both sides, and I was driven out of my kingdom by Olric."

The words were said without rancour. It seemed to me that this loss meant little to the old king, as if it was a small thing to lose a kingdom. In truth, his words irritated me. I had lost a great deal in that battle.

"On this journey I have discovered something in these last years of my life."

He looked again around all at his hearth, and paused for a while. When he spoke again, his voice was quiet and firm, and he spoke in the Saxon tongue:

"I have understood this: that the exercise of power, when it is unchained by human love, is the cause of all evil in this world."

Again his words irritated me; he had ruled and lost a kingdom, only to discover this simple truth that all right-thinking men understand. Many good men had been lost to enable him to understand it. So it is with those who seek power, so it would always be.

As I looked back to him, I saw that he was regarding me closely, a gentle affection playing about his eyes.

"I see that I do not speak plainly enough for you, Briton."

I shrugged my shoulders.

"Let me explain to you my meaning again, in a different way, for it now seems to me that you and my daughter, above all others, may be capable of understanding me."

I glanced at Ulla. She too regarded me with her proud head held high and poised, then looked at her father, who spoke on:

"In these last seasons of my life I have had cause to reflect upon some words spoken to me by Acha a long time ago now. She said to me that in this life we must all choose between the dark and the light. I have chosen to head towards the light, to take the path to the light."

Now Ceawlin stopped speaking. Ulla lowered her head, and I saw that a great peace seemed to pass over her features. I looked hard at the old king, and for a moment I remembered my thoughts after Wodensberg. Then, with a slight movement of my head, I nodded silently at the old man.

We had understood each other.

Ceawlin was silent for a while. Then, clearly deciding to move on from his thoughts, he looked at each of us – his daughter and me.

"I have brought you both here to tell you this for a reason. My grandson, Cadwalla . . ."

We could see that even to mention his grandson by name was a cause of delight to the old man.

". . . is of my own direct line. Others will already be plotting against him, for such is the nature of these things. Even now, there are others who would challenge Olric. Already Cuthwulf, my long-dead brother's son, makes plans against Olric, and all of the signs are that the strife will continue. The Britons and the Hwiccas who joined with Olric at Wodensberg even now demand power and status, for it was their arms that gave Olric the victory."

Ceawlin then looked at Ulla and me.

"So, your son will have trials to face in his life, and he will be pursued by those who seek power. How then do you see it, what are your thoughts?"

I looked at Ulla, and at the old Gevissa king.

"I will speak plainly, then Ulla will tell us what she thinks, for we may see this matter differently."

Ulla said nothing, just continued to stare into the glowing embers of the fire.

"For me, I would have it that my children play no part in these matters. I have known some part of your life, king, and I have worked as your thegn in the land of the Franks. It seems to me that this life of kings has very little human profit in it, for none of them were ever content, and all were in strife always. No man spoke his mind plainly – all was deceit and intrigue. What small happiness they ever achieved was swept away in months."

I looked then at Crida.

"If my sons are warriors, then so be it, for that is the right way, that is how a man remains free, and how he wins sufficient status in this world to lift his head high and to sit in peace around his own hearth."

Crida stirred and looked across at me, he too nodding in silent agreement.

"But I do not want my children to seek power in this life. To my mind it is finally the path of the fool, there is nothing in it, and no good will come to that man who follows it."

All were quiet. Ulla then looked up at us all.

"My husband speaks wise words, as he always does. But I remember a time when my father was a great king, when he cared for his people, when their needs were uppermost in his mind, before the dark times."

Ceawlin had lowered his head as she spoke.

"So I also know that good kingship is not just the power-lust, that there is good work that can be done, but that the risks are high. There is dissent everywhere. All think they know best, and all will plot for their own ends, their own advancement."

Ulla was always the daughter of a king.

"I would ask my father, what are your thoughts in this matter? What is best for our son?"

The old man looked at his daughter with gratitude. He then got to his feet slowly.

"For me, Ulla, your husband speaks wise words. There is a great ferment going on in this land, and all is in a state of change. Such is the strength of this ferment that I believe it will not be resolved in our lifetime, or in the lifetimes of our children, or even our children's grandchildren. Maybe in a thousand years there might be one who can make sense of it."

He passed his hand down his lean face.

"My advice to you would be to play no part in these kingship battles. Keep away from the intrigues of this time, have no part of them. There is nothing in it for the wise. Many men will be broken on these wheels before the forces let loose in this land are resolved."

We all looked at the old once bewildered king, and we saw that he talked of his own failed attempt to make sense of the forces that had been let loose in Britain.

"My counsel would be to look to the strength of your own family, make it strong, but keep away from the affairs of kings."

We had all three of us spoken our minds. I had found a strange ally in the old king himself, for what he said made sense to me, and I hoped for the sake of our children that those words made sense to Ulla also.

It was clear that Ceawlin had now said what he had wanted to say, and that some burden had been lifted from him.

Just then a Saxon warrior came in to the room and said something to Crida, who immediately stood up and left the hut.

We talked then for some time of our sons and daughter, of their characters, of how they already saw the world in different ways.

"Cadwalla is all action and deed. He thinks quickly about matters, then acts.

Then he forgets and moves on to the next thing. But Cuthan is a quiet boy; he will pick up a stone and look at it for minutes, before quietly replacing it back on the ground, exactly in the same place, with great care."

By now Ulla and I had warmed to our subject, and the old king listened with a quiet dignity to this talk of his family.

"But it is our daughter Acha . . ."

At the mention of this sacred name, Ceawlin's eyes flickered momentarily. ". . . who is the real character amongst them. She is imperious and tells all what to do! She takes no nonsense from the lads! I think that she follows her mother in this . . ."

So we talked. The fire danced in the stones as we told the old king of our lives together, Ulla alive with the thrill of telling her father of the new life around her. Ceawlin soaked it all up, delighting in this talk of the future, a future from which he had thought himself forever exiled.

The boughs had begun to burn low in their beckets on the wall, when Crida came back into the hut, and indicated that he might speak with Ceawlin.

The two men left the hut for a few moments, only for Ceawlin to reappear, deep concern written upon his lined, lean face.

"It would seem that my warriors and I were followed in my anxiety to reach you today. Olric's war-bands are in the area – this camp has been discovered."

As he talked, I leapt to my feet.

Ceawlin spoke quickly, decisively.

"Go. Take up your arms, there will be fighting. Daughter, fear not, my people and I will protect the children with our lives, and we will find some way of getting them far from this place."

We ran back to the hut where the children slept. Even as we did so, we could see by the still strong glare from the cauldrons that all was unrest in the camp. Men everywhere reached for their arms, and donned mail shirts and helmets, and the women ran for the huts. Even as we reached the hut, we could see that some warriors on the outer edge of the camp were already engaged in a skirmish. A war-band of perhaps fifty men had appeared through the woods, and fierce fighting had broken out in that place.

"Get yourself, Peg and the children over to your father's huts. Do it now!"

I watched as Ulla and Peg ran across the compound with the children and pushed through the throng of warriors now gathering outside of the old king's hut.

Then Ceawlin appeared, and I saw that he had put on his battle rig, for he wore the wolf's head crest on his helmet of gold and niello, and he bore it too on his shield and on his mail shirt. Behind him stood his shoulder-men, and they too wore the wolf's head crest on their battle shields. He shouted across to me:

"One final time I will bear arms. I do so to protect my family, and for no other reason."

I lifted *Saesbane* from its sheath and I too strode over to the old king's hut and

I stood with him then. Ceawlin made a sign to his shoulder-men, and I took my place at the side of the old Gevissa king, who nodded to me.

"Warrior, it is with pride that I take my place at your side. Let us do what must be done."

Together we went to meet the war-band sent by Olric to finish the old king, now his sworn enemy. But now, by threatening Ceawlin, he threatened my children, so that now he would reckon with me and my family too. So, with Saxons, I once more strode out to meet Saxons, and the battle was joined.

Fierce fighting raged there, and many were killed.

In the thick of the melee Ceawlin and his shoulder-men fought with great skill, learnt over many years of battle and conquest. Just then Crida fell, downed by a flat stroke from an axe. Yet still he fought from where he lay on his side, sweeping his sword before him. In a second I was there at his side, and *Saesbane* did its work, driving back three of the marauders, then leaving them there unmoving.

I looked down at the shoulder-guard; I smiled, and helped the dark warrior to his feet. I said:

"For my brother's life, after Fethan Leag."

He too smiled, and nodded, then we both turned and strode back into the fray.

Soon enough, Olric's men fell back.

But then we heard the sound of a horn, and we could see more men behind those that we were fighting, and now we heard that battle had been joined on the far side of the camp. It was then that we realised that we faced several war-bands, not just one. We had arrived in Ceawlin's camp at the worst of times, for it now seemed that Olric had sent a huge force to finally finish off his enemy.

Still we fought, and not one of us took a backward step. Olric's men, reinforced or not, could not get through us. By my side fought the old Gevissa king, and I could see what had made him the renowned warrior that the verses spoke about. For his skills were like those once displayed by the Roman mercenary, and I could see that he too had long been trained in the battle arts, for Olric's men fell like wooden skittles before him, and he fought like a man thirty winters less than his age.

But still Olric's men came at us and we fought them there. We then heard again three loud blasts of a Saxon horn, and Olric's men fell back in front of us. We leant on our swords. It had taken much from us but many of Olric's warriors lay vanquished before us, even though Ceawlin's men too had taken many casualties.

Ceawlin called out to me and I walked over to him.

His face now showed his age. It had been a mighty physical effort for the old king, but still the battle-spirit raged in him. At his side lay old Willem, mortally wounded.

"They merely regroup. You must take Ulla and the children, and you must go from this place now. Go now. We will cover your path for as long as we are able."

I looked at the old king and knew that he spoke the truth. It was the best chance that Ulla and the children would have of safety.

Ceawlin part-turned away from me then. He looked down at the stricken form of his comrade, barely hiding the great anguish that passed through his face as he did so.

I put my head into Ceawlin's hut and told Ulla and Peg to get the children, for we were leaving.

"And my father?"

"He will protect our retreat."

Ulla looked at the children, then looked again at me. I shouted at her then.

"Ulla, we must go, right now, or they will be lost!"

She made up her mind, grabbed hold of the children and we stepped out into the clearing.

Ulla went to Crida and said something to him, her hand trailing gently down his right arm. Then she went over to her father, held his head in her hands, and said something quietly to him.

The old king smiled and gently kissed her forehead.

Ceawlin spoke quietly to me then.

"Go. Take your children. I am glad that we finally sat at the same hearth. Take care of my daughter, she who is your wife. If the gods are kind, I too will soon be joined with mine."

I grasped his arm, looked once more into the lean, thought-tormented face. He smiled at me then, the unsettled wise smile of one whose journey in this life may have finally run its course.

"Go now, look after them, my son."

Then we heard the howls of Olric's war-band as they renewed their attack, and he turned to meet his enemy. Wild-haired Crida, his remaining shoulder-man, strode out at his side.

We ran for our lives from that clearing, down paths in the dark of the night. Slowly the sound of fighting behind us grew less; still we ploughed on through the pitch-black forest, stumbling here and there, as we sought safety in that strange place.

We ran for some time, and the battle sounds had faded way behind us. We came out onto the rim of the small lake that we had seen when we arrived. The bright full moon poured its strange bluesilver half-light over us and the rim of the lake. Not a sound could now be heard. We lay low there, gasping for breath, the children looking up with white faces into the eyes of their father and mother.

After a little while, we heard the sound of running. We could just make out a band of perhaps six men, no more, come into the space between the forest and the lake.

I gestured to Ulla, Peg and the children not to move. Nobody breathed. The

Saxons started to beat the bushes in which we lay. Ulla closed her eyes. My fingers closed tight over the hilt of *Saesbane*. Then one of the Saxons shouted to his comrades.

"Here it is. Quick, help me with it."

We heard the sounds of something heavy being hauled out of the undergrowth, not twenty paces from where we lay. Peering through the leaves, I could see that they had pulled up a small boat, and even now were pushing it out onto the waters of the lake.

Soon the sounds of their retreat faded into the night air.

Ulla looked at me, her eyes wide open in the gloom.

"Can we risk going back?"

"Too soon to tell. I think that we should wait for first light."

This we decided to do, and Ulla, Peg and the children got what sleep they could, as we lay there in bushes by the side of the lake.

I must have fallen into a dreamless sleep myself, for I was woken up by the first grey rays of the early morning sun as it fell over the lake, and the events of the previous day flooded back into my mind. I looked anxiously about me and saw with relief that my wife and my children slept quietly by my side. Even then the great danger that we had faced crashed in on me properly for the first time. I looked up and realised then that the lake was assailed by the cries of birds. From every corner came their cries – geese, heron, gulls – all greeting the new day in front of them, and the curious affairs of men meant nothing to them.

I woke up Ulla and the children, and very cautiously we made our way back to the old king's camp, taking no chances, stopping from time to time as we moved along the track.

Soon enough we were looking out onto the old camp of the king. I gestured to Ulla that she and the children should stay back.

A sight of real devastation met my eyes. Bodies lay everywhere, men and women, even some children too, lay strewn about the compound. But it seemed as if Ceawlin and his warriors had prevailed, for even as I looked I could see other men and women, with children, walking about the compound, collecting their belongings, loading up carts and horses, fleeing from this place now that it had been discovered by Olric's forces.

I went back for my family, and together we moved down into the compound. We headed for Ceawlin's hut. We could see no sign of the old king. Two warriors stood outside of his hut, and looked at us with some relief when we appeared, for they now lived in fear of the return of Olric's men.

I asked them what had become of the old king.

One of the warriors, who was not young, looked at me with sadness in his eyes and beckoned me go on into the hut. I looked then at Ulla, and asked her to stay outside with the children.

The dead body of the old king lay there, with both of his shoulder-men laid out at his side. Their bodies looked massive laid out in the small hut.

They had taken the helmet from Ceawlin's head. Otherwise he still lay there in his battle clothes, a warrior at the last, as he had lived. I looked at him, and his stone, monumental face seemed to me to be at peace, for all of the madness had left him at the end.

Later I brought his daughter into the hut. As she saw him and her friend, she fell to one knee, and reached out one arm to touch the bier on which her father lay.

"Fader, fader, fader . . ."

She spoke in the Aenglish language, and for some reason I momentarily pictured her as a young girl, daughter of a powerful king, explaining her Aenglish ways to me in the garden of her father's hall, her proud head tilted upwards, placing her trust in me, a Briton she had barely met. Much had happened to us both since those first meetings.

I left her alone there, sobbing for the dead Gevissa king and her wild friend.

We built a pyre and placed the three of them, the old king and his two shoulder-men, on a bier and burnt their bodies then, the few survivors in the camp standing with us, and Ulla and the children by my side. Young Cadwalla stared silently at the dissolution and wreck of the body of his grandfather, the old Wessex king. I could but imagine what thoughts assailed his young and lively mind then, his pale face solemn in the glow.

No other sound disturbed that place – no wolf-howl, no bird-cry, no other natural sound of any kind – just a great human lament that went up amongst those who remained. The old women who had survived wrung their hair. Some remembered when this warrior had once been young, and vital, and who had become even then a great king, and they feared what the future must now bring to them. This man had been brought low by a cruel fate, and by his own weakness which proved he was but human, like the rest of us, and they cried out in their despair that their gods had played with him for their diversion.

Later, we collected the ashes in three urns, in the Gevissa way. We put the urns into the ground, and into the pit we placed the old king's sword, his mail shirt and shield, the great helmet inlaid with gold and *niello*, which was a sign of their kings. On all of these things the proud black silhouette of the wolf's head stood prominent. We gave the same honour and dignity to his shoulder-men, Willem and Crida, those two who had stood by his side in all things, good and bad, proving by this that they were true shoulder-men.

Then we covered that space with the moist soil of the earth, and built a small mound over it, and this place deep in the Forest of Baer we called Ceawlin's Barrow, after the style of his people.

Then all left that place, having done honour to the old Gevissa king as best we could, in the time that was allowed to us.

*

We travelled north with as much speed as the wagon and the need for caution would allow.

By the end of the second day we had reached the north edge of the Ridgeway in the Vale of the White Horse. We would take this track for a few miles before meeting up again with the Corinium to Cunetio road, then head north-west back to Corinium and the western border of the Hwicca lands.

I knew of an old hill fort just below the great white horse carved there into the hillside and we decided to camp there for the night. The day was already closing when I pointed to my left, saying to my family:

"In that copse there, surrounded by the high trees, lies the barrow of the ancients. We are nearly at the fort."

We looked across to the copse; the high trees swayed gently in the breeze. It was early in the spring season and the day, which had become grey and overcast, had begun to grow cold towards evening.

As I drew alongside the covered wagon, I could see that Ulla had produced blankets, and I watched her as she wrapped each child in the red, green and woad-blue wools. She had been very quiet since we had left Ceawlin's camp; she had barely spoken to me, lost in her own thoughts. Now I looked across at her dark hair, held in two long plaits to the side of her head, as she tended to our children. Her full figure caused delightful shapes to appear in her dark-blue gown as she knelt towards each child. On her delicate shoulders she wore furs, which emphasised the curve of her hips. Finishing her task, she turned and saw me looking at her.

"We will camp here for the night. By noon tomorrow we should be well into the land of the Hwiccas, and soon after that back across the Powys border."

Ulla nodded but barely looked at me.

"Ulla, what is it?"

She looked at me then. The regal set of her eyes, the light-gold of her skin, the fine structure of the high set cheekbones – to me she had become even more beautiful than when I had first seen her in her father's hall after Deorham. Her figure was fuller since the birth of our children, even more womanly. The old proud temper flashed through her eyes as she spoke to me.

"So much has happened to me since I first met you. Our union has caused such pain to so many: the loss of your brother and mine; to be taken away from my people; to be banished by my own father, a king amongst my people. Now, just when I find him again, restored to his true self – to have him snatched away from me again! It is almost unbearable!"

She looked away from me, and stroked the hair of her daughter.

I said nothing.

A little while later I held up my arm:

"See now, the dusk is growing. This will do. Let us set up a fire here, eat and bed down for the night. We will need a full day's travel to get back home tomorrow."

We had left the Ridgeway and descended into a valley. To our immediate left-hand side was a low range of hills, more like high mounds, that were imprinted with a strangely undulating pattern. Below these was a dip in the valley, and out of it rose the fort, which was in truth but a flattened hilltop surrounded by defensive ditches. We worked our way around to the north-facing side. Here there was a lee below the fort where we could build a fire without fear of detection.

Soon enough we had a fire burning. We had chosen a small hollow in the lee, part of the defensive ditch dug around the old fort. The fort was at our backs and before us rose the hill of the white horse, although here we were too close to the ancient carving to see its full outline. If we climbed up to the fort in daylight we knew that we would be able to see southwards almost back to the downs that stretch to the sea.

We had taken some bread and cheese when we had left Ceawlin's camp. We ate it now greedily, for we had barely eaten during the day. Cadwalla sat there with Ulla and me, quietly staring into the flames.

Cadwalla had said very little since we had left Ceawlin's camp, and I worried for him. Now he continued to stare into the flames, saying nothing. He looked at me now.

"Father, I'm glad I met Grandpa before he died."

I said nothing, just looked into the innocent eyes of my son, still no more than eight winters in age.

"I did not like the fire though. Grandpa's face went black first, before . . ."

He held his small hands over his eyes in a sudden childish movement.

"Now then, Caddy lad, I have a little tale for you . . ."

Cadwalla looked at me. He enjoyed my stories.

"You remember the ancient barrow surrounded by trees that we passed a few furlongs down the Ridgeway?"

"Yes, you pointed it out to us all."

"That's it. Well, you see those horses over there? If we were to take them back to that place, and tied them to a tree, what would happen?"

My son thought for a moment.

"They would be stolen by Grandpa's enemies."

"No, not that. Try again."

Cadwalla stared into the flames.

"Nothing would happen. It's a trick question."

"No. Try again."

My son looked sideways at me.

"I give up. What would happen?"

I leaned towards the fire.

"Each one of the horses would have been shod with new shoes!"

Cadwalla's eyes opened wide.

"But there is more. What else would you find?"

Cadwalla shrugged his shoulders, his eyes still wide and mystified.

"Tied to each horse will be a new sword and a new shield, all glittering with the shine of stars. No man can break them. No man can shatter them."

Cadwalla clapped his hands together and exclaimed with delight at the story.

"Now then, boy, what do you think of that then? A ghost blacksmith! Not bad heh? All the people around here know this story. If you leave your horse in that place and return the next morning – new shoes! New sword and shield! Glittering! Unbreakable! There is a smithy who comes to do his work in the night, but whom nobody has ever seen!"

Cadwalla looked down the track with wide eyes and open mouth for a while.

Then he looked at me.

"That is a good story, Father."

But a little later, he turned his face back to the fire, and stared into the flames. He looked up at his mother:

"Where is Grandpa now?"

"He is in the heavens, with the grandma you did not meet."

"What is it like in the heavens?"

"Much like here, but there love comes first."

Across the flames, Ulla looked at me, and I nodded, barely perceptibly.

My son looked again into the flames. Soon he brought his hands over his eyes, again with the same childish movement. Then he looked up at me again:

"Will Uncle Cormac be guarding the far fields tonight?"

I looked up into the myriad of stars that were set out in the heavens above us.

"Aye lad. Tonight and every night he will be guarding the far fields for us, keeping an eye on those shadowlands."

The boy seemed somehow comforted by this reply, and soon after his chin dropped to his chest. I carried him to the wagon and lay him down next to his brother and sister, and Ulla climbed up next to him. I pulled the blankets closer around them both.

"Good night, my love."

But Ulla said nothing.

I walked back to the hearth.

I knew that Ulla had been much affected by the loss of her father. I knew too that she was also wracked with questions about her own conduct in all of these matters. Now too, for the first time since Deorham, it seemed that she questioned the pact which we had made to each other so long ago.

I pulled up my travel blanket and soon fell into a dreamless sleep.

*

The next morning I awoke first. A watery sun was already high, and that curious misted half-light that often reigns in the first few minutes of daylight in the spring months fell lazily over the plateau. It looked as if we had lost the heavy grey clouds of the previous day.

A keen breeze blew into my face as I walked across to the wagon. The early mist was already lifting, although light cloud obscured the full power of the sun. For the first time I could appreciate properly the commanding view from the fort of the surrounding valleys and hills. I was struck by the great silence in that place. No bird cried, no dog barked.

When I reached the wagon I saw with a shock that Ulla was not in it. Nor was Cadwalla nor Acha. Cuthan still slept soundly; I saw that his eyes flickered quickly on his frowning face, and I knew that he was still deep in the dream realms. But neither my wife nor my other children could be seen.

A sense of fear gripped me.

I raced up to the summit of the fort-mound. My eyes scanned around the plateau on which I stood. Looking south, even though the day was still shrouded in the light mist, I could see the green plains fall away before me. In one or two farm compounds, white smoke whispered tentatively of people making ready for the new day.

Turning around, I could see, maybe one or two hundred paces directly up in front of me, three human figures. They were stood on the crest of the windswept hill on which was picked out the great white horse of the ancients.

Even from this distance it was clear to me that the figures were Ulla, Cadwalla and Acha. They were looking back down over my head. From their higher vantage point, they would be able to see even more of the valleys, the plains and the gentle wooded slopes of the land that the Gevissa king had ruled for so many years.

Slowly I made my way up to them. I saw Ulla point out something to our children, and they stared off into the distance. As I walked up to them, the morning breeze gently lifted up the now-loosened coal-black hair of my wife, so that it streamed out behind her. Her deep-indigo gown billowed, pressing back against her body. The swirling breeze brought me the words that she spoke to our son and daughter:

"Yes, that's right, all of it. He was a great king who ruled over all of the hills and the fields and the valleys of this wonderful land, everywhere that you can see around you, even all the way back down to the mighty seas . . ."

"Ulla?"

The Gevissa princess turned towards me then. She held out her hand to me and I took it. We stood there with our son and daughter before us, each of us with a hand upon their shoulders, looking out over the Vale of the White Horse.

Ulla spoke without looking at me:

"What do you think happened to my father, in truth?"

I thought awhile.

"Who can say what so much power does to a man? Ulla, I do not know. Maybe in the thousand years that your father spoke of, this land may produce some great verseman who will be able to make some sense of it."

I fell silent.

I looked at her proud profile – this daughter of the late Saxon king who would be Bretwalda. Life, love, some laughter, much loss and leave-taking. Who amongst us can explain any of it? We can only go on, keeping clear sight of those things we hold most precious.

I hoisted Cadwalla onto my shoulders. Acha threw her arms about her mother's waist and pressed in close to her.

"If we are lucky, there is new life out of love. These children are the future and the hope for us all."

Ulla rested her hand upon her daughter's head, then turned to me and smiled.

Just then the sun burst out through the mist, and the vast open space around us was lit up with the glorious new light of a fresh spring morning.

Acknowledgements and Afterword

The three lines of poetry quoted by Rhuadrac in his **ADDRESS** are taken from 'Beowulf', A New Translation, by Seamus Heaney, 1999. Although the Old English original has survived for many hundreds of years, the words quoted have the stamp of the great Irish poet himself. It is perhaps possible that a man living in the days of Rhuadrac, with access to the Gevissa halls, may have heard an early oral version of the poem that we now know as Beowulf spoken aloud.

The description of young Pallas given by Rhuadrac to Veos at p. 128 is taken from 'Virgil, The Aeneid', A New Prose Translation by David West, 1990. For Gavin's strategic thinking before Deorham, I am indebted to a paper "The Battle of Deorham" by T.G.P Hallett, Vol. 8 62-73 Transactions of the Bristol and Gloucestershire Archaeological Society.

In general I attempted to correct the less accurate claims regarding this era made by several Victorian historians by reference to the work done by Sir Frank Stenton in his 'Anglo-Saxon England' and other more recent scholarship on the period; any inaccuracies that survive are down to the writer. Details of artefacts, jewellery, mosaics etc are generally accurate i.e evidence survives of such objects.

Nevertheless, this is a story, not a history.

On the other hand, a writer perhaps has a responsibility to make at least plausible use of historic events and names. Therefore the attempt has been made where possible to maintain a degree of historical accuracy. So, from the scarce historical record, events *could* have happened in this way. Deorham. Fethen leag, Wodensberg – all of these battles did take place if the few paragraphs given to them in the English Chronicles are to be believed. Ceawlin, king of the Gevissas, was apparently present at these events, and it would appear that he ruled his Wessex kingdom in the years circa 560-592.

For those readers who are interested in the history of the period and wish to read more, then they can easily get hold of the scant history by using the timeline at the front of the book. Be advised though: with the Victorian historians particularly, you will be entering a field as ferocious in its way as the hand to hand combat scenes depicted in this book; a place where champions are traduced with regularity, and whole squadrons of historians are despatched by their opponents with a ruthless efficiency that would have done either Cormac or Torquato credit.

A few changes to the (possible) historical record have been made; for example, various ancient regnal lists indicate that Uthwine may have been either a brother or a son to Ceawlin. The same is true of Cutha. They may even have been the same person. The record is not clear. The story has deliberately moved away from a family relationship between Uthwine and Ceawlin, so that they become allied Saxon and Engel, and therefore perhaps more subject to the strains and tensions that one imagines might have existed between allies at this time of conquest and settlement. Cutha is made the son of Ceawlin (which may be historically accurate), because it suited the design of the story.

All of the characters, with a few exceptions as to name (but not as to character), are created by the author; there was no Rhuadrac or Ulla, no Cormac or Torquato, no Ethna or Aisha or Cadolan, no war-band, no Gregor and Megwei, no doomed Oisin, Singer-of-Songs, not even little Fintan, quietly playing his lyre for the last time on the eve of battle. Nor any of the rest of them, either. But, astonishing thought that it is, people perhaps a little like these must have taken part in these events, before being swept away by the great roar of history.

The few exceptions include: Ceawlin, Farinmael, Condidan, Conmael, Brocmael, Kynon, Aidan, Selyf Sargaddau. These names are taken from the record, and belonged to real persons, even though the characters ascribed to them in this book are devised for the purpose of the story; for all of them there is at least some evidence in near contemporary records that people with these names existed, such as in the pages of the English Chronicles or the work of the Venerable Bede.

Did Ceawlin lose his way in the manner described? Who can say? The record (such as it is) suggests a loss of a grip on power in the last few years of his allegedly long reign that sits awkwardly with the steady progression apparently made before that point. Such a loss of grip on power seems to be not unusual in these kingships, which rested on the strength of individual personality and very little else. As the king grew old, so often did the grip on power grow less.

Story-tellers are most interested in trying to imagine, and convey, at least a sense of what it might have been like to be alive in those times. This is admittedly a very selective process; for example, anybody who has read *Gregory's* History of the Franks will be struck by what appears to be the casual physical cruelty of that age. Perhaps this was equally true of the Britain of that time, but it is not a reality that Rhuadrac chooses to dwell upon; throughout, he sees what he wants to see.

Again, to add a layer of authenticity to the story, the reader can travel to Dyrham, north of Bath, walk up the lane leading to the ancient St Peter's Church, and head off along the Cotswold Way public footpath in the direction of Hinton Hill. There, at the top of the valley, they will find the site for Farinmael's short speech on the eve of the Battle of Deorham. Also, behind it, through the short copse, the wide open plateau where in the story the battle subsequently takes place.

The reader can still visit the amazing remains of the lost city of Uriconium, now near to the village of Wroxeter, and see for themselves the superb work done by those charged with its preservation. Many may be surprised at the technical capacity of the Romans, particularly in building, almost two thousand years ago. Readers can also go to Fethan leag (usually now thought to be at Stoke Lyne near Bicester) and Silchester (south west of Reading), the latter again a fascinating place to see, being as it is the only intact site of a complete Roman wall and amphitheatre in this country. So too can the visitor see the Hill of the White Horse, and the hill fort beneath it, and also nearby Waylands Smithy, that remarkable place. Finally, Wodensberg is thought by most scholars to be the place called Adam's Grave in the Vale of Pewsey, another place, like Wayland's Smithy, which has at its centre a long barrow of the ancients.

About the Author

Tom O'Rourke is married with two grown up children. He has a degree in English Literature from Cardiff University and in Law from Nottingham Trent. *West Briton Story* is his debut novel.